Oxford World's Classics edition of *The Woodlanders*.

NANCY BARRINEAU teaches English at the University of North
Caroli...

OXFORD WORLD'S CLASSICS

*For over 100 years Oxford World's Classics have brought
readers closer to the world's great literature. Now with over 700
titles—from the 4,000-year-old myths of Mesopotamia to the
twentieth century's greatest novels—the series makes available
lesser-known as well as celebrated writing.*

*The pocket-sized hardbacks of the early years contained
introductions by Virginia Woolf, T. S. Eliot, Graham Greene,
and other literary figures which enriched the experience of reading.
Today the series is recognized for its fine scholarship and
reliability in texts that span world literature, drama and poetry,
religion, philosophy and politics. Each edition includes perceptive
commentary and essential background information to meet the
changing needs of readers.*

OXFORD WORLD'S CLASSICS

THOMAS HARDY

Tess of the d'Urbervilles

Edited by
JULIET GRINDLE *and* SIMON GATRELL

With a new Introduction by
PENNY BOUMELHA

Notes by
NANCY BARRINEAU

OXFORD
UNIVERSITY PRESS

OXFORD
UNIVERSITY PRESS

Great Clarendon Street, Oxford OX2 6DP

Oxford University Press is a department of the University of Oxford.
It furthers the University's objective of excellence in research, scholarship,
and education by publishing worldwide in

Oxford New York

Auckland Cape Town Dar es Salaam Hong Kong Karachi
Kuala Lumpur Madrid Melbourne Mexico City Nairobi
New Delhi Shanghai Taipei Toronto

With offices in

Argentina Austria Brazil Chile Czech Republic France Greece
Guatemala Hungary Italy Japan South Korea Poland Portugal
Singapore Switzerland Thailand Turkey Ukraine Vietnam

Oxford is a registered trade mark of Oxford University Press
in the UK and in certain other countries

Published in the United States
by Oxford University Press Inc., New York

Text © Oxford University Press 1983
Introduction and Select Bibliography © Penny Boumelha 2005
Note on the Text © Simon Gatrell 1988
Explanatory Notes © Nancy Barrineau 1988
Chronology © Patricia Ingham 2002

The moral rights of the author have been asserted

Database right Oxford University Press (maker)

First published as a World's Classics paperback 1988
Reissued as an Oxford World's Classics paperback 1998
New edition 2005

British Library Cataloguing in Publication Data

Data available

Library of Congress Cataloging in Publication Data

Data available

ISBN 0–19–284069–X

2

Typeset in Ehrhardt by
RefineCatch Limited, Bungay, Suffolk
Printed in Great Britain by
Clays Ltd., St. Ives plc., Suffolk

CONTENTS

GENERAL EDITOR'S PREFACE

The first concern in the Oxford World's Classics editions of Hardy's works has been with the texts. Individual editors have compared every version of the novel or stories that Hardy might have revised, and have noted variant readings in words, punctuation, and styling in each of these substantive texts; they have thus been able to exclude much that their experience suggests that Hardy did not intend. In some cases this is the first time that the novel has appeared in a critical edition purged of errors and oversights; where possible Hardy's manuscript punctuation is used, rather than what his compositors thought he should have written.

Some account of the editors' discoveries will be found in the Note on the Text in each volume, while the most interesting revisions their work has revealed are included as an element of the Explanatory Notes. In some cases a Clarendon Press edition of the novel provides a wealth of further material for the reader interested in the way Hardy's writing developed from manuscript to final collected edition.

I should like to thank Shirley Tinkler for her help in drawing the maps that accompany each volume.

SIMON GATRELL

HARDY'S WESSEX
OF THE NOVELS AND POEMS

0   10   20
Miles

River Thames

NORTH

Lumsdon •   • Christminster

The Brown House
• Alfredston

MID-

• Cresscombe
River Thames

Castle
Royal

• Marygreen

WESSEX

Marlbury Downs

Gaymead • • Aldbrickham

• Kennetbridge

WESSEX

• Inkpen Beacon

Stoke Barehills •

Quartershot

The Great
Plain

• Weydon
Priors

• Icenway
House

Stonehenge •

UPPER

• Stour Head

• Wintoncester

Leddenton
Shaston
• Marlott   ▲ Wingreen
The Chase   The Slopes
Trantridge Cross   Chaseborough
Stourcastle
Bulbarrow   Knollingwood Hall
Shottsford
Flintcombe   Forum   Lornton
Ash   Yensholt   Inn
Weatherbury   Warborne
Kingsbere   Welland R. Stour
WESSEX
Egdon Heath
Talbothays Anglebury
Dairies Wellbridge
Nether Minton
Ormelo Cor vesgate
Culmond
Cove

Fernel Hall
• Deansleigh
Park

WESSEX

• Southampton

• Portsmouth

Melchester

• Solentsea

Bramshurst
The Great
Forest
Chene Manor

• Sandbourne

• Knollsea

The
Island

• Lightship

The   Channel

LEGEND
● TOWNS AND VILLAGES
■ HOUSES
▲ HILLS
✕ EARTHWORKS
CRESTON WESSEX NAME
PRESTON REAL NAME
--- COUNTY BOUNDARY
⋯ LAND OVER 400 FEET

0   5 Mis
0   5 Kms

●GLASTON

■Marshal's Elm

●TONEBOROUGH
(TAUNTON)

●CAMELOT
(CADBURY)

●IVELCHESTER (ILCHESTER)
●VAGG HOLLOW

●TINTINHULL

●MILLPOOL
(MILBORNE
PORT)

OUTER WESSEX

●MONTISLOPE
(MONTACUTE)

Hendford
Hill
●IVELL
(YEOVIL)

●SHERTON ABBEY
(SHERBORNE)

●NARROBORNE

●ESTMINSTER
(YETMINSTER)

BLACKMORE VALE
or
Vale of the Little

●CHARD

●CREWKERNE

KING'S HINTOCK
(MELBURY
OSMUND)

●CATKNOLL
(CHETNOLE)

●LITTLE HINTOCK

▲Bubb Down
High Stag▲

Dogbury
Hill▲

●NEWLAND
BUCKLAND

EVERSHEAD
●(EVERSHOT)

OWLSCOMBE
(BATCOMBE)

●NETHERHAY

Toller Down▲

Kingcomb
Hill▲

ABBOT'S CERNEL
●(CERNE
ABBAS)

LOWER WESSEX

Lewesdon
▲Hill
▲Pilsdon
Pen

●EMMINSTER
(BEAMINSTER)

▲Norcombe
Hill

SOUTH

●BROAD SYDLINCH
(SYDLING ST NICHOLAS)

LONG

Marshwood Vale

Whitesheel
Hill▲

CHALK NEWTON
●(MAIDEN NEWTON)
R. FROME or VAR

▲Haggardon
Hill

SCRIMPTON
●(FRAMPTON)

●CHARMLEY
(CHARMINSTER

●PORT BREDY
(BRIDPORT)

CASTERBRIDGE
●(DORCHESTER)
MAI-DUN CASTLE✕ ●DURNOVER
(MAIDEN (FORDINGTON)
Black'on CASTLE)

PO'SHAM

●ABBOTSEA
(ABBOTSBURY)

●UPWEY

●BINCOMBE
BROADWEY CRESTON
(PRESTON)

Wooton Vale

●BUDMOUTH REGIS
(WEYMOUTH)

STREET OF WELLS
(FORTUNESWELL)
●EAST

THE ISLE
(ISLE OF

THE WESSEX OF
TESS OF THE D'URBERVILLES

INTRODUCTION

Readers who do not wish to learn details of the plot will prefer to treat the Introduction as an Epilogue.

I

Tess of the d'Urbervilles has held in the imagination of generations of readers a deserved place in the great series of novels of sexual tragedy that nineteenth-century Europe produced. Like Flaubert's *Madame Bovary* or Tolstoy's *Anna Karenina*, the novel takes its title from its heroine, held in intense single focus, and its plot structure from her sexual and marital history. That plot, almost elemental in its simplicity, draws resonance from its recapitulation of familiar elements of folk tale and myth. There are no sub-plots to parallel or contrast with Tess's story, and virtually no plot elements that do not bear directly upon her fate. There can seem something transcendent of history about the vividness of such figures and their narrative environments, but in fact a reading of *Tess* is enriched by an understanding of how intimately it is related to the moral debates and fictional developments of its time of writing. It is important that the novel is not set in the unspecific 'once upon a time' of fairy tale, but embeds its folk elements squarely in the context of recognizable English society of the nineteenth century. The changing conditions of rural labour, factional disputes within the Church of England, the class structure of society, the National School movement, all take their place beside the mythological, biblical, and folk allusions to ensure that the novel bestows a challenging contemporaneity upon its tale of the maiden seduced and abandoned. Added to that realism is the strain of moral—even polemical—commentary which repeatedly insists to the reader that Tess has done nothing wrong. Given these elements of the novel, it is perhaps not surprising that it has from the outset polarized its readers into supporters and detractors.

By the 1890s, Hardy was a well-established and successful novelist whose preoccupation with female characters and implicitly sexual themes had already been widely noted, often with regret, as it appeared to some reviewers of the time to be slightly vulgar; Richard Le Gallienne, for example, comments that 'There is one fault in

Mr Hardy's work that still jars . . . but which he can hardly be
expected to eradicate, as it is temperamental—a certain slight
coarseness of touch in his lovemaking . . . [H]is women and men
alike are always somewhat too obviously animal.'[1] But in the latter
part of the nineteenth century, matters relating to gender and sexuality moved to the centre of public debate, with such developments as
the introduction of civil divorce and the subsequent press interest in
divorce cases, the rise of what is now called first-wave feminism, the
campaigns against the double standard and child prostitution and
the related raising of the age of consent, the trial of Oscar Wilde, and
the emergence of the eugenics movement. Widespread public debate
on sexuality and the roles of women were, inevitably, both reflected
in and shaped by cultural forms. A period of considerable experi-
mentation in fiction brought forth feminist utopias like Florence
Dixie's *Gloriana* (1890), fantasies like Jane Hume Clapperton's
Margaret Dunmore (1888), polemical novels like Olive Schreiner's
The Story of an African Farm (1883), explorations of female
victimage or potential like Sarah Grand's *The Heavenly Twins*
(1893), and collections of impressionistic short stories like *Keynotes*
(1893) by Mary Dunne, writing as George Egerton. Many such
works were best-sellers in their time, and so were some works in the
inevitable wave of satires and ripostes which always accompany such
success. These works, and the very many like them, brought in from
the fringes to the heart of popular fiction such issues and experiences
as prostitution, rape, contraception, adultery, divorce, and childbirth. It was often assumed that women writers bore the primary
responsibility for introducing this frequently deplored sexual focus:
the essayist Hubert Crackanthorpe complained in 1894, for example,
that 'the society lady, dazzled by the brilliancy of her own conversation, and the serious-minded spinster, bitten by some sociological
theory, still decide . . . that fiction is the obvious medium through
which to astonish or improve the world'. Others took a more positive
view of these developments: 'It is only during the last twenty years
or so', wrote H. E. Harvey in 1896, 'that the voice of woman has
really been heard in literature.' Nevertheless, many male writers also
contributed to the emergence of the so-called New Fiction, with its
New Woman heroines and its openly sexual subject matter. Writers

[1] Richard Le Gallienne, *Retrospective Reviews. A Literary Log II 1893–1895*
(London, 1896), 80–3.

like Mark Rutherford and Francis Adams, George Moore and George Gissing, played their own role. Indeed, possibly the best-known of all the New Woman novels, *The Woman Who Did* (1895), was by the male Manx novelist Grant Allen (who, incidentally, praised *Tess of the d'Urbervilles* as a work 'of which every young girl and married woman in England ought to be given a copy').[2]

In this context, then, Hardy's career-long interest in writing about women took on a new edge of contemporaneity and controversy which seems to have emboldened him somewhat. Hardy had, on the whole, tried scrupulously to preserve a distance between himself, a living individual with opinions and beliefs, and his novels. It is with *Tess* that he willingly takes on a more overtly polemical stance, throwing down a challenge to his readers in his Explanatory Note to the novel:

I will just add that the story is sent out in all sincerity of purpose, as an attempt to give artistic form to a true sequence of things; and in respect of the book's opinions and sentiments, I would ask any too genteel reader, who cannot endure to have said what everybody nowadays thinks and feels, to remember a well-worn sentence of St Jerome's: If an offence come out of the truth, better is it that the offence come than the truth be concealed. (p. 3)

'What everybody now thinks and feels': the phrase makes very clear Hardy's sense that his novel lives in a context of current debate and evolving opinion. As a professional novelist who had long sought to walk a fine line between artistic integrity and success in the main-stream of publication, he was certainly no stranger to compromise, self-censorship, and editorial intervention. The best financial returns from fiction, at the end of the nineteenth century, were to be had from publication in serial form in a magazine of wide circulation, followed by a three-volume library edition of the text, and then a cheaper one-volume edition for general sales. American publication, generally in the same sequence, could be separately negotiated. Hardy had long since settled into this pattern when he began the manuscript of *Tess*, probably in September or October of 1888, when the setting and themes of the novel are called up by his diary notes

---

[2] Hubert Crackanthorpe, 'Reticence in Literature: Some Roundabout Remarks', *Yellow Book*, 2 (1894), 269; H. E. Harvey, 'Science as a Moral Guide', *Westminster Review*, 149 (1898), 186–93; Grant Allen, *The British Barbarians: A Hill-Top Novel* (London, 1895), 94.

recording visits to the Vale of Blackmoor and reflections upon the social decline of the Hardy family. In order to secure publication for his novels in the lucrative serial format, he had been obliged to omit or rewrite numerous scenes from his earlier works. But with his great last set of novels, from *The Woodlanders* to *The Well-Beloved*, the potentially controversial material is inextricable from their fundamental narrative impulse, and the editorial trimming to which they were subjected comes to look absurdly irrelevant.[3] In *Tess of the d'Urbervilles*, for example, the scene in which Angel Clare carries the dairymaids in turn through the puddles to spare their good shoes takes a different form in the serial version, in which he transports them in a wheelbarrow; and the first period of the relationship between Tess and Alec d'Urberville was presented for the sensibilities of magazine readers in the form of a marriage ceremony, falsified by Alec but believed by Tess to be real. The letter of the law of propriety is thus preserved, but nothing could disguise the fact that this is a novel which recounts the entrapment and downfall of a woman due to her poverty and her sexual attractiveness, and one which nevertheless insists that she is, in the words of its subtitle, 'A Pure Woman'.

Some of Hardy's difficulties in getting the novel into print at all resulted from just this aspect. Among those approached as possible publishers, Edward Arnold found it unacceptable because 'the plot involves frequent and detailed reference to immoral situations', while Mowbray Morris replied that 'the general impression left on me by reading your story is one of rather too much succulence'.[4] Similarly, early reviewers of the novel were not slow to take up Hardy's challenge to conventional morality, nor to see it as another example of the supposed immoral influence on wholesome English narrative of, variously, French fiction or Scandinavian drama, novels with a purpose, or New Women writers. This was not simply because it dealt with the sexual 'fall' of a naive young woman; after all, the plot of 'seduction and betrayal' had long been a tradition in English fiction. Commonly, though, the fallen woman had only two plot-shapes available to her: either death, or redemption through

---

[3] For a fuller description of the changes Hardy made to *Tess*, see the Note on the Text.

[4] Both quoted from J. T. Laird, *The Shaping of 'Tess of the d'Urbervilles'* (Oxford: Clarendon Press, 1975), 10–12.

self-sacrifice. The story of Tess Durbeyfield did not fit comfortably into either mould, though it certainly contained elements of both. Controversially, it showed a young woman whose feelings for her child were ambivalent, who sought recuperation rather than redemption, and dared to imagine that she could recommence her life, and who expected her new husband to react to her earlier sexual transgression exactly as she had responded to his. More daringly still, it showed its fallen woman knowingly repeating that fall, leaving behind the threshing machines and Arctic birds of her life as an agricultural labourer for the cashmere and frills of boarding-house life as Alec's mistress. The greatest challenge to contemporary sensibilities, however, came in the shape of the novel's subtitle: 'A Pure Woman'. This made it abundantly clear that the text was designed, not to set out Tess's story as a warning fable, but as a defence of her moral virtue. Responses were often partisan, according to the broader social views of the commentator. The feminist Clementina Black welcomed Hardy as 'one of that brave and clear-sighted minority' who understand that a woman's 'moral worth' does not boil down to chastity, while Mowbray Morris (in his review as in his earlier editorial rejection of the text) was contemptuous of the novel's insistence upon its heroine's attractiveness: 'Poor Tess's sensual qualifications for the part of heroine are paraded over and over again with a persistence like that of a horse-dealer egging on some wavering customer to a deal, or a slave-dealer appraising his wares to some full-blooded pasha.'[5] For these first readers, there was little doubt that *Tess of the d'Urbervilles* fitted fairly and squarely into the mould of the New Fiction.

II

Yet, if Hardy's novel owes something of its polemical boldness to contemporary ideological and artistic trends, it also draws deeply on the reservoir of themes and plot structures that had impelled his work from the outset. Romantic and sexual relationships across social boundaries lie at the very core of Hardy's fiction· boundaries of social class or education, of age or wealth, of legal contracts or

[5] Clementina Black, review of *Tess of the d'Urbervilles*, in *Illustrated London News*, 9 Jan. 1892, p. 50; Mowbray Morris, 'Culture and Anarchy', *Quarterly Review*, 174 (1892), 325.

degrees of kinship, at once fire and thwart the passion of his protagonists. Sometimes such differences are resolved—by the passage
of time, by a convenient death, by the moral maturing of one of the
lovers—to produce the more or less conventional happy ending of
relationship fulfilled: works like *Far from the Madding Crowd* or
Under the Greenwood Tree clearly fit this pattern. Sometimes, however, the differences are preserved in all their sharpness and lead to
the tragedies of unfulfilment, loss, and waste that are so prominent
in his last works. But out of all the panoply of plot mechanisms that
can be set in motion to drive lovers apart, it is to the social discourses
of class that Hardy returns with almost obsessive frequency. The
concern with cross-class romance holds the centre of his fiction,
flagged from the outset in the title of his first (unpublished and
subsequently lost) novel, 'The Poor Man and the Lady'. It is in *Tess
of the d'Urbervilles* that differences of class and the nature of class-
determined experience are given their most subtle and complex
examination in all of his fiction.

One place to begin with this issue is to ask the question: why is the
novel entitled *Tess of the d'Urbervilles* and not, say 'Tess Durbeyfield'?
The answer is directly related to the complexity of Tess's class position. The poverty of her family, the ease with which they are forced
into ruin and homelessness by episodes of misfortune, and Tess's
vulnerability to exploitation by landowners and the increasing mech-
anization of agriculture, all point clearly to her status as a member of
the rural proletariat of the late nineteenth century. But it is important to the novel that Tess's situation also depends upon the fact that
she is of decayed aristocratic lineage: the d'Urberville knights
amongst whose tombs she and her family seek refuge are *her* ancestors and not those of Alec d'Urberville, whose manufacturing family
has simply taken over the name in an attempt to add the patina of
antiquity to their newly acquired wealth. When her drunken father
and distracted mother, misunderstanding these social ups and
downs, send her to 'claim kin' with Alec, they instigate what turns
out to be her sexual downfall. At the same time, the novel repeatedly
draws attention to her education, superior by the standards applied
to rural women of the time, and to its effects upon her life. If the
shared name is the basis of her early perceived kinship with Alec,
then some degree of shared access to culture equally misleadingly
and tragically appears to give her kinship with Angel Clare.

Hi please
can this be
re-added to
Cataloge
Morbury Library.

It seems to have
been taken off &

poss last
copy

Many thanks
Marie x

Wakefield
Libraries
Know Your
Neighbourhood

Some critical readings of the novel have selectively focused their gaze upon one or other of these multiple aspects of Tess. Some have seen her as typifying the proletarianization of the peasantry and the destruction of stable agricultural communities; in such a reading, it does not especially matter that Tess is female, except in so far as it adds a culturally sanctioned pathos to her victimization. Other critics, taking the lead of D. H. Lawrence,[6] have concentrated their attention on her ancestry and have seen her as a kind of natural aristocrat, a refined sensibility trapped in the circumstances of a peasant, whose tragedy is deepened by the sense of historic decline. Others again have tracked through the many textual references to omens and legends, mythic foreshadowings and literary precursors, to construct a Tess who recapitulates cultural archetypes of the feminine from Patient Griselda to the highborn lady in disguise; in this version, her class position in turn is of negligible importance. None of these perspectives is entirely wrong, certainly, and all of them can be supported by episodes and vignettes from the text: Tess at the mercy of the dehumanizing threshing machine; Tess, eyes flashing, fighting back against Alec with a haughty swing of the heavy glove; Tess with her wedding-day happiness overshadowed by the ghostly rattle of the legendary d'Urberville coach. But as the novel's plot unfolds, the play of differences and similarities between Tess and her family past and present, Tess and her co-workers, Tess and her lovers, is what gives the novel its structure, at once driving and pursuing her from place to place. And it is the complexity of this interaction that gives the novel its fascination.

Nevertheless, what gives the novel its vividness and focus is its unwavering and single-minded concentration on the figure of Tess herself. The critic John Bayley has argued that 'Tess is the most striking embodiment in literature of the woman realised both as object and as consciousness, to herself and to others'.[7] The passionate intensity of the narrative mode seeks to evoke Tess in every particular: how she looks, how she sounds, how she breathes, how she moves, what she thinks, how she feels. With the rise of feminist

[6] See D. H. Lawrence, 'Study of Thomas Hardy', in *Phoenix: The Posthumous Papers of D. H. Lawrence*, ed. Edward D. Macdonald (1936; repr. London: Heinemann, 1961), 398–516.

[7] John Bayley, *An Essay on Hardy* (Cambridge: Cambridge University Press, 1978), 189.

criticism in more recent times, this aspect of the novel has become one of its most controversial features. There is, it has been argued, something reminiscent of sexual pursuit and possession in the very intensity of the gaze, something which turns the ostensibly ungendered narrative voice toward overtly desirous maleness. There is, for example, the fascination with her interiority, with plumbing 'the deepness of the ever-varying pupils', with 'the red interior of her mouth' (p. 187), with the 'feminine smoothness' of her arm as she works and it becomes 'scarified by the stubble, and bleeds' (p. 101). At the same time, the most fateful experiences of Tess's narrative career are linked by a chain of imagery of penetration, from the death of the horse Prince, impaled on the broken shaft of the cart, to the knife-thrust with which she retaliates to kill Alec and which leads ultimately to her execution. Time and again she is awakened from sleep or reverie to moments of violence, imaged in the continual interweaving of white and red that marks her from her opening appearance. Sometimes it can seem that there is no respite for Tess, no escape from the erotic gaze of the narrator whose fascination with her reduplicates that of her sexual pursuers. For many modern readers, the tightness of the narrative focus on the suffering, violated, bleeding Tess has become a source of discomfort. The reader can feel implicated in a dialectic of desire and victimization, in a way most forcefully and challengingly formulated by John Kincaid, for whom *Tess* becomes 'a titillating snuff movie we run in our own minds'.[8]

Yet this narrative appropriation is not all there is to be said about the novel's manipulation of its narrative voice and distance. If it often lingers over the texture of her hair or the lift of her upper lip, it can also draw back abruptly to see her as 'a fly on a billiard-table of indefinite length, and of no more consequence to the surroundings than that fly' (pp. 120–1). This metaphoric distancing of vision is paralleled by the many moments when the novel withholds narrative access to its heroine. It is, for example, notable that, at crucial moments in the plot, Tess is either asleep or withdrawn into her own inner world: when Prince dies, during her first sexual encounter with Alec, when the sleep-walking Angel buries his image of the virginal

---

[8] James Kincaid, '"You did not come": Absence, Death and Eroticism in *Tess*', in Regina Barreca (ed.), *Sex and Death in Victorian Literature* (Bloomington and Indianapolis: Indiana University Press, 1990), 29.

bride, when he returns, too late, to find her installed once more with Alec at The Herons, when she is taken away by the police from Stonehenge. Through the metaphor of unconsciousness, the novel permits its heroine a degree of resistance to the otherwise pervasive physical and psychological display through which she is constructed. Most notably, there is no direct narration of the crucial night in The Chase which could give the reader either a definitive commentary on the nature of the event or an evocation of Tess's experience of it. To some extent, of course, this is an inevitable moment of censorship (or self-censorship), as the explicit narration of a sexual encounter would have been unthinkable in the context of a magazine serial at this period. Beyond this, however, it is striking that the event which has probably the most ineluctable and far-reaching consequences of any in the novel occurs silently and invisibly between Phases. A crucial consequence of this is that the reader cannot know whether what occurs is a rape or a seduction. An earlier moment, when Alec persuades Tess to eat a strawberry, forced and out of season, that she is not sure she wants, provides a symbolic transposition of the sexual encounter. But the matter remains ambiguous: community gossip about rape—'A little more than persuading had to do wi' the coming o't' (p. 103)—is a late addition in the composition of the text, and the fact that Tess departs from Alec only 'some few weeks subsequent to the night ride in The Chase' (p. 87) provides contradictory evidence of some kind of acquiescence, at least. The novel withholds from the reader access to the formative event of its heroine's plot. Similarly, the moments when the narrative might most seem to require Tess to speak her own truth are in fact silent: for example, although Angel Clare's wedding-night confession is fully detailed, Tess's reciprocal account is not given, and the earlier letter in which she has set out the same events before her marriage to Angel is concealed from him by a narrative device (the letter slides under the mat) but also concealed from the reader by the manipulation of narrative voice. In other words, therefore, *Tess of the d'Urbervilles* does not set out the meaning for Tess herself of her story; instead, it examines at length the various ways in which others interpret her.

Fundamental to what Tess and her story mean for those around her, it appears, is the close association others are inclined to make between her and nature. What nature connotes is different in each case, and also evidently in each case gendered. One version of the natural, posited by the narrative commentary, is constructed by means of an implied contrast with the social and intellectual. In this version, Tess's actions and reactions can be attributed variously to instinct ('the women's instinct to hide'), appetite ('the "appetite for joy" '), or intuition ('the intuitive heart of woman'), all of them non-intellectual modes of knowledge explicitly associated with women (pp. 214, 208, 264). In this view, the association of women with nature serves to reduce their individuality and identity; whereas men working in the fields remain distinct, we are told, women in the same situation are 'part and parcel of outdoor nature' (p. 100). When this mode of commentary prevails, the reader is told that Tess's sexual experiences should not be subject to moral opprobrium, 'a sense of condemnation under an arbitrary law of society which had no foundation in Nature' (p. 298). For Angel Clare, on the other hand, what is natural is very precisely related to his social morality. For him, too, the idea of the natural depends for its significance upon a contrast with something else: that is, the natural is what is not artificial. It is rapidly made clear (to the reader, if not to Angel), however, that this particular perception of what is natural is itself a perception very much shaped by art. The 'nature' Angel values is seen through the lens of literature. In the phase of his happiness, he sees farm life as 'bucolic' and Tess as 'idyllic' (p. 222)—both terms drawn from the literary representation of nature—and he courts her precisely to win himself 'a mate from unconstrained Nature, and not from the abodes of Art' (p. 191). The moral weighting he gives to this binary opposition—natural is good, artificial is bad—is quite explicit here. But however 'unconstrained' his version of nature might be, it appears not to include sex, motherhood, and the loss of a child, all of them experiences which have shaped the woman he believes he loves, for her confession of them turns her immediately from a 'child of nature' (p. 252) to an embodiment of 'Nature, in her fantastic trickery' (p. 257). Alec d'Urberville's perhaps less complicated understanding of Tess, by contrast, is based in turn upon his response to 'her exceptional physical nature' (p. 263). The version of nature associated with Alec is very much focused on the biological processes of sexual instinct and reproduction, on the 'hiss of fertilization' (p. 164) and 'stir of germination' (p. 112) that characterize Talbothays, where the female dairy workers 'writhed feverishly under the oppressiveness of an emotion thrust on them by cruel Nature's law'

(p. 162). It is in the context of this construction of nature that Tess comes to think that 'in a physical sense this man alone was her husband' (p. 378), and that Angel Clare can describe him to Tess as 'your husband in Nature' (p. 262).

In other words, although the novel sets out and contrasts different possible understandings of nature, what they have in common as they converge in the figure of Tess is that each casts her as a representative of the 'nature' of woman, the sexual difference that in this novel enables all the male characters to project onto her their own various constructions of female sexuality. Whether they see her as a peasant or a princess, a temptress or a virgin, an erotic response from men appears inevitable, and it is this that pursues Tess from place to place, forcing her to disguise herself in self-protection against 'aggressive admiration' (p. 299) and leading her to a sense of relief at the harsh economic exploitation of Farmer Groby, 'that sort of attack being independent of sex' (p. 339). If Angel and Alec are apparently antithetical, they are also alike in their attempts to make Tess stand for the whole female sex. Alec believes that her behaviour is like that of all women, saying one thing and doing another, and she responds by asserting her individuality: ' "Did it never strike your mind that what every woman says some women may feel?" ' (p. 89). Angel prefers to cast her as 'a visionary essence of woman—a whole sex condensed into one typical form. He called her Artemis, Demeter, and other fanciful names . . .' (p. 146). Once more, her response is to insist upon her own uniqueness: ' "Call me Tess," she would say askance' (p. 146). Tess's attempt to claim her unique individuality is not successful, as neither of her lovers is able to separate his response to her from his understanding of the nature of women in general. It is important to the patterning of the novel that the dissolute and amoral Alec and the ascetic and intellectual Angel stand in essentially the same relationship to Tess. Angel, who plays the harp, and Alec, who wields a pitchfork, are not the opposites that this would suggest, but rather complement one another. Numerous elements of the novel stress this, including the way that they briefly exchange roles, so that Alec is converted to Evangelical Christianity and Angel invites the hapless Izz to accompany him to Brazil. The two characters are also linked by parallels: each drives Tess in a carriage while also pressing his attentions on her, and each feeds her with berries. Both experience Tess as an embodiment of woman and hence of sexuality; and if that is a great misfortune for her, it also leads them into extremity, causing one or the other to abandon his faith, to emigrate, to walk in his sleep, to be murdered. The inevitability of a sexual response from men is what crystallizes Tess's experience of herself as the 'nature' of woman. Endlessly provocative without intent, she comes to feel guilty by virtue of her female body alone: 'And there was revived in her the wretched sentiment which had often come to her before, that in inhabiting the fleshly tabernacle with which Nature had endowed her, she was somehow doing wrong' (p. 329).

III

It is likely that one of the reasons why *Tess of the d'Urbervilles* seemed so challenging to its first readers was the degree of its insistence—unusual in its time—upon the life of the body. The intensity of what might be called the narrative gaze upon Tess's body has been discussed above, but the novel is more generally imbued with a strong sense of material existence, of bodily needs, appetites, and instincts: episodes of cold and hunger, bleeding and breastfeeding, exhaustion and sleep, death and execution. On occasion, Tess tries to abstract her sense of self from her physical being, as when she talks of the ability to project the soul away from the body: 'lie on the grass at night and look straight up at some big bright star; and, by fixing your mind upon it, you will soon find that you are hundreds and hundreds o' miles away from your body, which you don't seem to want at all' (p. 136). Such dualism is repudiated by the novel's plot, which is at once motivated and enabled by the social circumstances (poverty, femaleness) that offer Tess only the choices of being a 'kept woman' or a labourer. Once she leaves the parental home, she must depend for her survival on what her own body can earn. Later in the novel, her whole family similarly depends upon what Tess's body is worth. Her sexual body and her working body figure alternately as the object of economic exchange, and it is this that renders her especially vulnerable to the interlocking effects of class and sexual exploitation. Sometimes these are expressed or experienced in a straightforwardly oppressive or hostile fashion—Farmer Groby's pitiless supervision of her work or the revenge of the sexual rival Car Darch—but they are imaged most poignantly, because most lovingly, in her two principal relationships, with Alec d'Urberville and with Angel Clare.

Of course, poverty, whether of a man or a woman, in any case brings its own levels of vulnerability. That this is compounded by Tess's femaleness is all too evident in that it is precisely the gendered body that leads to the sufferings and vicissitudes to which she is subjected. Most notably, it is only the fact that she is female that permits her virginity and its loss to be so central to the plot. Even in the agricultural setting of the novel, where cycles of season and fertility are everywhere apparent, the loss of a woman's virginity seems to parallel death as a physical event of irreversible consequence. The persistent association of the imagery of penetration with death, in this text, also seems to emphasize the extent to which Tess's first night with Alec in The Chase constitutes her social death. The novel returns repeatedly, both in Tess's reported consciousness and in the narrative commentary, to the possibility that human life itself moves to the cyclical rhythms of the natural world: 'The recuperative power which pervaded organic nature was surely not denied to maidenhead alone', hopes Tess at one point (p. 112). But, like the protagonists of Hardy's other late novels, she is not permitted the 'break of continuity between her earlier and present existence' (p. 327) which alone would enable her to escape the apparent fatedness of her downfall. Inhuman rhythms dominate in her story: the remorseless linearity of the narrative 'phases' to which she is subject, the cruel repetition of the social exploitations which propel her through them, the dying fall of the social decline of the d'Urberville family, the compulsive cycles of mythic re-enactment. From these arises the 'almost physical sense of an implacable past' (p. 327) that propels her back to Alec d'Urberville and thence to the gallows.

Tess's female body, we are told early in the novel, is 'beautiful feminine tissue, sensitive as gossamer, and practically blank as snow as yet', on which a 'coarse pattern' (p. 82) is to be inscribed. In this she represents in little the novel's broader sense of human history as a text materially incised, imaged in the 'Cross in Hand', where a human hand carved on a stone pillar stands graphically but inscrutably for the impress of human experience upon the natural landscape. Monuments of human culture preside over the stages of Tess's decline, culminating in the siting of her arrest at Stonehenge.

It is hardly an exaggeration to say that Tess is victimized by texts. The phases of her tragedy can be counted off by means of letters and quotations: the parish archives that alert Parson Tringham to her d'Urberville past, the text painter's flaming sign 'thy damnation slumbereth not', Joan Durbeyfield's well-meant but ill-conceived letter of advice, the biblical text that crystallizes the sense of a virtuous woman in the Clare household, Tess's confession that slips beneath the doormat, the series of written appeals and warnings and denunciations that Tess and others send to Angel in Brazil. This sense of the life overshadowed by the text gives a particular, perhaps sinister, significance to the novel's ending, when, in a scene explicitly alluding to Adam and Eve expelled from Eden in Milton's *Paradise Lost*, Liza-Lu emerges, potentially to re-enact, in the attenuated form of the 'half girl, half woman' (p. 419) that she is, her sister's story. Some of the cultural resonance of *Tess of the d'Urbervilles* derives from the interplay of its references to the irreversible biblical narrative of the Fall and to the cyclical repetitions of seasonal regeneration. Hardy's concluding invocation of *Paradise Lost* powerfully evokes the post-lapsarian world of knowing sexuality from which there is no return, but, simultaneously, sets up the sense that the cycle begins again by substituting for Tess her presumably still virginal sister. Tess is, it seems, replaceable, not only in the eyes of Angel Clare, and not only in her own (for it is she who urges her sister upon her husband), but in those of the reader, for whom a new narrative of the gendered body is adumbrated. Tragedy is, characteristically, a literary mode focused on the exceptional individual whose downfall leaves the world poorer, shaped by their absence. It is a final, poignant irony of *Tess* that its heroine, however vivid her presence and however moving her suffering, is denied at last the grandeur of such a traditional tragic ending.

Throughout the novel, Tess struggles to persuade herself and others of the uniqueness of her own life. Her education, sadly, has only taught her that 'there is set down in some old book somebody just like me, and . . . that I shall only act her part . . . The best is not to remember that your nature and your past doings have been just like thousands' and thousands', and that your coming life and doings 'll be like thousands' and thousands' ' (p. 142). The novel's interweaving of its literary and mythological allusions with its deployment of the metaphor of textuality encapsulates this sense of the meaning of Tess Durbeyfield: that her individual story is precisely not the unique destiny of the exceptional, but rather the potential fate of any member of her sex and class in a society so determined that what is written on the body can never be erased.

NOTE ON THE TEXT

THE text of this edition is that established for the Clarendon edition of the novel. The Oxford text is based on the manuscript of the novel, now in the British Library, that was used by the printer of the *Graphic* serialization, and which is marked with the stints that each of the compositors undertook. This decision was made on the grounds that Hardy's punctuation as there revealed is both very different from and more meaningful than that imposed upon his sense by the compositors of the novel's first and subsequent printings. Occasionally in the manuscript there are places where Hardy's punctuation is clearly inadequate—such as the omission of inverted commas to open or close a speech, or the omission of a full stop at the end of a sentence—and then the punctuation of the first printing has been accepted. The same procedure has been followed with the thirty-nine leaves that are missing from the manuscript, and were noted as missing by Hardy when he presented it in 1912 to what was then the British Museum Library. (In passing it is worth noting that the best explanation available to account for these missing leaves is that they bore Hardy's wife's handwriting, and that he removed them, wanting only his own script to appear in public collections; this certainly happened in the case of the manuscript of *The Mayor of Casterbridge*.)

The copy-text has further been emended by the addition of almost all of the substantive revisions that Hardy made to the novel at various stages. The exceptions will be noted in the very brief outline of the development of the novel between 1887 and 1928 that follows.

It was on 29 June 1887 that Hardy signed a contract with W. F. Tillotson & Son to write a serial for their Bolton fiction syndication bureau; he agreed to send them the first four instalments exactly two years later. We have no solid information about when Hardy began work on the novel. Notes preserved in *The Early Life of Thomas Hardy*[1] dating from September 1888 seem to indicate that he was at least thinking about the story then, but the first direct reference to work on what was to become *Tess* is in a letter to Tillotson of

[1] Published (with *The Later Years of Thomas Hardy*) as *The Life of Thomas Hardy* (London: Macmillan, 1964).

February 1889. At some date Hardy found that he would have to push back the date of submission to the end of September 1889, but in fact he managed to send about a half of the manuscript (then entitled 'Too Late Beloved') to Bolton on 9 September. It appears that the first sixteen chapters of the manuscript were set in type before anyone in the publisher's office read them. These chapters included Tess's violation, her illegitimate baby, and its baptism, and Tillotsons were shocked when they read them, and wrote to say that they could not publish the story. After an exchange of letters between author and publishers it was agreed that the contract between them should be cancelled.

What Hardy did as a result of this rejection is fascinating. The weekly illustrated magazine the *Graphic* had been pressing Hardy for a serial ever since the appearance there in 1886 of *The Mayor of Casterbridge*, and (simplifying complicated negotiations) Hardy offered in late October or early November 1889 to supply the magazine both with a full-length serial (half to be delivered by September 1891) and a shorter piece for a special Christmas Number, eventually to be the linked story sequence *A Group of Noble Dames* (the manuscript to be sent by July 1890). This offer was accepted in mid-November, and the dates were confirmed by the beginning of December. The correspondence shows that Hardy at no time hinted to the editor of the *Graphic* that he had already written half of the longer piece, and it is reasonable to assume that he realized he would have to do a fair amount of rewriting if his novel was to be acceptable to the conservative magazine.

There would be nothing out of the ordinary in this pattern of events, were it not that by the middle of November 1889 Hardy had offered the novel to the editors of two other magazines, Edward Arnold of *Murray's Magazine*, and Mowbray Morris of *Macmillan's Magazine*. Hardy sent both editors the manuscript. On 15 November Arnold rejected it on the grounds of its numerous immoral situations. Though at this time the *Graphic* was accepting the novel, Hardy sent the manuscript off to *Macmillan's Magazine*, and received from Mowbray Morris a letter of rejection based on grounds similar to those Arnold gave, dated 25 November. It is possible to suggest that Hardy was just ensuring that his half-written novel would be published somewhere, but an alternative explanation accounts more satisfyingly for all the evidence.

Hardy had already discussed with both Arnold and Morris the place of 'immoral' incidents in fiction and thus had good reason to expect that they would respond the way they did to the manuscript he sent them. It seems improbable that he expected either to accept the novel, especially when by 21 November he had already agreed with the *Graphic* payment for its English serialization (and remember that he never even mentioned the existence of the half-manuscript to the *Graphic*).

Why then should he have sent it to Arnold and Morris? It is interesting that certain key phrases in the letters from Arnold and Morris have been marked by Hardy in red ink, and these notes may provide a clue. In January 1890 Hardy published in the *New Review* an attack upon the contemporary conditions that were imposed on the publication of fiction in England. In 'Candour in English Fiction', Hardy condemned the narrow blindness of magazine editors and proprietors of circulating libraries who dictated that thick veils should be drawn over truths of human behaviour; and it may well have been that the seed from which this piece grew was the initial rejection of his novel by Tillotsons. The submission of the manuscript to Arnold and Morris would then have been made in the conscious expectation of rejection. We know that Hardy invited Morris to make a full commentary on what he read, and he would have used the replies of the editors as water to stimulate the growth of his anger, that sprouted eventually as 'Candour in English Fiction'.

Once Hardy had reached agreement with Arthur Locker, the editor of the *Graphic*, he probably set the novel aside in order to concentrate upon *A Group of Noble Dames*, and the trouble he experienced over the story-sequence had an important effect upon the development of what was to be *Tess of the d'Urbervilles*. In essence the Tillotson experience was repeated. The stories were set up in type and then read by the proprietor and editorial staff of the magazine. They were horrified, especially by the amount of pregnancy and childbirth, and in June 1890 demanded changes or new stories. Hardy made revisions, and for the first time in his career used a blue pencil on the manuscript to indicate to himself which parts of the original stories had been bowdlerized.

If Hardy had wondered how the *Graphic* would take to his Tess story, these events must have suggested an answer to him. He sent the magazine half of the manuscript of the novel a week late in early October 1890, and there were blue-pencil and pen markings all over it. These temporary alterations, however, represent only the surfaced portion of the iceberg of bowdlerization; both Tess's violation and the baptism of her child had been removed entirely from the manuscript, and were published as separate stories elsewhere. In the place of the former was a page or two now lost describing a ceremony of marriage performed between Alec and Tess by a friend of Alec's in the guise of a registrar; the latter was abandoned altogether. It seems inevitable also that the second half of the novel, after the confession scene at Wellbridge Manor, should have been written under a certain amount of constraint deriving from Hardy's knowledge of the prejudices of the *Graphic*'s editorial board.

Proof-sheets of the *Graphic* were sent to New York for *Harper's Bazaar*, and though Hardy could not reinstate the excised material, he deleted the false marriage and added a brief summary of the events in The Chase. He must have felt sympathetic to the American serialization, for he made a fair number of further changes for *Harper's Bazaar* that he did not offer for the English serialization. At least transatlantic readers would not imagine that Angel could reject Tess because she had failed to tell the difference between a real and a false official.

For the novel's first edition Hardy brought together most of the scattered parts of the manuscript, though the description of the dance in the hay-trusser's barn was for some opaque reason omitted; he reinstated many though not all of the blue-pencilled passages, and he made a thorough revision of the whole. The edition of a thousand copies was published in December 1891 by Osgood, McIlvaine. The novel was unexpectedly successful, and the printer, R. & R. Clark, had already distributed some of the type before the publishers could ask for a second impression. Hardy made a handful of changes, and the impression, partly reset, was published in February 1892. There rapidly followed two further impressions, and it was soon decided to issue the book in the cheaper one-volume form. For this resetting (called by the publishers the fifth edition of the novel) Hardy made a large number of changes, some of which are of considerable local significance—*Tess of the d'Urbervilles* is the only novel about which it seems reasonable to say that Hardy's initial creative impulse extended beyond the publication of the first edition.

When *Tess* was issued in 1895 as the first volume of Hardy's first collected edition (the Wessex Novels edition published by Osgood, McIlvaine), the plates made from the one-volume setting were used, and Hardy revised only sparingly.

In America the first edition of the novel did not appear until January 1892, the first of Hardy's novels to be covered by international copyright there. It was set from a variety of copy, and had none of Hardy's revisions for the English first edition; a few months later Harper issued a 'New and Revised' edition which included some of Hardy's major changes to the serial text; and in 1893 a third edition was issued that was loosely based on the English one-volume edition. None of these has any textual authority.

The next time that Hardy had a chance to revise the text was in 1900 when Harper, who had taken over from Osgood, McIlvaine, planned to publish a sixpenny paperback edition. By now Hardy was concentrating his attention on the writing of poetry, but he still found the time and the enthusiasm to make a substantial number of changes, including the first attempt to trivialize Alec d'Urberville's conversion to Evangelicalism.

In 1902 Macmillan replaced Harper as Hardy's English publisher, and swiftly issued an impression of the plates of the first collected edition with their own title-page. For *Tess* in this issue Hardy made a few revisions, most of them similar to those made two years earlier in the paperback text. It seems probable that only the fact that Macmillan's text was printed from plates prevented Hardy from making all of the paperback changes. This would seem like a good argument for including all of the paperback changes in an edited text, were it not that evidence associated with the resetting of the novel for the Wessex edition of 1912 suggests a different approach.

For this second collected edition Hardy used as copy an impression of the revised plates of the first collected edition. A sufficient number of the changes Hardy made in this copy are precisely those made in the paperback text to make it reasonably certain that he had by his side while rereading the novel either a list of the paperback changes or the copy that the paperback edition was set from. The implication is thus that those paperback changes not incorporated into the Wessex edition text were consciously rejected by Hardy, and have also been left out of the text as here edited. The only exceptions to this procedure occur when it can be shown that revisions in the paperback edition were constricted for inclusion in the Macmillan 1902 edition. In such circumstances the usually fuller paperback versions have been preferred.

The Wessex edition represents the last time that Hardy read through and revised the whole of the novel, but the few local revisions made for the American Autograph edition in 1915, the third impression of the Wessex edition in 1919, the Mellstock edition also in 1919, and those made in manuscript in Hardy's study copy of the first impression of the Wessex edition have also been included in this text.

Anyone who is interested in more details, either of the history of the text's development, or of the precise nature of the revisions made at each stage, should consult the introduction to the Clarendon edition of the novel.

S. G.

SELECT BIBLIOGRAPHY

Letters and Essays by Thomas Hardy

Hardy, Thomas, *Collected Letters*, ed. Richard Little Purdy and Michael Millgate, 7 vols. (Oxford: Clarendon Press, 1978–98).
—— *The Literary Notebooks of Thomas Hardy*, ed. Lennart A. Björk, 2 vols. (London and Basingstoke: Macmillan, 1995).
—— *Thomas Hardy's Personal Writings: Prefaces, Literary Opinions, Reminiscences*, ed. Harold Orel (London: Macmillan, 1967).

Biographies

Gibson, James, *Thomas Hardy* (Basingstoke: Macmillan, 1996).
Gittings, Robert, *Young Thomas Hardy* (London: Heinemann Educational, 1975).
—— *The Older Hardy* (London: Heinemann Educational, 1978).
Millgate, Michael, *Thomas Hardy: A Biography* (London: Oxford University Press, 1982).
—— 'Thomas Hardy: The Biographical Sources', in Dale Kramer (ed.), *The Cambridge Companion to Thomas Hardy* (Cambridge: Cambridge University Press, 1999), 1–18.
Pinion, Frank B., *Thomas Hardy: His Life and Friends* (Basingstoke: Macmillan, 1992).
Seymour-Smith, Martin, *Hardy* (London: Bloomsbury, 1994).
Widdowson, Peter, 'Thomas Hardy: A Partial Portrait', in his *On Thomas Hardy: Late Essays and Earlier* (London: Macmillan, 1998), 10–26.

Text, Composition, and Publishing Context of Tess of the d'Urbervilles

Feltes, N. N., *Modes of Production of Victorian Novels* (Chicago and London: University of Chicago Press, 1975).
Gatrell, Simon, *Hardy the Creator: A Textual Biography* (Oxford: Clarendon Press, 1998).
Jackson, Arlene M., *Illustration and the Novels of Thomas Hardy* (London: Macmillan, 1982).
Jacobus, Mary, 'Tess: the Making of a Pure Woman', in Susan Lipshitz (ed.), *Tearing the Veil: Essays in Femininity* (London: Routledge and Kegan Paul, 1978), 77–92.
Laird, J. T., *The Shaping of 'Tess of the d'Urbervilles'* (Oxford: Clarendon Press, 1975).
Roberts, Marguerite (ed.), *'Tess' in the Theatre: Two Dramatizations of*

'Tess of the d'Urbervilles' by Thomas Hardy, One by Lorimer Stoddard (Toronto: University of Toronto Press, 1950).

Rosenbaum, Barbara, *Index of English Literary Manuscripts*, vol. iv: *1800–1900*, part 2: *Hardy–Lamb* (London and New York: Mansell, 1990), 3–224.

Springer, Marlene, *Hardy's Use of Allusion* (London and Basingstoke: Macmillan, 1983).

Sutherland, J. A., *Victorian Novelists and their Publishers* (London: Athlone Press, 1976).

Taylor, Dennis, *Hardy's Literary Language and Victorian Philology* (Oxford: Clarendon Press, 1993).

Reviews and Critical Guides

Clarke, Graham (ed.), *Thomas Hardy: Critical Assessments*, 4 vols. (Mountfield, Sussex: Helm Information, 1993).

Cox, R. G. (ed.), *Thomas Hardy: The Critical Heritage* (London: Routledge and Kegan Paul, 1970).

Gerber, Helmut, and Davis, Eugene W. (eds.), *Thomas Hardy: An Annotated Bibliography of Writings About Him* (De Kalb: Northern Illinois University Press, 1973).

Harvey, Geoffrey, *The Complete Critical Guide to Thomas Hardy* (London and New York: Routledge, 2003).

Lerner, Laurence, and Holstrom, John (eds.), *Thomas Hardy and his Readers: A Selection of Contemporary Reviews* (New York: Barnes, 1968).

Critical Works on Hardy

Bayley, John, *An Essay on Hardy* (Cambridge: Cambridge University Press, 1978).

Boumelha, Penny, *Thomas Hardy and Women: Sexual Ideology and Narrative Form* (Brighton: Harvester Press, and New York: St Martins Press, 1982).

Bullen, J. B., *The Expressive Eye: Fiction and Perception in the Work of Thomas Hardy* (Oxford: Clarendon Press, 1986).

Garson, Marjorie, *Hardy's Fables of Integrity: Woman, Body, Text* (Oxford: Clarendon Press, 1991).

Goode, John, *Thomas Hardy: The Offensive Truth* (Oxford: Basil Blackwell, 1988).

Gregor, Ian, *The Great Web: The Form of Hardy's Major Fiction* (London: Faber and Faber, 1974).

Higonnet, Margaret R. (ed.), *The Sense of Sex: Feminist Perspectives on Hardy* (Urbana and Chicago: University of Illinois Press, 1993).

Ingham, Patricia, *Thomas Hardy: A Feminist Reading* (Hemel Hempstead: Harvester, 1989).

—— *Thomas Hardy*, Authors in Context (Oxford: Oxford University Press, 2003).

Kramer, Dale, *Thomas Hardy: The Forms of Tragedy* (London: Macmillan, 1975).

—— (ed.), *The Cambridge Companion to Thomas Hardy* (Cambridge: Cambridge University Press, 1999).

Levine, George, 'Shaping Hardy's Art: Vision, Class and Sex', in John Richetti (ed.), *The Columbia History of the British Novel* (New York: Columbia University Press, 1994), 533–59.

Lodge, David, 'Thomas Hardy as a Cinematic Novelist', in Lance St John Butler (ed.), *Thomas Hardy After Fifty Years* (London: Macmillan, 1977), 78–89.

Miller, J. Hillis, *Thomas Hardy: Distance and Desire* (Cambridge, Mass.: Harvard University Press, 1970).

Moore, Kevin Z., *The Descent of the Imagination: Postromantic Culture in the Later Novels of Thomas Hardy* (New York: New York University Press, 1990).

Morrell, Roy, *Thomas Hardy: The Will and the Way* (Kuala Lumpur: University of Malaysia Press, 1965).

Sumner, Rosemary, *Thomas Hardy: Psychological Novelist* (London: Macmillan, 1981).

Vigar, Penelope, *The Novels of Thomas Hardy: Illusion and Reality* (London: Athlone Press, 1974).

Widdowson, Peter, *Hardy in History: A Study in Literary Sociology* (London: Routledge, 1989).

Williams, Raymond, 'Thomas Hardy', in his *The English Novel from Dickens to Lawrence* (London: Chatto and Windus, 1970; repr. London: Hogarth Press, 1984), 95–118.

Wright, T. R., *Hardy and the Erotic* (London and Basingstoke: Macmillan, 1989).

Critical Essays on Tess of the d'Urbervilles

Freeman, Janet, 'Ways of Looking at Tess', *Studies in Philology*, 79 (1982), 311–23.

Greenslade, William, 'The Lure of Pedigree and the Menaces of Heredity in *Tess of the d'Urbervilles* and *Jude the Obscure*', in his *Degeneration, Culture and the Novel 1880–1940* (Cambridge: Cambridge University Press, 1994), 151–81.

Harris, Margaret, 'Thomas Hardy's *Tess of the d'Urbervilles*: Faithfully

Presented by Roman Polanski?', *Sydney Studies in English*, 7 (1981–2), 115–22.

Higonnet, Margaret R., 'A Woman's Story: Tess and the Problem of Voice', in her *The Sense of Sex: Feminist Perspectives on Hardy* (Urbana and Chicago: University of Illinois Press, 1993), 14–31.

—— 'Introduction', in Thomas Hardy, *Tess of the d'Urbervilles*, ed. Tim Dolin (London: Penguin, 1998).

Kincaid, James, ' "You did not come": Absence, Death and Eroticism in *Tess*', in Regina Barreca (ed.), *Sex and Death in Victorian Literature* (Bloomington and Indianapolis: Indiana University Press, 1990), 9–31.

Law, Jules, 'A "Passing Corporeal Blight": Political Bodies in *Tess of the d'Urbervilles*', *Victorian Studies*, 40 (1997), 245–70.

Lodge, David, 'Tess, Nature and the Voices of Hardy', in his *Language of Fiction: Essays in Criticism and Verbal Analysis of the English Novel* (London: Routledge and Kegan Paul, 1966), 164–88.

Miller, J. Hillis, '*Tess of the d'Urbervilles*: Repetition as Immanent Design', in his *Fiction and Repetition: Seven English Novels* (Oxford: Basil Blackwell, 1982), 116–46.

Morton, Peter R., '*Tess of the d'Urbervilles*: A Neo-Darwinian Reading', *Southern Review*, 7 (1974), 38–50.

Paris, Bernard J., ' "A Confusion of Many Standards": Conflicting Value Systems in *Tess of the d'Urbervilles*', *Nineteenth-Century Fiction*, 24 (1969), 57–79.

Pykett, Lyn, 'Ruinous Bodies: Women and Sexuality in Hardy's Late Fiction', *Critical Survey*, 5 (1993), 157–66.

Rogers, Shannon L., 'Medievalism in the Last Novels of Thomas Hardy: New Wine in Old Bottles', *English Literature in Transition*, 42 (1999), 298–316.

Sadoff, Dianne Fallon, 'Looking at Tess: The Female Figure in Two Narrative Media', in Margaret R. Higonnet (ed.), *The Sense of Sex: Feminist Perspectives on Hardy* (Urbana and Chicago: University of Illinois Press, 1993), 149–71.

Shideler, Ross, 'Hardy: Marriage and the Darkening Darwinian World', in his *Questioning the Father: From Darwin to Zola, Ibsen, Strindberg, and Hardy* (Stanford: Stanford University Press, 1999), 135–69.

Shires, Linda M., 'The Radical Aesthetic of *Tess of the d'Urbervilles*', in Dale Kramer (ed.), *The Cambridge Companion to Thomas Hardy* (Cambridge: Cambridge University Press, 1999), 145–63.

Shumaker, Jeanette, 'Breaking with the Conventions: Victorian Confession Novels and *Tess of the d'Urbervilles*', *English Literature in Transition*, 37 (1994), 445–62.

Silverman, Kaja, 'History, Figuration and Female Subjectivity in *Tess of the d'Urbervilles*', *Novel*, 18 (1984), 5–28.

Tanner, Tony, 'Colour and Movement in Hardy's *Tess of the d'Urbervilles*', *Critical Quarterly*, 10 (1968), 219–39; repr. in R. P. Draper (ed.), *Hardy: The Tragic Novels. A Casebook* (London: Macmillan, 1968), 182–208.

Widdowson, Peter, ' "Moments of Vision": Postmodernizing *Tess of the d'Urbervilles*; or, *Tess of the d'Urbervilles* Faithfully Presented by Peter Widdowson', in his *On Thomas Hardy: Late Essays and Earlier* (London: Macmillan, 1998), 115–33.

Further Reading in Oxford World's Classics

Hardy, Thomas, *Desperate Remedies*, ed. Patricia Ingham.

—— *Far from the Madding Crowd*, ed. Suzanne B. Falck-Yi and Linda M. Shires.

—— *An Indiscretion in the Life of an Heiress and Other Stories*, ed. Pamela Dalziel.

—— *Jude the Obscure*, ed. Patricia Ingham.

—— *Life's Little Ironies*, ed. Alan Manford and Norman Page.

—— *The Mayor of Casterbridge*, ed. Dale Kramer and Pamela Dalziel.

—— *A Pair of Blue Eyes*, ed. Alan Manford.

—— *The Return of the Native*, ed. Simon Gatrell and Margaret Higonnet.

—— *Selected Poetry*, ed. Samuel Hynes.

—— *Two on a Tower*, ed. Suleiman M. Ahmad.

—— *Under the Greenwood Tree*, ed. Simon Gatrell.

—— *The Well-Beloved*, ed. Tom Hetherington.

—— *Wessex Tales*, ed. Kathryn King.

—— *The Woodlanders*, ed. Dale Kramer and Penny Boumelha.

A CHRONOLOGY OF THOMAS HARDY

	Life	*Historical and Cultural Background*
1835		Telegraph comes into use.
1837		William IV dies and is succeeded by Victoria.
1838		Anti-Corn Law League set up.
1839		Chartist riots.
1840	2 June: Thomas Hardy born, Higher Bockhampton, Dorset, eldest child of a builder, Thomas Hardy, and Jemima Hand, who have been married for less than six months. Younger siblings: Mary (b. 1841), Henry (b. 1851), Katharine (Kate) (b. 1856).	Victoria marries the German prince, Albert. Penny postage instituted. Charles Dickens, *The Old Curiosity Shop* serialized Charles Darwin, *The Voyage of HMS Beagle*
1842		Underground labour banned for women and children. Robert Browning, *Dramatic Lyrics* Alfred Tennyson, *Poems*
1843		Dickens, *A Christmas Carol* John Ruskin, *Modern Painters*
1844		Factory Act limiting working hours for women and children. Robert Chambers, *Vestiges of the Natural History of Creation* (popularizing an evolutionary view)
1845		John Henry Newman joins the Roman Catholic Church. Benjamin Disraeli, *Sybil* F. Engels, *Condition of the Working Classes in England in 1844*
1846		'Railway Mania' year: 272 Railway Acts passed. Repeal of the Corn Laws which have protected farm prices. Irish potato famine (1845–9) kills over a million people.
1847		Ten Hour Factory Act (limiting working hours). Charlotte Brontë, *Jane Eyre* Emily Brontë, *Wuthering Heights*

Life	*Historical and Cultural Background*
1848–56 Schooling in Dorset.	
1848	Chartist Petition to Parliament and end of Chartism. Year of revolutions in Europe.
	Public Health Act (inspired by Edwin Chadwick's Report into the Sanitary Conditions of the Working Classes).
	Pre-Raphaelite Brotherhood founded.
	Dickens, *Dombey and Son*
	Elizabeth Gaskell, *Mary Barton*
	Anne Brontë, *The Tenant of Wildfell Hall*
	William Makepeace Thackeray, *Vanity Fair*
	Marx and Engels, *The Communist Manifesto*
1850	Public Libraries Act.
	Dickens, *David Copperfield*
	Tennyson, *In Memoriam*
1851	The Great Exhibition at the Crystal Palace in Hyde Park, supported by Prince Albert, a great success.
	Ruskin, *The Stones of Venice*
1852	Thackeray, *Henry Esmond*
1853	Vaccination against smallpox becomes compulsory.
	Dickens, *Bleak House*
	Charlotte Brontë, *Villette*
	Gaskell, *Cranford*
	Matthew Arnold, *Poems*
1854	Outbreak of the Crimean War: Britain and France defend European interests in the Middle East against Russia; Florence Nightingale goes out to Scutari in the Crimea.
	Dickens, *Hard Times*
1855	Gaskell, *North and South*
	Anthony Trollope, *The Warden* (first of the Barchester novels)
1856 Hardy watches the hanging of Martha Browne for the murder of her husband (thought to be remembered in the death of Tess Durbeyfield on the gallows).	Crimean War ends; Victoria Cross for bravery instituted.
	Elizabeth Barrett Browning, *Aurora Leigh* (lengthy and melodramatic verse narrative of a woman writer's life)

Life	Historical and Cultural Background
1856–62 Articled to Dorchester architect John Hicks; later his assistant; late 1850s, important friendship with Horace Moule (eight years older, middle class, and Cambridge educated) who becomes his intellectual mentor and encourages his self-education in the classics.	
1857	Matrimonial Causes Act makes divorce possible without an Act of Parliament, but on unequal terms for men and women. Dickens, *Little Dorrit* Trollope, *Barchester Towers* Gustave Flaubert, *Madame Bovary*
1858	Indian Mutiny crushed. George Eliot, *Scenes of Clerical Life*
1859	Darwin, *The Origin of Species* Samuel Smiles, *Self-Help* J. S. Mill, *Liberty* Dickens, *A Tale of Two Cities* Eliot, *Adam Bede* Tennyson, *Idylls of the King*
1860	Cobden Act extends free trade. Eliot, *The Mill on the Floss* Wilkie Collins, *The Woman in White*
1861	Death of Prince Albert: Victoria goes into seclusion. Outbreak of American Civil War. Dickens, *Great Expectations* Eliot, *Silas Marner* Francis Palgrave, *Golden Treasury* (much quoted by Hardy) Isabella Beeton, *Book of Household Management* (sells over 60,000 copies in one year)
1862 Employed as a draughtsman by London architect, Arthur Blomfield. Self-education continues, including earlier English writers.	Mary Elizabeth Braddon, *Lady Audley's Secret* (the best known of the lurid sensational novels of the 1860s)

	Life	Historical and Cultural Background
1863		Work begins on first London underground (steam) railway. Football Association founded as professional sport. The Metropolitan Line is developed. Thackeray dies. Eliot, *Romola* Mill, *Utilitarianism* in book form
1864		Albert Memorial is constructed. Newman, *Apologia Pro Vita Sua* Trollope, *Can You Forgive Her?* (the first of the political series, the Palliser novels)
1865		Founding by William Booth of what becomes the Salvation Army. End of American Civil War. Dickens, *Our Mutual Friend*
1866		After the defeat of the Reform Bill to extend the vote: rioting in Hyde Park. Eliot, *Felix Holt, the Radical* Gaskell, *Wives and Daughters* (left unfinished at her death)
1867	Returns to Dorset as a jobbing architect. He works for Hicks on church restoration.	Second Reform Act increases voters to two million; Mill tries to include women in the Bill but fails. Paris Exhibition. Trollope, *The Last Chronicle of Barset* (last of the Barchester novels) Marx, *Das Kapital*
1868	Completes his first novel 'The Poor Man and the Lady' but it is rejected for publication (see 1878).	Founding of the Trades Union Congress. Collins, *The Moonstone* Browning, *The Ring and the Book*
1869	Works for the architect Crickmay in Weymouth, again on church restoration.	Suez Canal opened. Founding of Girton College. Arnold, *Culture and Anarchy* Mill, *The Subjection of Women*
1870	After many youthful infatuations thought to be referred to in early poems, he meets Emma Lavinia Gifford, his future wife, on a professional visit to St Juliot in north Cornwall.	Married Women's Property Act gives wives the right to keep their earnings. Elementary Education Act enabling local authorities to set up schools. Dickens dies, leaving. *The Mystery of Edwin Drood* unfinished. D. G. Rossetti, *Poems*

Life	*Historical and Cultural Background*
1871	*Desperate Remedies* published in volume form by Tinsley Brothers.	Legalizing of trade unions. First Impressionist Exhibition in Paris. Religious tests abolished at Oxford, Cambridge, and Durham universities. Eliot, *Middlemarch* Darwin, *The Descent of Man*
1872	*Under the Greenwood Tree* published in volume form by Tinsley Brothers.	
1873	*A Pair of Blue Eyes* (based on his meeting with Emma) and previously serialized in *Tinsley's Magazine*. Horace Moule commits suicide in Cambridge.	Mill, *Autobiography* Walter Pater, *Studies in the History of the Renaissance* (encouraging 'Art for Art's sake' and an impetus towards the later Aesthetic Movement)
1874	*Far from the Madding Crowd* (previously serialized in the *Cornhill Magazine*). Hardy marries Emma and sets up house in Surbiton, London. (They have no children, to Hardy's regret, and she never gets on with his family.)	Factory Act.
1875	Emma and Hardy return to Swanage in Dorset.	Artisans' Dwellings Act (providing housing for the 'respectable poor' or 'artisans'). Efficient system of compulsory vaccination of children against smallpox introduced. Trollope, *The Way We Live Now* (fierce satire on contemporary society and its greed)
1876	*The Hand of Ethelberta* (previously serialized in the *Cornhill Magazine*) published in volume form.	Disraeli creates Victoria Empress of India. Alexander Graham Bell patents the telephone. Invention of the phonograph. Eliot, *Daniel Deronda* Henry James, *Roderick Hudson*
1878	*The Return of the Native* (previously serialized in *Belgravia*) published in volume form.	London University grants degrees to women for the first time.

	Life	*Historical and Cultural Background*
1878	The Hardys move back to London (Tooting). Serialized version of part of the unpublished first novel appears in *Harper's Weekly* in New York as *An Indiscretion in the Life of an Heiress* (never included in his collected works).	G. H. Lewes dies.
1879		Beginning of a long though intermittent economic depression in Britain, lasting into the 1890s. William Morris's lecture, *The Art of the People*, explaining ideas which led later to the Arts and Crafts Movement in the latter part of the century. Henrik Ibsen, *A Doll's House* James, *Daisy Miller*
1880	*The Trumpet-Major* (previously serialized in *Good Words*) published in volume form. Hardy is ill for many months.	Gladstone becomes Prime Minister for the second time. George Eliot and Gustave Flaubert die. Education Act makes elementary education compulsory. Charles Parnell demands home rule for Ireland. George Gissing, *Workers in the Dawn* Tennyson, *Ballads and Other Poems* Trollope, *The Duke's Children* (last of the Palliser novels)
1881	*A Laodicean* (previously serialized in *Harper's New Monthly Magazine*) published in volume form. The Hardys return to Dorset, living at first in Wimborne.	Death of Carlyle. 'Otto' safety bicycle patented: Hardy and Emma become keen cyclists. By the 1890s many have succumbed to 'bicycle mania'. Ibsen, *Ghosts* (involving syphilis but later seen by Queen Victoria) James, *Portrait of a Lady*
1882	*Two on a Tower* (previously serialized in the *Atlantic Monthly*) published in volume form.	
1882–90		Parliament repeatedly vetoes votes for women.
1883		Andrew Mearns, *The Bitter Cry of Outcast London* (exposé of poverty)
1884	Hardy becomes a Justice of the Peace and serves as a magistrate in Dorchester.	Third Reform Bill. Founding of the Fabian Society.

Life	Historical and Cultural Background
1885	The Hardys move for the last time: to a house, Max Gate, outside Dorchester, designed by Hardy and built by his brother.	Death of General Gordon at Khartoum. Criminal Law Amendment Act (raises age of consent to 16).
1886	*The Mayor of Casterbridge* (previously serialized in the *Graphic*) published in volume form.	Repeal of the Contagious Diseases Act. Irish Home Rule Act.
1887	*The Woodlanders* (previously serialized in *Macmillan's Magazine*) published in volume form. Hardy begins to visit London for 'the Season'. Visit to Italy.	Victoria's Golden Jubilee.
1888	*Wessex Tales.* Visit to Paris.	Matthew Arnold dies.
1889		London dock strike. Robert Browning dies. William Booth, *Life and Labour of the People in London* (exhaustive documentary account) starts publication G. B. Shaw, *Fabian Essays on Socialism* Ibsen, *A Doll's House* staged in London Gissing, *The Nether World*
1890		Decline of the circulating libraries and the death of the three-volume novel. William Morris founds the Kelmscott Press. Housing of the Working Classes Act. Oscar Wilde, *The Picture of Dorian Gray* Ibsen, *Hedda Gabler*
1891	*Tess of the d'Urbervilles* (previously serialized in censored form in the *Graphic*) published in volume form. It simultaneously enhances his reputation as a novelist and causes a scandal because of its advanced views on sexual conduct. *A Group of Noble Dames* (tales) also published.	

Life	*Historical and Cultural Background*
1892	Hardy's father, Thomas, dies. Serialized version of *The Well-Beloved*, entitled *The Pursuit of the Well-Beloved*, published in the *Illustrated London News*. Hardy's estrangement from Emma increases.	Death of Alfred Tennyson. Wilde, *Lady Windermere's Fan* Rudyard Kipling, *Barrack-Room Ballads*
1892–3	*Our Exploits at West Poley*, a long tale for boys, published in an American periodical, *The Household*. Serial version of *The Pursuit of the Well-Beloved*—virtually a different novel from the later book version.	
1893	Meets Florence Henniker, one of several society women with whom he had intense friendships. Collaborates with her on *The Spectre of the Real* (published 1894).	Keir Hardie sets up the Independent Labour Party. Wilde, *A Woman of No Importance*
1894	*Life's Little Ironies* (tales).	Kipling, *The Jungle Book*
1895	*Jude the Obscure* appears in volume form: a savage attack on marriage which worsens relations with Emma. Serialized previously in *Harper's New Monthly Magazine* in bowdlerized form. It receives both eulogistic and vitriolic reviews. The latter are a factor in his ceasing to write novels.	Oscar Wilde jailed for homosexual offences; serves three years. The first Bristol electric tramway. Wilde, *The Importance of Being Earnest* H. G. Wells, *The Time-Machine*
1895–6	First collected edition: the Wessex Novels (16 volumes). This includes the first book edition of *Jude the Obscure*.	
1896		Locomotive on the Highways Act (car speed maximum 14 m.p.h.). Death of William Morris. Wells, *The Island of Dr Moreau*

	Life	*Historical and Cultural Background*
1897	*The Well-Beloved*, a newly rewritten version of the 1892 serial, added to the Wessex Novels as volume XVII. From now on he only publishes the poetry he has been writing since the 1860s.	Queen Victoria's Diamond Jubilee. Existing suffrage organizations unite as National Union of Women's Suffrage Societies. Havelock Ellis, *Sexual Inversion*
1898	*Wessex Poems and Other Verses.* Hardy and Emma continue to live at Max Gate but are now estranged and 'kept separate'.	Germany begins the building of a large battle fleet. Britain responds by doing the same. Wilde released from prison. Wilde, *The Ballad of Reading Gaol*
1899–1902		Boer War in South Africa over the Transvaal gold mines; Britain crushes the Boers.
1900		Labour Representation Committee set up to get Labour candidates into Parliament. Wilde and Ruskin die.
1901	*Poems of the Past and the Present* (post-dated 1902)	Victoria dies and is succeeded by Edward VII.
1902	Macmillan becomes his publisher.	James, *The Wings of the Dove*
1903		First manned flight by Wright brothers in the USA. Motor Car Act raises speed limit to 20 m.p.h. James, *The Ambassadors*
1904	Hardy's mother Jemima, the single most important influence in his life, dies. Part 1 of *The Dynasts* (epic drama in verse on Napoleon) published.	Anglo-French Entente. James, *The Golden Bowl*
1905	At about this time Hardy meets Florence Emily Dugdale, his future second wife, then aged 26. She is soon a friend of Hardy and Emma, and his part-time secretary.	Increased trade-union activity. E. M. Forster, *Where Angels Fear to Tread*
1906	Part 2 of *The Dynasts*.	Thirty Labour MPs are elected in General Election.
1907		Anglo-Russian Entente. Act allowing marriage with deceased wife's sister. First London cinema. Forster, *The Longest Journey*.

	Life	*Historical and Cultural Background*
1908	Part 3 of *The Dynasts* completes the work.	Non-contributory state pension is set up. Forster, *A Room with a View*
1909	*Time's Laughingstocks and Other Verses.*	Housing and Town Planning Act (to help provide working-class housing). Labour Exchanges Act (seeking employment previously difficult).
1910	Is awarded the Order of Merit, having previously refused a knighthood. Also receives the Freedom of Dorchester.	Edward VII dies and is succeeded by George V.
1911		National Insurance Act. D. H. Lawrence, *The White Peacock*
1912	27 November: Emma dies, still estranged. Her death triggers the writing of Hardy's finest love lyrics, *Poems of 1912–1913*, about their early time together in Cornwall which he now revisits.	William Morris produces first cheap Morris Oxford car. George V attends first Royal Command Variety Performance.
1912–13	Publication of a major collected edition of novels and verse by Hardy: the Wessex Edition (24 volumes).	
1913	*A Changed Man and Other Tales.*	A suffragette throws herself under the King's horse at the Derby. Lawrence, *Sons and Lovers*
1914	10 February: Hardy marries Florence Dugdale (who was hurt by the poems written about Emma after her death). *Satires of Circumstance*; *The Dynasts: Prologue and Epilogue.*	Start of First World War. A million copies of books now available in free public libraries. James Joyce, *Dubliners*
1914–15		Joyce, *A Portrait of the Artist as a Young Man*
1915	Mary, Hardy's sister, dies. His distant relative, Frank George, is killed at Gallipoli.	Virginia Woolf, *The Voyage Out* Lawrence, *The Rainbow*
1916	*Selected Poems*	Self-proclamation of an independent Irish Republic.
1917	*Moments of Vision and Miscellaneous Verses*	T. S. Eliot, *Prufrock and Other Observations*

	Life	*Historical and Cultural Background*
1918		First World War ends. Vote extended to men over 21 and some women over 30. Those Irish who want independence set up their own parliament, the Dáil, and the Irish 'troubles' begin. British troops ruthlessly repress the rebels. Education Act raises the school-leaving age to 14 and extends education for some to 16.
1919		Russian Revolution helps stir up working-class militancy. First satisfactory contraceptive for women is devised.
1919–20	Mellstock Edition of novels and verse (37 volumes).	
1920		Increased social awareness is indicated by extension of National Insurance against unemployment. Lawrence, *Women in Love*
1921		Ireland splits into new republic and the North, which remains part of the United Kingdom.
1922	*Late Lyrics and Earlier with Many Other Verses*	BBC is set up. Joyce, *Ulysses* Woolf, *Jacob's Room* T. S. Eliot, *The Waste Land*
1923	*The Famous Tragedy of the Queen of Cornwall* (drama). Florence Henniker dies. The Prince of Wales, the future Edward VIII (later the Duke of Windsor), visits Max Gate.	
1924	Dramatized version of *Tess* performed at Dorchester. Hardy is infatuated with the local woman, Gertrude Bugler, who plays Tess.	First Labour Government formed by Ramsay MacDonald. Forster, *A Passage to India*
1925	*Human Shows, Far Phantasies, Songs and Trifles.*	Woolf, *Mrs Dalloway* and *The Common Reader* (essays)
1926		May: General Strike, lasting 9 days. James Ramsay MacDonald forms a coalition government which he leads until 1935 but is expelled from the Labour Party who refuse to support it.
1927		Invention of talking pictures. Woolf, *To the Lighthouse*

Life	*Historical and Cultural Background*
1928	11 January: Hardy dies. His heart is buried in Emma's grave at Stinsford, his ashes in Westminster Abbey. *Winter Words in Various Moods and Metres* published posthumously. Hardy's brother, Henry, dies.	Vote is extended to women over 21. Lawrence, *Lady Chatterley's Lover* Woolf, *Orlando*
1928–30	Hardy's autobiography is completed by his second wife and published on his instructions under her name.	
1937	Florence, Hardy's second wife, dies.	
1940	Hardy's last sibling, Kate, dies.	

TESS OF THE D'URBERVILLES

A PURE WOMAN
FAITHFULLY PRESENTED BY
THOMAS HARDY

". . . Poor wounded name! My bosom as a bed
Shall lodge thee."—W. SHAKESPEARE*

EXPLANATORY NOTE
TO THE
FIRST EDITION

THE main portion of the following story appeared—with slight modifications—in the *Graphic* newspaper: other chapters, more especially addressed to adult readers, in the *Fortnightly Review* and the *National Observer*, as episodic sketches. My thanks are tendered to the editors and proprietors of those periodicals for enabling me now to piece the trunk and limbs of the novel together, and print it complete, as originally written two years ago.

I will just add that the story is sent out in all sincerity of purpose, as an attempt to give artistic form to a true sequence of things; and in respect of the book's opinions and sentiments, I would ask any too genteel reader, who cannot endure to have said what everybody nowadays thinks and feels, to remember a well-worn sentence of St Jerome's: If an offence come out of the truth, better is it that the offence come than that the truth be concealed.

November 1891.   T. H.

PREFACE
TO THE
FIFTH AND LATER EDITIONS

THIS novel being one wherein the great campaign of the heroine begins after an event in her experience which has usually been treated as fatal to her part of protagonist, or at least as the virtual ending of her enterprises and hopes, it was quite contrary to avowed conventions that the public should welcome the book, and agree with me in holding that there was something more to be said in fiction than had been said about the shaded side of a well-known catastrophe. But the responsive spirit in which *Tess of the d'Urbervilles* has been received by the readers of England and America, would seem to prove that the plan of laying down a story on the lines of tacit opinion, instead of making it to square with the merely vocal formulæ of society, is not altogether a wrong one, even when exemplified in so unequal and partial an achievement as the present. For this responsiveness I cannot refrain from expressing my thanks; and my regret is that, in a world where one so often hungers in vain for friendship, where even not to be wilfully misunderstood is felt as a kindness, I shall never meet in person these appreciative readers, male and female, and shake them by the hand.

I include amongst them the reviewers—by far the majority—who have so generously welcomed the tale. Their words show that they, like the others, have only too largely repaired my defects of narration by their own imaginative intuition.

Nevertheless, though the novel was intended to be neither didactic nor aggressive, but in the scenic parts to be representative simply, and in the contemplative to be oftener charged with impressions than with convictions, there have been objectors both to the matter and to the rendering.

The more austere of these maintain a conscientious difference of opinion concerning, among other things, subjects fit for art, and reveal an inability to associate the idea of the sub-title adjective with any but the artificial and derivative meaning which has resulted to it from the ordinances of civilization. They ignore the meaning of the word in Nature, together with all aesthetic claims upon it, not to mention the spiritual interpretation afforded by the finest side of their own Christianity. Others dissent on grounds which are intrinsically no more than an assertion that the novel embodies the views of life prevalent at the end of the nineteenth century, and not those of an earlier and simpler generation—an assertion which I can only hope may be well founded. Let me repeat that a novel is an impression, not an argument; and there the matter must rest; as one is reminded by a passage which occurs in the letters of Schiller to Goethe on judges of this class: "They are those who seek only their own ideas in a representation, and prize that which should be as higher than what is. The cause of the dispute, therefore, lies in the very first principles, and it would be utterly impossible to come to an understanding with them." And again: "As soon as I observe that any one, when judging of poetical representations, considers anything more important than the inner Necessity and Truth, I have done with him."

In the introductory words to the first edition I suggested the possible advent of the genteel person who would not be able to endure something or other in these pages. That person duly appeared among the aforesaid objectors. In one case he felt upset that it was not possible for him to read the book through three times, owing to my not having made that critical effort which "alone can prove the salvation of such an one." In another, he objected to such vulgar articles as the Devil's pitchfork, a lodging-house carving-knife, and a shame-bought parasol, appearing in a respectable story. In another place he was a gentleman who turned Christian for half-an-hour the better to express his grief that a disrespectful phrase about the Immortals should have been used; though the same innate gentility compelled him to excuse the author in words of pity that one cannot be too thankful for: "He does but give us of his best." I can assure this great critic that to exclaim illogically against the gods, singular or plural, is not such an original sin of mine as he seems to imagine. True, it may have some local originality; though if Shakespeare were an authority on history, which perhaps he is not, I could show that the sin was introduced into Wessex as early as the Heptarchy* itself. Says Glo'ster in *Lear*, otherwise Ina, king of that country:

> As flies to wanton boys are we to the gods;
> They kill us for their sport.*

The remaining two or three manipulators of *Tess* were of the predetermined sort whom most writers and readers would gladly forget; professed literary boxers, who put on their convictions for the occasion; modern "Hammers of Heretics";* sworn Discouragers, ever on the watch to prevent the tentative half-success from becoming the whole success later on; who pervert plain meanings, and grow personal under the name of practising the great historical method. However, they may have causes to advance, privileges to guard, traditions to keep going; some of which a mere tale-teller, who writes down how the things of the world strike him, without any ulterior intentions whatever, has overlooked, and may by pure inadvertence have run foul of when in the least aggressive mood. Perhaps some passing perception, the outcome of a dream-hour, would if generally acted on, cause such an assailant considerable inconvenience with respect to position, interests, family, servant, ox, ass, neighbour, or neighbour's wife. He therefore valiantly hides his personality behind a publisher's shutters, and cries "Shame!" So densely is the world thronged that any shifting of positions, even the best warranted advance, galls somebody's kibe.* Such shiftings often begin in sentiment, and such sentiment sometimes begins in a novel.

July 1892.

The foregoing remarks were written during the early career of this story, when a spirited public and private criticism of its points was still fresh to the feelings. The pages are allowed to stand for what they are worth, as something once said; but probably they would not have been written now. Even in the short time which has elapsed since the book was first published, some of the critics who provoked the reply have "gone down into silence", as if to remind one of the infinite unimportance of both their say and mine.

In the present edition it may be well to state, in response to inquires from readers interested in landscape, pre-historic antiquities, and especially old English architecture, that the description of these backgrounds in this and its companion novels has been done from the real. Many features of the first two kinds have been given under their existing names; for instance, the Vale of Blackmoor or Blakemore, Hambledon Hill, Bulbarrow, Nettlecombe Tout, Dogbury Hill, High-Stoy, Bubb-Down Hill, The Devil's Kitchen, Cross-in-Hand, Long-Ash Lane, Benvill Lane, Giant's Hill, Crimmercrock Lane, and Stonehenge. The rivers Froom or Frome, and Stour, are, of course, well known as such. And in planning the stories the idea was that large towns and points tending to mark the outline of Wessex—such as Bath, Plymouth, The Start, Portland Bill, Southampton, &c.—should be named outright. The scheme was not greatly elaborated, but, whatever its value, the names remain still.

In respect of places described under fictitious or ancient names—for reasons that seemed good at the time of writing—discerning persons have affirmed in print that they clearly recognize the originals: such as Shaftesbury in "Shaston", Sturminster Newton in "Stourcastle", Dorchester in "Casterbridge", Salisbury in "Melchester", Salisbury Plain in "The Great Plain", Cranbourne in "Chaseborough", Cranbourne Chase in "The Chase", Beaminster in "Emminster", Bere Regis in "Kingsbere", Woodbury Hill in "Greenhill", Wool Bridge in "Wellbridge", Hartfoot or Harput Lane in "Stagfoot Lane", Hazelbury in "Nuttlebury", Bridport in "Port-Bredy", Maiden Newton in "Chalk Newton", a farm near Nettlecombe Tout in "Flintcomb-Ash", Sherborne in "Sherton Abbas", Milton Abbey in "Middleton Abbey", Cerne Abbas in "Abbot's Cernel", Evershot in "Evershead", Taunton in "Toneborough", Bournemouth in "Sandbourne", Winchester in "Wintoncester", and so on. I shall not be the one to contradict them; I accept their statements as at least an indication of their real and kindly interest in the scenes.

January 1895

The present edition of this novel contains a few pages that have never appeared in any previous edition. When the detached episodes were collected as stated in the preface of 1891, these pages were overlooked, though they were in the original manuscript. They occur in Chapter X.

Respecting the sub-title, to which allusion was made above, I may add that it was appended at the last moment, after reading the final proofs, as being the estimate left in a candid mind of the heroine's character—an estimate that nobody would be likely to dispute. It was disputed more than anything else in the book. *Melius fuerat non scribere.** But there it stands.

The novel was first published complete, in three volumes, in November 1891.

March 1912.   T. H.

CONTENTS

PHASE THE FIRST

THE MAIDEN

PHASE THE FIRST

THE MAIDEN

I

ON an evening in the latter part of May a middle-aged man was walking homeward from Shaston to the village of Marlott, in the adjoining Vale of Blakemore or Blackmoor. The pair of legs that carried him were rickety, and there was a bias in his gait which inclined him somewhat to the left of a straight line. He occasionally gave a smart nod, as if in confirmation of some opinion; though he was not thinking of anything in particular. An empty egg-basket was slung upon his arm, the nap of his hat was ruffled, a patch being quite worn away at its brim where his thumb came in taking it off. Presently he was met by an elderly parson astride on a grey mare, who, as he rode, hummed a wandering tune.

"Good-night t'ee," said the man with the basket.

"Good-night, Sir John," said the parson.

The pedestrian, after another pace or two, halted, and turned round.

"Now, sir, begging your pardon; we met last market-day on this road about this time, and I zaid 'Good-night,' and you made reply '*Good-night, Sir John*', as now."

"I did," said the parson.

"And once before that—near a month ago."

"I may have."

"Then what might your meaning be in calling me 'Sir John' these different times, when I be plain Jack Durbeyfield the haggler?"*

The parson rode a step or two nearer. "It was only my whim," he said; and, after a moment's hesitation: "It was on account of a discovery I made some little time ago, whilst I was hunting up pedigrees for the new county history. I am Parson Tringham, the antiquary, of Stagfoot Lane. Don't you really know, Durbeyfield, that you are the lineal representative of the ancient and knightly family of the d'Urbervilles, who derive their descent from Sir Pagan

d'Urberville, that renowned knight who came from Normandy with
William the Conqueror, as appears by Battle Abbey Roll?"

"Never heard it before, sir!"

"Well—it's true. . . . Throw up your chin a moment, so that I may
catch the profile of your face better. Yes, that's the d'Urberville nose
and chin—a little debased.—Your ancestor was one of the twelve
knights who assisted the Lord of Estremavilla in Normandy in his
conquest of Glamorganshire. Branches of your family held manors
over all this part of England; their names appear in the Pipe Rolls in
the time of King Stephen.* In the reign of King John one of them was
rich enough to give a manor to the Knights Hospitallers; and in
Edward the Second's time your forefather Brian was summoned to
Westminster to attend the great Council there. You declined a little
in Oliver Cromwell's time, but to no serious extent, and in Charles
the Second's reign* you were made Knights of the Royal Oak for your
loyalty. Aye, there have been generations of Sir Johns among you,
and if knighthood were hereditary like a baronetcy—as it practically
was in old times, when men were knighted from father to son—you
would be Sir John now."

"Ye don't say so!"

"In short," concluded the parson decisively smacking his leg with
his switch, "there's hardly such another family in England!"

"Daze my eyes, and isn't there," said Durbeyfield. "And here have
I been knocking about year after year from pillar to post as if I was no
more than the commonest feller in the parish. . . . And how long hev
this news about me been knowed, Pa'son Tringham?"

The clergyman explained that as far as he was aware, it had quite
died out of knowledge, and could hardly be said to be known at all.
His own investigations had begun on a day in the preceding spring
when having been engaged in tracing the vicissitudes of the
d'Urberville family he had observed Durbeyfield's name on his
waggon, and had thereupon been led to make inquiries about his
father and grandfather till he had no doubt on the subject. "At first I
resolved not to disturb you with such a useless piece of information," said he. "However our impulses are too strong for our
judgment sometimes. I thought you might perhaps know something
of it all the while."

"Well, I have heard once or twice, 'tis true, that my family had
seen better days afore they came to Blackmoor. But I took no notice

o't, thinking it to mean that we had once kept two horses where we now keep only one. I've got a wold silver spoon, and a wold graven seal at home, too; but Lord, what's a spoon and seal? . . . And to think that I and these noble d'Urbervilles were one flesh all the time. 'Twas said that my gr't-granfer had secrets, and didn't care to talk of where he come from. . . . And where do we raise our smoke now, parson, if I may make so bold; I mean, where do we d'Urbervilles live?"

"You don't live anywhere. You are extinct—as a county family."

"That's bad."

"Yes—what the mendacious family chronicles call extinct in the male line—that is, gone down—gone under."

"Then where do we lie?"

"At Kingsbere-sub-Greenhill: rows and rows of you in your vaults, with your effigies, under Purbeck-marble canopies."

"And where be our family mansions and estates?"

"You haven't any."

"Oh? No lands neither?"

"None; though you once had 'em in abundance, as I said, for your family consisted of numerous branches. In this county there was a scat of yours at Kingsbere, and another at Sherton, and another at Millpond, and another at Lullstead, and another at Wellbridge."

"And shall we ever come into our own again?"

"Ah—that I can't tell!"

"And what had I better do about it, sir?" asked Durbeyfield after a pause.

"Oh—nothing, nothing; except chasten yourself with the thought of 'how are the mighty fallen.'* It is a fact of some interest to the local historian and genealogist, nothing more. There are several families among the cottagers of this county of almost equal lustre. Good-night."

"But you'll turn back and have a quart of beer wi' me on the strength o't, Pa'son Tringham? There's very pretty brew in tap at The Pure Drop—though, to be sure, not so good as at Rolliver's."

"No thank you—not this evening Durbeyfield. You've had enough already." Concluding thus the parson rode on his way, with doubts as to his discretion in retailing this curious bit of lore.

When he was gone Durbeyfield walked a few steps in a profound reverie, and then sat down upon the grassy bank by the roadside depositing his basket before him. In a few minutes a youth appeared in the distance, walking in the same direction as that which had been pursued by Durbeyfield; the latter on seeing him held up his hand, and the lad quickened his pace and came near.

"Boy—take up that basket! I want 'ee to go on an errand for me."

The lath-like stripling frowned. "Who be you, then, John Durbeyfield, to order me about and call me boy? You know my name as well as I know yours!"

"Do you, do you! That's the secret—that's the secret! Now obey my orders, and take the message I'm going to charge 'ee wi'. . . . Well, Fred, I don't mind telling you that the secret is that I'm one of a noble race—it has been just found out by me this present afternoon, p.m." And as he made the announcement Durbeyfield, declining from his sitting position, luxuriously stretched himself out upon the bank among the daisies.

The lad stood before Durbeyfield and contemplated his length from crown to toe.

"Sir John d'Urberville—that's who I am," continued the prostrate man: "that is if knights were baronets—which they be. 'Tis recorded in history all about me. Dost know of such a place, lad, as Kingsbere-sub-Greenhill?"

"Ees. I've been there to Greenhill Fair."

"Well; under the church of that city there lie—"

" 'Tisn't a city—the place I mean; leastwise 'twaddn' when I was there—'twas a little one-eyed blinking sort o' place—"

"Never you mind the place, boy—that's not the question before us. Under the church of that there parish lie my ancestors— hundreds of 'em—in coats of mail and jewels—in gr't lead coffins weighing tons and tons. There's not a man in the county o' South-Wessex that's got grander and nobler skillentons in his family than I."

"Oh?"

"Now take up that basket, and goo on to Marlott, and when you've come to The Pure Drop Inn, tell 'em to send a horse-and-carriage to me immed'ately, to carry me hwome. And in the bottom o' the carriage they be to put a noggin o' rum in a small bottle and chalk it up to my account. And when you've done that goo on to my house with the basket, and tell my wife to put away that washing, because she needn't finish it, and wait till I come hwome, as I've news to tell her."

As the lad stood in a dubious attitude Durbeyfield put his hand in his pocket and produced a shilling, one of the chronically few that he possessed. "Here's for your labour, lad."

This made a difference in the young man's estimate of the position. "Yes, Sir John. Thank 'ee. Anything else I can do for 'ee, Sir John?"

"Tell 'em at hwome that I should like for supper, well, lamb's fry if they can get it; and if they can't, black-pot; and if they can't get that, well, chitterlings will do."

"Yes, Sir John."

The boy took up the basket and as he set out the notes of a brass band were heard from the direction of the village. "What's that?" said Durbeyfield. "Not on account o' I?"

" 'Tis the women's club-walking,* Sir John. Why your da'ter is one o' the members."

"To be sure—I'd quite forgot it in my thoughts of greater things. Well, vamp on to Marlott, will ye, and order that carriage, and maybe I'll drive round and inspect the club."

The lad departed, and Durbeyfield lay waiting on the grass and daisies in the evening sun. Not a soul passed that way for a long while, and the faint notes of the band were the only human sounds audible within the rim of blue hills.

II

THE village of Marlott lay amid the north-eastern undulations of the beautiful Vale of Blakemore or Blackmoor aforesaid—an engirdled and secluded region, for the most part untrodden as yet by tourist or landscape-painter, though within a four hours' journey from London.

It is a vale whose acquaintance is best made by viewing it from the summits of the hills that surround it—except perhaps during the droughts of summer. An unguided ramble into its recesses in bad weather is apt to engender dissatisfaction with its narrow, tortuous, and miry ways.

This fertile and sheltered tract of country, in which the fields are never brown and the springs never dry, is bounded on the south by the bold chalk ridge that embraces the prominences of Hambledon Hill, Bulbarrow, Nettlecombe-Tout, Dogbury, High-Stoy, and Bubb-Down. The traveller from the coast who, after plodding northward for a score of miles over calcareous downs and corn-lands, suddenly reaches the verge of one of these escarpments, is surprised and delighted to behold, extended like a map beneath him, a country differing absolutely from that which he has passed through. Behind him the hills are open, the sun blazes down upon fields so large as to give an unenclosed character to the landscape, the lanes are white, the hedges low and plashed, the atmosphere colourless. Here in the valley the world seems to be constructed upon a smaller and more delicate scale; the fields are mere paddocks, so reduced that from this height their hedgerows appear a network of dark green threads overspreading the paler green of the grass. The atmosphere beneath is languorous, and is so tinged with azure that what artists call the middle-distance partakes also of that hue, while the horizon beyond is of the deepest ultramarine. Arable lands are few and limited; with but slight exceptions the prospect is a broad rich mass of grass and trees, mantling minor hills and dales within the major. Such is the Vale of Blackmoor.

The district is of historic no less than of topographical interest. The Vale was known in former times as the Forest of White Hart, from a curious legend of King Henry the Third's reign, in which the killing by a certain Thomas de la Lynd of a beautiful white hart which the king had run down and spared, was made the occasion of a heavy fine.* In those days, and till comparatively recent times, the country was densely wooded. Even now traces of its earlier condition are to be found in the old oak copses and irregular belts of timber that yet survive upon its slopes, and the hollow-trunked trees that shade so many of its pastures.

The forests have departed, but some old customs of their shades remain. Many however linger only in a metamorphosed or disguised form. The May-Day dance, for instance, was to be discerned, on the afternoon under notice, in the guise of the club-revel, or "club-walking", as it was there called.

It was an interesting event to the younger inhabitants of Marlott, though its real interest was not observed by the participators in the ceremony. Its singularity lay less in the retention of a custom of walking in procession and dancing on each anniversary than in the members being solely women. In men's clubs such celebrations were though expiring, less uncommon: but either the natural shyness of the softer sex, or a sarcastic attitude on the part of male relatives, had denuded such women's clubs as remained (if any other did) of this their glory and consummation. The club of Marlott alone lived to uphold the local Cerealia.* It had walked for hundreds of years, if not as benefit-club, as votive sisterhood of some sort; and it walked still.

The banded ones were all dressed in white gowns—a gay survival from Old-Style days,* when cheerfulness and Maytime were synonyms—days before the habit of taking long views had reduced emotions to a monotonous average. Their first exhibition of themselves was in a processional march of two and two round the parish. Ideal and real clashed slightly as the sun lit up their figures against the green hedges and creeper-laced house-fronts; for, though the whole troop wore white garments, no two whites were alike among them. Some approached pure blanching; some had a bluish pallor; some worn by the older characters (which had possibly lain by folded for many a year) inclined to a cadaverous tint, and to a Georgian style.

In addition to the distinction of a white frock every woman and girl carried in her right hand a peeled willow-wand, and in her left a bunch of white flowers. The peeling of the former, and the selection of the latter, had been an operation of personal care.

There were a few middle-aged and even elderly women in the train, their silver-wiry hair and wrinkled faces, scourged by time and trouble, having almost a grotesque, certainly a pathetic, appearance in such a jaunty situation. In a true view, perhaps, there was more to be gathered and told of each anxious and experienced one, to whom the years were drawing nigh when she should say, "I have no pleasure in them," than of her juvenile comrades. But let the elder be passed over here for those under whose bodices the life throbbed quick and warm.

The young girls formed, indeed, the majority of the band, and their heads of luxuriant hair reflected in the sunshine every tone of gold, and black, and brown. Some had beautiful eyes, others a beautiful nose, others a beautiful mouth and figure: few, if any, had all. A difficulty of arranging their lips in this crude exposure to public scrutiny, an inability to balance their heads, and to dissociate self-consciousness from their features, was apparent in them, and showed that they were genuine country girls, unaccustomed to many eyes.

And as each and all of them were warmed without by the sun, so each had a private little sun for her soul to bask in; some dream, some affection, some hobby, at least some remote and distant hope which, though perhaps starving to nothing, still lived on, as hopes will. Thus they were all cheerful, and many of them merry.

They came round by The Pure Drop Inn, and were turning out of the high road to pass through a wicket-gate into the meadows, when one of the women said:

"The Lord-a-Lord! Why, Tess Durbeyfield, if there isn't thy father riding hwome in a carriage!"

A young member of the band turned her head at the exclamation. She was a fine and handsome girl—not handsomer than some others, possibly—but her mobile peony mouth and large innocent eyes added eloquence to colour and shape. She wore a red ribbon in her hair, and was the only one of the white company who could boast of such a pronounced adornment. As she looked round Durbeyfield was seen moving along the road in a chaise belonging to The Pure Drop, driven by a frizzle-headed brawny damsel with her gown-sleeves rolled above her elbows. This was the cheerful servant of that establishment, who, in her part of factotum, turned groom and ostler at times. Durbeyfield, leaning back, and with his eyes closed luxuriously, was waving his hand above his head and singing in a slow recitative: "I've-got-a-gr't-family-vault-at-Kingsbere—and-knighted-forefathers-in-lead-coffins-there!"

The clubbists tittered, except the girl called Tess—in whom a slow heat seemed to rise at the sense that her father was making himself foolish in their eyes. "He's tired, that's all," she said hastily, "and he has got a lift home, because our own horse has to rest to-day."

"Bless thy simplicity, Tess," said her companions. "He's got his market-nitch.* Haw-haw!"

"Look here; I won't walk another inch with you, if you say any jokes about him!" Tess cried, and the colour upon her cheeks spread over her face and neck. In a moment her eyes grew moist, and her glance drooped to the ground. Perceiving that they had really pained her they said no more, and order again prevailed. Tess's pride would not allow her to turn her head again, to learn what her father's meaning was, if he had any; and thus she moved on with the whole body to the enclosure where there was to be dancing on the green. By the time the spot was reached she had recovered her equanimity, and tapped her neighbour with her wand, and talked as usual.

Tess Durbeyfield at this time of her life was a mere vessel of emotion untinctured by experience. The dialect was on her tongue to some extent, despite the village school; the characteristic intonation of that dialect, for this district, being the voicing approximately rendered by the syllable UR, probably as rich an utterance as any to be found in human speech. The pouted-up deep red mouth to which this syllable was native had hardly as yet settled into its definite shape, and her lower lip had a way of thrusting the middle of her top one upward, when they closed together after a word.

Phases of her childhood lurked in her aspect still. As she walked along to-day, for all her bouncing handsome womanliness, you could sometimes see her twelfth year in her cheeks, or her ninth sparkling from her eyes; and even her fifth would flit over the curves of her mouth now and then.

Yet few knew, and still fewer considered this. A small minority, mainly strangers, would look long at her in casually passing by, and grow momentarily fascinated by her freshness, and wonder if they would ever see her again; but to almost everybody she was a fine and picturesque country girl, and no more.

Nothing was seen or heard further of Durbeyfield in his triumphal chariot under the conduct of the ostleress, and the club having entered the allotted space, dancing began. As there were no men in the company the girls danced at first with each other, but when the hour for the close of labour drew on, the masculine inhabitants of the village together with other idlers and pedestrians, gathered round the spot and appeared inclined to negotiate for a partner.

Among these on-lookers were three young men of a superior class, carrying small knapsacks strapped to their shoulders and stout sticks in their hands. Their general likeness to each other and their consecutive ages would almost have suggested that they might be, what in fact they were, brothers. The eldest wore the white tie, high waistcoat, and thin-brimmed hat of the regulation curate; the second was the normal undergraduate; the appearance of the third and youngest would hardly have been sufficient to characterize him; there was an uncribbed, uncabined,* aspect in his eyes and attire, implying that he had hardly as yet found the entrance to his professional groove. That he was a desultory, tentative student of something and everything might only have been predicated of him.

These three brethren told casual acquaintance that they were spending their Whitsun* holidays in a walking-tour through the Vale of Blackmoor, their course being south-westerly from the town of Shaston on the north-east.

They leant over the gate by the highway, and inquired as to the meaning of the dance and the white-frocked maids. The two elder of the brothers were plainly not intending to linger more than a moment; but the spectacle of a bevy of girls dancing without male partners seemed to amuse the third, and make him in no hurry to move on. He unstrapped his knapsack, put it with his stick on the hedge-bank, and opened the gate.

"What are you going to do, Angel?" asked the eldest.

"I am inclined to go and have a fling with them. Why not all of us—just for a minute or two—it will not detain us long?"

"No, no; nonsense!" said the first. "Dancing in public with a troop of country hoydens—suppose we should be seen! Come along, or it will be dark before we get to Stourcastle, and there's no place we can sleep at nearer than that; besides, we must get through another chapter of *A Counterblast to Agnosticism** before we turn in, now I have taken the trouble to bring the book."

"All right—I'll overtake you and Cuthbert in five minutes; don't stop; I give my word that I will, Felix."

The two elder reluctantly left him and walked on, taking their brother's knapsack to relieve him in following, and the youngest entered the field.

"This is a thousand pities," he said gallantly to two or three of the girls nearest him, as soon as there was a pause in the dance. "Where are your partners, my dears?"

"They've not left off work yet," answered one of the boldest. "They'll be here by-and-by. Till then will you be one, sir?"

"Certainly. But what's one among so many!"

"Better than none. 'Tis melancholy work facing and footing it to one of your own sort, and no clipsing and colling at all! Now, pick and choose."

" 'Ssh—don't be so for'ard!" said a shyer girl.

The young man thus invited glanced them over, and attempted some discrimination; but as the group were all so new to him he could not very well exercise it. He took almost the first that came to hand, which was not the speaker, as she had expected; nor did it happen to be Tess Durbeyfield. Pedigree, ancestral skeletons, monumental record, the d'Urberville lineaments, did not help Tess in her life's battle as yet, even to the extent of attracting to her a dancing-partner over the heads of the commonest peasantry. So much for Norman blood unaided by Victorian lucre.

The name of the eclipsing girl, whatever it was, has not been handed down; but she was envied by all as the first who enjoyed the luxury of a masculine partner that evening. Yet such was the force of example that the village young men, who had not hastened to enter the gate while no intruder was in the way, now dropped in quickly, and soon the couples became leavened with rustic youth to a marked extent, till at length the plainest woman in the club was no longer compelled to foot it on the masculine side of the figure.

The church clock struck, when suddenly the student said that he must leave—he had been forgetting himself—he had to join his companions. As he fell out of the dance his eyes lighted on Tess Durbeyfield, whose own large orbs wore, to tell the truth, the faintest aspect of reproach that he had not chosen her. He too was sorry then that, owing to her backwardness, he had not observed her; and with that in his mind he left the pasture.

On account of his long delay he started in a flying run down the lane westward, and had soon passed the hollow, and mounted the next rise. He had not yet overtaken his brothers, but he paused to get breath; and looked back. He could see the white figures of the girls in the green enclosure, whirling about as they had whirled when he was among them. They seemed to have quite forgotten him already.

All of them, except, perhaps, one. This white shape stood apart by the hedge alone. From her position he knew it to be the pretty maiden with whom he had not danced. Trifling as the matter was, he yet instinctively felt that she was hurt by his oversight. He wished that he had asked her; he wished that he had inquired her name. She was so modest, so expressive, she had looked so soft in her thin white gown that he felt he had acted stupidly.

However, it could not be helped, and turning, and bending himself to a rapid walk, he dismissed the subject from his mind.

As for Tess Durbeyfield, she did not so easily dislodge the incident from her consideration. She had no spirit to dance again for a long time, though she might have had plenty of partners; but, ah! they did not speak so nicely as the strange young man had done. It was not till the rays of the sun had absorbed the young stranger's retreating figure on the hill that she shook off her temporary sadness and answered her would-be partner in the affirmative.

She remained with her comrades till dusk, and participated with a certain zest in the dancing; though, being heart-whole as yet, she enjoyed treading a measure purely for its own sake; little divining when she saw "the soft torments, the bitter sweets, the pleasing pains, and the agreeable distresses"* of those girls who had been wooed and won, what she herself was capable of in that kind. The struggles and wrangles of the lads for her hand in a jig were an amusement to her—no more; and when they became fierce she rebuked them.

She might have stayed even later, but the incident of her father's odd appearance and manner returned upon the girl's mind to make her anxious, and wondering what had become of him she dropped away from the dancers and bent her steps towards the end of the village at which the parental cottage lay.

While yet many score yards off, other rhythmic sounds than those she had quitted became audible to her; sounds that she knew well— so well. They were a regular series of thumpings from the interior of the house, occasioned by the violent rocking of a cradle upon a stone floor, to which movement a feminine voice kept time by singing, in a vigorous gallopade, the favourite ditty of "The Spotted Cow"*—

> I saw her lie do'—own in yon'—der green gro'—ove;
> Come, love!' and I'll tell' you where!'

The cradle-rocking and the song* would cease simultaneously for a moment, and an exclamation at highest vocal pitch would take the place of the melody.

"God bless thy diment* eyes! And thy waxen cheeks! And thy cherry mouth! And thy Cubit's* thighs! And every bit o' thy blessed body!"

After this invocation the rocking and the singing would recommence, and "The Spotted Cow" proceed as before. So matters stood when Tess opened the door, and paused upon the mat within it surveying the scene.

The interior, in spite of the melody, struck upon the girl's senses with an unspeakable dreariness. From the holiday gaieties of the field—the white gowns, the nosegays, the willow-wands, the whirling movements on the green, the flash of gentle sentiment towards the stranger—to the yellow melancholy of this one-candled spectacle, what a step! Besides the jar of contrast, there came to her a chill self-reproach that she had not returned sooner, to help her mother in these domesticities, instead of indulging herself out-of-doors.

There stood her mother amid the group of children, as Tess had left her, hanging over the Monday washing-tub, which had now, as always, lingered on to the end of the week. Out of that tub had come the day before—Tess felt it with a dreadful sting of remorse—the very white frock upon her back which she had so carelessly greened about the skirt on the damping grass—which had been wrung up and ironed by her mother's own hands.

As usual, Mrs Durbeyfield was balanced on one foot beside the tub, the other being engaged in the aforesaid business of rocking her youngest child. The cradle-rockers had done hard duty for so many years, under the weight of so many children, on that flag-stone floor, that they were worn nearly flat, in consequence of which a huge jerk accompanied each swing of the cot, flinging the baby from side to side like a weaver's shuttle, as Mrs Durbeyfield, excited by her song, trod the rocker with all the spring that was left in her after a long day's seething in the suds.

Nick-knock, nick-knock went the cradle: the candle-flame stretched itself tall, and began jigging up and down; the water dribbled from the matron's elbows, and the song galloped on to the end of the verse, Mrs Durbeyfield regarding her daughter the while. Even now, when burdened with a young family, Joan Durbeyfield was a passionate lover of tune. No ditty floated into Blackmoor Vale from the outer world but Tess's mother caught up its notation in a week.

There still faintly beamed from the woman's features something of the freshness, and even the prettiness, of her youth; rendering it probable that the personal charms which Tess could boast of were in main part her mother's gift, and therefore unknightly, unhistorical.

"I'll rock the cradle for 'ee, mother," said the daughter gently. "Or I'll take off my best frock and help you wring up? I thought you had finished long ago."

Her mother bore Tess no ill-will for leaving the house-work to her single-handed efforts for so long: indeed, Joan seldom upbraided her thereon at any time, feeling but slightly the lack of Tess's assistance whilst her instinctive plan for relieving herself of her labours lay in postponing them. To-night, however, she was even in a blither mood than usual. There was a dreaminess, a preoccupation, an exaltation, in the maternal look which the girl could not understand.

"Well I'm glad you've come," her mother said as soon as the last note had passed out of her. "I want to go and fetch your father; but what's more'n that, I want to tell 'ee what have happened. Y'll be fess enough, my poppet, when th'st know!" (Mrs Durbeyfield habitually spoke the dialect: her daughter, who had passed the sixth standard in the National school* under a London-trained mistress, spoke two languages; the dialect at home, more or less; ordinary English abroad and to persons of quality.)

"Since I've been away?" Tess asked.

"Ay!"

"Had it anything to do with father's making such a mommet of himself in thik carriage this afternoon?—Why did 'er? I felt inclined to sink into the ground with shame!"

"That wer all a part of the larry! We've been found to be the greatest gentlefolk in the whole county—reaching all back long before Oliver Grumble's time—to the days of the Pagan Turks—with monuments and vaults and crests and 'scutcheons, and the Lord knows what-all. In Saint Charles's days we was made Knights o' the Royal Oak, our real name being d'Urberville. . . . Don't that make your bosom plim? 'Twas on this account that your father rode home in the vlee; not because he'd been drinking, as people supposed."

"I'm glad of that. . . . Will it do us any good, mother?"

"O yes. 'Tis thoughted that great things may come o't. No doubt a mampus of volk of our own rank will be down here in their carriages as soon as 'tis known. Your father learnt it on his way hwome from Shaston, and he has been telling me the whole pedigree of the matter."

"Where is father now?" asked Tess suddenly.

Her mother gave irrelevant information by way of answer. "He called to see the doctor to-day in Shaston. It is not consumption at all, it seems. It is fat round his heart 'a says. There, it is like this." Joan Durbeyfield as she spoke curved a sodden thumb and forefinger to the shape of the letter C, and used the other forefinger as a pointer.—" 'At the present moment,' he says to your father, 'your heart is enclosed all round there, and all round there: this space is still open', 'a says. 'As soon as it do meet, so' "—Mrs Durbeyfield closed her fingers into a circle complete—" 'off you will go like a shadder Mr Durbeyfield,' 'a says. 'You mid last ten years: you mid go off in ten months or ten days.' "

Tess looked alarmed. Her father possibly to go behind the eternal cloud so soon notwithstanding this sudden greatness! "But where *is* father?" she asked again.

Her mother put on a deprecating look. "Now don't you be bursting out angry! The poor man—he felt so rafted after his uplifting by the pa'son's news—that he went up to Rolliver's half-an-hour ago. He do want to get up his strength for his journey to-morrow with that load of beehives, which must be delivered, family or no. He'll have to start shortly after twelve to-night, as the distance is so long."

"Get up his strength!" said Tess impetuously, the tears welling to her eyes. "O my God! Go to a public-house to get up his strength! And you as well agreed as he, mother!"

Her rebuke and her mood seemed to fill the whole room, and to impart a cowed look to the furniture, and candle, and children playing about, and to her mother's face.

"No," said the latter touchily, "I be not agreed. I have been waiting for 'ee to bide and keep house while I go to fetch him."

"I'll go."

"O no, Tess. You see, it would be no use."

Tess did not expostulate. She knew what her mother's objection meant. Mrs Durbeyfield's jacket and bonnet were already hanging slily upon a chair by her side, in readiness for this contemplated jaunt, the reason for which the matron deplored more than its necessity.

"And take the *Compleat Fortune-Teller** to the outhouse," Joan continued, rapidly wiping her hands, and donning the garments.

The *Compleat Fortune-Teller* was an old thick volume, which lay on a table at her elbow, so worn by pocketing that the margins had reached the edge of the type. Tess took it up, and her mother started.

This going to hunt up her shiftless husband at the inn was one of Mrs Durbeyfield's still extant enjoyments in the muck and muddle of rearing children. To discover him at Rolliver's, to sit there for an hour or two by his side, and dismiss all thought and care of the children during the interval, made her happy. A sort of halo, an occidental glow, came over life then. Troubles and other realities took on themselves a metaphysical impalpability, sinking to mere mental phenomena for serene contemplation, and no longer stood as pressing concretions which chafed body and soul. The youngsters, not immediately within sight, seemed rather bright and desirable appurtenances than otherwise; the incidents of daily life were not without humorousness and jollity in their aspect there. She felt a little as she had used to feel when she sat by her now wedded husband in the same spot during his wooing, shutting her eyes to his defects of character, and regarding him only in his ideal presentation as lover.

Tess being left alone with the younger children went first to the outhouse with the fortune-telling book, and stuffed it into the thatch. A curious fetishistic fear of this grimy volume on the part of her mother prevented her ever allowing it to stay in the house all night; and hither it was brought back whenever it had been consulted. Between the mother, with her fast-perishing lumber of superstitions, folk-lore, dialect, and orally transmitted ballads, and the daughter, with her trained National teachings and Standard knowledge under an infinitely Revised Code, there was a gap of two hundred years as ordinarily understood. When they were together the Jacobean and the Victorian ages were juxtaposed.

Returning along the garden-path Tess mused on what her mother could have wished to ascertain from the book on this particular day. She guessed the recent ancestral discovery to bear upon it, but did not divine that it solely concerned herself. Dismissing this, however, she busied herself with sprinkling the linen dried during the daytime, in company with her nine-year-old brother Abraham, and her sister Eliza-Louisa of twelve and a half, called "Liza-Lu", the youngest ones being put to bed. There was an interval of four years and more between Tess and the next of the family, the two who had filled the gap having died in their infancy, and this lent her a deputy-maternal attitude when she was alone with her juniors. Next in juvenility to Abraham came two more girls, Hope and Modesty; then a boy of three; and then the baby, who had just completed his first year.

All these young souls were passengers in the Durbeyfield ship— entirely dependent on the judgment of the two Durbeyfield adults for their pleasures, their necessities, their health, even their existence. If the heads of the Durbeyfield household chose to sail into difficulty, disaster, starvation, disease, degradation, death, thither were these half-dozen little captives under hatches compelled to sail with them—six helpless creatures, who had never been asked if they wished for life on any terms, much less if they wished for it on such hard conditions as were involved in being of the shiftless house of Durbeyfield. Some people would like to know whence the poet whose philosophy is in these days deemed as profound and trustworthy as his song is breezy and pure, gets his authority for speaking of "Nature's holy plan."

It grew later, and neither father nor mother reappeared. Tess looked out of the door, and took a mental journey through Marlott. The village was shutting its eyes. Candles and lamps were being put out everywhere: she could inwardly behold the extinguisher, and the extended hand.

Her mother's fetching simply meant one more to fetch. Tess began to perceive that a man in indifferent health, who proposed to start on a journey before one in the morning, ought not to be at an inn at this late hour celebrating his ancient blood. "Abraham," she said to her little brother, "do you put on your hat—you bain't afraid?—and go up to Rolliver's, and see what has gone wi' father and mother."

The boy jumped promptly from his seat, and opened the door; and the night swallowed him up. Half-an-hour passed yet again; neither man woman nor child returned. Abraham, like his parents, seemed to have been limed and caught by the ensnaring inn. "I must go myself," she said.

Liza-Lu then went to bed, and Tess, locking them all in, started on her way up the dark and crooked lane or street not made for hasty progress, a street laid out before inches of land had value, and when one-handed clocks sufficiently subdivided the day.

IV

ROLLIVER's inn, the single alehouse at this end of the long and broken village, could only boast of an off-licence;* hence, as nobody could legally drink on the premises, the amount of overt accommodation for consumers was strictly limited to a little board about six inches wide and two yards long, fixed to the garden-palings by pieces of wire, so as to form a ledge. On this board, thirsty strangers deposited their cups as they stood in the road and drank, and threw the dregs on the dusty ground to the pattern of Polynesia,* and wished they could have a restful seat inside.

Thus the strangers. But there were also local customers who felt the same wish; and where there's a will there's a way.

In a large bedroom upstairs, the window of which was thickly curtained with a great woollen shawl lately discarded by the landlady Mrs Rolliver, were gathered on this evening nearly a dozen persons, all seeking beatitude; all old inhabitants of the nearer end of Marlott, and frequenters of this retreat. Not only did the distance to The Pure Drop, the fully licenced tavern at the further part of the dispersed village, render its accommodation practically unavailable for dwellers at this end; but the far more serious question, the quality of the liquor, confirmed the opinion hereabout that it was better to drink with Rolliver in a corner of the housetop than with the other landlord in a wide house.*

A gaunt four-post bedstead which stood in the room afforded sitting-space for several persons gathered round three of its sides; a couple more men had elevated themselves on a chest of drawers; another rested on the oak-carved "cwoffer"; two on the wash-stand; another on the night-stool; and thus all were somehow seated at their ease. The stage of mental comfort to which they had arrived at this hour was one wherein their souls expanded beyond their skins, and spread their personalities warmly through the room. In this process the chamber and its furniture grew more and more dignified and luxurious, the shawl hanging at the window took upon itself the richness of tapestry, the brass handles of the chest of drawers were as golden knockers, and the carved bedposts seemed to have some kinship with the magnificent pillars of Solomon's temple.*

Mrs Durbeyfield, having quickly walked hitherward after parting from Tess, opened the front door, crossed the downstairs room, which was in deep gloom, and then unfastened the stair-door like one whose fingers knew the tricks of the latches well. Her ascent of the crooked staircase was a slower process, and her face, as it rose into the light above the last stair, encountered the gaze of all the party assembled in the bedroom.

"—Being a few private friends I've asked in to keep up club-walking at my own expense," the landlady exclaimed at the sound of footsteps, as glibly as a child repeating the catechism, while she peered over the stairs. "Oh—'tis you, Mrs Durbeyfield—Lard—how you frightened me!—I thought it might be some gaffer sent by gover'ment."

Mrs Durbeyfield was welcomed with glances and nods by the remainder of the conclave, and turned to where her husband sat. He was humming absently to himself in a low tone: "I be—as good as—some folk here and there! I've got a great family vault at Kingsbere-sub-Greenhill, and finer skillentons than any man—in Wessex!"

"I've something to tell 'ee that's come into my head about that—a grand projick!" whispered his cheerful wife. "Here, John, don't 'ee see me?" She nudged him while he, looking through her as through a window-pane, went on with his recitative.

"Hush! Don't 'ee sing so loud, my good man," said the landlady; "in case any member of the gover'ment should be passing, and take away my licends."

"He's told 'ee what's happened to us, I suppose?" asked Mrs Durbeyfield.

"Yes—in a way. D'ye think there's any money hanging by it?"

"Ah, that's the secret," said Joan Durbeyfield sagely. "However, 'tis well to be kin to a coach, even if you don't ride in 'en." She dropped her public voice and continued in a low tone to her husband: "I've been thinking, since you brought the news, that there's a great rich lady out by Trantridge, on the edge o' The Chase, of the name of d'Urberville."

"Hey—what's that?" said Sir John.

She repeated the information. "That lady must be our relation," she said; "and my projick is to send Tess to claim kin."

"There *is* a lady of the name, now you mention it," said Durbeyfield. "Pa'son Tringham didn't think of that. . . . But she's nothing beside we—a junior branch of us, no doubt, hailing long since King Norman's day."

While this question was being discussed neither of the pair noticed, in their preoccupation, that little Abraham had crept into the room, and was awaiting an opportunity of asking them to return. "She is rich. And she'd be sure to take notice o' the maid," continued Mrs Durbeyfield. "And 'twill be a very good thing. I don't see why two branches o' one family should not be on visiting terms."

"Yes; and we'll all claim kin!" said Abraham brightly from under the bedstead. "And we'll all go and see her when Tess has gone to live with her; and we'll ride in her coach, and wear black clothes!"

"How do you come here, child? What nonsense be ye talking! Go away and play on the stairs till father and mother be ready! . . . Well, Tess ought to go to this other member of our family. She'd be sure to win the lady—Tess would. And likely enough 'twould lead to some noble gentleman marrying her. In short, I know it."

"How?"

"I tried her fate in the *Fortune-Teller*, and it brought out that very thing! . . . You should ha' seen how pretty she looked to-day; her skin is as sumple as a duchess's."

"What says the maid herself to going?"

"I've not asked her. She don't know there is any such lady relation yet. But it would certainly put her in the way of a grand marriage, and she won't say nay to going."

"Tess is queer."

"But she's tractable at bottom. Leave her to me."

Though this conversation had been private, sufficient of its import reached the understandings of those around to suggest to them that the Durbeyfields had weightier concerns to talk of now than common folks had, and that Tess, their pretty eldest daughter, had fine prospects in store.

"Tess is a fine figure o' fun, as I said to myself to-day when I zeed her vamping round parish with the rest," observed one of the elderly boozers in an undertone. "But Joan Durbeyfield must mind that she don't get green malt in floor."* It was a local phrase which had a peculiar meaning, and there was no reply.

The conversation became inclusive, and presently other footsteps were heard crossing the room below.

"—Being a few private friends asked in to-night to keep up

club-walking at my own expense." The landlady had rapidly re-used the formula she kept on hand for intruders before she recognized that the newcomer was Tess.

Even to her mother's gaze the girl's young features looked sadly out of place amid the alcoholic vapours which floated here as no unsuitable medium for wrinkling middle-age; and hardly was a reproachful flash from Tess's dark eyes needed to make her father and mother rise from their seats, hastily finish their ale, and descend the stairs behind her, Mrs Rolliver's caution following their footsteps.

"No noise, please, if ye'll be so good, my dears; or I mid lose my licends, and be summons'd, and I don't know what all! . . . 'Night t'ye!"

They went home together, Tess holding one arm of her father, and Mrs Durbeyfield the other. He had, in truth, drunk very little: not a fourth of the quantity which a systematic tippler could carry to church on a Sunday afternoon without a hitch in his eastings or genuflexions; but the weakness of Sir John's constitution made mountains of his petty sins in this kind. On reaching the fresh air he was sufficiently unsteady to incline the row of three at one moment as if they were marching to London and at another as if they were marching to Bath—which produced a comical effect, frequent enough in families on nocturnal homegoings; and, like most comical effects, not quite so comic after all. The two women valiantly disguised these forced excursions and countermarches as well as they could from Durbeyfield their cause, and from Abraham, and from themselves; and so they approached by degrees their own door, the head of the family bursting suddenly into his former refrain as he drew near, as if to fortify his soul at sight of the smallness of his present residence:

"I've' got' a fam'-ily vault' at Kings'-bere!"

"Hush—don't be so silly, Jacky," said his wife. "Yours is not the only family that was of 'count in wold days. Look at the Anktells, and Horseys, and the Tringhams themselves—gone to seed a'most as much as you—though you was bigger folks than they, that's true. Thank God, I was never of no family, and have nothing to be ashamed of in that way!"

"Don't you be so sure o' that. From your nater 'tis my belief you've disgraced yourselves more than any o' us, and was kings and queens outright at one time."

Tess turned the subject by saying what was far more prominent in her own mind at the moment than thoughts of her ancestry: "I am afraid father won't be able to take the journey with the beehives to-morrow so early."

"I? I shall be all right in an hour or two," said Durbeyfield.

It was eleven o'clock before the family were all in bed, and two o'clock next morning was the latest hour for starting with the bee-hives if they were to be delivered to the retailers in Casterbridge before the Saturday market began, the way thither lying by bad roads over a distance of between twenty and thirty miles, and the horse and waggon being of the slowest. At half-past one Mrs Dur-beyfield came into the large bedroom where Tess and all her little brothers and sisters slept.

"The poor man can't go," she said to her eldest daughter, whose great eyes had opened the moment her mother's hand touched the door.

Tess sat up in bed, lost in a vague interspace between a dream and this information.

"But somebody must go," she replied. "It is late for the hives already. Swarming will soon be over for the year; and if we put off taking 'em till next week's market the call for 'em will be past, and they'll be thrown on our hands."

Mrs Durbeyfield looked unequal to the emergency. "Some young feller, perhaps, would go? One of them who were so much after dancing with 'ee yesterday," she presently suggested.

"O no—I wouldn't have it for the world!" declared Tess proudly. "And letting everybody know the reason—such a thing to be ashamed of! I think *I* could go if Abraham could go with me to kip me company."

Her mother at length agreed to this arrangement. Little Abraham was aroused from his deep sleep in a corner of the same apartment, and made to put on his clothes while still mentally in the other world. Meanwhile Tess had hastily dressed herself; and the twain, lighting a lantern, went out to the stable. The rickety little waggon was already laden, and the girl led out the horse Prince, only a degree less rickety than the vehicle.

The poor creature looked wonderingly round at the night, at the lantern, at their two figures, as if he could not believe that at that hour, when every living thing was intended to be in shelter and at rest, he was called upon to go out and labour. They put a stock of candle-ends into the lantern, hung the latter to the off-side of the load, and directed the horse onward, walking at his shoulder at first during the uphill parts of the way, in order not to overload an animal of so little vigour. To cheer themselves as well as they could, they made an artificial morning with the lantern, some bread and butter, and their own conversation, the real morning being far from come. Abraham, as he more fully awoke (for he had moved in a sort of trance so far), began to talk of the strange shapes assumed by the various dark objects against the sky; of this tree that looked like a raging tiger springing from a lair; of that which resembled a giant's head.

When they had passed the little town of Stourcastle, dumbly somnolent under its thick brown thatch, they reached higher ground. Still higher, on their left, the elevation called Bulbarrow or Bealbarrow, well-nigh the highest in South Wessex, swelled into the sky, engirdled by its earthen trenches. From hereabout the long road was fairly level for some distance onward. They mounted in front of the waggon, and Abraham grew reflective.

"Tess!" he said in a preparatory tone, after a silence.

"Yes, Abraham."

"Bain't you glad that we've become gentlefolk?"

"Not particular glad."

"But you be glad that you 'm going to marry a gentleman?"

"What?" said Tess, lifting her face.

"That our great relation will help 'ee to marry a gentleman."

"I? Our great relation? We have no such relation. What has put that into your head?"

"I heard 'em talking about it up at Rolliver's when I went to find father. There's a rich lady of our family out at Trantridge, and mother said that if you claimed kin with the lady, she'd put 'ee in the way of marrying a gentleman."

His sister became abruptly still, and lapsed into a pondering silence. Abraham talked on, rather for the pleasure of utterance than for audition, so that his sister's abstraction was of no account. He leant back against the hives, and with upturned face made observation on the stars, whose cold pulses were beating amid the black hollows above, in serene dissociation from these two wisps of human life. He asked how far away those twinklers were, and whether God was on the other side of them. But ever and anon his childish prattle recurred to what impressed his imagination even more deeply than the wonders of creation. If Tess were made rich by marrying a gentleman, would she have money enough to buy a spy-glass so large that it would draw the stars as near to her as Nettlecombe-Tout?

The renewed subject, which seemed to have impregnated the whole family, filled Tess with impatience.

"Never mind that now!" she exclaimed.

"Did you say the stars were worlds, Tess?"

"Yes."

"All like ours?"

"I don't know; but I think so. They sometimes seem to be like the apples on our stubbard-tree.* Most of them splendid and sound—a few blighted."

"Which do we live on—a splendid one or a blighted one?"

"A blighted one."

" 'Tis very unlucky that we didn't pitch on a sound one, when there were so many more of 'em!"

"Yes."

"Is it like that *really*, Tess?" said Abraham, turning to her much impressed, on reconsideration of this rare information. "How would it have been if we had pitched on a sound one?"

"Well, father wouldn't have coughed and creeped about as he does, and wouldn't have got too tipsy to go this journey; and mother wouldn't have been always washing, and never getting finished."

"And you would have been a rich lady ready-made, and not have had to be made rich by marrying a gentleman?"

"O Aby, don't—don't talk of that any more!"

Left to his reflections Abraham soon grew drowsy. Tess was not skilful in the management of a horse, but she thought that she could take upon herself the entire conduct of the load for the present, and allow Abraham to go to sleep if he wished to do so. She made him a sort of nest in front of the hives, in such a manner that he could not fall, and, taking the reins into her own hands, jogged on as before.

Prince required but slight attention, lacking energy for superfluous movements of any sort. With no longer a companion to distract her, Tess fell more deeply into reverie than ever, her back leaning against the hives. The mute procession past her shoulders of trees and hedges became attached to fantastic scenes outside reality, and the occasional heave of the wind became the sigh of some immense sad soul, conterminous with the universe in space, and with history in time.

Then examining the mesh of events in her own life, she seemed to see the vanity of her father's pride; the gentlemanly suitor awaiting herself in her mother's fancy; to see him as a grimacing personage, laughing at her poverty, and her shrouded knightly ancestry. Everything grew more and more extravagant, and she no longer knew how time passed. A sudden jerk shook her in her seat, and Tess awoke from the sleep into which she, too, had fallen.

They were a long way further on than when she had lost consciousness, and the waggon had stopped. A hollow groan, unlike anything she had ever heard in her life, came from the front, followed by a shout of "Hoi, there!"

The lantern hanging at her waggon had gone out, but another was shining in her face—much brighter than her own had been. Something terrible had happened. The harness was entangled with an object which blocked the way.

In consternation Tess jumped down, and discovered the dreadful truth. The groan had proceeded from her father's poor horse Prince. The morning mail-cart, with its two noiseless wheels, speeding along these lanes like an arrow, as it always did, had driven into her slow and unlighted equipage. The pointed shaft of the cart had entered the breast of the unhappy Prince like a sword; and from the wound his life's blood was spouting in a stream, and falling with a hiss into the road.

In her despair Tess sprang forward and put her hand upon the hole, with the only result that she became splashed from face to skirt with the crimson drops. Then she stood helplessly looking on. Prince also stood firm and motionless as long as he could; till he suddenly sank down in a heap.

By this time the mail-cart man had joined her, and began dragging and unharnessing the hot form of Prince. But he was already dead; and seeing that nothing more could be done immediately, the mail-cart man returned to his own animal, which was uninjured.

"You was on the wrong side," he said. "I am bound to go on with the mail-bags, so that the best thing for you to do is to bide here with your load. I'll send somebody to help you as soon as I can. It is getting daylight, and you have nothing to fear."

He mounted and sped on his way; while Tess stood and waited. The atmosphere turned pale, the birds shook themselves in the hedges, arose, and twittered: the lane showed all its white features, and Tess showed hers, still whiter. The huge pool of blood in front of her was already assuming the iridescence of coagulation; and when the sun rose a hundred prismatic hues were reflected from it. Prince lay alongside still and stark; his eyes half open, the hole in his chest looking scarcely large enough to have let out all that had animated him.

" 'Tis all my doing—all mine!" the girl cried, gazing at the spectacle. "No excuse for me—none. What will mother and father live on now? Aby, Aby!" She shook the child, who had slept soundly through the whole disaster. "We can't go on with our load—Prince is killed!"

When Abraham realized all, the furrows of fifty years were extemporized on his young face.

"Why, I danced and laughed only yesterday!" she went on to herself. "To think that I was such a fool!"

" 'Tis because we be on a blighted star, and not a sound one, isn't it, Tess?" murmured Abraham through his tears.

In silence they waited through an interval which seemed endless. At length a sound, and an approaching object, proved to them that the driver of the mail-cart had been as good as his word. A farmer's man from near Stourcastle came up leading a strong cob.* He was harnessed to the waggon of beehives in the place of Prince, and the load taken on towards Casterbridge.

The evening of the same day saw the empty waggon reach again the spot of the accident. Prince had lain there in the ditch since the morning; but the place of the blood-pool was still visible in the middle of the road, though scratched and scraped over by passing vehicles. All that was left of Prince was now hoisted into the waggon he had formerly hauled, and with his hoofs in the air and his shoes shining, in the setting sunlight he retraced the eight or nine miles to Marlott.

Tess had gone back earlier. How to break the news was more than she could think. It was a relief to her tongue to find from the faces of her parents that they already knew of their loss, though this did not

lessen the self-reproach which she continued to heap upon herself
for her negligence.

But the very shiftlessness of the household rendered the
misfortune a less terrifying one to them than it would have been to a
striving family, though in the present case it meant ruin, and in the
other it would only have meant inconvenience. In the Durbeyfield
countenances there was nothing of the red wrath that would have
burnt upon the girl from parents more ambitious for her welfare.
Nobody blamed Tess as she blamed herself.

When it was discovered that the knacker and tanner would give
only a very few shillings for Prince's carcase because of his decrepi-
tude, Durbeyfield rose to the occasion.

"No," said he stoically; "I won't sell his old body. When we
d'Urbervilles was Knights in the land we didn't sell our chargers for
cat's meat. Let 'em keep their shillings! He've served me well in his
lifetime, and I won't part from him now."

He worked harder the next day in digging a grave for Prince in the
garden than he had worked for months to grow a crop for his family.
When the hole was ready Durbeyfield and his wife tied a rope round
the horse, and dragged him up the path towards it, the children
following in funeral train. Abraham and Liza-Lu sobbed, Hope and
Modesty discharged their grief in loud blares which echoed from the
walls; and when Prince was tumbled in they gathered round the
grave. The breadwinner had been taken away from them; what would
they do?

"Is he gone to heaven?" asked Abraham between the sobs.

Then Durbeyfield began to shovel in the earth, and the children
cried anew. All except Tess. Her face was dry and pale as though she
regarded herself in the light of a murderess.

V

THE haggling business, which had mainly depended on the horse, became disorganized forthwith. Distress, if not penury, loomed in the distance. Durbeyfield was what was locally called a slack-twisted fellow; he had good strength to work at times; but the times could not be relied on to coincide with the hours of requirement; and having been unaccustomed to the regular toil of the day-labourer he was not particularly persistent when they did so coincide.

Tess, meanwhile, as the one who had dragged her parents into this quagmire, was silently wondering what she could do to help them out of it: and then her mother broached her scheme. "We must take the ups wi' the downs, Tess," said she; "and never could your high blood have been found out at a more called-for moment. You must try your friends. Do ye know that there is a very rich Mrs d'Urberville living on the outskirts o' The Chase, who must be our relation? You must go to her and claim kin, and ask for some help in our trouble."

"I shouldn't care to do that," says Tess. "If there is such a lady 'twould be enough for us if she were friendly—not to expect her to give us help."

"You could win her round to do anything, my dear. Besides, perhaps there's more in it than you know of. I've heard what I've heard, good-now."

The oppressive sense of the harm she had done led Tess to be more deferential than she might otherwise have been to the maternal wish; but she could not understand why her mother should find such satisfaction in contemplating an enterprise of, to her, such doubtful profit. Her mother might have made inquiries, and have discovered that this Mrs d'Urberville was a lady of unequalled virtues and charity. But Tess's pride made the part of poor relation one of particular distaste to her.

"I'd rather try to get work," she murmured.

"Durbeyfield, you can settle it," said his wife turning to where he sat in the background. "If you say she ought to go she will go."

"I don't like my children going and making themselves beholden to strange kin," murmured he. "I'm the head of the noblest branch o' the family, and I ought to live up to it."

His reasons for staying away were worse to Tess than her own objections to going. "Well, as I killed the horse, mother," she said mournfully, "I suppose I ought to do something. I don't mind going and seeing her. But you must leave it to me about asking for help. And don't go thinking about her making a match for me—it is silly."

"Very well said, Tess," observed her father, sententiously.

"Who said I had such a thought?" asked Joan.

"I fancy it is in your mind, mother. But I'll go."

Rising early next day she walked to the hill-town called Shaston, and there took advantage of a van which twice in the week ran from Shaston eastward to Chaseborough, passing near Trantridge, the parish in which the vague and mysterious Mrs d'Urberville had her residence.

Tess Durbeyfield's route on this memorable morning lay amid the north-eastern undulations of the Vale in which she had been born, and in which her life had unfolded. The Vale of Blackmoor was to her the world, and its inhabitants the races thereof. From the gates and stiles of Marlott she had looked down its length in the wondering days of infancy, and what had been mystery to her then was not much less than mystery to her now. She had seen daily from her chamber-window towers, villages, faint white mansions; above all the town of Shaston standing majestically on its height; its windows shining like lamps in the evening sun. She had hardly ever visited the place, only a small tract even of the Vale and its environs being known to her by close inspection. Much less had she been far outside the valley. Every contour of the surrounding hills was as personal to her as that of her relatives' faces; but for what lay beyond her judgment was dependent on the teaching of the village school, where she had held a leading place at the time of her leaving, a year or two before this date.

In those early days she had been much loved by others of her own sex and age, and had used to be seen about the village as one of three—all nearly of the same year—walking home from school side by side, Tess the middle one—in a pink print pinafore, of a finely reticulated pattern, worn over a stuff frock that had lost its original colour for a nondescript tertiary—marching on upon long stalky legs, in tight stockings which had little ladder-like holes at the knees, torn by kneeling in the roads and banks in search of vegetable and mineral treasures; her then earth-coloured hair hanging like pot-hooks; the arms of the two outside girls resting round the waist of Tess; her arms on the shoulders of the two supporters.

As Tess grew older, and began to see how matters stood, she felt quite a Malthusian* towards her mother for thoughtlessly giving her so many little sisters and brothers, when it was such a trouble to nurse and provide for them. Her mother's intelligence was that of a happy child: Joan Durbeyfield was simply an additional one, and that not the eldest, to her own long family of waiters on Providence.

However, Tess became humanely beneficent towards the small ones, and to help them as much as possible she used, as soon as she left school, to lend a hand at haymaking or harvesting on neighbouring farms; or, by preference, at milking or butter-making processes, which she had learnt when her father had owned cows; and being deft-fingered it was a kind of work in which she excelled.

Every day seemed to throw upon her young shoulders more of the family burdens, and that Tess should be the representative of the Durbeyfields at the d'Urberville mansion came as a thing of course. In this instance it must be admitted that the Durbeyfields were putting their fairest side outward.

She alighted from the van at Trantridge Cross, and ascended on foot a hill in the direction of the district known as The Chase; on the borders of which, as she had been informed, Mrs d'Urberville's seat, The Slopes, would be found. It was not a manorial home in the ordinary sense, with fields and pastures and a grumbling farmer out of whom the owner had to squeeze an income for himself and his family by hook or by crook: it was more, far more; a country-house built for enjoyment pure and simple, with not an acre of troublesome land attached to it beyond what was required for residential purposes and for a little fancy farm kept in hand by the owner, and tended by a bailiff.

The crimson brick lodge came first in sight, up to its eaves in dense evergreens. Tess thought this was the mansion itself till, passing through the side-wicket with some trepidation, and onward to a point at which the drive took a turn, the house proper stood in full view. It was of recent erection, indeed almost new, and of the same rich red colour that formed such a contrast with the evergreens of the lodge. Far behind the corner of the house—which rose like a geranium bloom against the subdued colours around—stretched the soft azure landscape of The Chase—a truly venerable tract of forest land; one of the few remaining woodlands in England of undoubted primæval date, wherein Druidical mistletoe was still found on aged oaks, and where enormous yew-trees, not planted by the hand of man, grew as they had grown when they were pollarded for bows. All this sylvan antiquity however, though visible from The Slopes, was outside the immediate boundaries of the estate.

Everything on this snug property was bright, thriving, and well-kept: acres of glass houses stretched down the inclines to the copses at their feet. Everything looked like money—like the last coin issued from the Mint. The stables, partly screened by Austrian pines and Evergreen Oaks and fitted with every late appliance were as dignified as chapels-of-ease.* On the extensive lawn stood an ornamental tent, its door being towards her.

Simple Tess Durbeyfield stood at gaze, in a half-alarmed attitude, on the edge of the gravel sweep. Her feet had brought her onward to this point before she had quite realized where she was; and now all was contrary to her expectation. "I thought we were an old family; but this is all new!" she said in her artlessness. She wished that she had not fallen in so readily with her mother's plans for "claiming kin", and had endeavoured to get assistance nearer home.

The d'Urbervilles—or Stoke-d'Urbervilles, as they at first called themselves—who owned all this, were a somewhat unusual family to find in such an old-fashioned part of the country. Parson Tringham had spoken truly when he said that our shambling John Durbeyfield was the only real and lineal representative of the old d'Urberville family existing in the country or near it: he might have added, what he knew very well, that the Stoke-d'Urbervilles were no more d'Urbervilles of the true tree than he was himself. Yet it must be admitted that this family formed a very good stock whereon to regraft a name which sadly wanted such renovation.

When old Mr Simon Stoke, latterly deceased, had made his fortune as an honest merchant (some said money-lender) in the North, he decided to settle as a county man in the South of England out of hail of his business district; and in doing this he felt the necessity of recommencing with a name that would not too readily identify him with the smart tradesman of the past, and that would be less commonplace than the original bald stark words. Conning for an hour in the British Museum the pages of works devoted to extinct, half-extinct, obscured, and ruined families appertaining to the quarter of England in which he proposed to settle he considered that *d'Urberville* looked and sounded as well as any of them: and d'Urberville accordingly was annexed to his own name for himself and his heirs eternally. Yet he was not an extravagant-minded man in this, and in constructing his family tree on the new basis was duly reasonable in framing his intermarriages and aristocratic links, never inserting a single title above a rank of strict moderation.

Of this work of imagination poor Tess and her parents were naturally in ignorance—much to their discomfiture—indeed, the very possibility of such annexations was unknown to them; who supposed that though to be well-favoured might be the gift of fortune, a family name came by nature.

Tess still stood hesitating like a bather about to make his plunge, hardly knowing whether to retreat or to persevere, when a figure came forth from the dark triangular door of the tent. It was that of a tall young man, smoking.

He had an almost swarthy complexion, with full lips, badly moulded, though red and smooth, above which was a well-groomed black moustache with curled points, though his age could not be more than three- or four-and-twenty. Despite the touches of barbarism in his contours there was a singular force in the gentleman's face, and in his bold rolling eye.

"Well, my beauty, what can I do for you?" said he, coming forward. And perceiving that she stood quite confounded: "Never mind me. I am Mr d'Urberville. Have you come to see me or my mother?"

This embodiment of a d'Urberville and a namesake differed even more from what Tess had expected than the house and grounds had differed. She had dreamed of an aged and dignified face, the sublimation of all the d'Urberville lineaments, furrowed with incarnate memories, representing in hieroglyphic the centuries of her family's and England's history. But she screwed herself up to the work in hand, since she could not get out of it, and answered, "I came to see your mother, sir."

"I am afraid you cannot see her—she is an invalid," replied the present representative of the spurious house—for this was Mr Alec, the only son of the lately deceased gentleman.—"Cannot I answer your purpose? What is the business you wish to see her about?"

"It isn't business—it is—I can hardly say what!"

"Pleasure?"

"O no. . . . . Why, sir, if I tell you, it will seem—." Tess's sense of a certain ludicrousness in her errand was now so strong that, notwithstanding her awe of him, and her general discomfort at being here, her rosy lips curved towards a smile, much to the attraction of the swarthy Alexander. "It is so very foolish," she stammered; "I fear I can't tell you."

"Never mind—I like foolish things. Try again my dear," said he kindly.

"Mother asked me to come," Tess continued; "and, indeed, I was in the mind to do so myself likewise. But I did not think it would be like this. I came, sir, to tell you that we are of the same family as you."

"Ho.—Poor relations?"

"Yes."

"Stokes?"

"No. D'Urbervilles."

"Ay, ay: I mean d'Urbervilles."

"Our names are worn away to Durbeyfield: but we have several proofs that we are d'Urbervilles. Antiquarians hold we are: and—and—we have an old seal, marked with a ramping lion on a shield, and a castle over him. And we have a very old silver spoon, round in the bowl like a little ladle, and marked with the same castle. But it is so worn that mother uses it to stir the pea-soup."

"A castle argent is certainly my crest," said he blandly. "And my arms a lion rampant."

"And so mother said we ought to make ourselves beknown to you—as we've lost our horse by a bad accident—and are the oldest branch o' the family."

"Very kind of your mother, I'm sure. And I, for one, don't regret her step." Alec looked at Tess as he spoke in a way that made her blush a little. "And so, my pretty girl, you've come on a friendly visit to us, as relations?"

"I suppose I have," faltered Tess, looking uncomfortable again.

"Well—there's no harm in it. Where do you live? What are you?"

She gave him brief particulars; and responding to further inquiries told him that she was intending to go back by the same carrier who had brought her.

"It is a long while before he returns past Trantridge Cross. Supposing we walk round the grounds to pass the time, my pretty Coz?"

Tess wished to abridge her visit as much as possible; but the young man was pressing, and she consented to accompany him. He conducted her about the lawns, and flower-beds, and conservatories; and thence to the fruit-garden and green-houses, where he asked her if she liked strawberries.

"Yes," said Tess. "When they come."

"They are already here." D'Urberville began gathering specimens of the fruit for her, handing them back to her as he stooped: and presently selecting a specially fine product of the "British Queen" variety he stood up and held it by the stem to her mouth.

"No, no!" she said quickly, putting her fingers between his hand and her lips. "I would rather take it in my own hand."

"Nonsense!" he insisted; and in a slight distress she parted her lips and took it in.

They had spent some time wandering desultorily thus, Tess eating in a half-pleased, half-reluctant state whatever d'Urberville offered her. When she could consume no more of the strawberries he filled her little basket with them: and then the two passed round to the rose-trees, whence he gathered blossoms and gave her to put in her bosom. She obeyed like one in a dream, and when she could affix no more he himself tucked a bud or two into her hat, and heaped her basket with others in the prodigality of his bounty. At last, looking at his watch, he said, "Now, by the time you have had something to eat, it will be time for you to leave, if you want to catch the carrier to Shaston. Come here, and I'll see what grub I can find."

Stoke-d'Urberville took her back to the lawn and into the tent, where he left her, soon reappearing with a basket of light luncheon, which he put before her himself. It was evidently the gentleman's wish not to be disturbed in this pleasant *tête-à-tête* by the servantry.

"Do you mind my smoking?" he asked.

"O, not at all, sir."

He watched her pretty and unconscious munching through the skeins of smoke that pervaded the tent, and Tess Durbeyfield did not divine, as she innocently looked down at the roses in her bosom, that there behind the blue narcotic haze was potentially the "tragic mischief" of her drama—one who stood fair to be the blood-red ray in the spectrum of her young life. She had an attribute which amounted to a disadvantage just now; and it was this that caused Alec d'Urberville's eyes to rivet themselves upon her. It was a luxuriance of aspect, a fulness of growth, which made her appear more of a woman than she really was. She had inherited the feature from her mother without the quality it denoted. It had troubled her mind occasionally, till her companions had said that it was a fault which time would cure.

She soon had finished her lunch. "Now I am going home, sir," she said, rising.

"And what do they call you?" he asked, as he accompanied her along the drive till they were out of sight of the house.

"Tess Durbeyfield down at Marlott."

"And you say your people have lost their horse?"

"I—killed him!" she answered, her eyes filling with tears as she gave particulars of Prince's death. "And I don't know what to do for father on account of it!"

"I must think if I cannot do something. My mother must find a berth for you. But, Tess, no nonsense about 'd'Urberville': 'Durbeyfield' only, you know—quite another name."

"I wish for no better, sir," said she with something of dignity.

For a moment—only for a moment—when they were in the turning of the drive, between the tall rhododendrons and conifers, before the lodge became visible, he inclined his face towards her as if—. But no: he thought better of it; and let her go.

Thus the thing began. Had she perceived this meeting's import she might have asked why she was doomed to be seen and coveted that day by the wrong man, and not by some other man, the right and desired one in all respects—as nearly as humanity can supply the right and desired; yet to him who amongst her acquaintance might have approximated to this kind, she was but a transient impression half-forgotten.

In the ill-judged execution of the well-judged plan of things the call seldom produces the comer, the man to love rarely coincides with the hour for loving. Nature does not often say "See!" to her poor creature at a time when seeing can lead to happy doing; or reply "Here" to a body's cry of "Where?" till the hide-and-seek has become an irksome, outworn game. We may wonder whether, at the acme and summit of the human progress, these anachronisms will be corrected by a finer intuition, a closer interaction of the social machinery than that which now jolts us round and along; but such completeness is not to be prophesied, or even conceived as possible. Enough that in the present case, as in millions, it was not the two halves of a perfect whole that confronted each other at the perfect moment: a missing counterpart wandered independently about the earth waiting in crass obtuseness till the late time came. Out of which maladroit delay sprang anxieties, disappointments, shocks, catastrophes, and passing strange destinies.

When d'Urberville got back to the tent he sat down astride on a chair, reflecting, with a pleased gleam in his face. Then he broke into a loud laugh.

"Well—I'm damned! What a funny thing! Ha-ha-ha! And what a crumby girl!"

VI

TESS went down the hill to Trantridge Cross, and inattentively waited to take her seat in the van returning from Chaseborough to Shaston. She did not know what the other occupants said to her as she entered, though she answered them; and when they had started anew she rode along with an inward and not an outward eye.

One among her fellow travellers addressed her more pointedly than any had spoken before: "Why—you be quite a posy! And such roses in early June!"

Then she became aware of the spectacle she presented to their surprised vision: roses at her breast; roses in her hat; roses and strawberries in her basket to the brim. She blushed, and said confusedly that the flowers had been given to her: when the passengers were not looking she stealthily removed the more prominent blooms from her hat and placed them in the basket, where she covered them with her handkerchief. Then she fell to reflecting again, and in looking downwards a thorn of the rose remaining in her breast accidentally pricked her chin. Like all the cottagers in Blackmoor Vale Tess was steeped in fancies and prefigurative superstitions: she thought this an ill-omen—the first she had noticed that day.

The van travelled only so far as Shaston, and there were several miles of pedestrian descent from that mountain-town into the Vale to Marlott. Her mother had advised her to stay here for the night, at the house of a cottage-woman they knew, if she should feel too tired to come on; and this Tess did; not descending to her home till the following afternoon.

When she entered the house she perceived in a moment from her mother's triumphant manner that something had occurred in the interim.

"O yes—I know all about it. I told 'ee it would be all right, and now 'tis proved!"

"Since I've been away? What has?" said Tess rather wearily.

Her mother surveyed the girl up and down with arch approval, and went on banteringly, "So you've brought 'em round!"

"How do you know, mother?"

"I've had a letter."

Tess then remembered that there would have been time for this.

"They say—Mrs d'Urberville says—that she wants you to look after a little fowl-farm which is her hobby. But this is only her artful way of getting 'ee there without raising your hopes. She's going to own 'ee as kin—that's the meaning o't."

"But I didn't see her."

"You zid somebody I suppose?"

"I saw her son."

"And did he own 'ee?"

"Well—he called me Coz."

"Ah—I knew it! . . . Jacky—he called her Coz!" cried Joan to her husband. "Well, he spoke to his mother, of course, and she do want 'ee there."

"But I don't know that I am apt at tending fowls," said the dubious Tess.

"Then I don't know who is apt. You've ben born in the business, and brought up in it. They that be born in a business always know more about it than any prentice. Besides, that's only just a show of something for you to do, that you midn't feel beholden."

"I don't altogether think I ought to go," said Tess thoughtfully. "Who wrote the letter? Will you let me look at it?"

"Mrs d'Urberville wrote it. Here it is."

The letter was in the third person, and briefly informed Mrs Durbeyfield that her daughter's services would be useful to that lady in the management of her poultry-farm, that a comfortable room would be provided for her if she could come, and that the wages would be on a liberal scale if they liked her.

"O—that's all," said Tess.

"You couldn't expect her to throw her arms round 'ee, an' to kiss and to coll 'ee all at once."

Tess looked out of the window. "I would rather stay here with father and you," she said.

"But why?"

"I'd rather not tell you why, mother—indeed I don't quite know why."

A week afterwards she came in one evening from an unavailing search for some light occupation in the immediate neighbourhood. Her idea had been to get together sufficient money during the summer to purchase another horse. Hardly had she crossed the threshold before one of the children danced across the room saying "The gentleman 's been here!"

Her mother hastened to explain, smiles breaking from every inch of her person. Mrs d'Urberville's son had called on horseback, having been riding by chance in the direction of Marlott. He had wished to know, finally, in the name of his mother, if Tess could really come to manage the old lady's fowl-farm or not, the lad who had hitherto superintended the birds having proved untrustworthy. "Mr d'Urberville says you must be a good girl if you are at all as you appear; he knows you must be worth your weight in gold. He is very much interested in 'ee—truth to tell."

Tess seemed for the moment really pleased to hear that she had won such high opinion from a stranger, when in her own esteem she had sunk so low. "It is very good of him to think that," she murmured. "And if I was quite sure how it would be living there, I would go any-when."

"He is a mighty handsome man."

"I don't think so," said Tess coldly.

"Well—there's your chance whether or no. And I'm sure he wears a beautiful diamond ring!"

"Yes," said little Abraham brightly from the window-bench. "And I seed it! And it did twinkle when he put his hand up to his mistarshers. . . . Mother, why did our grand relation keep on putting his hand up to his mistarshers?"

"Hark at that child!" cried Mrs Durbeyfield with parenthetic admiration.

"Perhaps to show his diamond ring," murmured Sir John dreamily from his chair.

"I'll think it over," said Tess leaving the room.

"Well—she's made a conquest o' the younger branch of us, straight off," continued the matron to her husband. "And she's a fool if she don't follow it up."

"I don't quite like my children going away from home," said the haggler. "As the head of the family the rest ought to come to me."

"But do let her go, Jacky," coaxed his poor witless wife. "He's struck wi' her—you can see that. He called her Coz. He'll marry her, most likely, and make a lady of her; and then she'll be what her forefathers was."

John Durbeyfield had more conceit than energy or health, and this supposition was pleasant to him. "Well—perhaps that's what young Mr d'Urberville means," he admitted; "and sure enough he mid have serious thoughts about improving his blood by linking on to the old line. . . . Tess, the little rogue! And have she really paid 'em a visit to such an end as this!"

Meanwhile Tess was walking thoughtfully among the gooseberry bushes in the garden, and over Prince's grave. When she came in her mother pursued her advantage. "Well, what be you going to do?" she asked.

"I wish I had seen Mrs d'Urberville," said Tess.

"I think you mid as well settle it. Then you'll see her soon enough."

Her father coughed in his chair.

"I don't know what to say!" answered the girl restlessly. "It is for you to decide. I killed the old horse, and I suppose I ought to do something to get ye a new one. But—but—I don't quite like Mr d'Urberville being there!"

The children who had made use of this idea of Tess being taken up by their wealthy kinsfolk (which they imagined the other family to be) as a species of dolorifuge after the death of the horse, began to cry at Tess's reluctance, and teased and reproached her for hesitating.

"Tess won't go-o-o and be made a la-a-dy of!—no, she says she wo-o-on't!" they wailed, with square mouths. "And we shan't have a nice new horse, and lots o' golden money to buy fairlings! And Tess won't look pretty in her best cloze no mo-o-ore!"

Her mother chimed in to the same tune: a certain way she had of making her labours in the house seem heavier than they were by prolonging them indefinitely, also weighed in the argument. Her father alone preserved an attitude of neutrality.

"I will go," said Tess at last.

Her mother could not repress her consciousness of the nuptial Vision conjured up by the girl's consent. "That's right! For such a pretty maid as 'tis, this is a fine chance!"

Tess smiled crossly.

"I hope it is a chance for earning money. It is no other kind of chance. You had better say nothing of that silly sort about parish."

Mrs Durbeyfield did not promise. She was not quite sure that she did not feel proud enough, after the visitor's remarks, to say a good deal.

Thus it was arranged; and the young girl wrote, agreeing to be ready to set out on any day on which she might be required. She was duly informed that Mrs d'Urberville was glad of her decision, and that a spring-cart should be sent to meet her and her luggage at the top of the Vale on the day after the morrow, when she must hold herself prepared to start. Mrs d'Urberville's handwriting seemed rather masculine.

"A cart?" murmured Joan Durbeyfield doubtingly. "It might have been a carriage for her own kin!"

Having at last taken her course Tess was less restless and abstracted, going about her business with some self-assurance in the thought of acquiring another horse for her father by an occupation which would not be onerous. She had hoped to be a teacher at the school, but the fates seemed to decide otherwise. Being mentally older than her mother she did not regard Mrs Durbeyfield's matrimonial hopes for her in a serious aspect for a moment. The light-minded woman had been discovering good matches for her daughter almost from the year of her birth.

VII

ON the morning appointed for her departure Tess was awake before dawn—at the marginal minute of the dark when the grove is still mute, save for one prophetic bird who sings with a clear-voiced conviction that he at least knows the correct time of day, the rest preserving silence as if equally convinced that he is mistaken. She remained upstairs packing till breakfast-time, and then came down in her ordinary weekday clothes, her Sunday apparel being carefully folded in her box.

Her mother expostulated. "You will never set out to see your folks without dressing up more the dand than that?"

"But I am going to work!" said Tess.

"Well, yes," said Mrs Durbeyfield; and in a private tone, "at first there mid be a little pretence o't. . . . But I think it will be wiser of 'ee to put your best side outward," she added.

"Very well; I suppose you know best," replied Tess with calm abandonment. And to please her parent the girl put herself quite in Joan's hands, saying serenely, "Do what you like with me, mother."

Mrs Durbeyfield was only too delighted at this tractability. First she fetched a great basin, and washed Tess's hair with such thoroughness that when dried and brushed it looked twice as much as at other times. She tied it with a broader pink ribbon than usual. Then she put upon her the white frock that Tess had worn at the club-walking, the airy fulness of which, supplementing her enlarged *coiffure*, imparted to her developing figure an amplitude which belied her age, and might cause her to be estimated as a woman when she was not much more than a child.

"I declare there's a hole in my stocking heel!" said Tess.

"Never mind holes in your stockings—they don't speak! When I was a maid, so long as I had a pretty bonnet the devil might ha' found me in heels."

Her mother's pride in the girl's appearance led her to step back like a painter from his easel, and survey her work as a whole. "You must zee yourself!" she cried. "It is much better than you was t'other day."

As the looking-glass was only large enough to reflect a very small portion of Tess's person at one time, Mrs Durbeyfield hung a black cloak outside the casement, and so made a large reflector of the panes, as it is the wont of bedecking cottagers to do. After this she went downstairs to her husband, who was sitting in the lower room.

"I'll tell 'ee what 'tis, Durbeyfield," said she, exultingly, "he'll never have the heart not to love her. But whatever you do, don't zay too much to Tess of his fancy for her, and this chance she has got. She is such an odd maid that it mid zet her against him, or against going there, even now. . . . If all goes well I shall certainly be for making some return to that pa'son at Stagfoot Lane for telling us—dear good man!"

However, as the moment for the girl's setting out drew nigh, when the first excitement of the dressing had passed off, a slight misgiving found place in Joan Durbeyfield's mind. It prompted the matron to say that she would walk a little way—as far as to the point where the acclivity from the valley began its first steep ascent to the outer world. At the top Tess was going to be met with the spring-cart sent by the Stoke-d'Urbervilles, and her box had already been wheeled ahead towards this summit by a lad with trucks, to be in readiness.

Seeing their mother put on her bonnet the younger children clamoured to go with her. "I do want to walk a little-ways wi' Sissy, now she's going to marry our gentleman-cousin, and wear fine cloze!"

"Now," said Tess flushing and turning quickly, "I'll hear no more o' that! Mother, how could you ever put such stuff into their heads?"

"Going to work my dears, for our rich relation, and help get enough money for a new horse," said Mrs Durbeyfield pacifically.

"Good-bye, father," said Tess, with a lumpy throat.

"Good-bye, my maid," said Sir John, raising his head from his breast as he suspended his nap, induced by a slight excess this morning in honour of the occasion. "Well, I hope my young friend will like such a comely sample of his own blood. . . . And tell'n, Tess, that being sunk, quite, from our former grandeur, I'll sell him the title—yes, sell it—and at no onreasonable figure."

"Not for less than a thousand pound!" cried Lady Durbeyfield.

"Tell'n—I'll take a thousand pound. . . . Well, I'll take less, when I come to think o't. He'll adorn it better than a poor lammicken feller like myself can. Tell'n he shall hae it for a hundred. . . . But I won't stand upon trifles—tell'n he shall hae it for fifty—for twenty pound!

Yes twenty pound—that's the lowest. Dammy, family honour is family honour, and I won't take a penny less!"

Tess's eyes were too full and her voice too choked to utter the sentiments that were in her. She turned quickly, and went out.

So the girls and their mother all walked together, a child on each side of Tess, holding her hand, and looking at her meditatively from time to time, as at one who was about to do great things; her mother just behind with the smallest; the group forming a picture of honest beauty flanked by innocence, and backed by simple-souled vanity. They followed the way till they reached the beginning of the ascent, on the crest of which the vehicle from Trantridge was to receive her, this limit having been fixed to save the horse the labour of the last slope. Far away behind the first hills the cliff-like dwellings of Shaston broke the line of the ridge. Nobody was visible in the elevated road which skirted the ascent, save the lad whom they had sent on before them, sitting on the handle of the barrow that contained all Tess's worldly possessions.

"Bide here a bit, and the cart will soon come, no doubt," said Mrs Durbeyfield. "Yes—I see it yonder!"

It had come—appearing suddenly from behind the forehead of the nearest upland, and stopping beside the boy with the barrow. Her mother and the children thereupon decided to go no further; and bidding them a hasty good-bye Tess bent her steps up the hill.

They saw her white shape draw near to the spring-cart, on which her box was already placed. But before she had quite reached it another vehicle shot out from a clump of trees on the summit, came round the bend of the road there, passed the luggage-cart, and halted beside Tess, who looked up as if in great surprise.

Her mother perceived, for the first time, that the second vehicle was not a humble conveyance like the first, but a spick-and-span gig or dog-cart, highly varnished and equipped. The driver was a young man of three- or four-and-twenty, with a cigar between his teeth; wearing a dandy cap, drab jacket, breeches of the same hue, white neckcloth, stick-up collar, and brown driving-gloves—in short he was the handsome horsey young buck who had visited Joan a week or two before to get her answer about Tess.

Mrs Durbeyfield clapped her hands like a child. Then she looked down, then stared again. Could she be deceived as to the meaning of this?

"Is dat the gentleman-kinsman who'll make Sissy a lady?" asked the youngest child.

Meanwhile the muslined form of Tess could be seen standing still, undecided, beside this turn-out, whose owner was talking to her. Her seeming indecision was, in fact, more than indecision: it was misgiving. She would have preferred the humble cart. The young man dismounted, and appeared to urge her to ascend. She turned her face down the hill to her relatives and regarded the little group. Something seemed to quicken her to a determination; possibly the thought that she had killed Prince. She suddenly stepped up; he mounted beside her, and immediately whipped on the horse. In a moment they had passed the slow cart with the box, and disappeared behind the shoulder of the hill.

Directly Tess was out of sight, and the interest of the matter as a drama was at an end, the little ones' eyes filled with tears. The youngest child said, "I wish poor, poor Tess wasn't gone away to be a lady!" and lowering the corners of his lips burst out crying. The new point of view was infectious, and the next child did likewise, and then the next, till the whole three of them wailed loud.

There were tears also in Joan Durbeyfield's eyes as she turned to go home. But by the time that she had got back to the village she was passively trusting to the favour of accident. However, in bed that night she sighed, and her husband asked her what was the matter.

"Oh—I don't know exactly," she said. "I was thinking that perhaps it would ha' been better if Tess had not gone."

"Oughtn't ye to have thought of that before?"

"Well—'tis a chance for the maid. . . . Still, if 'twere the doing again, I wouldn't let her go till I had found out whether the gentleman is really a good-hearted young man and choice over her as his kinswoman."

"Yes, you ought, perhaps, to ha' done that," snored Sir John.

Joan Durbeyfield always managed to find consolation somewhere: "Well, as one of the genuine stock, she ought to make her way with 'en, if she plays her trump card aright. And if he don't marry her afore he will after. For that he's all afire wi' love for her any eye can see."

"What's her trump card? Her d'Urberville blood, you mean?"

"No, stupid; her face—as 'twas mine."

VIII

HAVING mounted beside her, Alec d'Urberville drove rapidly along the crest of the first hill, chatting compliments to Tess as they went, the cart with her box being left far behind. Rising still, an immense landscape stretched around them on every side; behind, the green valley of her birth; before, a grey country of which she knew nothing except from her first brief visit to Trantridge. Thus they reached the verge of an incline down which the road stretched in a long straight descent of nearly a mile.

Ever since the accident with her father's horse Tess Durbeyfield, courageous as she naturally was, had been exceedingly timid on wheels; the least irregularity of motion startled her. She began to get uneasy at a certain recklessness in her conductor's driving.

"You will go down slow, sir, I suppose?" she said with attempted unconcern.

D'Urberville looked round upon her, nipped his cigar with the tips of his large white centre-teeth, and allowed his lips to smile slowly of themselves.

"Why—Tess," he answered, after another whiff or two; "it isn't a brave bouncing girl like you who asks that? Why, I always go down at full gallop. There's nothing like it for raising your spirits."

"But perhaps you need not now?"

"Ah," he said, shaking his head, "there are two to be reckoned with. It is not me alone. Tib has to be considered, and she has a very queer temper."

"Who?"

"Why this mare. I fancy she looked round at me in a very grim way just then—didn't you notice it?"

"Don't try to frighten me sir," said Tess stiffly.

"Well, I don't. If any living man can manage this horse I can—I won't say any living man can do it—but if such has the power, I am he."

"Why do you have such a horse?"

"Ah—well may you ask it! It was fate I suppose. . . . Tib has killed one chap; and just after I bought her she nearly killed me. And then, take my word for it, I nearly killed her. But she's touchy

still, very touchy; and one's life is hardly safe behind her sometimes."

They were just beginning to descend; and it was evident that the
horse, whether of her own will or of his (the latter being the more
likely) knew so well the reckless performance expected of her that
she hardly required a hint from behind.

Down, down they sped, the wheels humming like a top, the
dog-cart rocking right and left, its axis acquiring a slightly oblique
set in relation to the line of progress; the figure of the horse rising
and falling in undulations before them. Sometimes a wheel was off
the ground, it seemed for many yards: sometimes a stone was sent
spinning over the hedge, and flinty sparks from the horse's hoofs
outshone the daylight. The aspect of the straight road enlarged with
their advance, the two banks dividing like a splitting stick; one
rushing past at each shoulder.

The wind blew through Tess's white muslin to her very skin, and
her washed hair flew out behind. She was determined to show no
open fear, but she clutched d'Urberville's rein-arm.

"Don't touch my arm! We shall be thrown out if you do! Hold on
round my waist!"

She grasped his waist; and so they reached the bottom. "Safe
thank God, in spite of your fooling!" said she, her face on fire.

"Tess—fie! That's temper!" said d'Urberville.

" 'Tis truth!"

"Well, you need not let go your hold of me so thanklessly the
moment you feel yourself out of danger."

She had not considered what she had been doing; whether he were
man or woman, stick or stone, in her involuntary hold on him.
Recovering her reserve she sat without replying, and thus they
reached the summit of another declivity. "Now then again," said
d'Urberville.

"No, no," said Tess. "Show more sense, do, please."

"But when people find themselves on one of the highest points in
the county, they must get down again," he retorted. He loosened
rein, and away they went a second time. D'Urberville turned his face
to her as they rocked, and said in playful raillery: "Now then: put
your arms round my waist again as you did before, my beauty."

"Never!" said Tess independently, holding on as well as she could
without touching him.

"Let me put one little kiss on those holmberry lips,* Tess; or even on that warmed cheek, and I'll stop—on my honour, I will!"

Tess, surprised beyond measure, slid further back still on her seat, at which he urged the horse anew, and rocked her the more.

"Will nothing else do?" she cried at length, in desperation, her large eyes staring at him like those of a wild animal. This dressing her up so prettily by her mother had apparently been to lamentable purpose.

"Nothing, dear Tess," he replied.

"Oh, I don't know—very well; I don't mind!" she panted miserably.

He drew rein, and as they slowed he was on the point of imprinting the desired salute, when, as if hardly yet aware of her own modesty, she dodged aside. His arms being occupied with the reins there was left him no power to prevent her manœuvre.

"Now, damn it—I'll break both our necks!" swore her capriciously passionate companion. "So you can go from your word like that, you young witch, can you?"

"Very well," said Tess, "I'll not move since you be so determined! But I—thought you would be kind to me, and protect me, as my kinsman!"

"Kinsman be hanged! Now!"

"But I don't want anybody to kiss me, sir!" she implored, a big tear beginning to roll down her face, and the corners of her mouth trembling in her attempts not to cry. "And I wouldn't ha' come if I had known!"

He was inexorable, and she sat still, and d'Urberville gave her the kiss of mastery. No sooner had he done so than she flushed with shame, took out her handkerchief, and wiped the spot on her cheek that had been touched by his lips. His ardour was nettled at the sight, for the act on her part had been unconsciously done.

"You are mighty sensitive for a cottage girl!" said the young man.

Tess made no reply to this remark, of which, indeed, she did not quite comprehend the drift, unweeting of the snub she had administered by her instinctive rub upon her cheek. She had, in fact, undone the kiss, as far as such a thing was physically possible. With a dim sense that he was vexed she looked steadily ahead as they trotted on near Melbury Down and Wingreen, till she saw to her consternation that there was yet another descent to be undergone.

"You shall be made sorry for that!" he resumed, his injured tone still remaining, as he flourished the whip anew. "Unless, that is, you agree willingly to let me do it again, and no handkerchief."

She sighed. "Very well sir!" she said. "Ah—let me get my hat!"

At the moment of speaking her hat had blown off into the road, their present speed on the upland being by no means slow. D'Urberville pulled up, and said he would get it for her; but Tess was down on the other side.

She turned back and picked up the article. "You look prettier with it off, upon my soul, if that's possible," he said contemplating her over the back of the vehicle. "Now then—up again! . . . What's the matter?"

The hat was in place, and tied, but Tess had not stepped forward. "No, sir," she said, revealing the red and ivory of her mouth as her eye lit in defiant triumph. "Not again, if I know it!"

"What—you won't get up beside me?"

"No. I shall walk."

" 'Tis five or six miles yet to Trantridge."

"I don't care if 'tis dozens. Besides, the cart is behind."

"You artful hussy! Now, tell me—didn't you make that hat blow off on purpose? I'll swear you did!"

Her strategic silence confirmed his suspicion.

Then d'Urberville cursed and swore at her, and called her everything he could think of for the trick. Turning the horse suddenly he tried to drive back upon her, and so hem her in between the gig and the hedge. But he could not do this, short of injuring her.

"You ought to be ashamed of yourself for using such wicked words!" cried Tess with spirit, from the top of the hedge into which she had scrambled. "I don't like 'ee at all! I hate and detest you! I'll go back to mother, I will."

D'Urberville's bad temper cleared up at sight of hers; and he laughed heartily. "Well—I like you all the better," he said. "Come, let there be peace. I'll never do it any more against your will. My life upon it now!"

Still Tess could not be induced to remount. She did not, however, object to his keeping his gig alongside her; and in this manner, at a slow pace, they advanced towards the village of Trantridge. From time to time d'Urberville exhibited a sort of fierce distress at the sight of the tramping he had driven her to undertake by his misdemeanour. She might, in truth, have safely trusted him now; but he had forfeited her confidence for the time, and she kept on the ground, progressing thoughtfully, as if wondering whether it would be wiser to return home. Her resolve, however, had been taken, and it seemed vacillating even to childishness to abandon it now, unless for graver reasons. How could she face her parents, get back her box, and disconcert the whole scheme for the rehabilitation of her family, on such sentimental grounds?

A few minutes later the chimneys of The Slopes appeared in view; and in a snug nook to the right the poultry-farm and cottage of Tess's destination.

IX

THE community of fowls to which Tess had been appointed as supervisor, purveyor, nurse, surgeon, and friend, made its head-quarters in an old thatched cottage standing in an enclosure that had once been a garden, but was now a trampled and sanded square. The house was overrun with ivy, its chimney being enlarged by the boughs of the parasite to the aspect of a ruined tower. The lower rooms were entirely given over to the birds, who walked about them with a proprietary air, as though the place had been built by them-selves, and not by certain dusty copyholders* who now lay east and west in the churchyard. The descendants of these bygone owners felt it almost as a slight to their family when the house which had so much of their affection, had cost so much of their forefathers' money, and had been in their possession for several generations before the d'Urbervilles came and built here, was indifferently turned into a fowl-house by Mrs Stoke-d'Urberville as soon as the property fell into hand according to law. " 'Twas good enough for Christians in grandfather's time," they said.

The rooms wherein dozens of infants had wailed at their nursing now resounded with the tapping of nascent chicks. Distracted hens in coops occupied spots where formerly stood chairs supporting sedate agriculturists. The chimney-corner and once blazing hearth was now filled with inverted beehives in which the hens laid their eggs; while out-of-doors the plots that each succeeding householder had care-fully shaped with his spade, were torn by the cocks in wildest fashion.

The garden in which the cottage stood was surrounded by a wall, and could only be entered through a door.

When Tess had occupied herself about an hour the next morning in altering and improving the arrangements, according to her skilled ideas as the daughter of a professed poulterer, the door in the wall opened, and a servant in white cap and apron entered. She had come from the manor-house.

"Mrs d'Urberville wants the fowls as usual," she said; but perceiving that Tess did not quite understand, she explained: "Mis'ess is a old lady, and blind."

"Blind!" said Tess.

Almost before her misgiving at the news could find time to shape itself she took, under her companion's direction, two of the most beautiful of the Hamburghs in her arms, and followed the maid-servant, who had likewise taken two, to the adjacent mansion, which, though ornate and imposing, showed traces everywhere on this side that some occupant of its chambers could bend to the love of dumb creatures—feathers floating within view of the front, and hen-coops standing on the grass.

In a sitting-room on the ground-floor, ensconced in an armchair with her back to the light, was the owner and mistress of the estate, a white-haired woman of not more than sixty, or even less, wearing a large cap. She had the mobile face frequent in those whose sight has decayed by stages, has been laboriously striven after, and reluctantly let go, rather than the stagnant mien apparent in persons long sightless or born blind. Tess walked up to this lady with her feathered charges—one sitting on each arm.

"Ah; you are the young woman come to look after my birds?" said Mrs d'Urberville, recognizing a new footstep. "I hope you will be kind to them. My bailiff tells me you are quite the proper person. Well, where are they? Ah, this is Strut! But he is hardly so lively to-day, is he? He is alarmed at being handled by a stranger, I suppose. And Phena too—yes, they are a little frightened—aren't you, dears? But they will soon get used to you."

While the old lady had been speaking Tess and the other maid, in obedience to her gestures, had placed the fowls severally in her lap, and she had felt them over from head to tail, examining their beaks, their combs, the manes of the cocks, their wings, and their claws. Her touch enabled her to recognize them in a moment, and to discover if a single feather were crippled or draggled. She handled their crops, and knew what they had eaten, and if too little or too much; her face enacting a vivid pantomime of the criticisms passing in her mind.

The birds that the two girls had brought in were duly returned to the yard, and the process was repeated till all the pet cocks and hens had been submitted to the old woman—Hamburghs, Bantams, Cochins, Brahmas, Dorkings,* and such other sorts as were in fashion just then—her perception of each visitor being seldom at fault as she received the bird upon her knees.

It reminded Tess of a Confirmation, in which Mrs d'Urberville was the bishop, the fowls the young people presented, and herself and the maidservant the parson and curate of the parish bringing them up. At the end of the ceremony Mrs d'Urberville abruptly asked Tess, wrinkling and twitching her face into undulations: "Can you whistle?"

"Whistle, ma'am?"

"Yes, whistle tunes."

Tess could whistle, like most other country girls, though the accomplishment was one which she did not care to profess in genteel company. However, she blandly admitted that such was the fact.

"Then you will have to practise it every day. I had a lad who did it very well, but he has left. I want you to whistle to my bullfinches; as I cannot see them I like to hear them, and we teach 'em airs that way.—Tell her where the cages are, Elizabeth.—You must begin to-morrow, or they will go back in their piping. They have been neglected these several days."

"Mr d'Urberville whistled to 'em this morning, ma'am," said Elizabeth.

"He! Pooh!"

The old lady's face creased into furrows of repugnance, and she made no further reply.

Thus the reception of Tess by her fancied kinswoman terminated, and the birds were taken back to their quarters. The girl's surprise at Mrs d'Urberville's manner was not great: for since seeing the size of the house she had expected no more. But she was far from being aware that the old lady had never heard a word of the so-called kinship. She gathered that no great affection flowed between the blind woman and her son. But in that, too, she was mistaken. Mrs d'Urberville was not the first mother compelled to love her offspring resentfully, and to be bitterly fond.

In spite of the unpleasant initiation of the day before, Tess inclined to the freedom and novelty of her new position in the morning when the sun shone, now that she was once installed there; and she was curious to test her powers in the unexpected direction asked of her, so as to ascertain her chance of retaining her post. As soon as she was alone within the walled garden she sat herself down on a coop, and seriously screwed up her mouth for the long-neglected practice. She found her former ability to have degenerated to the production of a hollow rush of wind through the lips, and no clear note at all.

She remained fruitlessly blowing and blowing, wondering how she could have so grown out of the art which had come by nature; till she became aware of a movement among the ivy-boughs which cloaked the garden-wall no less than the cottage. Looking that way she beheld a form springing from the coping into the plot. It was Alec d'Urberville, whom she had not set eyes on since he had conducted her the day before to the door of the gardener's cottage where she had lodgings.

"Upon my honour," cried he, "there was never before such a beautiful thing in nature or art as you look, 'cousin' Tess. ['Cousin' had a faint ring of mockery.] I have been watching you from over the wall—sitting like *Im*-patience on a monument,* and pouting up that pretty red mouth to whistling shape, and whooing and whooing, and privately swearing, and never being able to produce a note. Why, you are quite cross because you can't do it!"

"I may be cross, but I didn't swear."

"Ah—I understand why you are trying—those bullies! My mother wants you to carry on their musical education. How selfish of her!—as if attending to these curst cocks and hens here were not enough work for any girl. I would flatly refuse, if I were you."

"But she wants me particularly to do it, and to be ready by to-morrow morning."

"Does she? Well then—I'll give you a lesson or two."

"O no you won't," said Tess withdrawing towards the door.

"Nonsense; I don't want to touch you. See—I'll stand on this side of the wire-netting, and you can keep on the other; so you may feel quite safe. Now, look here; you screw up your lips too harshly. There 'tis;—so."

He suited the action to the word, and whistled a line of "Take O take those lips away."* But the allusion was lost upon Tess.

"Now try," said d'Urberville.

She attempted to look reserved; her face put on a sculptural severity. But he persisted in his demand, and at last, to get rid of him, she did put up her lips as directed for producing a clear note; laughing distressfully, however, and then blushing with vexation that she had laughed.

He encouraged her with "Try again!"

Tess was quite serious, painfully serious by this time; and she tried—ultimately and unexpectedly emitting a real round sound. The momentary pleasure of success got the better of her; her eyes enlarged, and she involuntarily smiled in his face.

"That's it! Now I have started you you'll go on beautifully. There—I said I would not come near you; and in spite of such temptation as never before fell to mortal man I'll keep my word.— Tess, do you think my mother a queer old soul?"

"I don't know much of her yet, sir."

"You'll find her so; she must be, to make you learn to whistle to her bullfinches. I am rather out of her books just now, but you will be quite in favour if you treat her live-stock well. Good-morning. If you meet with any difficulties and want help here, don't go to the bailiff; come to me."

It was in the economy of this *régime* that Tess Durbeyfield had undertaken to fill a place. Her first day's experiences were fairly typical of those which followed through many succeeding days. A familiarity with Alec d'Urberville's presence—which that young man carefully cultivated in her by playful dialogue, and by jestingly calling her his cousin when they were alone—removed much of her original shyness of him, without, however, implanting any feeling which could engender shyness of a new and tenderer kind. But she was more pliable under his hands than a mere companionship would have made her, owing to her unavoidable dependence upon his mother, and, through that lady's comparative helplessness, upon him.

She soon found that whistling to the bullfinches in Mrs d'Urberville's room was no such onerous business when she had regained the art, for she had caught from her musical mother numerous airs that suited those songsters admirably. A far more satisfactory time than when she practised in the garden was this whistling by the cages each morning. Unrestrained by the young man's presence she threw up her mouth, put her lips near the bars, and piped away in easeful grace to the attentive listeners.

Mrs d'Urberville slept in a large four-post bedstead hung with heavy damask curtains, and the bullfinches occupied the same apartment, where they flitted about freely at certain hours, and made little white spots on the furniture and upholstery. Once while Tess was at the window where the cages were ranged, giving her lesson as usual, she thought she heard a rustling behind the bed. The old lady was not present, and turning round the girl had an impression that the toes of a pair of boots were visible below the fringe of the curtains. Thereupon her whistling became so disjointed that the listener, if such there were, must have discovered her suspicion of his presence. She searched the curtains every morning after that, but never found anybody within them. Alec d'Urberville had evidently thought better of his freak to terrify her by an ambush of that kind.

X

EVERY village has its idiosyncracy, its constitution, often its own code of morality. The levity of some of the younger women in and about Trantridge was marked, and was perhaps symptomatic of the choice spirit who ruled The Slopes in that vicinity. The place had also a more abiding defect; it drank hard. The staple conversation on the farms around was on the uselessness of saving money; and smockfrocked arithmeticians, leaning on their ploughs or hoes, would enter into calculations of great nicety to prove that parish relief was a fuller provision for a man in his old age than any which could result from savings out of their wages during a whole lifetime.

The chief pleasure of these philosophers lay in going every Saturday night when work was done to Chaseborough, a decayed market-town two or three miles distant; and, returning in the small hours of the next morning, to spend Sunday in sleeping off the dyspeptic effects of the curious compounds sold to them as beer by the monopolizers of the once independent inns.

For a long time Tess did not join in the weekly pilgrimages. But under pressure from matrons not much older than herself—for a field-man's wages being as high at twenty-one as at forty, marriage was early here—Tess at length consented to go. Her first experience of the journey afforded her more enjoyment than she had expected, the hilariousness of the others being quite contagious after her monotonous attention to the poultry-farm all the week. She went again, and again. Being graceful and interesting, standing moreover on the momentary threshold of womanhood, her appearance drew down upon her some sly regards from loungers in the streets of Chaseborough; hence, though sometimes her journey to the town was made independently, she always searched for her fellows at nightfall, to have the protection of their companionship homeward.

This had gone on for a month or two when there came a Saturday in September, on which a fair and a market coincided; and the pilgrims from Trantridge sought double delights at the inns on that account. Tess's occupations made her late in setting out, so that her comrades reached the town long before her. It was a fine September evening, just before sunset, when yellow lights struggle with blue shades in hair-like lines, and the atmosphere itself forms a prospect, without aid from more solid objects, except the innumerable winged insects that dance in it. Through this low-lit mistiness Tess walked leisurely along.

She did not discover the coincidence of the market with the fair till she had reached the place, by which time it was close upon dusk. Her limited marketing was soon completed; and then as usual she began to look about for some of the Trantridge cottagers.

At first she could not find them, and she was informed that most of them had gone to what they called a private little jig at the house of a hay-trusser and peat-dealer who had transactions with their farm. He lived in an out-of-the-way nook of the townlet, and in trying to find her course thither her eyes fell upon Mr d'Urberville standing at a street-corner.

"What—my beauty—You here so late?" he said.

She told him that she was simply waiting for company homeward.

"I'll see you again," said he over her shoulder as she went on down the back lane.

Approaching the hay-trusser's she could hear the fiddled notes of a reel proceeding from some building in the rear; but no sound of dancing was audible, an exceptional state of things for these parts, where as a rule the stamping drowned the music. The front door being open she could see straight through the house into the garden at the back as far as the shades of night would allow; and nobody appearing to her knock she traversed the dwelling and went up the path to the outhouse whence the sound had attracted her.

It was a windowless erection used for storage, and from the open door there floated into the obscurity a mist of yellow radiance, which at first Tess thought to be illuminated smoke. But on drawing nearer she perceived that it was a cloud of dust, lit by candles within the outhouse, whose beams upon the haze carried forward the outline of the doorway into the wide night of the garden.

When she came close and looked in she beheld indistinct forms racing up and down to the figure of the dance, the silence of their footfalls arising from their being overshod in "scroff"—that is to say the powdery residuum from the storage of peat and other products, the stirring of which by their turbulent feet created the nebulosity that involved the scene. Through this floating fusty *débris* of peat and hay, mixed with the perspirations and warmth of the dancers, and forming together a sort of vegeto-human pollen, the muted fiddles feebly pushed their notes, in marked contrast to the spirit with which the measure was trodden out. They coughed as they danced, and laughed as they coughed. Of the rushing couples there could barely be discerned more than the high lights—the indistinctness shaping them to satyrs clasping nymphs—a multiplicity of Pans whirling a multiplicity of Syrinxes; Lotis attempting to elude Priapus, and always failing.

At intervals a couple would approach the doorway for air, and the haze no longer veiling their features, the demigods resolved themselves into the homely personalities of her own next-door neighbours. Could Trantridge in two or three short hours have metamorphosed itself thus madly!

Some Sileni* of the throng sat on benches and hay-trusses by the wall; and one of them recognized her.

"The maids don't think it respectable to dance at The Flower-de-Luce," he explained; "they don't like to let everybody see which be their fancy-men. Besides, the house sometimes shuts up just when their jints begin to get greased. So we come here and send out for liquor."

"But when be any of you going home?" asked Tess with some anxiety.

"Now—a'most directly. This is all but the last jig."

She waited. The reel drew to a close, and some of the party were in the mind for starting. But others would not, and another dance was formed. This surely would end it, thought Tess. But it merged in yet another. She became restless and uneasy; yet having waited so long it was necessary to wait longer; on account of the fair the roads were dotted with roving characters of possibly ill intent: and though not fearful of measurable dangers she feared the unknown. Had she been near Marlott she would have had less dread.

"Don't ye be nervous, my dear good soul!" expostulated between his coughs a young man with a wet face, and his straw hat so far back upon his head that the brim encircled it like the nimbus of a saint. "What's yer hurry? To-morrow is Sunday, thank God, and we can sleep it off in church time. Now, have a turn with me?"

She did not abhor dancing, but she was not going to dance here. The movement grew more passionate. The fiddlers behind the luminous pillar of cloud now and then varied the air by playing on the wrong side of the bridge, or with the back of the bow. But it did not matter; the panting shapes spun onwards.

They did not vary their partners if their inclination were to stick to previous ones. Changing partners simply meant that a satisfactory choice had not as yet been arrived at by one or other of the pair, and by this time every couple had been suitably matched. It was then that the ecstasy and the dream began, in which emotion was the matter of the universe, and matter but an adventitious intrusion likely to hinder you from spinning where you wanted to spin.

Suddenly there was a dull thump on the ground: a couple had fallen, and lay in a mixed heap. The next couple, unable to check its progress, came toppling over the obstacle. An inner cloud of dust rose around the prostrate figures amid the general one of the room, in which a twitching entanglement of arms and legs was discernible.

"You shall catch it for this, my gentleman, when you get home!" burst in female accents from the human heap—those of the unhappy partner of the man whose clumsiness had caused the mishap; she happened also to be his recently married wife—in which assortment there was nothing unusual at Trantridge, as long as any affection remained between wedded couples; and indeed it was not uncustomary in their later lives, to avoid making odd lots of the single people between whom there might be a warm understanding.

A loud laugh from behind Tess's back in the shade of the garden united with the titter within the room. She looked round, and saw the red coal of a cigar: Alec d'Urberville was standing there alone. He beckoned to her, and she reluctantly retreated towards him.

"Well, my beauty, what are you doing here?"

She was so tired after her long day, and her walk, that she confided her trouble to him—that she had been waiting, ever since he saw her, to have their company home, because the road at night was strange to her. "But it seems they will never leave off; and I really think I will wait no longer."

"Certainly do not. I have only a saddle-horse here to-day; but come to The Flower-de-Luce, and I'll hire a trap, and drive you home with me."

Tess, though flattered, had never quite got over her original mistrust of him; and, despite their tardiness, she preferred to walk home with the workfolk. So she answered that she was much obliged to him, but would not trouble him. "I have said that I will wait for 'em, and they will expect me to now."

"Very well, Miss Independence; please yourself. . . . Then I shall not hurry. . . . My good Lord, what a kick-up they are having there!"

He had not put himself forward into the light, but some of them had perceived him, and his presence led to a slight pause, and a consideration of how the time was flying. As soon as he had re-lit a cigar and walked away, the Trantridge people began to collect themselves from amid those who had come in from other farms; and prepared to leave in a body. Their bundles and baskets were gathered up, and half an hour later, when the clock-chime sounded a quarter past eleven, they were straggling along the lane which led up the hill towards their homes.

It was a three-mile walk, along a dry white road, made whiter to-night by the light of the moon.

Tess soon perceived as she walked in the flock, sometimes with this one, sometimes with that, that the fresh night air was producing staggerings and serpentine courses among the men who had partaken too freely; some of the more careless women also were wandering in their gait—to wit, a dark virago, Car Darch, dubbed Queen of Spades, till lately a favourite of d'Urberville's; Nancy, her sister, nicknamed the Queen of Diamonds; and the young married woman who had already tumbled down. Yet however terrestrial and lumpy their appearance just now to the mean unglamoured eye, to themselves the case was different. They followed the road with a sensation that they were soaring along in a supporting medium, possessed of original and profound thoughts; themselves and surrounding nature forming an organism of which all the parts harmoniously and joyously interpenetrated each other. They were as sublime as the moon and stars above them; and the moon and stars were as ardent as they.

Tess, however, had undergone such painful experiences of this kind in her father's house that the discovery of their condition spoilt the pleasure she was beginning to feel in the moonlight journey. Yet she stuck to the party, for reasons above given.

In the open highway they had progressed in scattered order; but now their route was through a field-gate, and the foremost finding a difficulty in opening it, they closed up together.

This leading pedestrian was Car the Queen of Spades, who carried a wicker basket containing her mother's groceries, her own draperies, and other purchases for the week. The basket being large and heavy, Car had placed it for convenience of porterage on the top of her head, where it rode on in jeopardized balance as she walked with arms akimbo.

"Well. . . . Whatever is that a-creeping down thy back, Car Darch?" said one of the group suddenly.

All looked at Car. Her gown was a light cotton print, and from the back of her head a kind of rope could be seen descending to some distance below her waist, like a Chinaman's queue.

" 'Tis her hair falling down," said another.

No: it was not her hair; it was a black stream of something oozing from her basket; and it glistened like a slimy snake in the cold still rays of the moon.

" 'Tis treacle," said an observant matron.

Treacle it was. Car's poor old grandmother had a weakness for the sweet stuff; honey she had in plenty out of her own hives; but treacle was what her soul desired, and Car had been about to give her a treat of surprise. Hastily lowering the basket the dark girl found that the vessel containing the syrup had been smashed within.

By this time there had arisen a shout of laughter at the extraordinary appearance of Car's back; which irritated the dark queen into getting rid of the disfigurement by the first sudden means available and independently of the help of the scoffers. She rushed excitedly into the field they were about to cross, and flinging herself flat on her back upon the grass began to wipe her gown as well as she could by spinning horizontally on the herbage and dragging herself over it upon her elbows.

The laughter rang louder: they clung to the gate, to the posts, rested on their staves, in the weakness engendered by their convulsions at the spectacle of Car. Our heroine, who had hitherto held her peace, at this wild moment could not help joining in with the rest.

It was a misfortune—in more ways than one. No sooner did the dark queen hear the soberer, richer note of Tess among those of the other work-people than a long smouldering sense of rivalry inflamed her to madness. She sprang to her feet, and closely faced the object of her dislike.

"How darest th' laugh at me, hussy!" she cried.

"I couldn't really help it—when t'others did," apologized Tess, still tittering.

"Ah—th'st think th' beest everybody, dostn't—because th' beest first favourite with He just now! But stop a bit, my lady, stop a bit! I'm as good as two of such! Look here—here's at 'ee!"

To Tess's horror the dark queen began stripping off the bodice of her gown—which for the added reason of its ridiculed condition she was only too glad to be free of—till she had bared her plump neck, shoulders, and arms to the moonshine, under which they looked as luminous and beautiful as some Praxitelean creation,* in their possession of the faultless rotundities of a lusty country girl. She closed her fists, and squared up at Tess.

"Indeed then—I shall not fight!" said the latter majestically; "and if I had known you was of that sort I wouldn't have so let myself down as to come with such a whorage as this is!"

The rather too inclusive speech brought down a torrent of vituperation from other quarters upon fair Tess's unlucky head, particularly from the Queen of Diamonds, who, having stood in the relations to d'Urberville that Car had also been suspected of, united with the latter against the common enemy. Several other women also chimed in, with an animus which none of them would have been so fatuous as to show but for the rollicking evening they had passed. Thereupon, finding Tess unfairly browbeaten, the husbands and lovers tried to make peace by defending her; but the result of that attempt was directly to increase the war.

Tess was indignant and ashamed. She no longer minded the loneliness of the way and the lateness of the hour; her one object was to get away from the whole crew as soon as possible. She knew well enough that the better among them would repent of their passion next day. They were all now inside the field, and she was edging back to rush off alone when a horseman emerged almost silently from the corner of the hedge that screened the road, and Alec d'Urberville looked round upon them.

"What the devil is all this row about, workfolk?" he asked.

The explanation was not readily forthcoming; and in truth he did not require any. Having heard their voices while yet some way off he had ridden creepingly forward, and learnt enough to satisfy himself.

Tess was standing apart from the rest, near the gate. He bent over towards her. "Jump up behind me," he whispered, "and we'll get shot of the screaming cats in a jiffy!"

She felt almost ready to faint, so vivid was her sense of the crisis. At almost any other moment of her life she would have refused such proffered aid and company, as she had refused them several times before; and now the loneliness would not of itself have forced her to do otherwise. But coming as the invitation did at the particular juncture when fear and indignation at these adversaries could be transformed by a spring of the foot into a triumph over them she abandoned herself to her impulse, climbed the gate, put her toe upon his instep, and scrambled into the saddle behind him. The pair were speeding away into the distant grey by the time that the contentious revellers became aware of what had happened.

The Queen of Spades forgot the stain on her bodice, and stood beside the Queen of Diamonds and the new-married staggering young woman—all with a gaze of fixity in the direction in which the horse's tramp was diminishing into silence on the road.

"What be ye looking at?" asked a man who had not observed the incident.

"Ho-ho-ho!" laughed dark Car.

"Hee-hee-hee!" laughed the tippling bride, as she steadied herself on the arm of her fond husband.

"Heu-heu-heu!" laughed dark Car's mother, stroking her moustache as she explained laconically, "Out of the frying-pan into the fire!"

Then these children of the open air, whom even excess of alcohol could scarce injure permanently, betook themselves to the field-path; and as they went there moved onward with them, around the shadow of each one's head, a circle of opalized light, formed by the moon's rays upon the glistening sheet of dew. Each pedestrian could see no halo but his or her own, which never deserted the head-shadow whatever its vulgar unsteadiness might be; but adhered to it, and persistently beautified it; till the erratic motions seemed an inherent part of the irradiation and the fumes of their breathing a component of the night's mist: and the spirit of the scene, and of the moonlight, and of Nature, seemed harmoniously to mingle with the spirit of wine.

XI

THE twain cantered along for some time without speech, Tess as she clung to him still panting in her triumph, yet in other respects dubious. She had perceived that the horse was not the spirited one he sometimes rode, and felt no alarm on that score, though her seat was precarious enough despite her tight hold of him. She begged him to slow the animal to a walk, which Alec accordingly did.

"Neatly done, was it not, dear Tess," he said by and by.

"Yes!" said she. "I am sure I ought to be much obliged to you."

"And are you?"

She did not reply.

"Tess, why do you always dislike my kissing you?"

"I suppose—because I don't love you."

"You are quite sure?"

"I am angry with you sometimes."

"Ah, I half feared as much." Nevertheless Alec did not object to that confession. He knew that anything was better than frigidity. "Why haven't you told me when I have made you angry?"

"You know very well why. Because I cannot help myself here."

"I haven't offended you often by love-making?"

"You have sometimes."

"How many times?"

"You know as well as I—too many times."

"Every time I have tried?"

She was silent, and the horse ambled along for a considerable distance, till a faint luminous fog, which had hung in the hollows all the evening, became general, and enveloped them. It seemed to hold the moonlight in suspension, rendering it more pervasive than in clear air. Whether on this account, or from absent-mindedness or from sleepiness, she did not perceive that they had long ago passed the point at which the lane to Trantridge branched from the highway, and that her conductor had not taken the Trantridge track.

She was inexpressibly weary. She had risen at five o'clock every morning of that week, had been on foot the whole of each day, and on this evening had, in addition, walked the three miles to Chaseborough, waited three hours for her neighbours without eating or drinking, her impatience to start them preventing either; she had then walked a mile of the way home, and had undergone the excitement of the quarrel, till, with the slow progress of their steed, it was now nearly one o'clock. Only once, however, was she overcome by actual drowsiness. In that moment of oblivion her head sank gently against him.

D'Urberville stopped the horse, withdrew his feet from the stirrups, turned sideways on the saddle, and enclosed her waist with his arm to support her.

This immediately put her on the defensive, and with one of those sudden impulses of reprisal to which she was liable she gave him a little push from her. In his ticklish position he nearly lost his balance and only just avoided rolling over into the road, the horse, though a powerful one, being fortunately the quietest he rode.

"That is devilish unkind," he said. "I mean no harm—only to keep you from falling."

She pondered suspiciously; till, thinking that this might after all be true, she relented and said quite humbly "I beg your pardon, sir."

"I won't pardon you unless you show some confidence in me. Good God!" he burst out, "what am I, to be repulsed so by a mere chit like you? For near three mortal months have you trifled with my feelings, eluded me, and snubbed me; and I won't stand it!"

"I'll leave you to-morrow, sir."

"No you will not leave me to-morrow! Will you, I ask once more, show your belief in me by letting me clasp you with my arm? Come, between us two and nobody else; now. We know each other well; and you know that I love you, and think you the prettiest girl in the world, which you are. Mayn't I treat you as a lover?"

She drew a quick pettish breath of objection, writhing uneasily on her seat, looked far ahead, and murmured, "I don't know—I wish—how can I say yes or no, when—"

He settled the matter by clasping his arm round her as he desired—and Tess expressed no further negative. Thus they sidled slowly onward till it struck her they had been advancing for an unconscionable time—far longer than was usually occupied by the short journey from Chaseborough, even at this walking pace, and that they were no longer on hard road, but in a mere trackway.

"Why—where be we?" she exclaimed.

"Passing by a wood."

"A wood—what wood? Surely we are quite out of the road?"

"A bit of The Chase—the oldest wood in England. It is a lovely night, and why should we not prolong our ride a little?"

"How could you be so treacherous!" said Tess between archness and real dismay, and getting rid of his arm by pulling open his fingers one by one, though at the risk of slipping off herself. "Just when I've been putting such trust in you, and obliging you to please you, because I thought I had wronged you by that push. Please set me down, and let me walk home."

"You cannot walk home, darling, even if the air were clear. We are miles away from Trantridge, if I must tell you, and in this growing fog you might wander for hours among these trees."

"Never mind that," she coaxed. "Put me down, I beg you. I don't mind where it is, only let me get down, sir, please!"

"Very well then, I will—on one condition. Having brought you here to this out-of-the-way place, I feel myself responsible for your safe conduct home, whatever you may yourself feel about it. As to your getting to Trantridge without assistance, it is quite impossible; for to tell the truth, dear, owing to this fog which so disguises everything, I don't quite know where we are myself. Now if you will promise to wait beside the horse, while I walk through the bushes till I come to some road or house, and ascertain exactly our whereabouts, I'll deposit you here willingly. When I come back I'll give you full directions, and if you insist upon walking you may; or you may ride—at your pleasure."

She accepted these terms, and slid off on the near side, though not till he had stolen a cursory kiss. He sprang down on the other side.

"I suppose I must hold the horse," said she.

"O no—it's not necessary," replied Alec, patting the panting creature. "He's had enough of it for to-night."

He turned the horse's head into the bushes, hitched him on to a bough, and made a sort of couch or nest for her in the deep mass of dead leaves. "Now, you sit there," he said. "The leaves have not got damp as yet. Just give an eye to the horse—it will be quite sufficient."

He took a few steps away from her, but returning said, "By the bye, Tess; your father has a new cob to-day. Somebody gave it to him."

"Somebody? You!"

D'Urberville nodded.

"O how very good of you that is!" she exclaimed with a painful sense of the awkwardness of having to thank him just then.

"And the children have some toys."

"I didn't know—you ever sent them anything!" she murmured, much moved. "I almost wish you had not—yes, I almost wish it!"

"Why, dear?"

"It—hampers me so."

"Tessy—don't you love me ever so little now?"

"I'm grateful," she reluctantly admitted. "But I fear I do not—" The sudden vision of his passion for herself as a factor in this result so distressed her that, beginning with one slow tear, and then following with another, she wept outright.

"Don't cry, dear, dear one! Now sit down here, and wait till I come." She passively sat down amid the leaves he had heaped, and shivered slightly. "Are you cold?" he asked.

"Not very—a little."

He touched her with his fingers, which sank into her as into down. "You have only that puffy muslin dress on—how's that?"

"It's my best summer one. 'Twas very warm when I started, and I didn't know I was going to ride, and that it would be night."

"Nights grow chilly in September. Let me see." He pulled off a light overcoat that he had worn, and put it round her tenderly. "That's it—now you'll feel warmer," he continued. "Now my pretty, rest there: I shall soon be back again."

Having buttoned the overcoat round her shoulders he plunged into the webs of vapour which by this time formed veils between the trees. She could hear the rustling of the branches as he ascended the adjoining slope, till his movements were no louder than the hopping of a bird, and finally died away. With the setting of the moon the pale light lessened, and Tess became invisible as she fell into reverie upon the leaves where he had left her.

In the meantime Alec d'Urberville had pushed on up the slope to clear his genuine doubt as to the quarter of The Chase they were in. He had, in fact, ridden quite at random for over an hour, taking any turning that came to hand in order to prolong companionship with her, and giving far more attention to Tess's moonlit person than to any wayside object. A little rest for the jaded animal being desirable he did not hasten his search for landmarks. A clamber over the hill into the adjoining vale brought him to the fence of a highway whose

contours he recognized, which settled the question of their whereabouts. D'Urberville thereupon turned back; but by this time the
moon had quite gone down, and, partly on occount of the fog, The
Chase was wrapped in thick darkness, although morning was not far
off. He was obliged to advance with outstretched hands, to avoid
contact with the boughs, and discovered that to hit the exact spot
from which he had started was at first entirely beyond him. Roaming
up and down, round and round, he at length heard a slight movement of the horse close at hand; and the sleeve of his overcoat
unexpectedly caught his foot.

"Tess!" said d'Urberville.

There was no answer. The obscurity was now so great that he could
see absolutely nothing but a pale nebulousness at his feet, which
represented the white muslin figure he had left upon the dead leaves.
Everything else was blackness alike. D'Urberville stooped; and heard
a gentle regular breathing. He knelt, and bent lower, till her breath
warmed his face, and in a moment his cheek was in contact with hers.
She was sleeping soundly, and upon her eyelashes there lingered tears.

Darkness and silence ruled everywhere around. Above them rose
the primeval yews and oaks of The Chase, in which were poised
gentle roosting birds in their last nap; and about them stole the
hopping rabbits and hares. But, might some say, where was Tess's
guardian angel? where was the Providence of her simple faith?
Perhaps, like that other god of whom the ironical Tishbite spoke, he
was talking, or he was pursuing, or he was in a journey, or he was
sleeping and not to be awaked.*

Why it was that upon this beautiful feminine tissue, sensitive as
gossamer, and practically blank as snow as yet, there should have
been traced such a coarse pattern as it was doomed to receive; why so
often the coarse appropriates the finer thus, the wrong man the
woman, the wrong woman the man, many thousand years of
analytical philosophy have failed to explain to our sense of order.
One may, indeed, admit the possibility of a retribution lurking in the
present catastrophe. Doubtless some of Tess d'Urberville's mailed
ancestors rollicking home from a fray had dealt the same measure
even more ruthlessly towards peasant girls of their time. But though
to visit the sins of the fathers* upon the children may be a morality
good enough for divinities, it is scorned by average human nature;
and it therefore does not mend the matter.

As Tess's own people down in those retreats are never tired of saying among each other in their fatalistic way: "It was to be." There lay the pity of it. An immeasurable social chasm was to divide our heroine's personality thereafter from that previous self of hers who stepped from her mother's door to try her fortune at Trantridge poultry-farm.

END OF PHASE THE FIRST

PHASE THE SECOND

MAIDEN NO MORE

PHASE THE SECOND

MAIDEN NO MORE

XII

THE basket was heavy and the bundle was large, but she lugged them along like a person who did not find her especial burden in material things. Occasionally she stopped to rest in a mechanical way by some gate or post; and then, giving the baggage another hitch upon her full round arm, went steadily on again.

It was a Sunday morning in late October, about four months after Tess Durbeyfield's arrival at Trantridge, and some few weeks subsequent to the night ride in The Chase. The time was not long past daybreak, and the yellow luminosity upon the horizon behind her back lighted the ridge towards which her face was set—the barrier of the vale wherein she had of late been a stranger—which she would have to climb over to reach her birthplace. The ascent was gradual on this side, and the soil and scenery differed much from those within Blakemore Vale. Even the character and accent of the two peoples had shades of difference, despite the amalgamating effects of a roundabout railway; so that though less than twenty miles from the place of her sojourn at Trantridge, her native village had seemed a far-away spot. The field-folk shut in there traded northward and westward, travelled, courted, and married northward and westward, thought northward and westward; those on this side mainly directed their energies and attention to the east and south.

The incline was the same down which d'Urberville had driven with her so wildly on that day in June. Tess went up the remainder of its length without stopping, and on reaching the edge of the escarpment gazed over the familiar green world beyond, now half veiled in mist. It was always beautiful from here; it was terribly beautiful to Tess to-day, for since her eyes last fell upon it she had learnt that the serpent hisses where the sweet birds sing, and her views of life had been totally changed for her by the lesson. Verily another girl than the simple one she had been at home was she who, bowed by thought, stood still here, and turned to look behind her. She could not bear to look forward into the Vale.

Ascending by the long white road that Tess herself had just laboured up she saw a two-wheeled vehicle, beside which walked a man who held up his hand to attract her attention.

She obeyed the signal to wait for him with unspeculative repose; and in a few minutes man and horse stopped beside her.

"Why did you slip away by stealth like this?" said d'Urberville with upbraiding breathlessness. "On a Sunday morning too, when people were all in bed! I only discovered it by accident, and I have been driving like the deuce to overtake you!—Just look at the mare! Why go off like this—you know that nobody wished to hinder your going? And how unnecessary it has been for you to toil along on foot, and encumber yourself with this heavy load! I have followed like a madman, simply to drive you the rest of the distance, if you won't come back?"

"I shan't come back," said she.

"I thought you wouldn't—I said so! Well then, put up your baskets, and let me help you on."

She listlessly placed her basket and bundle within the dog-cart, and stepped up; and they sat side by side. She had no fear of him now; and in the cause of her confidence her sorrow lay.

D'Urberville mechanically lit a cigar, and the journey was continued with broken, unemotional conversation on the commonplace objects by the wayside. He had quite forgotten his struggle to kiss her when, in the early summer, they had driven in the opposite direction along the same road. But she had not, and she sat now like a puppet, replying to his remarks in monosyllables. After some miles they came in view of the clump of trees beyond which the village of Marlott stood. It was only then that her still face showed the least emotion, a tear or two beginning to trickle down.

"What are you crying for?" he coldly asked.

"I was only thinking that I was born over there," murmured Tess.

"Well—we must all be born somewhere."

"I wish I had never been born—there or anywhere else."

"Pooh! Well, if you didn't wish to come to Trantridge why did you come?"

She did not reply.

"You didn't come for love of me, that I'll swear."

" 'Tis quite true. If I had gone for love o' you, if I had ever sincerely loved you, if I loved you still, I should not so loathe and hate myself for my weakness as I do now! . . . My eyes were dazed by you for a little, and that was all."

He shrugged his shoulders. She resumed—

"I didn't understand your meaning till it was too late."

"That's what every woman says."

"How can you dare to use such words!" she cried, turning impetuously upon him, her eyes flashing as the latent spirit (of which he was to see more some day) awoke in her. "My God, I could knock you out of the gig! Did it never strike your mind that what every woman says some women may feel?"

"Very well," he said laughing. "I am sorry to wound you. I did wrong—I admit it." He dropped into some little bitterness as he continued: "Only you needn't be so everlastingly flinging it in my face. I am ready to pay to the uttermost farthing. You know you need not work in the fields or dairies again. You know you may clothe yourself with the best, instead of in the bald plain way you have lately affected, as if you couldn't get a ribbon more than you earn."

Her lip lifted slightly, though there was little scorn as a rule in her large and impulsive nature. "I have said I will not take anything more from you, and I will not—I cannot! I *should* be your creature to go on doing that; and I won't!"

"One would think you were a princess from your manner in addition to a true and original d'Urberville,—ha-ha! . . . Well, Tess dear, I can say no more. I suppose I am a bad fellow—a damn bad fellow. I was born bad, and I have lived bad, and I shall die bad, in all probability. But, upon my lost soul, I won't be bad towards you again, Tess. And if certain circumstances should arise—you understand—in which you are in the least need, the least difficulty, send me one line, and you shall have by return whatever you require. I may not be at Trantridge—I am going to London for a time—I can't stand the old woman. But all letters will be forwarded."

She said that she did not wish him to drive her further, and they stopped just under the clump of trees. D'Urberville alighted, and lifted her down bodily in his arms, afterwards placing her articles on the ground beside her. She bowed to him slightly, her eye just lingering in his; and then she turned to take the parcels for departure.

Alec d'Urberville removed his cigar, bent towards her, and said, "You are not going to turn away like that, dear? Come!"

"If you wish," she answered indifferently. "See how you've mastered me!" She thereupon turned round and lifted her face to his, and remained like a marble term* while he imprinted a kiss upon her cheek—half-perfunctorily, half as if zest had not yet quite died out. Her eyes vaguely rested upon the remotest trees in the lane while the kiss was given, as though she were nearly unconscious of what he did.

"Now the other side—for old acquaintance' sake."

She turned her head in the same passive way, as one might turn at the request of a sketcher or hairdresser, and he kissed the other side, his lips touching cheeks that were damp and smoothly chill as the skin of the mushrooms in the fields around.

"You don't give me your mouth and kiss me back. You never willingly do that—you'll never love me, I fear."

"I have said so, often. It is true. I have never really and truly loved you, and I think I never can." She added mournfully: "Perhaps of all things a lie on this thing would do the most good to me now; but I have honour enough left, little as 'tis, not to tell that lie. If I did love you I may have the best o' causes for letting you know it. But I don't."

He emitted a laboured breath, as if the scene were getting rather oppressive to his heart, or to his conscience, or to his gentility. "Well—you are absurdly melancholy, Tess. I have no reason for flattering you now, and I can say plainly that you need not be so sad. You can hold your own for beauty against any woman of these parts, gentle or simple; I say it to you as a practical man and well-wisher. If you are wise you will show it to the world more than you do, before it fades . . . . And yet—Tess, will you come back to me? Upon my soul I don't like to let you go like this!"

"Never, never! I made up my mind as soon as I saw—what I ought to have seen sooner; and I won't come."

"Then good-morning my four-months' cousin—good-bye!"

He leapt up lightly, arranged the reins, and was gone between the tall red-berried hedges.

Tess did not look after him, but slowly wound along the crooked lane. It was still early, and though the sun's lower limb was just free of the hill, his rays, ungenial and peering, addressed the eye rather than the touch as yet. There was not a human soul near. Sad October and her sadder self seemed the only two existences haunting that lane.

As she walked, however, some footsteps approached behind her, the footsteps of a man; and owing to the briskness of his advance he was close at her heels and had said "Good morning" before she had been long aware of his propinquity. He appeared to be an artizan of some sort, and carried a tin pot of red paint in his hand. He asked in a business-like manner if he should take her basket, which she permitted him to do, walking beside him.

"It is early to be astir, this Sabbath morn," he said cheerfully.

"Yes," said Tess.

"When most people are at rest from their week's work."

She also assented to this.

"Though I do more real work to-day than all the week besides."

"Do you?"

"All the week I work for the glory of man, and on Sunday for the glory of God. That's more real than the other—hey? I have a little to do here at this stile." The man turned as he spoke to an opening at the roadside leading into a pasture. "If you'll wait a moment," he added, "I shall not be long."

As he had her basket she could not well do otherwise, and she waited, observing him. He set down her basket and the tin pot, and, stirring the paint with the brush that was in it, began painting large square letters on the middle board of the three composing the stile; placing a comma after each word, as if to give pause while that word was driven well home to the reader's heart,

THY, DAMNATION, SLUMBERETH, NOT.
2 PET. ii. 3.

Against the peaceful landscape, the pale decaying tints of the copses, the blue air of the horizon, and the lichened stile-boards, these staring vermillion words shone forth. They seemed to shout themselves out, and make the atmosphere ring. Some people might have cried "Alas, poor Theology!" at the hideous defacement the last grotesque phase of a creed which had served mankind well in its time. But the words entered Tess with accusatory horror: it was as if this man had known her recent history; yet he was a total stranger.

Having finished his text he picked up her basket, and she mechanically resumed her walk beside him.

"Do you believe what you paint?" she asked in low tones.

"Believe that text? Do I believe in my own existence!"

"But," said she tremulously, "suppose your sin was not of your own seeking?"

He shook his head. "I cannot split hairs on that burning query," he said. "I have walked hundreds of miles this past summer, painting these texes on every wall, gate, and stile in the length and breadth of this district: I leave their application to the hearts of the people who read 'em."

"I think they are horrible!" said Tess. "Crushing, killing!"

"That's what they are meant to be!" he replied in a trade voice. "But you should read my hottest ones—them I kips for slums and seaports. They'd make ye wriggle! Not but what this is a very good tex for rural districts . . . . Ah—there's a nice bit of blank wall up by that barn standing to waste. I must put one there—one that it will be good for dangerous young females like yerself to heed. Will ye wait, missy?"

"No," said she; and taking her basket Tess trudged on. A little way forward she turned her head. The old grey wall began to advertise a similar fiery lettering to the first, with a strange and unwonted mien, as if distressed at duties it had never before been called upon to perform. It was with a sudden flush that she read and realized what was to be the inscription he was now half-way through—

THOU, SHALT, NOT, COMMIT—

Her cheerful friend saw her looking, stopped his brush, and shouted—

"If you want to ask for edification on these things of moment, there's a very earnest good man going to preach a charity-sermon to-day in the parish you are going to—Mr Clare, of Emminster. I'm not of his persuasion now, but he's a good man, and he'll expound as well as any parson I know. 'Twas he began the work in me."

But Tess did not answer; she throbbingly resumed her walk, her eyes fixed on the ground. "Pooh—I don't believe God said such things!" she murmured contemptuously when her flush had died away.

A plume of smoke soared up suddenly from her father's chimney, the sight of which made her heart ache. The aspect of the interior, when she reached it, made her heart ache more. Her mother, who had just come downstairs, turned to greet her from the fireplace, where she was kindling "rendlewood" (barked-oak) twigs under the breakfast kettle. The young children were still above, as was also her father, it being Sunday morning, when he felt justified in lying an additional half-hour.

"Well!—my dear Tess!" exclaimed her surprised mother, jumping up and kissing the girl. "How be ye? I didn't see you till you was in upon me! Have you come home to be married?"

"No, I have not come for that, mother."

"Then for a holiday?"

"Yes—for a holiday; for a long holiday," said Tess.

"What, isn't your cousin going to do the handsome thing?"

"He's not my cousin, and he's not going to marry me."

Her mother eyed her narrowly.

"Come, you have not told me all," she said.

Then Tess went up to her mother, put her face upon Joan's neck, and told.

"And yet th'st not got him to marry 'ee!" reiterated her mother. "Any woman would have done it but you, after that!"

"Perhaps any woman would, except me."

"It would have been something like a story to come back with, if you had!" continued Mrs Durbeyfield, ready to burst into tears of vexation. "After all the talk about you and him which has reached us here, who would have expected it to end like this! Why didn't ye think of doing some good for your family instead o' thinking only of yourself? See how I've got to teave and slave, and your poor weak father with his heart clogged like a dripping-pan.* I did hope for something to come out o' this! To see what a pretty pair you and he made that day when you drove away together four months ago! See what he has given us—all, as we thought, because we were his kin. But if he's not, it must have been done because of his love for 'ee. And yet you've not got him to marry!"

Get Alec d'Urberville in the mind to marry her. He marry *her*! On matrimony he had never once said a word. And what if he had? How a convulsive snatching at social salvation might have impelled her to answer him she could not say. But her poor foolish mother little knew her present feeling towards this man. Perhaps it was unusual in the circumstances, unlucky, unaccountable; but there it was; and this, as she had said, was what made her detest herself. She had never wholly cared for him, she did not at all care for him now. She had dreaded him, winced before him, succumbed to adroit advantages he took of her helplessness; then, temporarily blinded by his ardent manners, had been stirred to confused surrender awhile: had suddenly despised and disliked him, and had run away. That was all. Hate him she did not quite; but he was dust and ashes to her, and even for her name's sake she scarcely wished to marry him.

"You ought to have been more careful, if you didn't mean to get him to make you his wife!"

"O mother, my mother!" cried the agonized girl, turning passionately upon her parent as if her poor heart would break. "How could I be expected to know? I was a child when I left this house four months ago. Why didn't you tell me there was danger in men-folk? Why didn't you warn me? Ladies know what to fend hands against, because they read novels that tell them of these tricks; but I never had the chance o' learning in that way, and you did not help me."

Her mother was subdued. "I thought if I spoke of his fond feelings, and what they might lead to, you would be hontish wi' him, and lose your chance," she murmured, wiping her eyes with her apron. "Well, we must make the best of it, I suppose. 'Tis nater, after all, and what do please God."

XIII

THE event of Tess Durbeyfield's return from the manor of her bogus kinsfolk was rumoured abroad, if rumour be not too large a word for a space of a square mile. In the afternoon several young girls of Marlott, former schoolfellows and acquaintances of Tess, called to see her; arriving dressed in their best starched and ironed, as became visitors to a person who had made a transcendent conquest (as they supposed); and sat round the room looking at her with great curiosity. For the fact that it was this said thirty-first cousin Mr d'Urberville who had fallen in love with her, a gentleman not altogether local, whose reputation as a reckless gallant and heartbreaker was beginning to spread beyond the immediate boundaries of Trantridge, lent Tess's supposed position, by its fearsomeness, a far higher fascination than it would have exercised if unhazardous.

Their interest was so deep that the younger ones whispered when her back was turned; "How pretty she is—and how that best frock do set her off! I believe it cost an immense deal, and that it was a gift from him."

Tess, who was reaching up to get the tea-things from the corner-cupboard, did not hear these commentaries. If she had heard them she might soon have set her friends right on the matter. But her mother heard, and Joan's simple vanity, having been denied the hope of a dashing marriage, fed itself as well as it could upon the sensation of a dashing flirtation. Upon the whole she felt gratified, even though such a limited and evanescent triumph should involve her daughter's reputation; it might end in marriage yet, and in the warmth of her responsiveness to their admiration she invited her visitors to stay to tea.

Their chatter, their laughter, their good-humoured innuendoes, above all, their flashes and flickerings of envy, revived Tess's spirits also; and as the evening wore on she caught the infection of their excitement, and grew almost gay. The marble hardness left her face, she moved with something of her old bounding step, and flushed in all her young beauty.

At moments, in spite of thought, she would reply to their inquiries with a manner of superiority, as if recognizing that her experiences in the field of courtship had indeed been slightly enviable. But so far was she from being, in the words of Robert South,* "in love with her own ruin", that the illusion was transient as lightning; cold reason came back to mock her spasmodic weakness; the ghastliness of her momentary pride would convict her, and recall her to reserved listlessness again.

And the despondency of the next morning's dawn, when it was no longer Sunday, but Monday; and no best clothes; and the laughing visitors were gone, and she awoke alone in her old bed, the innocent younger children breathing softly around her. In place of the excitement of her return and the interest it had inspired, she saw before her a long and stony highway which she had to tread, without aid, and with little sympathy. Her depression was then terrible, and she could have hidden herself in a tomb.

In the course of a few weeks Tess revived sufficiently to show herself so far as was necessary to get to church one Sunday morning. She liked to hear the chanting—such as it was—and the old Psalms, and to join in the Morning Hymn. That innate love of melody, which she had inherited from her ballad-singing mother, gave the simplest music a power over her which could well-nigh drag her heart out of her bosom at times.

To be as much out of observation as possible for reasons of her own, and to escape the gallantries of the young men, she set out before the chiming began, and took a back seat under the gallery, close to the lumber, where only old men and women came, and where the bier stood on end among the churchyard tools.

Parishioners dropped in by twos and threes, deposited themselves in rows before her, rested three-quarters of a minute on their foreheads as if they were praying, though they were not; then sat up, and looked around. When the chants came on one of her favourites happened to be chosen among the rest—the old double chant "Langdon"*—but she did not know what it was called, though she would much have liked to know. She thought, without exactly wording the thought, how strange and godlike was a composer's power, who from the grave could lead through sequences of emotion, which he alone had felt at first, a girl like her who had never heard of his name, and never would have a clue to his personality.

The people who had turned their heads turned them again as the service proceeded; and at last observing her they whispered to each other. She knew what their whispers were about, grew sick at heart, and felt that she could come to church no more.

The bedroom which she shared with some of the children formed her retreat more continually than ever. Here, under her few square yards of thatch, she watched winds, and snows, and rains, gorgeous sunsets, and successive moons at their full. So close kept she that at length almost everybody thought she had gone away.

The only exercise that Tess took at this time was after dark; and it was then, when out in the woods, that she seemed least solitary. She knew how to hit to a hair's-breadth that moment of evening when the light and the darkness are so evenly balanced that the constraint of day and the suspense of night neutralize each other, leaving absolute mental liberty. It is then that the plight of being alive becomes attenuated to its least possible dimensions. She had no fear of the shadows; her sole idea seemed to be to shun mankind—or rather that cold accretion called the world, which, so terrible in the mass, is so unformidable, even pitiable, in its units.

On these lonely hills and dales her quiescent glide was of a piece with the element she moved in. Her flexuous and stealthy figure became an integral part of the scene. At times her whimsical fancy would intensify natural processes around her till they seemed a part of her own story. Rather they became a part of it; for the world is only a psychological phenomenon, and what they seemed they were. The midnight airs and gusts, moaning amongst the tightly-wrapped buds and bark of the winter twigs, were formulæ of bitter reproach. A wet day was the expression of irremediable grief at her weakness in the mind of some vague ethical being whom she could not class definitely as the God of her childhood, and could not comprehend as any other.

But this encompassment of her own characterization, based on shreds of convention, peopled by phantoms and voices antipathetic to her, was a sorry and mistaken creation of Tess's fancy—a cloud of moral hobgoblins by which she was terrified without reason. It was they that were out of harmony with the actual world, not she. Walking among the sleeping birds in the hedges, watching the skipping rabbits on a moonlit warren, or standing under a pheasant-laden bough, she looked upon herself as a figure of Guilt intruding into the haunts of Innocence. But all the while she was making a distinction where there was no difference. Feeling herself in antagonism she was quite in accord. She had been made to break an accepted social law, but no law known to the environment in which she fancied herself such an anomaly.

XIV

IT was a hazy sunrise in August. The denser nocturnal vapours, attacked by the warm beams, were dividing and shrinking into isolated fleeces within hollows and coverts, where they waited till they should be dried away to nothing.

The sun, on account of the mist, had a curious, sentient, personal look, demanding the masculine pronoun for its adequate expression. His present aspect, coupled with the lack of all human forms in the scene, explained the old-time heliolatries* in a moment. One could feel that a saner religion had never prevailed under the sky. The luminary was a golden-haired, beaming, mild-eyed, godlike creature, gazing down in the vigour and intentness of youth upon an earth that was brimming with interest for him.

His light a little later broke through chinks of cottage shutters, throwing stripes like red-hot pokers upon cupboards, chests of drawers, and other furniture within; and awakening harvesters who were not already astir.

But of all ruddy things that morning the brightest were two broad arms of painted wood which rose from the margin of a yellow corn-field hard by Marlott village. They with two others below, formed the revolving Maltese cross* of the reaping-machine, which had been brought to the field on the previous evening, to be ready for operations this day. The paint with which they were smeared, intensified in hue by the sunlight, imparted to them a look of having been dipped in liquid fire.

The field had already been "opened"; that is to say, a lane a few feet wide, had been hand-cut through the wheat along the whole circumference of the field, for the first passage of the horses and machine.

Two groups, one of men and lads, the other of women, had come down the lane just at the hour when the shadows of the eastern hedge-top struck the west hedge midway, so that the heads of the groups were enjoying sunrise while their feet were still in the dawn. They disappeared from the lane between the two stone posts which flanked the nearest field-gate.

Presently there arose from within a ticking like the love-making of the grasshopper. The machine had begun, and a moving concatenation of three horses and the aforesaid long rickety machine was visible over the gate, a driver sitting upon one of the hauling horses, and an attendant on the seat of the implement. Along one side of the field the whole wain went, the arms of the mechanical reaper revolving slowly, till it passed down the hill quite out of sight. In a minute it came up on the other side of the field at the same equable pace; the glistening brass star in the forehead of the fore-horse first catching the eye as it rose into view over the stubble, then the bright arms, and then the whole machine.

The narrow lane of stubble encompassing the field grew wider with each circuit, and the standing corn was reduced to smaller area as the morning wore on. Rabbits, hares, snakes, rats, mice, retreated inwards as into a fastness, unaware of the ephemeral nature of their refuge, and of the doom that awaited them later in the day when, their covert shrinking to a more and more horrible narrowness, they were huddled together friends and foes, till the last few yards of upright wheat fell also under the teeth of the unerring reaper, and they were every one put to death by the sticks and stones of the harvesters.

The reaping-machine left the fallen corn behind it in little heaps, each heap being of the quantity for a sheaf; and upon these the active binders in the rear laid their hands—mainly women, but some of them men in print shirts, and trousers supported round their waists by leather straps rendering useless the two buttons behind; which twinkled and bristled with sunbeams at every movement of each wearer, as if they were a pair of eyes in the small of his back.

But those of the other sex were the most interesting of this company of binders, by reason of the charm which is acquired by woman when she becomes part and parcel of outdoor nature, and is not merely an object set down therein as at ordinary times. A field-man is a personality afield; a field-woman is a portion of the field; she has somehow lost her own margin, imbibed the essence of her surrounding, and assimilated herself with it.

The women—or rather girls, for they were mostly young—wore drawn cotton bonnets with great flapping curtains to keep off the sun, and gloves to prevent their hands being wounded by the stubble. There was one wearing a pale pink jacket, another in a cream-coloured tight-sleeved gown, another in a petticoat as red as the arms of the reaping-machine; and others, older, in the brown-rough "wrapper" or overall—the old-established and most appropriate dress of the field-woman, which the young ones were abandoning. This morning the eye returns involuntarily to the girl in the pink cotton jacket, she being the most flexuous and finely-drawn figure of them all. But her bonnet is pulled so far over her brow that none of her face is disclosed while she binds, though her complexion may be guessed from a stray twine or two of dark brown hair which extends below the curtain of her bonnet. Perhaps one reason why she seduces casual attention is that she never courts it, though the other women often gaze around them.

Her binding proceeds with clock-like monotony. From the sheaf last finished she draws a handful of ears, patting their tips with her left palm to bring them even. Then stooping low she moves forward, gathering the corn with both hands against her knees, and pushing her left gloved hand under the bundle to meet the right on the other side, holding the corn in an embrace like that of a lover. She brings the ends of the bond together, and kneels on the sheaf while she ties it, beating back her skirts now and then when lifted by the breeze. A bit of her naked arm is visible between the buff leather of the gauntlet and the sleeve of her gown; and as the day wears on its feminine smoothness becomes scarified by the stubble, and bleeds.

At intervals she stands up to rest, and to retie her disarranged apron, or to pull her bonnet straight. Then one can see the oval face of a handsome young woman with deep dark eyes and long heavy clinging tresses, which seem to clasp in a beseeching way anything they fall against. The cheeks are paler, the teeth more regular, the red lips thinner than is usual in a country-bred girl.

It is Tess Durbeyfield, otherwise d'Urberville, somewhat changed—the same, but not the same; at the present stage of her existence living as a stranger and an alien here, though it was no strange land that she was in. After a long seclusion she had come to a resolve to undertake outdoor work in her native village, the busiest season of the year in the agricultural world having arrived, and nothing that she could do within the house being so remunerative for the time as harvesting in the fields.

The movements of the other women were more or less similar to Tess's, the whole bevy of them drawing together like dancers in a quadrille* at the completion of a sheaf by each, every one placing her sheaf on end against those of the rest, till a shock, or "stitch" as it was here called, of ten or a dozen was formed.

They went to breakfast, and came again, and the work proceeded as before. As the hour of eleven drew near a person watching her might have noticed that every now and then Tess's glance flitted wistfully to the brow of the hill, though she did not pause in her sheafing. On the verge of the hour the heads of a group of children, of ages ranging from six to fourteen, rose above the stubbly convexity of the hill.

The face of Tess flushed slightly, but still she did not pause.

The eldest of the comers, a girl who wore a triangular shawl, its corner draggling on the stubble, carried in her arms what at first sight seemed to be a doll, but proved to be an infant in long clothes. Another brought some lunch. The harvesters ceased working, took their provisions, and sat down against one of the shocks. Here they fell to, the men plying a stone jar freely, and passing round a cup.

Tess Durbeyfield had been one of the last to suspend her labours. She sat down at the end of the shock, her face turned somewhat away from her companions. When she had deposited herself a man in a rabbit-skin cap, and with a red handkerchief tucked into his belt, held the cup of ale over the top of the shock for her to drink. But she did not accept his offer. As soon as her lunch was spread she called up the big girl, who was her sister, Liza-Lu, and took the baby of her; who, glad to be relieved of the burden, went away to the next shock and joined the other children playing there. Tess, with a curiously stealthy yet courageous movement, and with a still rising colour, unfastened her frock and began suckling the child.

The men who sat nearest considerately turned their faces towards the other end of the field, some of them beginning to smoke; one, with absent-minded fondness, regretfully stroking the jar that would no longer yield a stream. All the women but Tess fell into animated talk, and adjusted the disarranged knots of their hair.

When the infant had taken its fill the young mother sat it upright in her lap, and looking into the far distance dandled it with a gloomy indifference that was almost dislike; then all of a sudden she fell to violently kissing it some dozens of times, as if she could never leave off, the child crying at the vehemence of an onset which strangely combined passionateness with contempt.

"She's fond of that there child, though she mid pretend to hate en, and say she wishes the baby and her too were in the churchyard," observed the woman in the red petticoat.

"She'll soon leave off saying that," replied the one in buff. "Lord, 'tis wonderful what a body can get used to o' that sort in time!"

"A little more than persuading had to do wi' the coming o't, I reckon. There were they that heard a sobbing one night last year in The Chase; and it mid ha' gone hard wi' a certain party if folks had come along."

"Well, a little more, or a little less, 'twas a thousand pities that it should have happened to she, of all others. But 'tis always the comeliest! The plain ones be as safe as churches—hey, Jenny?" The speaker turned to one of the group who certainly was not ill-defined as plain.

It was a thousand pities, indeed; it was impossible for even an enemy to feel otherwise on looking at Tess as she sat there, with her flower-like mouth and large tender eyes, neither black nor blue nor grey nor violet; rather all those shades together, and a hundred others, which could be seen if one looked into their irises—shade behind shade—tint beyond tint—around pupils that had no bottom; an almost standard woman, but for the slight incautiousness of character inherited from her race.

A resolution which had surprised herself had brought her into the fields this week for the first time during many months. After wearing and wasting her palpitating heart with every engine of regret that lonely inexperience could devise, common-sense had illumined her. She felt that she would do well to be useful again—to taste a new sweet independence at any price. The past was past; whatever it had been it was no more at hand. Whatever its consequences, time would close over them; they would all in a few years be as if they had never been, and she herself grassed down and forgotten. Meanwhile the trees were just as green as before; the birds sang and the sun shone as clearly now as ever. The familiar surroundings had not darkened because of her grief, nor sickened because of her pain.

She might have seen that what had bowed her head so profoundly—the thought of the world's concern at her situation— was founded on an illusion. She was not an existence, an experience, a passion, a structure of sensations, to anybody but herself. To all humankind besides Tess was only a passing thought. Even to friends she was no more than a frequently passing thought. If she made herself miserable the livelong night and day it was only this much to them—"Ah, she makes herself unhappy." If she tried to be cheerful, to dismiss all care, to take pleasure in the daylight, the flowers, the baby, she could only be this idea to them—"Ah, she bears it very well." Moreover, alone in a desert island would she have been wretched at what had happened to her? Not greatly. If she could have been just created, to discover herself as a spouseless mother, with no experience of life except as the parent of a nameless child, would the position have caused her to despair? No, she would have taken it calmly, and found pleasures therein. Most of the misery had been generated by her conventional aspect, and not by her innate sensations.

Whatever Tess's reasoning, some spirit had induced her to dress herself up neatly as she had formerly done, and come out into the fields, harvest-hands being greatly in demand just then. This was why she had borne herself with dignity, and had looked people calmly in the face at times, even when holding the baby in her arms.

The harvest-men rose from the shock of corn, and stretched their limbs, and extinguished their pipes. The horses, which had been unharnessed and fed, were again attached to the scarlet machine. Tess, having quickly eaten her own meal, beckoned to her eldest sister to come and take away the baby, fastened her dress, put on the buff gloves again, and stooped anew to draw a bond from the last completed sheaf for the tying of the next.

In the afternoon and evening the proceedings of the morning were continued, Tess staying on till dusk with the body of harvesters. Then they all rode home in one of the largest wagons, in the company of a broad tarnished moon that had risen from the ground to the eastwards, its face resembling the outworn gold-leaf halo of some worm-eaten Tuscan saint.* Tess's female companions sang songs, and showed themselves very sympathetic and glad at her reappearance out of doors, though they could not refrain from mischievously throwing in a few verses of the ballad about the maid who went to the merry green wood and came back in a changed state. There are counterpoises and compensations in life; and the event which had made of her a social warning had also for the moment made her the most interesting personage in the village to many. Their friendliness won her still further away from herself, their lively spirits were contagious, and she became almost gay.

But now that her moral sorrows were passing away a fresh one arose on the natural side of her which knew no social law. When she reached home it was to learn to her grief that the baby had been suddenly taken ill since the afternoon. Some such collapse had been probable, so tender and puny was its frame; but the event came as a shock nevertheless.

The baby's offence against society in coming into the world was forgotten by the girl-mother; her soul's desire was to continue that offence by preserving the life of the child. However, it soon grew clear that the hour of emancipation for that little prisoner of the flesh was to arrive earlier than her worst misgivings had conjectured. And when she had discovered this she was plunged into a misery which transcended that of the child's simple loss. Her baby had not been baptized.

Tess had drifted into a frame of mind which accepted passively the consideration that, if she should have to burn for what she had done, burn she must, and there was an end of it. Like all village girls she was well grounded in the Holy Scriptures, and had dutifully studied the histories of Aholah and Aholibah,* and knew the inferences to be drawn therefrom. But when the same question arose with regard to the baby it had a very different colour. Her darling was about to die, and no salvation.

It was nearly bedtime, but she rushed downstairs and asked if she might send for the parson. The moment happened to be one at which her father's sense of the antique nobility of his family was highest, and his sensitiveness to the smudge which Tess had set upon that nobility most pronounced, for he had just returned from his weekly booze at Rolliver's Inn. No parson should come inside his door, he declared, prying into his affairs just then, when, by her shame, it had become more necessary than ever to hide them. He locked the door and put the key in his pocket.

The household went to bed, and, distressed beyond measure, Tess retired also. She was continually waking as she lay, and in the middle of the night found that the baby was still worse. It was obviously dying—quietly and painlessly, but none the less surely.

In her misery she rocked herself upon the bed. The clock struck the solemn hour of one, that hour when fancy stalks outside reason, and malignant possibilities stand rock-firm as facts. She thought of the child consigned to the nethermost corner of hell as its double doom for lack of baptism and lack of legitimacy; saw the arch-fiend tossing it with his three-pronged fork, like the one they used for heating the oven on baking-days; to which picture she added many other quaint and curious details of torment sometimes taught the young in this Christian country. The lurid presentment so power-fully affected her imagination in the silence of the sleeping house that her night-gown became damp with perspiration, and the bedstead shook with each throb of her heart.

The infant's breathing grew more difficult, and the mother's mental tension increased. It was useless to devour the little thing with kisses; she could stay in bed no longer, and walked feverishly about the room.

"O merciful God, have pity, have pity upon my poor baby!" she cried. "Heap as much anger as you want to upon me, and welcome; but pity the child!"

She leant against the chest of drawers, and murmured incoherent supplications for a long while, till she suddenly started up. "Ah, perhaps baby can be saved! Perhaps it will be just the same!" She spoke so brightly that it seemed as though her face might have shone in the gloom surrounding her.

She lit a candle, and went to a second and a third bed under the wall, where she awoke her young sisters and brothers, all of whom occupied the same room. Pulling out the washing-stand so that she could get behind it, she poured some water from a jug, and made them kneel around, putting their hands together, with fingers exactly vertical. While the children, scarcely awake, awe-striken at her manner, their eyes growing larger and larger, remained in this position, she took the baby from her bed,—a child's child, so imma-ture as scarce to seem a sufficient personality to endow its producer with the maternal title. Tess then stood erect with the infant on her arm beside the basin, the next sister held the prayerbook open before her as the clerk at church held it before the parson; and thus the girl set about baptizing her child.

Her figure looked singularly tall and imposing as she stood in her long white night-gown, a thick cable of twisted dark hair hanging straight down her back to her waist. The kindly dimness of the weak candle abstracted from her form and features the little blemishes which sunlight might have revealed—the stubble-scratches upon her wrists, and the weariness of her eyes—her high enthusiasm having a transfiguring effect upon the face which had been her undoing, showing it as a thing of immaculate beauty, with a touch of dignity which was almost regal.

The little ones kneeling round, their sleepy eyes blinking and red, awaited her preparations full of a suspended wonder which their physical heaviness at that hour would not allow to become active. The most impressed of them said: "Be you really going to christen him, Tess?"

The girl-mother replied in a grave affirmative.

"What's his name going to be?"

She had not thought of that. But a name suggested by a phrase in the book of Genesis* came into her head as she proceeded with the baptismal service, and now she pronounced it:

"SORROW, I baptize thee in the name of the Father, and of the Son, and of the Holy Ghost." She sprinkled the water, and there was silence.

"Say 'Amen', children."

The tiny voices piped in obedient response: "A—men!"

Tess went on: "We receive this child"—and so forth—"and do sign him with the sign of the cross." Here she dipped her hand into the basin, and fervently drew an immense cross upon the baby with her forefinger; continuing with the customary sentences as to his manfully fighting against sin, the world, and the devil; and being a faithful soldier and servant unto his life's end. She duly went on with the Lord's Prayer, the children lisping it after her in a thin, gnat-like wail; till at the conclusion, raising their voices to clerk's pitch, they again piped into the silence, "A—men!"

Then their sister, with much augmented confidence in the efficacy of this sacrament, poured forth from the bottom of her heart the thanksgiving that follows, uttering it boldly and triumphantly, in the stopt-diapason note* which her voice acquired when her heart was in her speech, and which will never be forgotten by those who knew her.* The ecstasy of faith almost apotheosized her; it set upon her face a glowing irradiation and brought a red spot into the middle of each cheek; while the miniature candle-flame inverted in her eye-pupils shone like a diamond. The children gazed up at her with more and more reverence, and no longer had a will for questioning. She did not look like Sissy to them now, but as a being large, towering and awful, a divine personage with whom they had nothing in common.

Poor Sorrow's campaign against sin, the world, and the devil* was doomed to be of limited brilliancy—luckily perhaps for himself, considering his beginnings. In the blue of the morning that fragile soldier and servant breathed his last; and when the other children awoke they cried bitterly, and begged Sissy to have another pretty baby.

The calmness which had possessed Tess since the christening remained with her in the infant's loss. In the daylight, indeed, she felt her terrors about his soul to have been somewhat exaggerated; whether well-founded or not she had no uneasiness now, reasoning that if Providence would not ratify such an act of approximation she, for one, did not value the kind of heaven lost by the irregularity—either for herself or for her child.

So passed away Sorrow the Undesired—that intrusive creature, that bastard gift of shameless Nature who respects not the social law; a waif to whom eternal Time had been a matter of days merely; who knew not that such things as years and centuries ever were; to whom the cottage interior was the universe, the week's weather climate, new-born babyhood human existence, and the instinct to suck human knowledge.

Tess, who mused on the christening a good deal, wondered if it were doctrinally sufficient to secure a Christian burial for the child. Nobody could tell this but the parson of the parish, and he was a new-comer, and did not know her. She went to his house after dusk, and stood by the gate, but could not summon courage to go in. The enterprize would have been abandoned if she had not by accident met him coming homeward as she turned away. In the gloom she did not mind speaking freely.

"I should like to ask you something, sir."

He expressed his willingness to listen; and she told the story of the baby's illness and the extemporized ordinance. "And now, sir," she added earnestly, "can you tell me this—will it be just the same for him as if you had baptized him?"

Having the natural feelings of a tradesman at finding that a job he should have been called in for had been unskilfully botched by his customers among themselves, he was disposed to say no. Yet the dignity of the girl, the strange tenderness in her voice, combined to affect his nobler impulses—or rather those that he had left in him after ten years of endeavour to graft technical belief on actual scepticism. The man and the ecclesiastic fought within him, and the victory fell to the man.

"My dear girl," he said, "it will be just the same."

"Then will you give him a Christian burial?" she asked quickly.

The vicar felt himself cornered. Hearing of the baby's illness, he had conscientiously gone to the house after nightfall to perform the rite, and, unaware that the refusal to admit him had come from Tess's father and not from Tess, he could not allow the plea of necessity for its irregular administration.

"Ah—that's another matter," he said.

"Another matter—why?" asked Tess rather warmly.

"Well—I would willingly do so if only we two were concerned. But I must not—for certain reasons."

"Just for once, sir!"

"Really I must not."

"O sir!" She seized his hand as she spoke.

He withdrew it, shaking his head.

"Then I don't like you!" she burst out, "and I'll never come to your church no more!"

"Don't talk so rashly."

"Perhaps it will be just the same to him if you don't? . . . Will it be just the same? Don't for God's sake speak as saint to sinner, but as you yourself to me myself—poor me!"

How the Vicar reconciled his answer with the strict notions he supposed himself to hold on these subjects it is beyond a layman's power to tell, though not to excuse. Somewhat moved, he said in this case also—

"It will be just the same."

So the baby was carried in a small deal box, under an ancient woman's shawl, to the churchyard that night, and buried by lantern-light, at the cost of a shilling and a pint of beer to the sexton, in that shabby corner of God's allotment where He lets the nettles grow, and where all unbaptised infants, notorious drunkards, suicides, and others of the conjecturally damned are laid. In spite of the untoward surroundings, however, Tess bravely made a little cross of two laths and a piece of string, and having bound it with flowers, she stuck it up at the head of the grave one evening when she could enter the churchyard without being seen, putting at the foot also a bunch of the same flowers in a little jar of water to keep them alive. What matter was it that on the outside of the jar the eye of mere observation noted the words "Keelwell's Marmalade"? The eye of maternal affection did not see them in its vision of higher things.

XV

"BY experience," says Roger Ascham, "we find out a short way by a long wandering."* Not seldom that long wandering unfits us for further travel, and of what use is our experience to us then? Tess Durbeyfield's experience was of this incapacitating kind. At last she had learned what to do; but who would now accept her doing?

If before going to the d'Urbervilles' she had rigorously moved under the guidance of sundry gnomic texts* and phrases known to her and to the world in general, no doubt she would never have been imposed on. But it had not been in Tess's power—nor is it in anybody's power—to feel the whole truth of golden opinions while it is possible to profit by them. She—and how many more—might have ironically said to God with Saint Augustine, "Thou hast counselled a better course than thou hast permitted."

She remained in her father's house during the winter months, plucking fowls, or cramming turkeys and geese, or making clothes for her sisters and brothers out of some finery which d'Urberville had given her, and she had put by with contempt. Apply to him she would not. But she would often clasp her hands behind her head and muse when she was supposed to be working hard.

She philosophically noted dates as they came past in the revolution of the year: the disastrous night of her undoing at Trantridge with its dark background of The Chase; also the dates of the baby's birth and death; also her own birthday; and every other day individualized by incidents in which she had taken some share. She suddenly thought one afternoon, when looking in the glass at her fairness, that there was yet another date, of greater importance to her than those; that of her own death, when all these charms would have disappeared; a day which lay sly and unseen among all the other days of the year, giving no sign or sound when she annually passed over it; but not the less surely there. When was it? Why did she not feel the chill of each yearly encounter with such a cold relation? She had Jeremy Taylor's thought* that some time in the future those who had known her would say "It is the ——th, the day that poor Tess Durbeyfield died"; and there would be nothing singular to their minds in the statement. Of that day, doomed to be her terminus in time through all the ages, she did not know the place in month, week, season, or year.

Almost at a leap Tess thus changed from simple girl to complex woman. Symbols of reflectiveness passed into her face, and a note of tragedy at times into her voice. Her eyes grew larger and more eloquent. She became what would have been called a fine creature; her aspect was fair and arresting; her soul that of a woman whom the turbulent experiences of the last year or two had quite failed to demoralize. But for the world's opinion those experiences would have been simply a liberal education.

She had held so aloof of late that her trouble, never generally known, was nearly forgotten in Marlott. But it became evident to her that she could never be really comfortable again in a place which had seen the collapse of her family's attempt to "claim kin"—and through her, even closer union—with the rich d'Urbervilles. At least she could not be comfortable there till long years should have obliterated her keen consciousness of it. Yet even now Tess felt the pulse of hopeful life still warm within her; she might be happy in some nook which had no memories. To escape the past and all that appertained thereto was to annihilate it; and to do that she would have to get away.

Was once lost always lost really true of chastity? she would ask herself. She might prove it false if she could veil bygones. The recuperative power which pervaded organic nature was surely not denied to maidenhood alone.

She waited a long time without finding opportunity for a new departure. A particularly fine spring came round, and the stir of germination was almost audible in the buds; it moved her as it moved the wild animals, and made her passionate to go. At last, one day in early May, a letter reached her from a former friend of her mother's to whom she had addressed inquiries long before—a person whom she had never seen—that a skilful milkmaid was required at a dairy-house many miles to the southward, and that the dairyman would be glad to have her for the summer months.

It was not quite so far off as could have been wished; but it was probably far enough, her radius of movement and repute having been so small. To persons of limited spheres miles are as geographical degrees, parishes as counties, counties as provinces and kingdoms.

On one point she was resolved: there should be no more d'Urberville air-castles in the dreams and deeds of her new life. She would be the dairymaid Tess, and nothing more. Her mother knew Tess's feeling on this point so well, though no words had passed between them on the subject, that she never alluded to the knightly ancestry now.

Yet such is human inconsistency that one of the interests of the new place to her was the accidental virtue of its lying near her forefathers' country (for they were not Blakemore men, though her mother was Blakemore to the bone). The dairy called Talbothays, for which she was bound, stood not remotely from some of the former estates of the d'Urbervilles, near the great family vaults of her granddames and their powerful husbands. She would be able to look at them, and think not only that d'Urberville, like Babylon, had fallen,* but that the individual innocence of a humble descendant could lapse as silently. All the while she wondered if any strange good thing might come of her being in her ancestral land; and some spirit within her rose automatically as the sap in the twigs. It was unexpended youth, surging up anew after its temporary check, and bringing with it hope, and the invincible instinct towards self-delight.

END OF PHASE THE SECOND

PHASE THE THIRD

THE RALLY

PHASE THE THIRD

THE RALLY

XVI

On a thyme-scented, bird-hatching morning in May, between two and three years after the return from Trantridge—silent reconstructive years for Tess Durbeyfield—she left her home for the second time.

Having packed up her luggage so that it could be sent to her later, she started in a hired trap for the little town of Stourcastle, through which it was necessary to pass on her journey, now in a direction almost opposite to that of her first adventuring. On the curve of the nearest hill she looked back regretfully at Marlott and her father's house, although she had been so anxious to get away.

Her kindred dwelling there would probably continue their daily lives as heretofore, with no great diminution of pleasure in their consciousness, although she would be far off and they deprived of her smile. In a few days the children would engage in their games as merrily as ever, without the sense of any gap left by her departure. This leaving of the younger children she had decided to be for the best: were she to remain they would probably gain less good by her precepts than harm by her example.

She went through Stourcastle without pausing, and onward to a junction of highways, where she could await a carrier's van that ran to the south-west; for the railways which engirdled this interior tract of country had never yet struck across it. While waiting, however, there came along a farmer in his spring-cart, driving approximately in the direction that she wished to pursue. Though he was a stranger to her she accepted his offer of a seat beside him, ignoring that its motive was a mere tribute to her countenance. He was going to Weatherbury, and by accompanying him thither she could walk the remainder of the distance instead of travelling in the van by way of Casterbridge.

Tess did not stop at Weatherbury, after this long drive, further than to make a slight nondescript meal at noon, at a cottage to which the farmer recommended her. Thence she started on foot, basket in hand, to reach the wide upland of heath dividing this district from the low-lying meads of a further valley, in which the dairy stood that was the aim and end of her day's pilgrimage.

Tess had never before visited this part of the country, and yet she felt akin to the landscape. Not so very far to the left of her she could discern a dark patch in the scenery, which inquiry confirmed her in supposing to be trees, marking the environs of Kingsbere—in the church of which parish the bones of her ancestors—her useless ancestors—lay entombed.

She had no admiration for them now; she almost hated them for the dance they had led her; not a thing of all that had been theirs did she retain but the old seal and spoon. "Pooh—I have as much of mother as father in me!" she said. "All my prettiness comes from her, and she was only a dairymaid."

The journey over the intervening uplands and lowlands of Egdon when she reached them, was a more troublesome walk than she had anticipated, the distance being actually but a few miles. It was two hours, owing to sundry wrong turnings, ere she found herself on a summit commanding the long-sought-for vale,—the Valley of Great Dairies, the valley in which milk and butter grew to rankness, and were produced more profusely, if less delicately, than at her home— the verdant plain so well-watered by the river Var or Froom.

It was intrinsically different from the Vale of Little Dairies, Blackmoor Vale, which, save during her disastrous sojourn at Trantridge, she had exclusively known till now. The world was drawn to a larger pattern here. The enclosures numbered fifty acres instead of ten, the farmsteads were more extended, the groups of cattle formed tribes hereabout; there only families. These myriads of cows stretching under her eyes from the far east to the far west outnumbered any she had ever seen at one glance before. The green lea was speckled as thickly with them as a canvas by Van Alsloot or Sallaert* with burghers. The ripe hues of the red and dun kine absorbed the evening sunlight, which the white-coated animals returned to the eye in rays almost dazzling, even at the distant elevation on which she stood.

The bird's-eye perspective before her was not so luxuriantly beautiful, perhaps, as that other one which she knew so well; yet it was more cheering. It lacked the intensely blue atmosphere of the rival vale, and its heavy soils and scents; the new air was clear, bracing, ethereal. The river itself which nourished the grass and cows of these renowned dairies flowed not like the streams in Blackmoor. Those were slow, silent, often turbid; flowing over beds of mud into which the incautious wader might sink and vanish unawares. The Froom waters were clear as the pure River of Life shown to the Evangelist,* rapid as the shadow of a cloud, with pebbly shallows that prattled to the sky all day long. There the water-flower was the lily; the crowfoot* here.

Either the change in the quality of the air from heavy to light, or the sense of being amid new scenes where there were no invidious eyes upon her, sent up her spirits wonderfully. Her hopes mingled with the sunshine in an ideal photosphere which surrounded her as she bounded along against the soft south wind. She heard a pleasant voice in every breeze, and in every bird's note seemed to lurk a joy.

Her face had latterly changed with changing states of mind, continually fluctuating between beauty and ordinariness, according as the thoughts were gay or grave. One day she was pink and flawless; another pale and tragical. When she was pink she was feeling less than when pale; her more perfect beauty accorded with her less elevated mood; her more intense mood with her less perfect beauty. It was her best face physically that was now set against the south wind.

The irresistible, universal, automatic tendency to find sweet pleasure somewhere, which pervades all life, from the meanest to the highest, had at length mastered Tess. Being even now only a young woman of twenty, one who mentally and sentimentally had not finished growing, it was impossible that any event should have left upon her an impression that was not in time capable of transmutation.

And thus her spirits, and her thankfulness, and her hopes, rose higher and higher. She tried several ballads, but found them inadequate; till, recollecting the psalter that her eyes had so often wandered over of a Sunday morning before she had eaten of the tree of knowledge, she chanted: "O ye Sun and Moon . . . O ye Stars . . . ye Green Things upon the Earth . . . ye Fowls of the Air . . . Beasts and Cattle . . . Children of Men . . . bless ye the Lord, praise Him and magnify Him for ever."*

She suddenly stopped and murmured, "But perhaps I don't quite know the Lord as yet."

And probably the half-unconscious rhapsody was a Fetichistic utterance in a Monotheistic setting; women whose chief companions are the forms and forces of outdoor Nature retain in their souls far more of the Pagan fantasy of their remote forefathers than of the systematized religion taught their race at later date. However, Tess found at least approximate expression for her feelings in the old *Benedicite** that she had lisped from infancy; and it was enough. Such high contentment with such a slight initial performance as that of having started towards a means of independent living was a part of the Durbeyfield temperament. Tess really wished to walk uprightly, while her father did nothing of the kind; but she resembled him in being content with immediate and small achievements, and in having no mind for laborious effort towards such petty social advancement as could alone be effected by a family so heavily handicapped as the once powerful d'Urbervilles were now.

There was, it should be said, the energy of her mother's unex-pended family, as well as the natural energy of Tess's years, rekindled after the experience which had so overwhelmed her for the time. Let the truth be told—women do as a rule live through such humili-ations, and regain their spirits, and again look about them with an interested eye. While there's life there's hope is a conviction not so entirely unknown to the "betrayed" as some amiable theorists would have us believe.

Tess Durbeyfield, then, in good heart, and full of zest for life, descended the Egdon slopes lower and lower towards the dairy of her pilgrimage.

The marked difference, in the final particular, between the rival vales now showed itself. The secret of Blackmoor was best discovered from the heights around: to read aright the valley before her it was necessary to descend into its midst. When Tess had accomplished this feat she found herself to be standing on a carpeted level, which stretched to the east and west as far as the eye could reach.

The river had stolen from the higher tracts and brought in particles to the vale all this horizontal land; and now, exhausted, aged, and attenuated, lay serpentining along through the midst of its former spoils.

Not quite sure of her direction Tess stood still upon the hemmed expanse of verdant flatness, like a fly on a billiard-table of indefinite length, and of no more consequence to the surroundings than that

fly. The sole effect of her presence upon the placid valley so far had
been to excite the mind of a solitary heron, which, after descending
to the ground not far from her path, stood with neck erect looking
at her.

Suddenly there arose from all parts of the lowland a prolonged
and repeated call: "Waow! waow! waow!" From the furthest east to
the furthest west the cries spread as if by contagion, accompanied in
some cases by the barking of a dog. It was not the expression of the
valley's consciousness that beautiful Tess had arrived, but the ordinary announcement of milking-time, half-past four o'clock, when the
dairymen set about getting in the cows.

The red and white herd nearest at hand, which had been phleg-
matically waiting for the call, now trooped towards the steading in
the background, their great bags of milk swinging under them as
they walked. Tess followed slowly in their rear, and entered the
barton by the open gate through which they had entered before her.
Long thatched sheds stretched round the enclosure, their slopes
encrusted with vivid green moss, and their eaves supported by
wooden posts rubbed to a glassy smoothness by the flanks of infinite
cows and calves of bygone years, now passed to an oblivion almost
inconceivable in its profundity. Between the posts were ranged the
milchers, each exhibiting herself at the present moment to a whimsical eye in the rear as a circle on two stalks, down the centre of
which a switch moved pendulum-wise; while the sun, lowering
itself behind this patient row, threw their shadows accurately
inwards upon the wall. Thus it threw shadows of these obscure and
homely figures every evening with as much care over each contour
as if it had been the profile of a court beauty on a palace wall;
copied them as diligently as it had copied Olympian shapes on
marble *façades* long ago; or the outline of Alexander, Cæsar, and the
Pharaohs.

They were the less restful cows that were stalled. Those that
would stand still of their own will were milked in the middle of the
yard, where many of such better behaved ones stood waiting now—
all prime milchers, such as were seldom seen out of this valley, and
not always within it; nourished by the succulent feed which the
water-meads supplied at this prime season of the year. Those of
them that were spotted with white reflected the sunshine in dazzling
brilliancy, and the polished brass knobs on their horns glittered with

something of military display. Their large veined udders hung
ponderous as sandbags, the teats sticking out like the legs of a gipsy's
crock; and as each animal lingered for her turn to arrive the milk
oozed forth and fell in drops to the ground.

XVII

THE dairymaids and men had flocked down from their cottages and out of the dairyhouse with the arrival of the cows from the meads; the maids walking in pattens, not on account of the weather, but to keep their shoes above the mulch of the barton. Each girl sat down on her three-legged stool, her face sideways, her right cheek resting against the cow, and looked musingly along the animal's flank at Tess as she approached. The male milkers, with hat-brims turned down, resting flat on their foreheads, and gazing on the ground, did not observe her.

One of these was a sturdy middle-aged man—whose long white "pinner" was somewhat finer and cleaner than the wraps of the others, and whose jacket underneath had a presentable marketing aspect—the master-dairyman of whom she was in quest, his double character as working milker and buttermaker here during six days, and on the seventh as a man in shining broad-cloth in his family pew at church, being so marked as to have inspired a rhyme:

> Dairyman Dick
> All the week:—
> On Sundays Mister Richard Crick.

Seeing Tess standing at gaze he went across to her.

The majority of dairymen have a cross manner at milking-time, but it happened that Mr Crick was glad to get a new hand—for the days were busy ones now—and he received her warmly; inquiring for her mother and the rest of the family—(though this as a matter of form merely, for in reality he had not been aware of Mrs Durbeyfield's existence till apprised of the fact by a brief business-letter about Tess).

"O—ay, as a lad I knowed your part o' the country very well," he said terminatively. "Though I've never been there since. And a aged woman of ninety that used to live nigh here, but is dead and gone long ago, told me that a family of some such name as yours in Blackmoor Vale came originally from these parts, and that 'twere a old ancient race that had all but perished off the earth—though the new generations didn't know it. But Lord, I took no notice of the old woman's ramblings, not I."

"O no—it is nothing," said Tess.

Then the talk was of business only.

"You can milk 'em clean, my maidy? I don't want my cows going azew at this time o' year."

She reassured him on that point, and he surveyed her up and down. She had been staying indoors a good deal, and her complexion had grown delicate.

"Quite sure you can stand it? 'Tis comfortable enough here for rough folk; but we don't live in a cowcumber frame."

She declared that she could stand it, and her zest and willingness seemed to win him over.

"Well, I suppose you'll want a dish o' tay, or victuals of some sort, hey? Not yet? Well, do as ye like about it. But faith, if 'twas I, I should be as dry as a kex wi' travelling so far."

"I'll begin milking now, to get my hand in," said Tess.

She drank a little milk as temporary refreshment—to the sur-prise—indeed, slight contempt—of Dairyman Crick, to whose mind it had apparently never occurred that milk was good as a beverage. "Oh, if ye can swaller that, be it so," he said indifferently, while one held up the pail that she sipped from. " 'Tis what I hain't touched for years—not I. Rot the stuff; it would lie in my innerds like lead. . . . You can try your hand upon she," he pursued, nodding to the nearest cow. "Not but what she do milk rather hard. We've hard ones and we've easy ones, like other folks. However, you'll find out that soon enough."

When Tess had changed her bonnet for a hood, and was really on her stool under the cow, and the milk was squirting from her fists into the pail, she appeared to feel that she really had laid a new foundation for her future. The conviction bred serenity, her pulse slowed, and she was able to look about her.

The milkers formed quite a little battalion of men and maids, the men operating on the hard-teated animals, the maids on the kindlier natures. It was a large dairy. There were nearly a hundred milchers under Crick's management, all told; and of the herd the master-dairyman milked six or eight with his own hands, unless away from home. These were the cows that milked hardest of all; for his journey-milkmen being more or less casually hired, he would not entrust this half-dozen to their treatment, lest, from indifference, they should not milk them fully; nor to the maids, lest they should fail in the same way for lack of finger-grip; with the result that in course of time the cows would "go azew"—that is, dry up. It was not the loss for the moment that made slack milking so serious, but that with the decline of demand there came decline, and ultimately cessation, of supply.

After Tess had settled down to her cow there was for a time no talk in the barton, and not a sound interfered with the purr of the milk-jets into the numerous pails, except a momentary exclamation to one or other of the beasts, requesting her to turn round or stand still. The only movements were those of the milkers' hands up and down, and the swing of the cows' tails. Thus they all worked on, encompassed by the vast flat mead which extended to either slope of the valley—a level landscape compounded of old landscapes long forgotten, and, no doubt, differing in character very greatly from the landscape they composed now.

"To my thinking," said the dairyman, rising suddenly from a cow he had just finished off, snatching up his three-legged stool in one hand and the pail in the other, and moving on to the next hard-yielder in his vicinity; "to my thinking, the cows don't gie down their milk to-day as usual. Upon my life, if Winker do begin keeping back like this, she'll not be worth going under by midsummer!"

" 'Tis because there's a new hand come among us," said Jonathan Kail. "I've noticed such things afore."

"To be sure. It may be so. I didn't think o't."

"I've been told that it goes up into their horns at such times," said a dairymaid.

"Well—as to going up into their horns," replied Dairyman Crick dubiously, as though even witchcraft might be limited by anatomical possibilities, "I couldn't say; I certainly could not. But as nott cows will keep it back as well as the horned ones, I don't quite agree to it. . . . Do ye know that riddle about the nott cows, Jonathan? Why do nott cows give less milk in a year than horned?"

"I don't!" interposed the milkmaid. "Why do they?"

"Because there bain't so many of 'em," said the dairyman. "Howsomever, these gam'sters do certainly keep back their milk today. Folks, we must lift up a stave or two—that's the only cure for't."

Songs were often resorted to in dairies hereabout as an enticement to the cows when they showed signs of withholding their usual yield; and the band of milkers at this request burst into melody—in purely business-like tones, it is true, and with no great spontaneity; the result, according to their own belief, being a decided improvement during the song's continuance. When they had gone through fourteen or fifteen verses of a cheerful ballad about a murderer who was afraid to go to bed in the dark because he saw certain brimstone flames around him, one of the male milkers said, "I wish singing on the stoop didn't use up so much of a man's wind! You should get your harp, sir—not but what a fiddle is best."

Tess, who had given ear to this, thought the words were addressed to the dairyman; but she was wrong. A reply, in the shape of "Why?" came as it were out of the belly of a dun cow in the stalls: it had been spoken by a milker behind the animal, whom she had not hitherto perceived.

"O yes; there's nothing like a fiddle," said the dairyman. "Though I do think that bulls are more moved by a tune than cows—at least that's my experience. . . . Once there was a old aged man over at Mellstock—William Dewy by name—one of the family that used to do a good deal of business as tranters over there, Jonathan, do ye mind?—I knowed the man by sight as well as I know my own brother, in a manner of speaking. Well, this man was a coming home-along from a wedding where he'd been playing his fiddle, one fine moonlight night, and for shortness' sake he took a cut across Forty-acres—a field lying that way—where a bull was out to grass. The bull seed William, and took after him, horns aground, begad; and though William runned his best, and hadn't *much* drink in him (considering 'twas a wedding, and the folks well off) he found he'd never reach the fence and get over in time to save himself. Well, as a last thought he pulled out his fiddle as he runned, and struck up a jig, turning to the bull, and backing towards the corner. The bull softened down, and stood still, looking hard at William Dewy, who fiddled on and on; till a sort of a smile stole over the bull's face. But no sooner did William stop his playing and turn to get over hedge than the bull would stop his smiling, and lower his horns towards the seat of William's breeches. Well, William had to turn about and play on, willy-nilly; and 'twas only three o'clock in the world, and 'a knowed that nobody would come that way for hours, and he so leery and tired that 'a didn't know what to do. When he had scraped till about four o'clock he felt that he verily would have to give over soon, and he said to himself, There's only this last tune between me and eternal welfare: Heaven save me, or I'm a done man. Well, then he called to mind how he'd seen the cattle kneel o' Christmas Eves in the dead o' night. It was not Christmas Eve then, but it came into his head to play a trick upon the bull. So he broke into the 'Tivity Hymn, just as at Christmas carol-singing; when lo and behold, down went the bull upon his bended knees, in his ignorance, just as if 'twere the true 'Tivity night and hour. As soon as his horned friend were down, William turned, clinked off like a long-dog, and jumped safe over hedge, before the praying bull had got on his feet again to take after him. William used to say that he'd seen a man look a fool a good many times, but never such a fool as that bull looked when he found his pious feelings had been played upon, and 'twas not Christmas Eve. . . . Yes, William Dewy, that was the man's name; and I can tell you to a foot where he's a lying in Mellstock churchyard at this very moment—just between the second yew-tree and the north aisle."

"It's a curious story; it carries us back to mediæval times, when faith was a living thing." The remark, singular for a dairy-yard, was murmured by the voice behind the dun cow; but as nobody understood the reference no notice was taken, except that the narrator seemed to think it might imply scepticism as to his tale.

"Well, 'tis quite true, sir, whether or no. I knowed the man well."

"O yes—I have no doubt of it," said the person behind the dun cow.

Tess's attention was thus attracted to the dairyman's interlocutor, of whom she could see but the merest patch owing to his burying his head so persistently in the flank of the milcher. She could not understand why he should be addressed as "sir" even by the dairyman himself. But no explanation was discernible; he remained under the cow long enough to have milked three, uttering a private ejaculation now and then, as if he could not get on.

"Take it gentle, sir; take it gentle," said the dairyman. " 'Tis knack not strength, that does it."

"So I find," said the other, standing up at last and stretching his arms. "I think I have finished her, however; though she made my fingers ache."

Tess could then see him at full length. He wore the ordinary white pinner and leather leggings of a dairy-farmer when milking, and his boots were clogged with the mulch of the yard; but this was all his local livery. Beneath it was something educated, reserved, subtle, sad, differing.

But the details of his aspect were temporarily thrust aside by the discovery that he was one whom she had seen before. Such vicissitudes had Tess passed through since that time that for a moment she could not remember where she had met him; and then it flashed upon her that he was the pedestrian who had joined in the club-dance at Marlott—the passing stranger who had come she knew not whence, had danced with others but not with her, had slightingly left her, and gone on his way with his friends.

The flood of memories brought back by this revival of an incident anterior to her troubles produced a momentary dismay lest, recognizing her also, her should by some means discover her story. But it passed away when she found no sign of remembrance in him. She saw by degrees that since their first and only encounter his mobile face had grown more thoughtful, and had acquired a young man's shapely moustache and beard—the latter of the palest straw colour where it began upon his cheeks, and deepening to a warm brown further from its root.

Under his linen milking-pinner he wore a dark velveteen jacket, cord breeches and gaiters, and a starched white shirt. Without the milking-gear nobody could have guessed what he was. He might with equal probability have been an eccentric landowner or a gentlemanly ploughman. That he was but a novice at dairy-work she had realized in a moment, from the time he had spent upon the milking of one cow.

Meanwhile many of the milkmaids had said to one another of the new-comer, "How pretty she is!" with something of real generosity and admiration, though with a half hope that the auditors would qualify the assertion—which, strictly speaking, they might have done, prettiness being an inexact definition of what struck the eye in Tess. When the milking was finished for the evening they straggled indoors, where Mrs Crick the dairyman's wife—who was too respectable to go out milking herself and wore a hot stuff gown in warm weather because the dairymaids wore prints—was giving an eye to the leads and things. Only two or three of the maids, Tess learnt, slept in the dairyhouse besides herself, most of the helpers going to their homes. She saw nothing at supper-time of the superior milker who had commented on the story, and asked no questions about him, the remainder of the evening being occupied in arranging her place in the bed-chamber. It was a large room over the milk-house, some thirty feet long, the sleeping-cots of the other three indoor milkmaids being in the same apartment. They were blooming young women, and, except one, rather older than herself. By bed-time Tess was thoroughly tired, and fell asleep immediately.

But one of the girls, who occupied an adjoining bed, was more wakeful than Tess, and would insist upon relating to the latter various particulars of the homestead into which she had just entered. The girl's whispered words mingled with the shades; and to Tess's drowsy mind they seemed to be generated by the darkness in which they floated.

"Mr Angel Clare—he that is learning milking, and that plays the harp—never says much to us. He is a pa'son's son, and is too much taken up wi' his own thoughts to notice girls. He is the dairyman's pupil—learning farming in all its branches. He has learnt sheep-farming at another place, and he's now mastering dairywork. . . . Yes, he is quite the gentleman-born. His father is the Reverent Mr Clare at Emminster—a good many miles from here."

"O—I have heard of him," said her companion, now awake. "A very earnest clergyman, is he not?"

"Yes—that he is—the earnestest man in all Wessex, they say—the last of the old Low-Church sort, they tell me—for all about here be what they call High. All his sons except our Mr Clare be made pa'sons too."

Tess had not at this hour the curiosity to ask why the present Mr Clare was not made a parson like his brethren, and gradually fell asleep again, the words of her informant coming to her along with the smell of the cheeses in the adjoining cheese-loft, and the measured dripping of the whey* from the wrings downstairs.

XVIII

ANGEL CLARE rises out of the past not altogether as a distinct figure, but as an appreciative voice, a long regard of fixed, abstracted eyes, and a mobility of mouth, somewhat too small and delicately lined for a man's, though with an unexpectedly firm close of the lower lip now and then; enough to do away with any inference of indecision. Nevertheless, something nebulous, preoccupied, vague, in his bearing and regard, marked him as one who probably had no very definite aim or concern about his material future. Yet as a lad people had said of him that he was one who might do anything if he tried.

He was the youngest son of his father, a poor parson at the other end of the country, and had arrived at Talbothays Dairy as a six-months' pupil, after going the round of some other farms, his object being to acquire a practical skill in the various processes of farming, with a view either to the Colonies, or the tenure of a home-farm, as circumstances might decide.

His entry into the ranks of the agriculturists and breeders was a step in the young man's career which had been anticipated neither by himself nor by others.

Mr Clare the elder, whose first wife had died and left him a daughter, married a second late in life. This lady had somewhat unexpectedly brought him three sons; so that between Angel, the youngest, and his father the vicar, there seemed to be almost a missing generation. Of these three boys the aforesaid Angel, the child of his old age, was the only son who had not taken a University degree, though he was the single one of them whose early promise might have done full justice to an academical training.

Some two or three years before Angel's appearance at the Marlott dance, on a day when he had left school, and was pursuing his studies at home, a parcel came to the vicarage from the local bookseller's, directed to the Reverend James Clare. The vicar having opened it and found it to contain a book, read a few pages; whereupon he jumped up from his seat and went straight to the shop with the book under his arm.

"Why has this been sent to my house?" he asked peremptorily, holding up the volume.

"It was ordered, sir."

"Not by me, or any one belonging to me, I am happy to say."

The shopkeeper looked into his order-book. "O, it has been misdirected, sir," he said. "It was ordered by Mr Angel Clare, and should have been sent to him."

Mr Clare winced as if he had been struck. He went home pale and dejected, and called Angel into his study. "Look into this book, my boy," he said. "What do you know about it?"

"I ordered it," said Angel simply.

"What for?"

"To read."

"How can you think of reading it?"

"How can I? Why—it is a system of philosophy. There is no more moral, or even religious, work published."

"Yes—moral enough; I don't deny that. But religious!—and for *you*, who intend to be a minister of the gospel!"

"Since you have alluded to the matter, father," said the son, with anxious thought upon his face, "I should like to say, once for all, that I should prefer not to take orders. I fear I could not conscientiously do so. I love the Church as one loves a parent. I shall always have the warmest affection for her. There is no institution for whose history I have a deeper admiration; but I cannot honestly be ordained her minister, as my brothers are, while she refuses to liberate her mind from an untenable redemptive theolatry."*

It had never occurred to the straightforward and simple-minded vicar that one of his own flesh and blood could come to this! He was stultified, shocked, paralyzed. And if Angel were not going to enter the Church, what was the use of sending him to Cambridge? The University, as a step to anything but ordination, seemed, to this man of fixed ideas, a preface without a volume. He was a man not merely religious, but devout; a firm believer—not as the phrase is now elusively construed by theological thimble-riggers* in the Church and out of it—but in the old and ardent sense of the Evangelical school: one who could

> —indeed opine
> That the Eternal and Divine
> Did, eighteen centuries ago
> In very truth . . .

Angel's father tried argument, persuasion, entreaty. "No, father; I cannot underwrite Article Four* (leave alone the rest) taking it 'in the literal and grammatical sense' as required by the Declaration; and therefore I can't be a parson in the present state of affairs," said Angel. "My whole instinct in matters of religion is towards reconstruction; to quote your favourite Epistle to the Hebrews, '*the removing of those things that are shaken, as of things that are made, that those things which cannot be shaken may remain.*' "*

His father grieved so deeply that it made Angel quite ill to see him. "What is the good of your mother and me economizing and stinting ourselves to give you a University education if it is not to be used for the honour and glory of God?" his father repeated.

"Why, that it may be used for the honour and glory of man, father."

Perhaps if Angel had persevered he might have gone to Cambridge like his brothers. But the vicar's view of that seat of learning as a stepping-stone to orders alone was quite a family tradition; and so rooted was this idea in his mind that perseverance began to appear to the sensitive son akin to an intent to misappropriate a trust, and wrong the pious heads of the household, who had been and were, as his father had hinted, compelled to exercise much thrift to carry out this uniform plan of education for the three young men.

"I will do without Cambridge," said Angel at last. "I feel that I have no right to go there in the circumstances."

The effects of this decisive debate were not long in showing themselves. He spent years and years in desultory studies, undertakings, and meditations; he began to evince considerable indifference to social forms and observances. The material distinctions of rank and wealth he increasingly despised. Even the "good old family", (to use a favourite phrase of a late local worthy) had no aroma for him unless there were good new resolutions in its representatives. As a balance to these austerities, when he went to live in London to see what the world was like, and with a view to practising a profession or business there, he was carried off his head and nearly entrapped by a woman much older than himself; though luckily he escaped not greatly the worse for the experience.

Early association with country solitudes had bred in him an unconquerable, and almost unreasonable, aversion to modern town-life, and shut him out from such success as he might have aspired to by following a mundane calling in the impracticability of the spiritual one. But something had to be done; he had wasted many valuable years; and having an acquaintance who was starting on a thriving life as a Colonial farmer it occurred to Angel that this might be a lead in the right direction. Farming—either in the Colonies, America, or at home—farming at any rate, after becoming well-qualified for the business by a careful apprenticeship; that was a vocation which would probably afford an independence without the sacrifice of what he valued even more than a competency—intellectual liberty.

So we find Angel Clare at six-and-twenty here at Talbothays as a student of kine, and, as there were no houses near at hand in which he could get a comfortable lodging, a boarder at the dairyman's.

His room was an immense attic which ran the whole length of the dairyhouse. It could only be reached by a ladder from the cheese-loft, and had been closed up for a long time till he arrived and selected it as his retreat. Here Clare had plenty of space, and could often be heard by the dairy-folk pacing up and down when the household had gone to rest. A portion was divided off at one end by a curtain, behind which was his bed, the outer part being furnished as a homely sitting-room.

At first he lived up above entirely, reading a good deal, and strumming upon an old harp which he had bought at a sale, saying when in a bitter humour that he might have to get his living by it in the streets some day. But he soon preferred to read human nature by taking his meals downstairs in the general dining-kitchen, with the dairyman and his wife, and the maids and men, who all together formed a lively assembly; for though but few milking hands slept in the house, several joined the family at meals. The longer Clare resided here the less objection had he to his company, and the more did he like to share quarters with them in common.

Much to his surprise he took, indeed, a real delight in their companionship. The conventional farm-folk of his imagination— personified in the newspaper press by the pitiable dummy known as Hodge—were obliterated after a few days' residence. At close quarters no Hodge was to be seen. At first, it is true, when Clare's intelligence was fresh from a contrasting society, these friends with whom he now hobnobbed seemed a little strange. Sitting down as a level member of the dairyman's household seemed, at the outset, an undignified proceeding. The ideas, the modes, the surroundings, appeared retrogressive and unmeaning. But with living on there, day after day, the acute sojourner became conscious of a new aspect in the spectacle. Without any objective change whatever, variety had taken the place of monotonousness. His host and his host's household, his men and his maids, as they became intimately known to Clare, began to differentiate themselves as in a chemical process. The thought of Pascal's was brought home to him: "A mesure qu'on a plus d'esprit, on trouve qu'il y a plus d'hommes originaux. Les gens du commun ne trouvent pas de différence entre les hommes."* The typical and unvarying Hodge* ceased to exist. He had been disintegrated into a number of varied fellow-creatures, beings of many minds, beings infinite in difference; some happy, many serene, a few depressed, one here and there bright even to genius, some stupid, others wanton, others austere; some mutely Miltonic, some potentially Cromwellian;* into men who had private views of each other, as he had of his friends; who could applaud or condemn each other, amuse or sadden themselves by the contemplation of each other's foibles or vices; men every one of whom walked in his own individual way the road to dusty death.

Unexpectedly he began to like the outdoor life for its own sake, and for what it brought, apart from its bearing on his own proposed career. Considering his position he became wonderfully free from the chronic melancholy which is taking hold of the civilized races with the decline of belief in a beneficient power. For the first time of late years he could read as his musings inclined him, without any eye to cramming for a profession; since the few farming handbooks which he deemed it desirable to master occupied him but little time.

He grew away from old associations, and saw something new in life and humanity. Secondarily he made close acquaintance with phenomena which he had before known but darkly—the seasons in their moods, morning and evening, night and noon, winds in their different tempers, trees, waters and mists, shades and silences, and the voices of inanimate things.

The early mornings were still sufficiently cool to render a fire acceptable in the large room wherein they breakfasted; and, by Mrs Crick's orders, who held that he was too genteel to mess at their table, it was Angel Clare's custom to sit in the yawning chimney-corner during the meal, his cup-and-saucer and plate being placed on a hinged flap at his elbow. The light from the low wide mullioned window opposite shone in upon his nook, and, assisted by a secondary light of cold blue quality which shone down the chimney, enabled him to read there easily whenever disposed to do so. Between Clare and the window was the table at which his companions sat, their munching profiles rising sharp against the panes; while to the side was the milk-house door, through which were visible the rectangular leads in rows, full to the brim with the morning's milk. At the further end the great churn could be seen revolving, and its slip-slopping heard—the moving power being discernible through the window in the form of a spiritless horse walking in a circle and driven by a boy.

For several days after Tess's arrival Clare, sitting abstractedly reading from some book, periodical, or piece of music just come by post, hardly noticed that she was present at table. She talked so little, and the other maids talked so much, that the babble did not strike him as possessing a new note; and he was ever in the habit of neglecting the particulars of an outward scene for the general impression. One day, however, when he had been conning one of his music scores, and by force of imagination was hearing the tune in his head, he lapsed into listlessness, and the music-sheet rolled to the hearth. He looked at the fire of logs, with its one flame pirouetting on the top in a dying dance after the breakfast cooking and boiling; and it seemed to jig to his inward tune; also at the two chimney crooks dangling down from the cotterel or cross-bar, plumed with soot which quivered to the same melody; also at the half-empty kettle whining an accompaniment. The conversation at the table mixed in with his phantasmal orchestra, till he thought, "What a fluty voice one of those milkmaids has. I suppose it is the new one." Clare looked round upon her, seated with the others.

She was not looking towards him. Indeed, owing to his long silence his presence in the room was almost forgotten.

"I don't—know about ghosts," she was saying. "But I do know that our souls can be made to go outside our bodies when we are alive."

The dairyman turned to her with his mouth full, his eyes charged with serious inquiry, and his great knife and fork (breakfasts were breakfasts here) planted erect on the table, like the beginning of a gallows. "What—really now? And is it so, maidy?" he said.

"A very easy way to feel 'em go," continued Tess, "is to lie on the grass at night, and look straight up at some big bright star; and by fixing your mind upon it you will soon find that you are hundreds and hundreds o' miles away from your body, which you don't seem to want at all."

The dairyman removed his hard gaze from Tess, and fixed it on his wife. "Now that's a rum thing, Christianner—hey? To think o' the miles I've vamped o' starlight nights these last thirty year, courting, or trading, or for doctor, or for nurse, and yet never had the least notion o' that till now, or feeled my soul rise so much as an inch above my shirt-collar."

The general attention being drawn to her, including that of the dairyman's pupil, Tess flushed, and remarking evasively that it was only a fancy, resumed her breakfast.

Clare continued to observe her. She soon finished her eating, and having a consciousness that Clare was regarding her began to trace imaginary patterns on the tablecloth with her forefinger, with the constraint of a domestic animal that perceives itself to be watched.

"What a fresh and virginal daughter of Nature that milkmaid is," he said to himself.

And then he seemed to discern in her something that was familiar, something which carried him back into a joyous and unforseeing past, before the necessity of taking thought had made the Heavens grey. He concluded that he had beheld her before; where he could not tell. A casual encounter during some country ramble it certainly had been; and he was not greatly curious about it. But the circumstance was sufficient to lead him to select Tess in preference to the other pretty milkmaids when he wished to contemplate contiguous womankind.

XIX

IN general the cows were milked as they presented themselves, without fancy or choice. But certain cows will show a fondness for a particular pair of hands, sometimes carrying this predilection so far as to refuse to stand at all except to their favourite, the pail of a stranger being unceremoniously kicked over.

It was Dairyman Crick's rule to insist on breaking down these partialities and aversions by constant interchange, since otherwise, in the event of a milkman or maid going away from the dairy, he was placed in a difficulty. The maids' private aims, however, were the reverse of the dairyman's rule, the daily selection by each damsel of the eight or ten cows to which she had grown accustomed, rendering the operation on their willing udders surprisingly easy and effortless.

Tess, like her compeers, soon discovered which of the cows had a preference for her style of manipulation, and her fingers having become delicate from the long domiciliary imprisonments to which she had subjected herself at intervals during the last two or three years, she would have been glad to meet the milchers' views in this respect. Out of the whole ninety-five there were eight in particular— Dumpling, Fancy, Lofty, Mist, Old Pretty, Young Pretty, Tidy, and Loud—who, though the teats of one or two were as hard as carrots, gave down to her with a readiness that made her work on them a mere touch of the fingers. Knowing, however, the dairyman's wish, she endeavoured conscientiously to take the animals just as they came, excepting the very hard yielders which she could not yet manage.

But she soon found a curious correspondence between the ostensibly chance position of the cows and her wishes in this matter, till she felt that their order could not be the result of accident. The dairyman's pupil had lent a hand in getting the cows together of late, and at the fifth or sixth time she turned her eyes, as she rested against the cow, full of sly inquiry upon him.

"Mr Clare—you have ranged the cows!" she said blushing; and in making the accusation symptoms of a smile gently lifted her upper lip in spite of her, so as to show the tips of her teeth, the lower lip remaining severely still.

"Well—it makes no difference," said he. "You will always be here to milk them."

"Do you think so? I *hope* I shall! But I don't *know*."

She was angry with herself afterwards, thinking that he, unaware of her grave reasons for liking this seclusion, might have mistaken her meaning. She had spoken so earnestly to him, as if his presence were somehow a factor in her wish. Her misgiving was such that at dusk, when the milking was over, she walked in the garden alone, to continue her regrets that she had disclosed to him her discovery of his considerateness.

It was a typical summer evening in June, the atmosphere being in such delicate equilibrium and so transmissive that inanimate objects seemed endowed with two or three senses, if not five. There was no distinction between the near and the far, and an auditor felt close to everything within the horizon. The soundlessness impressed her as a positive entity rather than as the mere negation of noise. It was broken by the strumming of strings.

Tess had heard those notes in the attic above her head. Dim, flattened, constrained by their confinement, they had never appealed to her as now, when they wandered in the still air with a stark quality like that of nudity. To speak absolutely, both instrument and execution were poor; but the relative is all, and as she listened Tess, like a fascinated bird, could not leave the spot. Far from leaving she drew up towards the performer, keeping behind the hedge that he might not guess her presence.

The outskirt of the garden in which Tess found herself had been left uncultivated for some years, and was now damp and rank with juicy grass which sent up mists of pollen at a touch, and with tall blooming weeds emitting offensive smells—weeds whose red and yellow and purple hues formed a polychrome as dazzling as that of cultivated flowers. She went stealthily as a cat through this profusion of growth, gathering cuckoo-spittle on her skirts, cracking snails that were underfoot, staining her hands with thistle-milk and slug-slime, and rubbing off upon her naked arms sticky blights which, though snow-white on the appletree-trunks, made madder stains on her skin; thus she drew quite near to Clare, still unobserved of him.

Tess was conscious of neither time nor space. The exaltation which she had described as being producible at will by gazing at a star, came now without any determination of hers; she undulated upon the thin notes of the second-hand harp, and their harmonies passed like breezes through her, bringing tears into her eyes. The floating pollen seemed to be his notes made visible, and the dampness of the garden the weeping of the garden's sensibility. Though near nightfall, the rank-smelling weed-flowers glowed as if they would not close, for intentness, and the waves of colour mixed with the waves of sound.

The light which still shone was derived mainly from a large hole in the western bank of cloud; it was like a piece of day left behind by accident, dusk having closed in elsewhere. He concluded his plaintive melody, a very simple performance, demanding no great skill; and she waited, thinking another might be begun. But, tired of playing, he had desultorily come round the fence, and was rambling up behind her. Tess, her cheeks on fire, moved away furtively, as if hardly moving at all.

Angel however saw her light summer gown; and he spoke, his low tones reaching her though he was some distance off.

"What makes you draw off in that way, Tess," said he. "Are you afraid?"

"O no, sir . . . not of outdoor things, especially just now, when the apple-blooth is falling, and everything so green."

"But you have your indoor fears—eh?"

"Well—yes, sir."

"What of?"

"I couldn't quite say."

"The milk turning sour?"

"No."

"Life in general?"

"Yes, sir."

"Ah—so have I, very often. This hobble of being alive is rather serious, don't you think so?"

"It is—now you put it that way."

"All the same I shouldn't have expected a young girl like you to see it so just yet. How is it you do?"

She maintained a hesitating silence.

"Come, Tess: tell me in confidence."

She thought that he meant what were the aspects of things to her, and replied shyly: "The trees have inquisitive eyes, haven't they?— that is, seem as if they had. And the river says 'Why do ye trouble me with your looks?' And you seem to see numbers of to-morrows just all in a line, the first of them the biggest and clearest, the others getting smaller and smaller as they stand further away; but they all seem very fierce and cruel and as if they said, 'I'm coming! Beware of me! Beware of me!' . . . But *you*, sir, can raise up dreams with your music, and drive all such horrid fancies away!"

He was surprised to find this young woman—who though but a milkmaid had just that touch of rarity about her which might make her the envied of her housemates—shaping such sad imaginings. She was expressing in her own native phrases—assisted a little by her sixth-standard training—feelings which might almost have been called those of the age—the ache of modernism. The perception arrested him less when he reflected that what are called advanced ideas are really in great part but the latest fashion in definition—a more accurate expression, by words in *-logy* and *-ism*, of sensations which men and women have vaguely grasped for centuries.

Still, it was strange that they should have come to her while yet so young; more than strange; it was impressive, interesting, pathetic. Not guessing the cause, there was nothing to remind him that experience is as to intensity, and not as to duration. Tess's passing corporeal blight had been her mental harvest.

Tess, on her part, could not understand why a man of clerical family and good education, and above physical want, should look upon it as a mishap to be alive. For the unhappy pilgrim Herself there was very good reason. But how could this admirable and poetic man ever have descended into the Valley of Humiliation, have felt with the man of Uz—as she herself had felt two or three years ago— "my soul chooseth strangling, and death rather than my life. I loathe it; I would not live alway."

It was true that he was at present out of his class. But she knew that was only because, like Peter the Great in a shipwright's yard, he was studying what he wanted to know.* He did not milk cows because he was obliged to milk cows, but because he was learning how to be a rich and prosperous dairyman, landowner, agriculturist, and breeder of cattle. He would become an American or Australian Abraham, commanding like a monarch his flocks and his herds, his spotted and his ring-straked, his menservants and his maids. At times, nevertheless, it did seem unaccountable to her that a decidedly bookish, musical, thinking young man should have chosen deliberately to be a farmer, and not a clergyman like his father and brothers.

Thus, neither having the clue to the other's secret, they were respectively puzzled at what each revealed, and awaited new knowledge of each other's character, and moods, without attempting to pry into each other's history.

Every day, every hour, brought to him one more little stroke of her nature, and to her one more of his. Tess was trying to lead a repressed life, but she little divined the strength of her own vitality.

At first Tess seemed to regard Angel Clare as an intelligence rather than as a man. As such she compared him with herself; and at every discovery of the abundance of his illuminations, of the distance between her own modest mental standpoint and the unmeasurable, Andean altitude of his, she became quite dejected, disheartened from all further effort on her own part whatever.

He observed her dejection one day when he had casually mentioned something to her about pastoral life in ancient Greece. She was gathering the buds called "lords and ladies"* from the bank while he spoke.

"Why do you look so woebegone all of a sudden?" he asked.

"O—'tis only—about my own self," she said, with a frail laugh of sadness, fitfully beginning to peel "a lady" meanwhile. "Just a sense of what might have been with me! My life looks as if it had been wasted for want of chances! When I see what you know, what you have read, and seen, and thought, I feel what a nothing I am! I'm like the poor Queen of Sheba who lived in the Bible. There is no more spirit in me."*

"Bless my soul, don't go troubling about that! Why," he said with some enthusiasm, "I should be only too glad, my dear Tess, to help you to anything in the way of history, or any line of reading you would like to take up—"

"It is a lady again," interrupted she, holding out the bud she had peeled.

"What?"

"I meant that there are always more ladies than lords when you come to peel them."

"Never mind about the lords and ladies: would you like to take up any course of study—history for example?"

"Sometimes I feel I don't want to know anything more about it than I know already."

"Why not?"

"Because what's the use of learning that I am one of a long row only—finding out that there is set down in some old book somebody just like me, and to know that I shall only act her part; making me sad, that's all. The best is not to remember that your nature and your past doings have been just like thousands' and thousands', and that your coming life and doings 'll be like thousands' and thousands'."

"What, really, then, you don't want to learn anything?"

"I shouldn't mind learning why—why the sun do shine on the just and the unjust alike,"* she answered, with a slight quaver in her voice. "But that's what books will not tell me."

"Tess; fie for such bitterness!" Of course he spoke with a conventional sense of duty only, for that sort of wondering had not been unknown to himself in bygone days. And as he looked at the unpractised mouth and lips, he thought that such a daughter of the soil could only have caught up the sentiment by rote. She went on peeling the lords and ladies till Clare, regarding for a moment the wave-like curl of her lashes as they drooped with her bent gaze on her soft cheek, lingeringly went away. When he was gone she stood awhile, thoughtfully peeling the last bud; and then, awakening from her reverie, flung it and all the crowd of floral nobility impatiently on the ground, in an ebullition of displeasure with herself for her *niai-series*, and with a quickening warmth in her heart of hearts.

How stupid he must think her! In an access of hunger for his good opinion she bethought herself of what she had latterly endeavoured to forget, so unpleasant had been its issues; the identity of her family with that of the knightly d'Urbervilles. Barren attribute as it was, disastrous as its discovery had been in many ways to her, perhaps Mr Clare as a gentleman and a student of history, would respect her sufficiently to forget her childish conduct with the lords and ladies, if he knew that those Purbeck-marble and alabaster people in Kingsbere Church really represented her own lineal forefathers: that she was no spurious d'Urberville compounded of money and ambition like those at Trantridge, but true d'Urberville to the bone.

But, before venturing to make the revelation, dubious Tess indirectly sounded the dairyman as to its possible effect upon

Mr Clare, by asking the former if Mr Clare had any great respect for old county families when they had lost all their money and land.

"Mr Clare," said the dairyman emphatically, "is one of the most rebellest rozums you ever knowed—not a bit like the rest of his family; and if there's one thing that he do hate more than another 'tis the notion of what's called a' old family. He says that it stands to reason that old families have done their spurt of work in past days, and can't have anything left in 'em now. There's the Billetts and the Drenkhards and the Greys and the St Quintins and the Hardys and the Goulds, who used to own the lands for miles down this valley; you could buy 'em all up now for an old song a'most. Why our little Retty Priddle here, you know, is one of the Paridelles—the old family that used to own lots o' the lands out by King's-Hintock now owned by the Earl o' Wessex, afore ever he or his was heard of. Well, Mr Clare found this out, and spoke quite scornful to the poor girl for days. 'Ah,' he says to her, 'you'll never make a good dairymaid! All your skill was used up ages ago in Palestine, and you must lie fallow for a thousand year to git strength for more deeds!'. . . . A boy came here t'other day asking for a job, and said his name was Matt, and when we asked him his surname, he said he'd never heard that 'a had any surname, and when we asked why, he said he supposed his folks hadn't been 'stablished long enough. 'Ah—you are the very boy I want!' says Mr Clare jumping up and shaking hands wi'en; 'I've great hopes of you;' and gave him half-a-crown. O no—he can't stomach old families."

After hearing this caricature of Clare's opinions poor Tess was glad that she had not said a word in a weak moment about her family—even though it was so unusually old as almost to have gone round the circle and become a new one. Besides, another dairy-girl was as good as she, it seemed, in that respect. She held her tongue about the d'Urberville vault, and the Knight of the Conqueror whose name she bore. The insight afforded into Clare's character suggested to her that it was largely owing to her supposed untraditional newness that she had won interest in his eyes.

XX

THE season developed and matured. Another year's instalment of flowers, leaves, nightingales, thrushes, finches and such ephemeral creatures, took up their positions where only a year ago others had stood in their place, when these were nothing more than germs and inorganic particles. Rays from the sunrise drew forth the buds and stretched them into long stalks, lifted up sap in noiseless streams, opened petals, and sucked out scents in invisible jets and breathings.

Dairyman Crick's household of maids and men lived on comfortably, placidly, even merrily. Their position was perhaps the happiest of all positions in the social scale, being above the line at which neediness ends, and below the line at which the *convenances* begin to cramp natural feeling, and the stress of threadbare modishness makes too little of enough.

Thus passed the leafy time, when arborescence seems to be the one thing aimed at out-of-doors; Tess and Clare unconsciously studied each other, ever balanced on the edge of a passion, yet apparently keeping out of it. All the while they were converging, under an irresistible law, as surely as two streams in one vale.

Tess had never in her recent life been so happy as she was now, possibly never would be so happy again. She was, for one thing, physically and mentally suited among these new surroundings. The sapling which had rooted down to a poisonous stratum on the spot of its sowing had been transplanted to a deeper soil. Moreover she, and Clare also, stood as yet on the debateable land between predilection and love; where no profundities have been reached; no reflections have set in, awkwardly inquiring, "Whither does this new current tend to carry me?—what does it mean to my future?—how does it stand towards my past?"

Tess was the merest stray phenomenon to Angel Clare as yet—a rosy, warming apparition, which had only just acquired the attribute of persistence in his consciousness. So he allowed his mind to be occupied with her, deeming his preoccupation to be no more than a philosopher's regard of an exceedingly novel, fresh and interesting specimen of womankind.

They met continually; they could not help it. They met daily in that strange and solemn interval, the twilight of the morning; in the violet or pink dawn; for it was necessary to rise early, so very early, here. Milking was done betimes; and before the milking came the skimming, which began at a little past three. It usually fell to the lot of some one or other of them to wake the rest, the first being aroused by an alarm-clock; and as Tess was the latest arrival and they soon discovered that she could be depended upon not to sleep through the alarm as the others did this task was thrust most frequently upon her. No sooner had the hour of three struck and whizzed, than she left her room and ran to the dairyman's door; then up the ladder to Angel's, calling him in a loud whisper; then woke her fellow milkmaids. By the time that Tess was dressed Clare was downstairs and out in the humid air; the remaining maids and the dairyman usually gave themselves another turn on the pillow, and did not appear till a quarter of an hour later.

The grey half-tones of daybreak are not the grey half-tones of the day's close, though the degree of their shade may be the same. In the twilight of the morning, light seems active, darkness passive; in the twilight of evening it is the darkness which is active and crescent, and the light which is the drowsy reverse.

Being so often—possibly not always by chance—the first two persons to get up at the dairy-house, they seemed to themselves the first persons up of all the world. In these early weeks of her residence here Tess did not skim, but went out of doors at once after rising, where he was generally awaiting her. The spectral, half-compounded, aqueous light which pervaded the open mead impressed them with a feeling of isolation, as if they were Adam and Eve. At this dim inceptive stage of the day Tess seemed to Clare to exhibit a dignified largeness both of disposition and physique, an almost regnant power—possibly because he knew that at that preternatural time hardly any woman so well-endowed in person as she was likely to be walking in the open air within the boundaries of his horizon; very few in all England. Fair women are usually asleep at midsummer dawns. She was close at hand, and the rest were nowhere.

The mixed, singular, luminous gloom in which they walked along together to the spot where the cows lay, often made him think of the Resurrection-hour. He little thought that the Magdalen might be at his side. Whilst all the landscape was in neutral shade, his companion's face, which was the focus of his eyes, rising above the mist-stratum, seemed to have a sort of phosphorescence upon it. She looked ghostly, as if she were merely a soul at large. In reality her face, without appearing to do so, had caught the cold gleam of day from the north-east; his own face, though he did not think of it, wore the same aspect to her.

It was then, as has been said, that she impressed him most deeply. She was no longer the milkmaid, but a visionary essence of woman— a whole sex condensed into one typical form. He called her Artemis, Demeter,* and other fanciful names, half-teasingly—which she did not like because she did not understand them.

"Call me Tess," she would say askance; and he did.

Then it would grow lighter, and her features would become simply feminine; they had changed from those of a divinity who could confer bliss to those of a being who craved it.

At these non-human hours they could get quite close to the water-fowl. Herons came, with a great bold noise as of opening doors and shutters, out of the boughs of a plantation which they frequented at the side of the mead; or, if already on the spot, hardily maintained their standing in the water as the pair walked by, watching them by moving their heads round in a slow, horizontal, passionless wheel, like the turn of puppets by clockwork.

They could then see the faint summer fogs in layers, woolly, level, and apparently no thicker than counterpanes, spread about the meadows in detached remnants of small extent. On the grey mois-ture of the grass were marks where the cows had lain through the night—dark-green islands of dry herbage the size of their carcases in the general sea of dew. From each island proceeded a serpentine trail, by which the cow had rambled away to feed after getting up, at the end of which trail they found her; the snoring puff from her nostrils when she recognized them making an intenser little fog of her own amid the prevailing one. Then they drove the animals back to the barton, or sat down to milk them on the spot, as the case might require.

Or perhaps the summer fog was more general, and the meadows lay like a white sea, out of which the scattered trees rose like danger-ous rocks. Birds would soar through it into the upper radiance, and hang on the wing sunning themselves, or alight on the wet rails subdividing the mead, which now shone like glass rods. Minute diamonds of moisture from the mist hung, too, upon Tess's eyelashes, and drops upon her hair, like seed pearls. When the day grew quite strong and commonplace these dried off her; moreover Tess then lost her strange and ethereal beauty; her teeth, lips, and eyes scintillated in the sunbeams, and she was again the dazzlingly fair dairymaid only, who had to hold her own against the other women of the world.

About this time they would hear Dairyman Crick's voice, lecturing the non-resident milkers for arriving late, and speaking sharply to old Deborah Fyander for not washing her hands:

"For Heaven's sake, pop thy hands under the pump, Deb! Upon my soul, if the London folk only knowed of thee and thy slovenly ways, they'd swaller their milk and butter more mincing than they do a'ready; and that's saying a good deal."

The milking progressed, till towards the end Tess and Clare, in common with the rest, could hear the heavy breakfast-table dragged out from the wall in the kitchen by Mrs Crick, this being the invariable preliminary to each meal; the same horrible scrape accompanying its return journey when the table had been cleared.

XXI

THERE was a great stir in the milk-house just after breakfast. The churn revolved as usual, but the butter would not come. Whenever this happened the dairy was paralyzed. Squish-squash echoed the milk in the great cylinder, but never arose the sound they waited for.

Dairyman Crick and his wife, the milkmaids Tess, Marian, Retty Priddle, Izz Huett, and the married ones from the cottages; also Mr Clare, Jonathan Kail, old Deborah, and the rest, stood gazing hopelessly at the churn; and the boy who kept the horse going outside put on moon-like eyes to show his sense of the situation. Even the melancholy horse himself seemed to look in at the window in inquiring despair at each walk round.

" 'Tis years since I went to Conjuror Trendle's son in Egdon— years," said the dairyman, bitterly. "And he was nothing to what his father had been. I have said fifty times, if I have said once, that I don't believe in en. And I *don't* believe in en, though 'a do cast folks' waters very true. But I shall have to go to 'n if he's alive. O yes, I shall have to go to 'n, if this sort of thing continnys!"

Even Mr Clare began to feel tragical at the dairyman's desperation.

"Conjuror Fall, t'other side of Casterbridge, that they used to call 'Wide-O', was a very good man when I was a boy," said Jonathan Kail. "But he's rotten as touchwood by now."

"My grandfather used to go to Conjuror Mynterne, out at Owlscombe; and a clever man a' were, so I've heard grandf'er say," continued Mr Crick. "But there's no such genuine folk about nowadays!"

Mrs Crick's mind kept nearer to the matter in hand. "Perhaps somebody in the house is in love," she said tentatively. "I've heard tell in my younger days that that will cause it. Why, Crick—that maid we had years ago, do ye mind—she that was in love wi' one of the milkers, do ye mind, and how the butter didn't come then—"

"Ah, yes, yes—but that isn't the rights o't. It had nothing to do with the love making. I can mind all about it—'twas the damage to the churn." He turned to Clare. "Jack Dollop, a 'hore's-bird of a fellow we had here as milker at one time, sir, courted a young woman over at Mellstock, and deceived her as he had deceived many afore.

But he had another sort o' woman to reckon wi' this time, and it was not the girl herself. One Holy Thursday,* of all days in the almanack, we was here as we mid be now, only there was no churning in hand, when we zid the girl's mother coming up to the door, wi' a great brass-mounted umbreller in her hand that would ha' felled an ox, and saying 'Do Jack Dollop work here?—because I want him! I have a big bone to pick with he, I can assure 'n!' And some way behind her mother walked Jack's young woman, crying bitterly into her hand-kercher.—'O Lard, here's a time!' said Jack, looking out o' winder at 'em. 'She'll murder me! Where shall I get—where shall I? Don't tell her where I be!' And with that he scrambled into the churn through the trap-door, and shut himself inside, just as the young woman's mother busted into the milk-house. 'The villain—where is he?' says she, 'I'll claw his face for 'n, let me only catch him!' Well, she hunted about everywhere, ballyragging Jack by side and by seam, Jack lying a'most stifled inside the churn, and the poor maid—or young woman rather—standing at the door crying her eyes out. I shall never forget it, never! 'Twould have melted a marble stone. But she couldn't find him nowhere at all."

The dairyman paused, and one or two words of comment came from the listeners.

Dairyman Crick's stories often seemed to be ended when they were not really so, and strangers were betrayed into premature inter-jections of finality; though old friends knew better. The narrator went on:

"Well, how the old woman should have had the wit to guess it, I could never tell, but she found out that he was inside that there churn. Without saying a word she took hold of the winch (it was turned by hand-power then) and round she swung him, and Jack began to flop about inside. 'O Lard! Stop the churn!—let me out!' says he popping out his head. 'I shall be churned into a pummy!' (he was a cowardly chap in his heart, as such men mostly be.)—'Not till ye make amends for ravaging her virgin innocence!' says the old woman. 'Stop the churn, you old witch!' screams he. 'You call me old witch, do ye, you deceiver!' says she, 'when ye ought to ha' been calling me mother-law these last five months!' And on went the churn, and Jack's bones rattled round again. Well, none of us ventured to interfere; and at last 'a promised to make it right wi' her. 'Yes—I'll be as good as my word,' he said. And so it ended that day."

While the listeners were smiling their comments there was a quick movement behind their backs, and they looked round. Tess, pale-faced, had gone to the door.

"How warm 'tis to-day!" she said almost inaudibly.

It was warm; and none of them connected her withdrawal with the reminiscences of the dairyman. He went forward, and opened the door for her, saying with tender raillery, "Why, maidy"—(he frequently, with unconscious irony, gave her this pet name)—"the prettiest milker I've got in my dairy; you mustn't get so fagged as this at the first breath of summer weather, or we shall be finely put-to for want of 'ee by dog-days, shan't we, Mr Clare."

"I was faint—and—I think I am better out o' doors," she said mechanically; and disappeared outside. Fortunately for her the milk in the revolving churn at that moment changed its squashing for a decided flick-flack.

" 'Tis coming!" cried Mrs Crick; and the attention of all was called off from Tess.

That fair sufferer soon recovered herself externally; but she remained much depressed all the afternoon. When the evening milking was done she did not care to be with the rest of them, and went out-of-doors, wandering along she knew not whither. She was wretched—O so wretched—at the perception that to her companions the dairyman's story had been rather a humorous narration than otherwise; none of them but herself seemed to see the sorrow of it; to a certainty, not one knew how cruelly it touched the tender place in her experience. The evening sun was now ugly to her, like a great inflamed wound in the sky. Only a solitary cracked-voiced reed-sparrow greeted her from the bushes by the river, in a sad, machine-made tone, resembling that of a past friend whose friendship she had outworn.

In these long June days the milkmaids, and, indeed, most of the household, went to bed at sunset or sooner, the morning work before milking being so early and heavy at a time of full pails. Tess usually accompanied her fellows upstairs. To-night, however, she was the first to go to their common chamber; and she had dozed when the other girls came in. She saw them undressing in the orange light of the vanished sun, which flushed their forms with its colour; she dozed again; but she was reawakened by their voices, and quietly turned her eyes towards them.

Neither of her three chamber-companions had got into bed. They were standing in a group, in their night-gowns, barefooted, at the window, the last red rays of the west still warming their faces and necks, and the walls around them. All were watching somebody in the garden with deep interest, their three faces close together: a jovial and round one, a pale one with dark hair, and a fair one whose tresses were auburn.

"Don't push—you can see as well as I," said Retty, the auburn haired and youngest girl, without removing her eyes from the window.

" 'Tis no use for you to be in love with him any more than me, Retty Priddle," said jolly-faced Marian the eldest, slily. "His thoughts be of other cheeks than thine."

Retty Priddle still looked; and the others looked again.

"There he is again!" cried Izz Huett, the pale girl with dark damp hair, and keenly cut lips.

"You needn't say anything, Izz," answered Retty. "For I zid you kissing his shade."

"*What* did you see her doing?" asked Marian.

"Why—he was standing over the whey-tub, to let off the whey, and the shade of his face came upon the wall behind, close to Izz, who was standing there filling a vat. She put her mouth against the wall and kissed the shade of his mouth; I zid her, though he didn't."

"O Izz Huett!" said Marian.

A rosy spot came into the middle of Izz Huett's cheek. "Well—there was no harm in it," she declared with attempted coolness. "And if I be in love wi'en, so is Retty too; and so be you, Marian, come to that."

Marian's full face could not blush past its chronic pinkness. "I!" she said. "What a tale! . . . Ah, there he is again! . . . Dear eyes—dear face—dear Mr Clare!"

"There—you've owned it!"

"So have you—so have we all," said Marian, with the dry frankness of complete indifference to opinion. "It is silly to pretend otherwise amongst ourselves, though we need not own it to other folks. I would just marry 'n to-morrow!"

"So would I—and more," murmured Izz Huett.

"And I too," whispered the more timid Retty.

The listener grew warm.

"We can't all marry him," said Izz.

"We shan't, either of us; which is worse still," said the eldest. "There he is again!" They all three blew him a silent kiss.

"Why?" asked Retty quickly.

"Because he likes Tess Durbeyfield best," said Marian lowering her voice. "I have watched him every day, and have found it out."

There was a reflective silence. "But she don't care anything for 'n?" at length breathed Retty.

"Well—I sometimes think that, too."

"But how silly all this is!" said Izz Huett impatiently. "Of course he won't marry any one of us, or Tess either—a gentleman's son, who's going to be a great landowner and farmer abroad! More likely to ask us to come wi'en as farm hands at so much a year!"

One sighed, and another sighed, and Marian's plump figure sighed biggest of all. Somebody in bed hard by sighed too. Tears came into the eyes of Retty Priddle, the pretty red-haired youngest— the last bud of the Paridelles, so important in the county annals. They watched silently a little longer, their three faces still close together as before, and the triple hues of their hair mingling. But the unconscious Mr Clare had gone indoors, and they saw him no more; and the shades beginning to deepen they crept into their beds. In a few minutes they heard him ascend the ladder to his own room.

Marian was soon snoring, but Izz did not drop into forgetfulness for a long time. Retty Priddle cried herself to sleep.

The deeper-passioned Tess was very far from sleeping even then. This conversation was another of the bitter pills she had been obliged to swallow that day. Scarce the least feeling of jealousy arose in her breast. For that matter she knew herself to have the preference. Being more finely formed, better educated, and, though the youngest except Retty, more woman than either, she perceived that only the slightest ordinary care was necessary for holding her own in Angel Clare's heart against these her candid friends. But the grave question was, ought she to do this? There was, to be sure, hardly the ghost of a chance for either of them, in a serious sense; but there was, or had been, a chance of one or the other inspiring him with a passing fancy for her, and enjoying the pleasure of his attentions while he stayed here. Such unequal attachments had led to marriage; and she had heard from Mrs Crick that Mr Clare had one day asked in a laughing way, what would be the use of his marrying a fine lady, and all the while ten thousand acres of Colonial pasture to feed, and cattle to rear, and corn to reap. A farm-woman would be the only sensible kind of wife for him. But whether Mr Clare had spoken seriously or not, why should she, who could never conscientiously allow any man to marry her now and who had religiously determined that she never would be tempted to do so, draw off Mr Clare's attention from other women, for the brief happiness of sunning herself in his eyes while he remained at Talbothays?

XXII

THEY came downstairs yawning next morning; but skimming and milking were proceeded with as usual, and they went indoors to breakfast. Dairyman Crick was discovered stamping about the house. He had received a letter, in which a customer had complained that the butter had a twang.

"And begad, so 't have!" said the dairyman, who held in his left hand a wooden slice, on which a lump of butter was stuck. "Yes—taste for yourself!"

Several of them gathered round him; and Mr Clare tasted, Tess tasted; also the other indoor milkmaids, one or two of the milking-men, and last of all Mrs Crick, who came out from the waiting breakfast-table. There certainly was a twang.

The dairyman, who had thrown himself into abstraction to better realize the taste, and so divine the particular species of noxious weed to which it appertained, suddenly exclaimed " 'Tis garlic! and I thought there wasn't a blade left in that mead!"

Then all the old hands remembered that a certain dry-mead, into which a few of the cows had been admitted of late, had, in years gone by, spoilt the butter in the same way. The dairyman had not recognized the taste at that time, and thought the butter bewitched.

"We must overhaul that mead," he resumed. "This mustn't continny!" All having armed themselves with old pointed knives they went out together. As the inimical plant could only be present in very microscopic dimensions to have escaped ordinary observation, to find it seemed rather a hopeless attempt in the stretch of rich grass before them. However, they formed themselves into line, all assisting, owing to the importance of the search; the dairyman at the upper end with Mr Clare, who had volunteered to help; then Tess, Marian, Izz Huett, and Retty; then Bill Lewell, Jonathan, and the married dairywomen—Beck Knibbs, with her woolly black hair and rolling eyes, and flaxen Frances, consumptive from the winter damps of the water-meads—who lived in their respective cottages.

With eyes fixed upon the ground they crept slowly across a strip of the field, returning a little further down in such a manner that, when they should have finished, not a single inch of the pasture but would have fallen under the eye of some one of them. It was a most tedious business, not more than half-a-dozen shoots of garlic being discoverable in the whole field; yet such was the herb's pungency that probably one bite of it by one cow had been sufficient to season the whole dairy's produce for the day.

Differing one from another in natures and moods so greatly as they did, they yet formed, bending, a curiously uniform row— automatic, noiseless; and an alien observer passing down the neighbouring lane might well have been excused for massing them as "Hodge". As they crept along, stooping low to discern the plant, a soft yellow gleam was reflected from the buttercups into their shaded faces, giving them an elfish moon-lit aspect, though the sun was pouring upon their backs in all the strength of noon.

Angel Clare, who communistically stuck to his rule of taking part with the rest in everything, glanced up now and then. It was not of course by accident that he walked next to Tess.

"Well—how are you?" he murmured.

"Very well thank you, sir," she replied demurely.

As they had been discussing a score of personal matters only half-an-hour before, the introductory style seemed a little superfluous. But they got no further in speech just then. They crept and crept, the hem of her petticoat just touching his gaiter, and his elbow sometimes brushing hers. At last the dairyman, who came next, could stand it no longer.

"Upon my soul and body, this here stooping do fairly make my back open and shut!" he exclaimed, straightening himself slowly with an excruciated look till quite upright. "And you, maidy Tess, you wasn't well a day or two ago—this will make your head ache finely. Don't do any more if you feel fainty—leave the rest to finish it."

Dairyman Crick withdrew, and Tess dropped behind. Mr Clare also stepped out of line, and began privateering about for the weed. When she found him near her, her very tension at what she had heard the night before made her the first to speak.

"Don't they look pretty!" she said.

"Who?"

"Izzy Huett and Retty."

Tess had moodily decided that either of these maidens would make a good farmer's wife, and that she ought to recommend them, and obscure her own wretched charms.

"Pretty? Well yes—they are pretty girls—fresh-looking. I have often thought so."

"Though, poor dears—prettiness won't last long."

"O no, unfortunately."

"They are excellent dairywomen."

"Yes: though not better than you."

"They skim better than I."

"Do they?"

Clare remained observing them—not without their observing him.

"She is colouring up," continued Tess heroically.

"Who?"

"Retty Priddle."

"Oh—why is that?"

"Because you are looking at her."

Self-sacrificing as her mood might be, Tess could not well go further and cry "Marry one of them, if you really do want a dairy-woman and not a lady; and don't think of marrying me." She followed Dairyman Crick, and had the mournful satisfaction of seeing that Clare remained behind.

From this day she forced herself to take pains to avoid him—never allowing herself, as formerly, to remain long in his company, even if their juxtaposition were purely accidental. She gave the other three every chance.

Tess was woman enough to realize from their avowals to herself that Angel Clare had the honour of all the dairymaids in his keeping, and her perception of his care to avoid compromising the happiness of either in the least degree, bred a tender respect in Tess for what she deemed, rightly or wrongly, the self-controlling sense of duty shown by him, a quality which she had never expected to find in one of the opposite sex, and in the absence of which more than one of the simple hearts who were his housemates might have gone weeping on her pilgrimage.

XXIII

THE hot weather of July had crept upon them unawares, and the atmosphere of the flat vale hung heavy as an opiate over the dairy-folk, the cows, and the trees. Hot steaming rains fell frequently, making the grass where the cows fed yet more rank, and hindering the late haymaking in the other meads.

It was Sunday morning; the milking was done; the outdoor milkers had gone home. Tess and the other three were dressing themselves rapidly, the whole bevy having agreed to go together to Mellstock Church—which lay some three or four miles distant from the dairyhouse. She had now been two months at Talbothays, and this was her first excursion.

All the preceding afternoon and night heavy thunderstorms had hissed down upon the meads; and washed some of the hay into the river; but this morning the sun shone out all the more brilliantly for the deluge; and the air was balmy and clear.

The crooked lane leading from their own parish to Mellstock ran along the lowest levels in a portion of its length, and when the girls reached the most depressed spot they found that the result of the rain had been to flood the lane over-shoe to a distance of some fifty yards. This would have been no serious hindrance on a week-day; they would have clicked through it in their high pattens and boots quite unconcerned; but on this day of vanity, this Sun's-day, when flesh went forth to coquet with flesh while hypocritically affecting business with spiritual things; on this occasion for wearing their white stockings and thin shoes, and their pink, white and lilac gowns, on which every mudspot would be visible, the pool was an awkward impediment. They could hear the church-bell calling—as yet nearly a mile off.

"Who would have expected such a rise in the river in summer-time!" said Marian, from the top of the roadside-bank on which they had climbed, and were maintaining a precarious footing in the hope of creeping along its slope till they were past the pool.

"We can't get there, anyhow, without walking right through it or else going round the Turnpike way; and that would make us so very late!" said Retty, pausing hopelessly.

"And I do colour up so hot, walking into church late, and all the people staring round," said Marian, "that I hardly cool down again till we get into the That it may please Thees."*

While they stood clinging to the bank they heard a splashing round the bend of the road, and presently appeared Angel Clare, advancing along the lane towards them through the water.

Four hearts gave a big throb simultaneously.

His aspect was probably as un-Sabbatarian a one as a dogmatic parson's son often presented; his attire being his dairy clothes, long wading-boots, a cabbage-leaf inside his hat to keep his head cool, with a thistle-spud* to finish him off.

"He's not going to church," said Marian.

"No—I wish he was," murmured Tess.

Angel, in fact, rightly or wrongly (to adopt the safe phrase of evasive controversialists) preferred sermons in stones to sermons in churches and chapels on fine summer days. This morning, moreover, he had gone out to see if the damage to the hay by the flood was considerable or not. On his walk he had observed the girls from a long distance—though they had been so occupied with their difficulties of passage as not to notice him. He knew that the water had risen at that spot, and that it would quite check their progress. So he had hastened on—with a dim idea of how he could help them, one of them in particular.

The rosy-cheeked, bright-eyed quartett looked so charming in their light summer attire—clinging to the roadside bank like pigeons on a roof-slope—that he stopped a moment to regard them before coming close. Their gauzy skirts had brushed up from the grass innumerable flies and butterflies which, unable to escape, remained caged in the transparent tissue as in an aviary. Angel's eye at last fell upon Tess, the hindmost of the four; she, being full of suppressed laughter at their dilemma, could not help meeting his glance radiantly.

He came beneath them in the water, which did not rise over his long boots; and stood looking at the entrapped flies and butterflies.

"Are you trying to get to church?" he said to Marian who was in front, including the next two in his remark, but avoiding Tess.

"Yes, sir; and 'tis getting late. And my colour do come up so—"

"I'll carry you through the pool—every Jill of you."

The whole four flushed, as if one heart beat through them.

"I think—you can't, sir," said Marian.

"It is the only way for you to get past. Stand still. Nonsense—you are not too heavy! I'd carry you all four together. Now, Marian—attend," he continued, "and put your arms round my shoulders, so. Now! Hold on. That's well done."

Marian had lowered herself upon his arm and shoulder as directed, and Angel strode off with her, his slim figure, as viewed from behind, looking like the mere stem to the great nosegay suggested by hers. They disappeared round the curve of the road, and only his sousing footsteps and the top ribbon of Marian's bonnet told where they were. In a few minutes he reappeared. Izz Huett was the next in order upon the bank.

"Here he comes," she murmured, and they could hear that her lips were dry with emotion. "And I have to put my arms round his neck and look into his face as Marian did."

"There's nothing in that," said Tess quickly.

"There's a time for everything," continued Izz, unheeding. "A time to embrace, and a time to refrain from embracing:* the first is now going to be mine."

"Fie—it is Scripture, Izz!"

"Yes," said Izz, "I've always a' ear at church for pretty verses." Angel Clare, to whom three-quarters of this performance was a commonplace act of kindness, now approached Izz. She quietly and dreamily lowered herself into his arms, and Angel methodically marched off with her. When he was heard returning for the third time Retty's throbbing heart could be almost seen to shake her. He went up to the red-haired girl, and while he was seizing her he glanced at Tess. His lips could not have pronounced more plainly, "It will soon be you and I!" Her comprehension appeared in her face: she could not help it: there was an understanding between them.

Poor little Retty, though by far the lightest weight, was the most troublesome of Clare's burdens. Marian had been like a sack of meal, a dead weight of plumpness, under which he had literally staggered. Izz had ridden sensibly and calmly; Retty was a bunch of hysterics.

However, he got through with the disquieted creature, deposited her, and returned. Tess could see over the hedge the distant three in a group, standing as he had placed them on the next rising ground. It was now her turn. She was embarrassed to discover that excitement at the proximity of Mr Clare's breath and eyes, which she had contemned in her companions, was intensified in herself; and as if fearful of betraying her secret she paltered with him at the last moment.

"I may be able to clim' along the bank, perhaps—I can clim' better than they. You must be so tired, Mr Clare."

"No, no, Tess!" said he quickly. And almost before she was aware she was seated in his arms and resting against his shoulder.

"Three Leahs to get one Rachel,"* he whispered.

"They are better women than I," she replied, magnanimously sticking to her resolve.

"Not to me," said Angel.

He saw her grow warm at this; and they went some steps in silence.

"I hope I am not too heavy," she said timidly.

"O no. You should lift Marian! Such a lump. You are like an undulating billow warmed by the sun. And all this fluff of muslin about you is the froth."

"It is very pretty—if I seem like that to you."

"Do you know that I have undergone three-quarters of this labour entirely for the sake of the fourth quarter?"

"No."

"I did not expect such an event to-day."

"Nor I. . . . The water came up so sudden."

That the rise in the water was what she understood him to refer to, the state of her breathing belied. Clare stood still, and inclined his face towards hers.

"O Tessy!" he exclaimed.

The girl's cheeks burned to the breeze, and she could not look into his eyes for her emotion. It reminded Angel that he was somewhat unfairly taking advantage of an accidental position; and he went no further with it. No definite words of love had crossed their lips as yet, and suspension at this point was desirable now. However he walked slowly, to make the remainder of the distance as long as possible; but at last they came to the bend, and the rest of their progress was in full view of the other three. The dry land was reached, and he set her down.

Her friends were looking with round thoughtful eyes at her and him, and she could see that they had been talking of her. He hastily bade them farewell, and splashed back along the stretch of submerged road.

The four moved on together as before, till Marian broke the silence by saying, "No—in all truth; we have no chance against her!" She looked joylessly at Tess.

"What do you mean?" asked the latter.

"He likes 'ee best—the very best! We could see it as he brought 'ee. He would have kissed 'ee, if you had encouraged him to do it, ever so little."

"No, no," said she.

The gaiety with which they had set out had somehow vanished; and yet there was no enmity or malice between them. They were generous young souls; they had been reared in the lonely country nooks where fatalism is a strong sentiment; and they did not blame her. Such supplanting was to be.

Tess's heart ached. There was no concealing from herself the fact that she loved Angel Clare, perhaps all the more passionately from knowing that the others had also lost their hearts to him. There is contagion in this sentiment, especially among women. And yet that same hungry heart of hers compassionated her friends. Tess's honest nature had fought against this; but too feebly; and the natural result had followed.

"I will never stand in your way, nor in the way of either of you!" she declared to Retty that night in the bedroom (her tears running down). "I can't help this, my dear! I don't think marrying is in his mind at all; but if he were even to ask me I should refuse him, as I should refuse any man."

"O would you? Why?" said wondering Retty.

"It cannot be. But I will be plain. Putting myself quite on one side I don't think he will choose either of you."

"I have never expected it—thought of it!" moaned Retty. "But O, I wish I was dead!"

The poor child, torn by a feeling which she hardly understood, turned to the other two girls who came upstairs just then. "We be friends with her again," she said to them. "She thinks no more of his choosing her than we do." So the reserve went off, and they were confiding and warm.

"I don't seem to care what I do now," said Marian, whose mood was tuned to its lowest bass. "I was going to marry a dairyman at Stickleford who's asked me twice; but—my soul—I would put an end to myself rather'n be his wife now! . . . Why don't ye speak, Izz?"

"To confess then," murmured Izz, "I made sure to-day that he was going to kiss me as he held me; and I lay still against his breast, hoping and hoping, and never moved at all. But he did not. I don't like biding here at Talbothays any longer. I shall go hwome."

The air of the sleeping-chamber seemed to palpitate with the hopeless passion of the girls. They writhed feverishly under the oppressiveness of an emotion thrust on them by cruel Nature's law—an emotion which they had neither expected nor desired. The incident of the day had fanned the flame that was burning the inside of their hearts out, and the torture was almost more than they could endure. The differences which distinguished them as individuals were abstracted by this passion, and each was but portion of one organism called sex. There was so much frankness and so little jealousy because there was no hope. Each one was a girl of fair common sense, and she did not delude herself with any vain conceits, or deny her love, or give herself airs, in the idea of outshining the others. The full recognition of the futility of their infatuation, from a social point of view; its purposeless beginning; its self-bounded outlook; its lack of everything to justify its existence in the eye of civilization (while lacking nothing in the eye of Nature); the one fact that it did exist, ecstasizing them to a killing joy; all this imparted to them a resignation, a dignity, which a practical and sordid expectation of winning him as a husband would have destroyed.

They tossed and turned on their little beds, and the cheese-wring dripped monotonously downstairs.

"B' you awake, Tess?" whispered one, half-an-hour later. It was Izz Huett's voice.

Tess replied in the affirmative; whereupon also Retty and Marian suddenly flung the bed-clothes off them, and sighed, "So be we!"

"I wonder what she is like—the lady they say his family have looked out for him."

"I wonder," said Izz.

"Some lady looked out for him?" gasped Tess, starting. "I have never heard o' that!"

"O yes—'tis whispered. A young lady of his own rank, chosen by his family: a doctor of divinity's daughter, near his father's parish of Emminster: he don't much care for her, they say. But he is sure to marry her."

They had heard so very little of this; yet it was enough to build up wretched dolorous dreams upon, there in the shade of the night. They pictured all the details of his being won round to consent, of the wedding preparations, of the bride's happiness, of her dress and veil, of her blissful home with him, when oblivion would have fallen upon themselves as far as he and their love were concerned. Thus they talked, and ached, and wept, till sleep charmed their sorrow away.

After this disclosure Tess nourished no further foolish thought that there lurked any grave and deliberate import in Clare's attentions to her. It was a passing summer love of her face, for love's own temporary sake—nothing more. And the thorny crown of this sad conception was that she whom he really did prefer in a cursory way to the rest, she who knew herself to be more impassioned in nature, cleverer, more beautiful than they, was in the eyes of propriety far less worthy of him than the homelier ones whom he ignored.

XXIV

Amid the oozing fatness and warm ferments of the Var Vale, at a season when the rush of juices could almost be heard below the hiss of fertilization, it was impossible that the most fanciful love should not grow passionate. The ready bosoms existing there were impregnated by their surroundings.

July passed over their heads, and the Thermidorean weather* which came in its wake seemed an effort on the part of Nature to match the state of hearts at Talbothays Dairy. The air of the place, so fresh in the spring, and early summer, was stagnant and enervating now. Its heavy scents weighed upon them, and at mid-day the landscape seemed lying in a swoon. Ethiopic scorchings browned the upper slopes of the pastures, but there was still bright green herbage here where the watercourses purled. And as Clare was oppressed by the outward heats so was he burdened inwardly by a waxing fervour of passion for the soft and silent Tess.

The rains having passed the uplands were dry. The wheels of the dairyman's spring-cart, as he sped home from market, licked up the pulverised surface of the highway, and were followed by white ribands of dust, as if they had set a thin powder-train on fire. The cows jumped wildly over the five-barred barton-gate, maddened by the gad-fly; Dairyman Crick kept his shirt-sleeves permanently rolled up from Monday to Saturday: open windows had no effect in ventilation without open doors, and in the dairy-garden the blackbirds and thrushes crept about under the currant-bushes rather in the manner of quadrupeds than of winged creatures. The flies in the kitchen were lazy, teasing, and familiar, crawling about in unwonted places, on the floor, into drawers, and over the backs of the milkmaids' hands. Conversations were concerning sunstroke; while butter-making, and still more butter-keeping, was a despair.

They milked entirely in the meads for coolness and convenience, without driving in the cows. During the day the animals obsequiously followed the shadow of the smallest tree as it moved round the stem with the diurnal roll; and when the milkers came they could hardly stand still for the flies.

On one of these afternoons four or five unmilked cows chanced to stand apart from the general herd, behind the corner of a hedge, among them being Dumpling and Old Pretty, who loved Tess's hands above those of any other maid. When she rose from her stool under a finished cow Angel Clare, who had been observing her for some time, asked her if she would take the aforesaid creatures next. She silently assented, and with her stool at arm's length, and the pail against her knee, went round to where they stood. Soon the sound of Old Pretty's milk fizzing into the pail came through the hedge, and then Angel felt inclined to go round the corner also, to finish off a hard-yielding milcher who had strayed there, he being now as capable of this as the dairyman himself.

All the men, and some of the women, when milking, dug their foreheads into the cows and gazed into the pail. But a few—mainly the younger ones—rested their heads sideways. This was Tess Durbeyfield's habit, her temple pressing the milcher's flank, her eyes fixed on the far end of the meadow with the quiet of one lost in meditation. She was milking Old Pretty thus, and the sun chancing to be on the milking-side is shone flat upon her pink-gowned form, and her white curtain-bonnet, and upon her profile, rendering it keen as a cameo cut from the dun background of the cow.

She did not know that Clare had followed her round, and that he sat under his cow watching her. The stillness of her head and features was remarkable; she might have been in a trance, her eyes open, yet unseeing. Nothing in the picture moved but Old Pretty's tail and Tess's pink hands, the latter so gently as to be a rhythmic pulsation only, as if they were obeying a reflex stimulus, like a beating heart.

How very lovable her face was to him. Yet there was nothing ethereal about it: all was real vitality, real warmth, real incarnation. And it was in her mouth that this culminated. Eyes almost as deep and speaking he had seen before, and cheeks perhaps as fair; brows as arched, a chin and throat almost as shapely; her mouth he had seen nothing to equal on the face of the earth. To a young man with the least fire in him that little upward lift in the middle of her red top lip was distracting, infatuating, maddening. He had never before seen a woman's lips and teeth which forced upon his mind, with such persistent iteration, the old Elizabethan simile of roses filled with snow.* Perfect, he, as a lover, might have called them off hand. But no: they were not perfect. And it was the touch of the imperfect upon the would-be perfect that gave the sweetness, because it was that which gave the humanity.

Clare had studied the curves of those lips so many times that he could reproduce them mentally with ease; and now, as they again confronted him, clothed with colour and life, they sent an *aura* over his flesh, a breeze through his nerves, which well-nigh produced a qualm; and actually produced by some mysterious physiological process, a prosaic sneeze.

She then became conscious that he was observing her; but she would not show it by any change of position, though the curious dream-like fixity disappeared, and a close eye might easily have discerned that the rosiness of her face deepened, and then faded till only a tinge of it was left.

The influence that had passed into Clare like an excitation from the sky, did not die down. Resolutions, reticences, prudences, fears, fell back like a defeated battalion. He jumped up from his seat, and, leaving his pail to be kicked over if the milcher had such a mind, went quickly towards the desire of his eyes, and kneeling down beside her, clasped her in his arms.

Tess was taken completely by surprise, and she yielded to his embrace with unreflecting inevitableness. Having seen that it was really her lover who had advanced, and no one else, her lips parted and she sank upon him in her momentary joy, with something very like an ecstatic cry.

He had been on the point of kissing that too tempting mouth, but he checked himself, for tender conscience' sake. "Forgive me, Tess dear," he whispered. "I ought to have asked. I—did not know what I was doing. I do not mean it as a liberty. I am devoted to you, Tessy, dearest, in all sincerity!"

Old Pretty by this time had looked round, puzzled; and seeing two people crouching under her where, by immemorial custom, there should have been only one, lifted her hind leg crossly.

"She is angry—she doesn't know what we mean—she'll kick over the milk!" exclaimed Tess, gently striving to free herself, her eyes concerned with the quadruped's actions, her heart more deeply concerned with herself and Clare.

She slipped up from her seat, and they stood together, his arm still encircling her. Tess's eyes, fixed on distance, began to fill.

"Why do you cry, my darling?" he said.

"O—I don't know!" she murmured.

As she saw and felt more clearly the position she was in she became agitated and tried to withdraw.

"Well—I have betrayed my feelings, Tess, at last," said he with a curious sigh of desperation, signifying unconsciously that his heart had outrun his judgment. "That I—love you dearly and truly I need not say. But I—it shall go no further now—it distresses you—I am as surprised as you are. You will not think I have presumed upon your defencelessness—been too quick and unreflecting, will you?"

"N'—I can't tell."

He had allowed her to free herself; and in a minute or two the milking of each was resumed. Nobody had beheld the gravitation of the two into one; and when the dairyman came round by that screened nook, a few minutes later, there was not a sign to reveal that the markedly sundered pair were more to each other than mere acquaintance. Yet in the interval since Crick's last view of them something had occurred which changed the pivot of the universe for their two natures: something which, had he known its quality, the dairyman would have despised, as a practical man; yet which was based upon a more stubborn and resistless tendency than a whole heap of so-called practicalities. A veil had been whisked aside; the tract of each one's outlook was to have a new horizon thenceforward—for a short time or for a long.

END OF PHASE THE THIRD

PHASE THE FOURTH

THE CONSEQUENCE

PHASE THE FOURTH

THE CONSEQUENCE

XXV

CLARE, restless, went out into the dusk when evening drew on, she who had won him having retired to her chamber.

The night was as sultry as the day. There was no coolness after dark unless on the grass. Roads, garden-paths, the house fronts, the barton-walls, were warm as hearths, and reflected the noontide temperature into the noctambulist's face.

He sat on the east gate of the dairy-yard, and knew not what to think of himself. Feeling had indeed smothered judgment that day.

Since the sudden embrace, three hours before, the twain had kept apart. She seemed stilled, almost alarmed, at what had occurred, while the novelty, unpremeditation, mastery of circumstance disquieted him—palpitating contemplative being that he was. He could hardly realize their true relations to each other as yet, and what their mutual bearing should be before third parties thenceforward.

Angel had come as pupil to this dairy in the idea that his temporary existence here was to be the merest episode in his life, soon passed through and early forgotten; he had come as to a place from which as from a screened alcove he could calmly view the absorbing world without, and, apostrophizing it with Walt Whitman*—

> Crowds of men and women attired in the usual costumes,
> How curious you are to me!—

resolve upon a plan for plunging into that world anew. But, behold, the absorbing scene had been imported hither. What had been the engrossing world had dissolved into an uninteresting outer dumbshow; while here, in this apparently dim and unimpassioned place, novelty had volcanically started up—as it had never, for him, started up elsewhere.

Every window of the house being open Clare could hear across the yard each trivial sound of the retiring household. That dairyhouse, so humble, so insignificant, so purely, to him, a place of constrained sojourn that he had never hitherto deemed it of sufficient import-ance to be reconnoitred as an object of any quality whatever in the landscape; what was it now? The aged and lichened brick gables breathed forth "Stay!" The windows smiled, the door coaxed and beckoned, the creeper blushed confederacy. A personality within it was so far-reaching in her influence as to spread into and make the bricks, mortar, and whole overhanging sky throb with a burning sensibility. Whose was this mighty personality? A milkmaid's.

It was amazing, indeed, to find how great a matter the life of the obscure dairy had become to him. And though new love was to be held partly responsible for this it was not solely so. Many besides Angel have learnt that the magnitude of lives is not as to their external displacements, but as to their subjective experiences. The impressionable peasant leads a larger, fuller, more dramatic life than the pachydermatous king. Looking at it thus he found that life was to be seen of the same magnitude here as elsewhere.

Despite his heterodoxy, faults, and weaknesses, Clare was a man with a conscience. Tess was no insignificant creature to toy with and dismiss; but a woman living her precious life—a life which, to herself who endured or enjoyed it, possessed as great a dimension as the life of the mightiest to himself. Upon her sensations the whole world depended, to Tess: through her existence all her fellow-creatures existed, to her. The universe itself only came into being for Tess on the particular day in the particular year in which she was born.

This consciousness upon which he had intruded was the single opportunity of existence ever vouchsafed to Tess by an unsympathetic first cause; her all; her every and only chance. How then should he look upon her as of less consequence than himself; as a pretty trifle to caress and grow weary of; and not deal in the greatest seriousness with the affection which he knew that he had awakened in her—so fervid and so impressionable as she was under her reserve; in order that it might not agonize and wreck her?

To encounter her daily in the accustomed manner would be to develop what had begun. Living in such close relations, to meet meant to fall into endearment; flesh and blood could not resist it; and having arrived at no conclusion as to the issue of such a tendency, he decided to hold aloof for the present from occupations in which they would be mutually engaged. As yet the harm done was small.

But it was not easy to carry out the resolution never to approach her. He was driven towards her by every heave of his pulse.

He thought he would go and see his friends. It might be possible to sound them upon this. In less than five months his term here would have ended, and after a few additional months spent upon other farms he would be fully equipped in agricultural knowledge, and in a position to start on his own account. Would not a farmer want a wife, and should a farmer's wife be a drawing-room wax-figure, or a woman who understood farming? Notwithstanding the pleasing answer returned to him by the silence he resolved to go his journey.

One morning when they sat down to breakfast at Talbothays Dairy, some maid observed that she had not seen anything of Mr Clare that day.

"O no," said Dairyman Crick. "Mr Clare has gone hwome to Emminster to spend a few days wi' his kinsfolk."

For four impassioned ones around that table the sunshine of the morning went out at a stroke, and the birds muffled their song. But neither girl by word or gesture revealed her blankness.

"He's getting on towards the end of his time wi' me," added the dairyman with a phlegm which unconsciously was brutal; "and so I suppose he is beginning to see about his plans for elsewhere."

"How much longer is he to bide here?" asked Izz Huett, the only one of the gloom-stricken bevy who could trust her voice with the question.

The others waited for the dairyman's answer as if their lives hung upon it; Retty with parted lips, gazing on the table-cloth, Marian with heat added to her redness, Tess throbbing and looking out at the meads.

"Well, I can't mind the exact day without looking at my memorandum-book," replied Crick with the same intolerable unconcern. "And even that may be altered a bit. He'll bide to get a little practice in the calving, out at the straw-yard, for certain. He'll hang on till the end of the year, I should say."

Four months or so of torturing ecstasy in his society—of "pleasure girdled about with pain".* After that, the blackness of unutterable night.

At this moment of the morning Angel Clare was riding along a narrow lane ten miles distant from the breakfasters, in the direction of his father's vicarage at Emminster carrying as well as he could a little basket which contained some black puddings and a bottle of mead, sent by Mrs Crick with her kind respects to his parents. The white lane stretched before him, and his eyes were upon it; but they were staring into next year, and not at the lane. He loved her: ought he to marry her?—dared he to marry her? What would his mother and his brothers say? What would he himself say a couple of years after the event? That would depend upon whether the germs of staunch comradeship underlay the temporary emotion, or whether it were a sensuous joy in her form only, with no substratum of everlastingness.

His father's hill-surrounded little town, the Tudor church tower of red stone, the clump of trees near the vicarage, came at last into view beneath him, and he rode down towards the well-known gate. Casting a glance in the direction of the church before entering his home he beheld standing by the vestry-door a group of girls, of ages between twelve and sixteen, apparently awaiting the arrival of some other one, who in a moment became visible; a figure somewhat older than the school-girls, wearing a broad-brimmed hat, and highly-starched cambric morning-gown, with a couple of books in her hand.

Clare knew her well. He could not be sure that she observed him; he hoped she did not, so as to render it unnecessary that he should go and speak to her, blameless creature that she was. An overpowering reluctance to greet her made him decide that she had not seen him. The young lady was Miss Mercy Chant, the only daughter of his father's neighbour and friend, whom it was his parents' quiet hope that he might wed some day. She was great at Antinomianism* and Bible-classes, and was plainly going to hold a class now. Clare's mind flew to the impassioned, summer-steeped heathens in the Var Vale, their rosy faces court-patched with cow-droppings; and to one the most impassioned of them all.

It was on the impulse of the moment that he had resolved to trot over to Emminster, and hence had not written to apprise his mother and father; aiming however to arrive about the breakfast hour, before they should have gone out to their parish duties. He was a little late, and they had already sat down to the morning meal. The group at table jumped up to welcome him as soon as he entered. They were his father and mother, his brother the Reverend Felix—curate at a town in the adjoining county, home for the inside of a fortnight—and his other brother the Reverend Cuthbert, the classical scholar, and fellow and dean of his College, down from Cambridge for the long vacation. His mother appeared in a cap and silver spectacles, and his father looked what in fact he was, an earnest, God-fearing man, somewhat gaunt, in years about sixty-five, his pale face lined with thought and purpose. Over their heads hung the picture of Angel's sister, the eldest of the family, sixteen years his senior, who had married a missionary and gone out to Africa.

Old Mr Clare was a clergyman of a type which, within the last twenty years, has well-nigh dropped out of contemporary life. A spiritual descendant in the direct line from Wycliff, Huss, Luther, Calvin; an Evangelical of the Evangelicals, a conversionist,* a man of Apostolic simplicity in life and thought, he had in his raw youth made up his mind once for all on the deeper questions of existence, and admitted no further reasoning on them thenceforward. He was regarded even by those of his own date and school of thinking as extreme; while, on the other hand, those totally opposed to him were unwillingly won to admiration for his thoroughness, and for the remarkable power he showed in dismissing all question as to principles in his energy for applying them. He loved Paul of Tarsus, liked St John, hated St James as much as he dared, and regarded with mixed feelings Timothy, Titus, and Philemon. The New Testament was less a Christiad than a Pauliad to his intelligence— less an argument than an intoxication. His creed of determinism was such that it almost amounted to a vice, and quite amounted, on its negative side, to a renunciative philosophy which had cousinship with that of Schopenhauer and Leopardi. He despised the Canons and Rubric, swore by the Articles* and deemed himself consistent through the whole category—which in a way he might have been. One thing he certainly was; sincere.

To the æsthetic, sensuous, Pagan pleasure in natural life and lush womanhood which his son Angel had lately been experiencing in Var Vale, his temper would have been antipathetic in a high degree, had he either by inquiry or imagination been able to apprehend it. Once upon a time Angel had been so unlucky as to say to his father, in a moment of irritation, that it might have resulted far better for mankind if Greece had been the source of the religion of modern civilization, and not Palestine; and his father's grief was of that blank description which could not realize that there might lurk a thousandth part of a truth, much less a half-truth or a whole truth, in such a proposition. He had simply preached austerely at Angel for some time after. But the kindness of his heart was such that he never resented anything for long, and welcomed his son to-day with a smile which was a candidly sweet as a child's.

Angel sat down; and the place felt like home; yet he did not so much as formerly feel himself one of the family gathered there. Every time that he returned hither he was conscious of this divergence; and since he had last shared in the vicarage life it had grown even more distinctly foreign to his own than usual. Its transcendental aspirations—still unconsciously based on the geocentric view of things, a zenithal paradise, a nadiral hell*—were as foreign to his own as if they had been the dreams of people on another planet. Latterly he had seen only Life, felt only the great passionate pulse of existence, unwarped, uncontorted, untrammelled by those creeds which futilely attempt to check what wisdom would be content to regulate.

On their part they saw a great difference in him, a growing divergence from the Angel Clare of former times. It was chiefly a difference in his manner that they noticed just now, particularly his brothers. He was getting to behave like a farmer; he flung his legs about; the muscles of his face had grown more expressive; his eyes looked as much information as his tongue spoke, and more. The manner of the scholar had nearly disappeared; still more the manner of the drawing-room young man. A prig would have said that he had lost culture, and a prude that he had become coarse. Such was the contagion of domiciliary fellowship with the Talbothays nymphs and swains.

After breakfast he walked with his two brothers, non-Evangelical, well-educated, hall-marked young men, correct to their remotest fibre; such unimpeachable models as are turned out yearly by the lathe of a systematic tuition. They were both somewhat short-sighted, and when it was the custom to wear a single eyeglass and string they wore a single eyeglass and string; when it was the custom to wear a double glass they wore a double glass; when it was the custom to wear spectacles, they wore spectacles straightway, all without reference to the particular variety of defect in their own vision. When Wordsworth was enthroned they carried pocket copies; and when Shelley was belittled they allowed him to grow dusty on their shelves. When Correggio's Holy-Families were admired they admired Correggio's Holy-Families; when he was decried in favour of Velasquez they sedulously followed suit without any personal objection.

If these two noticed Angel's growing social ineptness, he noticed their growing mental limitations. Felix seemed to him all Church; Cuthbert all College. His Diocesan Synods and Visitations* were the mainsprings of the world to the one: Cambridge to the other. Each brother candidly recognized that there were a few unimportant scores of millions of outsiders in civilized society, persons who were neither university men nor churchmen; but they were to be tolerated rather than reckoned with and respected.

They were both dutiful and attentive sons, and were regular in their visits to their parents. Felix, though an offshoot from a far more recent point in the devolution of theology than his father, was less self-sacrificing and disinterested. More tolerant than his father of a contradictory opinion, in its aspect as a danger to its holder, he was less ready than his father to pardon it as a slight to his own teaching. Cuthbert was, upon the whole, the more liberal-minded: though, with greater subtlety, he had not so much heart.

As they walked along the hill-side Angel's former feeling revived in him; that whatever their advantages by comparison with himself, neither saw or set forth life as it really was lived. Perhaps, as with many men, their opportunities of observation were not so good as their opportunities of expression. Neither had an adequate conception of the complicated forces at work outside the smooth and gentle current in which they and their associates floated. Neither saw the difference between local truth and universal truth; that what the inner world said in their clerical and academic hearing was quite a different thing from what the outer world was thinking.

"I suppose it is farming or nothing for you now, my dear fellow," Felix was saying among other things, to his youngest brother, as he looked through his spectacles at the distant fields with sad austerity. "And therefore we must make the best of it. But I do entreat you to endeavour to keep as much as possible in touch with moral ideals. Farming, of course, means roughing it externally; but high thinking may go with plain living, nevertheless."

"Of course it may," said Angel. "Was it not proved nineteen hundred years ago—if I may trespass upon your domain a little?

Why should you think, Felix, that I am likely to drop my high thinking and my moral ideals?"

"Well—I fancied, from the tone of your letters, and our conversation,—it may be fancy only—that you were somehow losing intellectual grasp. Hasn't it struck you, Cuthbert?"

"Now, Felix," said Angel drily; "we are very good friends, you know; each of us treading our allotted circles; but if it comes to intellectual grasp, I think you as a contended dogmatist had better leave mine alone, and inquire what has become of yours."

They returned down the hill to dinner, which was fixed at any time at which their father's and mother's morning work in the parish was usually concluded. Convenience as regarded afternoon callers was the last thing to enter into the consideration of unselfish Mr and Mrs Clare; though the three sons were sufficiently in unison on this matter to wish that their parents would conform a little to modern notions.

The walk had made them hungry, Angel in particular, who was now an outdoor man, accustomed to the profuse *dapes inemptæ** of the dairyman's somewhat coarsely laden table. But neither of the old people had arrived, and it was not till the sons were almost tired of waiting that their parents entered. The self-denying pair had been occupied in coaxing the appetites of some of their sick parishioners whom they, somewhat inconsistently, tried to keep imprisoned in the flesh, their own appetites being quite forgotten.

The family sat down to table, and a frugal meal of cold viands was deposited before them. Angel looked round for Mrs Crick's black puddings which he had directed to be nicely grilled as they did them at the dairy, and of which he wished his father and mother to appreciate the marvellous herbal savours as highly as he did himself.

"Ah—you are looking for the black puddings, my dear boy," observed Clare's mother. "But I am sure you will not mind doing without them, as I am sure your father and I shall not, when you know the reason. I suggested to him that we should take Mrs Crick's kind present to the children of the man who can earn nothing just now because of his attacks of *delirium tremens*; and he agreed that it would be a great pleasure to them; so we did."

"Of course," said Angel cheerfully, looking round for the mead.

"I found the mead so extremely alcoholic," continued his mother, "that it was quite unfit for use as a beverage; but as valuable as rum or brandy in an emergency: so I have put it in my medicine-closet."

"We never drink spirits at this table on principle," added his father.

"But what shall I tell the dairyman's wife?" said Angel.

"The truth, of course," said his father.

"I rather wanted to say—we enjoyed the mead and the black puddings very much. She is a kind, jolly sort of body, and is sure to ask me, directly I return."

"You cannot, if we did not," Mr Clare answered lucidly.

"Ah—no. Though that mead was a drop of pretty tipple."

"A what?" said Cuthbert and Felix both.

"Oh—'tis an expression they use down at Talbothays," replied Angel blushing. He felt that his parents were right in their practice, if wrong in their want of sentiment, and said no more.

XXVI

IT was not till the evening, after family prayers, that Angel found opportunity of broaching to his father one or two subjects near his heart. He had strung himself up to the purpose while kneeling behind his brothers on the carpet, studying the little nails in the heels of their walking boots. When the service was over they went out of the room with their mother, and Mr Clare and himself were left alone.

The young man first discussed with the elder his plans for the attainment of his position as a farmer on an extensive scale—either in England or in the Colonies. His father then told him that, as he had not been put to the expense of sending Angel up to Cambridge, he had felt it his duty to set by a sum of money every year towards the purchase or lease of land for him some day, that he might not feel himself unduly slighted. "As far as worldly wealth goes," continued his father, "you will no doubt stand far superior to your brothers in a few years."

This considerateness on old Mr Clare's part led Angel onward to the other and dearer subject. He observed to his father that he was then six-and-twenty, and that when he should start in the farming business he would require eyes in the back of his head to see to all matters—some one would be necessary to superintend the domestic labours of his establishment whilst he was afield. Would it not be well, therefore, for him to marry?

His father seemed to think this idea not unreasonable. And then Angel put the question: "What kind of wife do you think would be best for me, as a thrifty hard-working farmer?"

"A truly Christian woman, who will be a help and a comfort to you in your goings-out and your comings-in. Beyond that, it really matters little. Such an one can be found; indeed my earnest-minded friend and neighbour Dr Chant—"

"But ought she not primarily to be able to milk cows, churn good butter, make immense cheeses; know how to sit hens and turkeys, and rear chickens, to direct a field of labourers in an emergency, and estimate the value of sheep and calves?"

"Yes; a farmer's wife; yes, certainly. It would be desirable."

Mr Clare the elder had plainly never thought of these points before. "I was going to add," he said, "that, for a pure and saintly woman, you will not find one more to your true advantage, and certainly not more to your mother's mind and my own, than your friend Mercy, whom you used to show a certain interest in. It is true that my neighbour Chant's daughter has lately caught up the fashion of the younger clergy round about us, for decorating the communion-table—altar as I was shocked to hear her call it one day—with flowers and other stuff on festival occasions. But her father, who is quite as opposed to such flummery as I—says that can be cured. It is a mere girlish outbreak, which I am sure will not be permanent."

"Yes, yes: Mercy is good and devout, I know. But father, don't you think that a young woman equally pure and virtuous as Miss Chant, but one who, in place of that lady's ecclesiastical accomplishments, understands the duties of farm life as well as a farmer himself, would suit me infinitely better?"

His father persisted in his conviction that a knowledge of a farmer's wife's duties came second to a Pauline view of humanity; and the impulsive Angel, wishing to honour his father's feelings and to advance the cause of his heart at the same time, grew specious. He said that fate or providence had thrown in his way a woman who possessed every qualification to be the helpmate of an agriculturist, and was decidedly of a serious turn of mind. He would not say whether or not she had attached herself to the sound Low-Church school of his father; but she would probably be open to conviction on that point; she was a regular church-goer, of simple faith; honest-hearted, receptive, intelligent, graceful to a degree, chaste as a vestal, and in personal appearance exceptionally beautiful.

"Is she of a family such as you would care to marry into—a lady, in short?" asked his startled mother, who had come softly into the study during the conversation.

"She is not what in common parlance is called a lady," said Angel unflinchingly; "for she is a cottager's daughter, as I am proud to say. But she *is* a lady, nevertheless—in feeling and nature."

"Mercy Chant is of a very good family."

"Pooh—what's the advantage of that, mother!" said Angel quickly. "How is family to avail the wife of a man who has to rough it as I have and shall have to do?"

"Mercy is accomplished. And accomplishments have their charm," returned his mother, looking at him through her silver spectacles.

"As to external accomplishments, what will be the use of them in the life I am going to lead: while as to her reading, I can take that in hand. She'll be apt pupil enough, as you would say if you knew her. She's brim-full of poetry—actualized poetry, if I may use the expression. She *lives* what paper-poets only write. . . . And she is an unimpeachable Christian, I am sure; perhaps of the very tribe, genus, and species you desire to propagate."

"O Angel—you are mocking!"

"Mother, I beg pardon. But as she really does attend Church almost every Sunday morning, and is a good Christian girl, I am sure you will tolerate any social short-comings for the sake of that quality, and feel that I may do worse than choose her." Angel waxed quite earnest on that rather automatic orthodoxy in his beloved Tess, which (never dreaming that it might stand him in such good stead) he had been prone to slight when observing it practised by her and the other milkmaids, because of its obvious unreality amid beliefs essentially naturalistic.

In their sad doubts as to whether their son had himself any right whatever to the title he claimed for the unknown young woman Mr and Mrs Clare began to feel it as an advantage not to be over-looked that she at least was sound in her views; especially as the conjunction of the pair must have arisen by an act of providence; for Angel never would have made orthodoxy a condition of his choice. They said finally that it was better not to act in a hurry, but that they would not object to see her.

Angel therefore refrained from declaring more particulars now. He felt that, single-minded and self-sacrificing as his parents were, there yet existed certain latent prejudices of theirs, as middle-class people, which it would require some tact to overcome. For though legally at liberty to do as he chose, and though their daughter-in-law's qualifications could make no practical difference to their lives, in the probability of her living far away from them, he wished for affection's sake not to wound their sentiment in the most important decision of his life.

He observed his own inconsistencies in dwelling upon accidents in Tess's life as if they were vital features. It was for herself that he loved Tess; her soul, her heart, her substance—not for her skill in the dairy, her aptness as his scholar, and certainly not for her simple, formal faith-professions. Her unsophisticated, open-air existence required no varnish of conventionality to make it palatable to him. He held that education had as yet but little affected the beats of emotion and impulse on which domestic happiness depends. It was probable that, in the lapse of ages, improved systems of moral and intellectual training would appreciably, perhaps considerably, elevate the involuntary, and even the unconscious, instincts of human nature; but up to the present day, culture, as far as he could see, might be said to have affected only the mental epiderm of those lives which had been brought under its influence. This belief was confirmed by his experience of women, which, having latterly been extended from the cultivated middle class into the rural community, had taught him how much less was the intrinsic difference between the good and wise woman of one social stratum and the good and wise woman of another social stratum, than between the good and bad, the wise and the foolish, of the same stratum or class.

It was the morning of his departure. His brothers had already left the vicarage, to proceed on a walking-tour in the north, whence one was to return to his college, and the other to his curacy. Angel might have accompanied them, but preferred to rejoin his sweetheart at Talbothays. He would have been an awkward member of the party; for though the most appreciative humanist, the most ideal religionist, even the best-versed Christologist, of the three, there was alienation in the standing consciousness that his squareness would not fit the round hole that had been prepared for him. To neither Felix nor Cuthbert had he ventured to mention Tess.

His mother made him sandwiches, and his father accompanied him, on his own mare, a little way along the road. Having fairly well advanced his own affairs, Angel listened in a willing silence as they jogged on together through the shady lanes, to his father's account of his parish difficulties, and the coldness of brother clergymen whom he loved, because of his strict interpretations of the New Testament by the light of what they deemed a pernicious Calvinistic doctrine. "Pernicious!" said Mr Clare with genial scorn; and he proceeded to recount experiences which would show the absurdity of that idea. He told of wondrous conversions of evil livers of which he had been the instrument, not only amongst the poor, but amongst the rich and well-to-do; and he also candidly admitted many failures.

As an instance of the latter he mentioned the case of a young upstart squire named d'Urberville, living some forty miles off in the neighbourhood of Trantridge.

"Not one of the ancient d'Urbervilles of Kingsbere and other places?" asked his son. "That curiously historic, worn-out family, with its ghostly legend of the coach-and-four?"

"O no. The original d'Urbervilles decayed and disappeared sixty or eighty years ago—at least I believe so. This seems to be a new family which has taken the name; for the credit of the former knightly line I hope they are spurious, I'm sure. But it is odd to hear you express interest in old families. I thought you set less store by them even than I."

"You misapprehend me, father; you often do," said Angel with a little impatience. "Politically I am sceptical as to the virtue of their being old. Some of the wise even among themselves 'exclaim against their own succession' as Hamlet puts it,* but lyrically, dramatically, and even historically, I am tenderly attached to them."

This distinction, though by no means a subtle one, was yet too subtle for Mr Clare the elder, and he went on with the story he had been about to relate; which was that after the death of the senior so-called d'Urberville the young man developed the most culpable passions, though he had a blind mother whose condition should have made him know better. A knowledge of his career having come to the ears of Mr Clare, when he was in that part of the country preaching missionary sermons, he boldly took occasion to speak to the delinquent on his spiritual state. Though he was a stranger, occupying another's pulpit, he had felt this to be his duty, and took for his text the words from St Luke: "Thou fool, this night thy soul shall be required of thee." The young man much resented this directness of attack, and in the war of words which followed when they met he did not scruple publicly to insult Mr Clare, without respect for his grey hairs.

Angel flushed with distress. "Dear father," he said sadly, "I wish you would not expose yourself to such gratuitous pain from scoundrels!"

"Pain?" said his father, his rugged face shining in the ardour of self-abnegation. "The only pain to me was pain on his account, poor foolish young man. Do you suppose his incensed words could give me any pain, or even his blows?—'Being reviled we bless; being persecuted we suffer it: being defamed we entreat: we are made as the filth of the world, and as the offscouring of all things unto this day.'*—Those ancient and noble words to the Corinthians are strictly true of this present hour."

"Not blows, father. He did not proceed to blows?"

"No—he did not. Though I have borne blows from men in a mad state of intoxication."

"No!"

"A dozen times, my boy. What then? I have saved them from the guilt of murdering their own flesh and blood thereby. And they have lived to thank me, and praise God."

"May this young man do the same!" said Angel fervently. "But I fear otherwise, from what you say."

"We'll hope, nevertheless," said Mr Clare. "And I continue to pray for him—though on this side of the grave we shall probably never meet again. But after all one of those poor words of mine may spring up in his heart as a good seed, some day."

Now, as always, Clare's father was sanguine as a child; and though the younger could not accept his parent's narrow dogma, he revered his practice and recognized the hero under the pietist. Perhaps he revered his father's practice even more now than ever seeing that, in the question of making Tessy his wife, his father had not once thought of inquiring whether she were well-provided or penniless. The same unworldliness was what had necessitated Angel's getting a living as a farmer, and would probably keep his brothers in the position of poor parsons for the term of their activities; yet Angel admired it none the less. Indeed, despite his own heterodoxy, Angel often felt that he was nearer to his father on the human side than was either of his brethren.

XXVII

AN up-hill and down-dale ride of twenty-odd miles through a garish mid-day atmosphere brought him in the afternoon to a detached knoll a mile or two west of Talbothays, whence he again looked into that green trough of sappiness and humidity, the valley of the Var or Froom. Immediately he began to descend from the upland to the fat alluvial soil below, the atmosphere grew heavier; the languid perfume of the summer fruits, the mists, the hay, the flowers, formed therein a vast pool of odour which at this hour seemed to make the animals, the very bees and butterflies, drowsy. Clare was now so familiar with the spot that he knew the individual cows by their names when, a long distance off, he saw them dotted about the meads. It was with a sense of luxury that he recognized his power of viewing life here from its inner side, in a way that had been quite foreign to him in his student-days; and much as he loved his parents he could not help being aware that to come here, as now, after an experience of home-life, affected him like throwing off splints and bandages; even the one customary curb on the humours of English rural societies being absent in this place, Talbothays having no resident landlord.

Not a human being was out-of-doors at the dairy. The denizens were all enjoying the usual afternoon nap of an hour or so, which the exceedingly early hours kept in summer-time rendered a necessity. At the door the wood-hooped pails, sodden and bleached by infinite scrubbings, hung like hats on a stand upon the forked and peeled limb of an oak fixed there for that purpose; all of them ready and dry for the evening milking. Angel entered and went through the silent passages of the house to the back quarters, where he listened for a moment. Sustained snores came from the cart-house, where some of the men were lying down; the grunt and squeal of sweltering pigs arose from the still further distance. The large-leaved rhubarb and cabbage-plants slept too, their broad limp surfaces hanging in the sun like half-closed umbrellas.

He unbridled and fed his horse, and as he re-entered the house the clock struck three. Three was the afternoon skimming-hour; and with the stroke Clare heard the creaking of the floor-boards above, and then the touch of a descending foot on the stairs. It was Tess's, who in another moment came down before his eyes.

She had not heard him enter, and hardly realized his presence there. She was yawning, and he saw the red interior of her mouth as if it had been a snake's. She had stretched one arm so high above her coiled-up cable of hair that he could see its satin delicacy above the sunburn; her face was flushed with sleep, and her eyelids hung heavy over their pupils. The brim-fulness of her nature breathed from her. It was a moment when a woman's soul is more incarnate than at any other time; when the most spiritual beauty bespeaks itself flesh; and sex takes the outside place in the presentation.

Then those eyes flashed brightly through their filmy heaviness, before the remainder of her face was well awake. With an oddly compounded look of gladness, shyness, and surprise, she exclaimed, "O, Mr Clare—how you frightened me—I—"

There had not at first been time for her to think of the changed relations which his declaration had introduced; but the full sense of the matter rose up in her face when she encountered Clare's tender look as he stepped forward to the bottom stair.

"Dear, darling Tessy!" he whispered, putting his arms round her, and his face to her flushed cheek. "Don't for Heaven's sake Mister me any more. I have hastened back so soon, because of you!"

Tess's excitable heart beat against his by way of reply; and there they stood upon the red-brick floor of the entry, the sun slanting in by the window upon his back, as he held her tightly to his breast, upon her inclining face, upon the blue veins of her temple, upon her naked arm, and her neck, and into the depths of her hair. Having been lying down in her clothes she was warm as a sunned cat. At first she would not look straight up at him, but her eyes soon lifted, and his plumbed the deepness of the ever-varying pupils, with their radiating fibrils of blue, and black, and grey, and violet, while she regarded him as Eve at her second waking might have regarded Adam.

"I've got to go a-skimming," she pleaded. "And I have on'y old Deb to help me to-day. Mrs Crick is gone to market with Mr Crick, and Retty is not well, and the others are gone out somewhere, and won't be home till milking."

As they retreated to the milk-house Deborah Fyander appeared on the stairs.

"I have come back, Deborah," said Mr Clare upwards. "So I can help Tess with the skimming; and as you are very tired, I am sure, you needn't come down till milking-time."

Possibly the Talbothays milk was not very thoroughly skimmed that afternoon. Tess was in a dream, wherein familiar objects appeared as having light and shade and position, but no particular outline. Every time she held the skimmer under the pump to cool it for the work, her hand trembled, the ardour of his affection being so palpable that she seemed to flinch under it like a plant in too burning a sun.

Then he pressed her again to his side, and when she had done running her forefinger round the leads to cut off the cream-edge, he cleaned it in nature's way; for the unconstrained manners of Talbothays dairy came convenient now. "I may as well say it now as later, dearest," he resumed gently. "I wish to ask you something, of a very practical nature, which I have been thinking of ever since that day last week in the meads. I shall soon want to marry, and, being a farmer, you see I shall require for my wife a woman who knows all about the management of farms. Will you be that woman Tessy?" He put it in that way that she might not think he had yielded to an impulse of which his head would disapprove.

She turned quite careworn. She had bowed to the inevitable result of proximity, the necessity of loving him; but she had not calculated upon this sudden corollary which, indeed, Clare had put before her without quite meaning himself to do it so soon. With pain that was like the bitterness of dissolution she murmured the words of her indispensable and sworn answer as an honourable woman. "O Mr Clare—I cannot be your wife—I cannot be!" The sound of her own decision seemed to break Tess's very heart, and she bowed her face in her grief.

"But Tess!" he said, amazed at her reply, and holding her still more greedily close. "Do you say no? Surely you love me?"

"O yes, yes! And I would rather be yours than anybody's in the world," returned the sweet and honest voice of the distressed girl. "But I *cannot* marry you."

"Tess," he said holding her at arm's length. "You are engaged to marry some one else!"

"No, no!"

"Then why do you refuse me?"

"I don't want to marry. I have not thought o' doing it. I cannot. I only want to love you."

"But why?"

Driven to subterfuge, she stammered—

"Your father is a parson, and your mother wouldn' like you to marry such as me. She will want you to marry a lady."

"Nonsense—I have spoken to them both. That was partly why I went home."

"I feel I cannot—never, never!" she echoed.

"Is it too sudden to be asked thus, my pretty?"

"Yes—I did not expect it."

"If you will let it pass, please, Tessy, I will give you time," he said. "It was very abrupt to come home and speak to you all at once. I'll not allude to it again for a while."

She again took up the shining skimmer, held it beneath the pump, and began anew. But she could not, as at other times, hit the exact under-surface of the cream with the delicate dexterity required, try as she might: sometimes she was cutting down into the milk, sometimes in the air. She could hardly see, her eyes having filled with two blurring tears drawn forth by a grief which, to this her best friend and dear advocate, she could never explain.

"I can't skim—I can't!" she said turning away from him.

Not to agitate and hinder her longer the considerate Clare began talking in a more general way. "You quite misapprehend my parents. They are the most simple-mannered people alive, and quite unambitious. They are two of the few remaining Evangelical school. Tessy, are you an Evangelical?"

"I don't know."

"You go to church very regularly, and our parson here is not very high,* they tell me."

Tess's ideas on the views of the parish clergyman, whom she heard every week, seemed to be rather more vague than Clare's, who had never heard him at all. "I wish I could fix my mind on what I hear there more firmly than I do," she remarked as a safe generality. "It is often a great sorrow to me."

She spoke so unaffectedly that Angel was sure in his heart that his father could not object to her on religious grounds, even though she did not know whether her principles were High, Low, or Broad.* He himself knew that, in reality, the confused beliefs which she held, apparently imbibed in childhood, were, if anything, Tractarian as to phraseology* and pantheistic as to essence. Confused or otherwise, to disturb them was his last desire:

> Leave thou thy sister, when she prays,
> 　Her early Heaven, her happy views;
> 　Nor thou with shadow'd hint confuse
> A life that leads melodious days.*

He had occasionally thought the counsel less honest than musical; but he gladly conformed to it now.

He spoke further of the incidents of his visit, of his father's mode of life, of his zeal for his principles; she grew serener, and the undulations disappeared from her skimming; as she finished one lead after another he followed her, and drew the plugs for letting down the milk.*

"I fancied you looked a little downcast, when you came in," she ventured to observe, anxious to keep away from the subject of herself.

"Yes. . . . Well, my father has been talking a good deal to me of his troubles and difficulties, and the subject always tends to depress me. He is so zealous that he gets many snubs and buffetings from people of a different way of thinking from himself, and I don't like to hear of such humiliations to a man of his age; the more particularly as I don't think earnestness does any good when carried so far. . . . He has been telling me of a very unpleasant scene in which he took part recently. He went as the deputy of some missionary society to preach in the neighbourhood of Trantridge, a place forty miles from here, and made it his business to expostulate with a lax young cynic he met somewhere about there—son of some landowner up that way—and who has a mother afflicted with blindness. My father addressed himself to the gentleman point-blank, and there was quite a disturbance. It was very foolish of my father, I must say, to intrude his conversation upon a stranger when the probabilities were so obvious that it would be useless. But whatever he thinks to be his duty, that he'll do, in season or out of season; and of course he makes many enemies, not only among the absolutely vicious, but among the easy-going, who hate being bothered. He says he glories in what happened, and that good may be done indirectly; but I wish he would not so wear himself out now he is getting old, and would leave such pigs to their wallowing."

Tess's look had grown hard and worn, and her ripe mouth tragical; but she no longer showed any tremulousness. Clare's revived thoughts of his father prevented his noticing her particularly; and so they went on down the white row of liquid rectangles till they had finished and drained them off; when the other maids returned, and took their pails, and Deb came to scald out the leads for the new milk. As Tess withdrew, to go afield to the cows, he said to her softly, "And my question, Tessy?"

"O no, no!" replied she with grave hopelessness, as one who had heard anew the turmoil of her own past in the allusion to Alec d'Urberville. "It *can't* be!"

She went out towards the mead, joining the other milkmaids with a bound, as if trying to make the open air drive away her sad constraint. All the girls drew onward to the spot where the cows were grazing in the further mead, the bevy advancing with the bold grace of wild animals—the reckless, unchastened motion of women accustomed to unlimited space—in which they abandoned themselves to the air as a swimmer to the wave. It seemed natural enough to him, now that Tess was again in sight, to choose a mate from unconstrained Nature, and not from the abodes of Art.

XXVIII

Her refusal, though unexpected, did not permanently daunt Clare. His experience of women was great enough for him to be aware that the negative often meant nothing more than the preface to the affirmative; and it was little enough for him not to know that in the manner of the present negative there lay a great exception to the dallyings of coyness. That she had already permitted him to make love to her he read as an additional assurance, not fully trowing that in fields and pastures to "sigh gratis" is by no means deemed waste;* love-making being here more often accepted inconsiderately and for its own sweet sake than in the carking anxious homes of the ambitious, where a girl's craving for an establishment paralyzes her healthy thought of a passion as an end.

"Tess, why did you say 'no' in such a positive way?" he asked her in the course of a few days.

She started. "Don't ask me. I told you why—partly. I am not good enough—not worthy enough."

"How? Not fine lady enough?"

"Yes—something like that," murmured she. "Your friends would scorn me."

"Indeed, you mistake them—my father and mother. As for my brothers I don't care—" He clasped his fingers behind her back to keep her from slipping away. "Now—you did not mean it, sweet? I am sure you did not! You have made me so restless that I cannot read, or play, or do anything. I am in no hurry, Tess, but I want to know—to hear from your own warm lips—that you will some day be mine—any time you may choose; but some day?"

She could only shake her head and look away from him.

Clare regarded her attentively, conned the characters of her face as if they had been hieroglyphics. The denial seemed real. "Then I ought not to hold you in this way—ought I? I have no right to you—no right to seek out where you are, or to walk with you! . . . . Honestly Tess, do you love any other man?"

"How can you ask!" she said with continued self-suppression.

"I almost know that you do not. But then, why do you repulse me?"

"I don't repulse you. I like you to—tell me you love me: and you may always tell me so as you go about with me—and never offend me!"

"But you will not accept me as a husband?"

"Ah—that's different—it is for your good, indeed my dearest! O believe me, it is only for your sake! I don't like to give myself the great happiness o' promising to be yours in that way—because—because I am *sure* I ought not to do it."

"But you will make me happy!"

"Ah—you think so, but you don't know."

At such times as this, apprehending the grounds of her refusal to be her modest sense of incompetence in matters social and polite, he would say that she was wonderfully well-informed and versatile—which was certainly true, her natural quickness, and her admiration for him, having led her to pick up his vocabulary, his accent, and fragments of his knowledge, to a surprising extent. After these tender contests, and her victory, she would go away by herself under the remotest cow, if at milking-time, or into the sedge, or into her room, if at a leisure interval, and mourn silently, not a minute after an apparently phlegmatic negative.

The struggle was so fearful: her own heart was so strongly on the side of his—two ardent hearts against one poor little conscience—that she tried to fortify her resolution by every means in her power. She had come to Talbothays with a made-up mind. On no account could she agree to a step which might afterwards cause bitter rueing to her husband for his blindness in wedding her. And she held that what her conscience had decided for her when her mind was unbiassed ought not to be overruled now.

"Why don't somebody tell him all about me?" she said. "It was only forty miles off—why hasn't it reached here? Somebody must know!"

Yet nobody seemed to know; nobody told him.

For two or three days no more was said. She guessed from the sad countenances of her chamber-companions that they regarded her not only as the favourite but as the chosen; but they could see for themselves that she did not put herself in his way.

Tess had never before known a time in which the thread of her life was so distinctly twisted of two strands, positive pleasure and positive pain. At the next cheese making the pair were again left alone together. The dairyman himself had been lending a hand; but Mr Crick, as well as his wife, seemed latterly to have acquired a suspicion of mutual interest between these two; though they walked so circumspectly that suspicion was but of the faintest. Anyhow the dairyman left them to themselves.

They were breaking up the masses of curd before putting them into the vats. The operation resembled the act of crumbling bread on a large scale; and amid the immaculate whiteness of the curds Tess Durbeyfield's hands showed themselves of the pinkness of the rose. Angel, who was filling the vats with his handfuls, suddenly ceased, and laid his hands flat upon hers. Her sleeves were rolled far above the elbow, and bending lower, he kissed the inside vein of her soft arm.

Although the early September weather was sultry, her arm, from her dabbling in the curds, was as cold and damp to his mouth as a new-gathered mushroom, and tasted of the whey. But she was such a sheaf of susceptibilities that her pulse was accelerated by the touch, her blood driven to her finger-ends and the cool arms flushed hot. Then, as though her heart had said, "Is coyness longer necessary? Truth is truth between man and woman, as between man and man," she lifted her eyes, and they beamed devotedly into his as her lip rose in a tender half-smile.

"Do you know why I did that, Tess?" he said.

"Because you love me very much!"

"Yes: and as a preliminary to a new entreaty."

"Not *again*!" She looked a sudden fear that her resistance might break down under her own desire.

"O Tessy!" he went on; "I *cannot* think why you are so tantalizing. Why do you disappoint me so? You seem almost like a coquette,— upon my life you do—a coquette of the first urban water! They blow hot and blow cold, just as you do; and it is the very last sort of thing to expect to find in a retreat like Talbothays. . . . And yet dearest," he quickly added, observing how the remark had cut her, "I know you to be the most honest, spotless creature that ever lived. So how can I suppose you a flirt? Tess, why don't you like the idea of being my wife, if you love me as you seem to do?"

"I have never said I don't like the idea, and I never could say it; because—it isn't true!" The stress now getting beyond endurance her lip quivered, and she was obliged to go away.

Clare was so pained and perplexed that he ran after, and caught her in the passage. "Tell me, tell me!" he said, passionately clasping her, in forgetfulness of his curdy hands. "Do tell me that you won't belong to anybody but me!"

"I will, I will tell you!" she exclaimed. "And I will give you a complete answer, if you will let me go now. I will tell you my experience—all about myself—all!"

"Your experiences, dear; yes, certainly; any number." He expressed assent in loving satire, looking into her face. "My Tess has, no doubt, almost as many experiences as that wild convolvulus out there on the garden hedge, that opened itself this morning for the first time.— Tell me anything; but don't use that wretched expression any more about not being worthy of me."

"I will try—not! And I'll give you my reasons to-morrow—next week."

"Say on Sunday?"

"Yes, on Sunday."

At last she got away, and did not stop in her retreat till she was in the thicket of pollard willows* at the lower side of the barton, where she could be quite unseen. Here Tess flung herself down upon the rustling undergrowth of spear-grass as upon a bed, and remained crouching in palpitating misery broken by momentary shoots of joy, which her fears about the ending could not altogether suppress.

In reality she was drifting into acquiescence. Every see-saw of her breath, every wave of her blood, every pulse singing in her ears, was a voice that joined with Nature in revolt against her scrupulousness. Reckless, inconsiderate acceptance of him; to close with him at the altar, revealing nothing, and chancing discovery; to snatch ripe pleasure before the iron teeth of pain could have time to shut upon her; that was what love counselled; and in almost a terror of ecstasy Tess divined that, despite her many months of lonely self-chastisement, wrestlings, communings, schemes to lead a future of austere isolation, love's counsel would prevail.

The afternoon advanced, and still she remained among the willows. She heard the rattle of taking down the pails from the forked stands; the "waow-waow!" which accompanied the getting together of the cows. But she did not go to the milking. They would see her agitation; and the dairyman, thinking the cause to be love alone, would good-naturedly tease her; and that harassment could not be borne.

Her lover must have guessed her overwrought state and invented some excuse for her non-appearance, for no inquiries were made or calls given. At half-past six the sun settled down upon the levels, with the aspect of a great forge in the heavens, and presently a monstrous pumpkin-like moon arose on the other hand. The pollard willows, tortured out of their natural shape by incessant choppings, became spiny-haired monsters as they stood up against it. She went in, and upstairs, without a light.

It was now Wednesday. Thursday came, and Angel looked thoughtfully at her from a distance, but intruded in no way upon her. The indoor milkmaids Marian and the rest seemed to guess that something definite was afoot, for they did not force any remarks upon her in the bedchamber. Friday passed; Saturday. To-morrow was the day.

"I shall give way—I shall say yes—I shall let myself marry him—I cannot help it!" she jealously panted, with her hot face to the pillow that night, on hearing one of the other girls sigh his name in her sleep. "I can't bear to let anybody have him but me! Yet it is a wrong to him, and may kill him when he knows! O my heart—O, O, O!"

XXIX

"Now who mid ye think I've heard news o' this morning?" said Dairyman Crick as he sat down to breakfast next day, with a riddling gaze round upon the munching men and maids. "Now just who mid ye think?"

One guessed, and another guessed. Mrs Crick did not guess, because she knew already.

"Well," said the dairyman, " 'tis that slack-twisted 'hore's-bird of a feller Jack Dollop. He's lately got married to a widow-woman."

"Not Jack Dollop? A villain—to think o' that!" said a milker.

The name entered quickly into Tess Durbeyfield's consciousness, for it was the name of the lover who had wronged his sweetheart, and had afterwards been so roughly used by the young woman's mother in the butter-churn.

"And has he married the valiant matron's daughter, as he promised?" asked Angel Clare absently, as he turned over the news-paper he was reading at the little table to which he was always banished by Mrs Crick, in her sense of his gentility.

"Not he, sir. Never meant to," replied the dairyman. "As I say, 'tis a widow-woman. And she had money it seems—fifty poun' a year or so; and that was all he was after. They were married in a great hurry; and then she told him that by marrying she had lost her fifty poun' a year. Just fancy the state o' my gentleman's mind at that news! Never such a cat-and-dog life as they've been leading ever since! Serves him well beright. But onluckily the poor woman gets the worst o't."

"Well, the silly body should have told en sooner that the ghost of her first man would trouble him," said Mrs Crick.

"Ay; ay," responded the dairyman indecisively. "Still, you can see exactly how 'twas: she wanted a home, and didn't like to run the risk of losing him. Don't ye think that was something like it, maidens?" He glanced towards the row of girls.

"She ought to ha' told him just before they went to church, when he could hardly have backed out," exclaimed Marian.

"Yes—she ought," agreed Izz.

"She must have seen what he was after, and should ha' refused him!" cried Retty spasmodically.

"And what do you say, my dear?" asked the dairyman of Tess.

"I think she ought—to have told him the true state of things—or else refused him—I don't know," replied Tess, the bread-and-butter choking her.

"Be cust if I'd have done either o't," said Beck Knibbs, a married helper from one of the cottages. "All's fair in love and war. I'd ha' married en just as she did, and if he'd said two words to me about not telling him beforehand anything whatsomdever about my first chap that I hadn't chose to tell, I'd ha' knocked him down wi' the rolling-pin—a scram little feller like he! Any woman could do it."

The laughter which followed this sally, was supplemented only by a sorry smile for form's sake from Tess. What was comedy to them was tragedy to her; and she could hardly bear their mirth. She soon rose from table, and with an impression that Clare would follow her, went along a little wriggling path, now stepping to one side of the irrigating channels, and now to the other, till she stood by the main stream of the Var. Men had been cutting the water-weeds higher up the river, and masses of them were floating past her—moving islands of green crowfoot, whereon she might almost have ridden; long locks of the weed had lodged against the piles driven to keep the cows from crossing.

Yes; there was the pain of it. This question of a woman telling her story—the heaviest of crosses to herself—seemed but amusement to others. It was as if people should laugh at martyrdom.

"Tessy!" came from behind her and Clare sprang across the gully alighting beside her feet. "My wife—soon!"

"No. No. I cannot. For your sake, O Mr Clare; for your sake, I say no."

"Tess!"

"Still I say no!" she repeated.

Not expecting this he had put his arm lightly round her waist the moment after speaking, beneath her hanging tail of hair. (The younger dairymaids, including Tess, breakfasted with their hair loose on Sunday mornings, before building it up extra high for attending church, a style they could not adopt when milking with their heads against the cows.) If she had said "Yes" instead of "No" he would have kissed her: it had evidently been his intention; but her determined negative deterred his scrupulous heart. Their condition of domiciliary comradeship put her, as the woman, to such disadvantage by its enforced intercourse, that he felt it unfair to her to exercise any pressure of blandishment, which he might have honestly employed had she been better able to avoid him. He released her momentarily imprisoned waist, and withheld the kiss.

It all turned on that release. What had given her strength to refuse him this time was solely the tale of the widow told by the dairyman; and that would have been overcome in another moment. But Angel said no more: his face was perplexed; he went away.

Day after day they met—somewhat less constantly than before; and thus two or three weeks went by. The end of September drew near; and she could see in his eye that he might ask her again.

His plan of procedure was different now—as though he had made up his mind that her negatives were, after all, only coyness and youth, startled by the novelty of the proposal. The fitful evasiveness of her manner when the subject was under discussion, countenanced the idea. So he played a more coaxing game; and while never going beyond words, or attempting the renewal of caresses, he did his utmost orally.

In this way Clare persistently wooed her in undertones like that of the purling milk—at the cow's side, at skimmings, at buttermakings, at cheesemakings, among broody poultry,* and among farrowing pigs—as no milkmaid was ever wooed before by such a man.

Tess knew that she must break down. Neither a religious sense of a certain moral validity in the previous union nor a conscientious wish for candour could hold out against it much longer. She loved him so passionately; and he was so godlike in her eyes; and being, though untrained, instinctively refined, her nature cried for his tutelary guidance. And thus, though Tess kept repeating to herself "I can never be his wife," the words were vain. A proof of her weakness lay in the very utterance of what calm strength would not have taken the trouble to formulate. Every sound of his voice beginning on the old subject stirred her with a terrifying bliss, and she coveted the recantation she feared.

His manner was—what man's is not—so much that of one who would love and cherish and defend her, under any conditions, changes, charges, or revelations, that her gloom lessened as she basked in it. The season meanwhile was drawing onward to the equinox, and though it was still fine the days were much shorter. The dairy had again worked by morning candlelight for a long time; and a fresh renewal of Clare's pleading occurred one morning between three and four.

She had run up in her bed-gown to his door to call him as usual: then had gone back to dress and call the others; and in ten minutes was walking to the head of the stairs with the candle in her hand. At the same moment he came down his steps from above in his shirt-sleeves and put his arm across the stair-way.

"Now, Miss Flirt, before you go down," he said peremptorily. "It is a fortnight since I spoke, and this won't do any longer. You *must* tell me what you mean, or I shall have to leave this house. My door was ajar just now, and I saw you. For your own safety I must go. You don't know. Well? Is it to be yes at last?"

"I am only just up, Mr Clare, and—it is too early to take me to task!" she pouted. "You need not call me Flirt. 'Tis cruel and untrue. Wait till by and by. Please wait till by and by! I will really think seriously about it between now and then. Now let me go downstairs!"

She looked a little like what he said she was as, holding the candle sideways, she tried to smile away the seriousness of his words.

"Call me Angel then, and not Mr Clare."

"Angel."

"Angel dearest—why not?"

" 'Twould mean that I agree, wouldn't it?"

"It would only mean that you love me, even if you cannot marry me; and you were so good as to own that long ago."

"Very well then: 'Angel dearest', if I *must*," she murmured looking at her candle, a roguish curl coming upon her mouth, notwithstanding her suspense.

Clare had resolved never to kiss her until he had obtained her promise; but somehow, as Tess stood there in her prettily tucked-up milking-gown, her hair carelessly heaped upon her head till there should be leisure to arrange it when skimming and milking were done, he broke his resolve, and brought his lips to her cheek for one moment. She passed downstairs very quickly, never looking back at him or saying another word. The other maids were already down, and the subject was not pursued. Except Marian they all looked wistfully and suspiciously at the pair in the sad yellow rays which the morning candles emitted, in contrast with the first cold signals of the dawn without.

When skimming was done—which, as the milk diminished with the approach of autumn, was a lessening process day by day—Retty and the rest went out. The lovers followed them.

"Our tremulous lives are so different from theirs, are they not," he musingly observed to her, as he regarded the three figures tripping before him through the frigid pallor of opening day.

"Not so very different, I think," she said.

"Why do you think that?"

"There are very few women's lives that are not—tremulous," Tess replied, pausing over the new word as if it impressed her. "There's more in those three than you think."

"What is in them?"

"Almost—either of 'em," she began, "would make—perhaps would make—a properer wife than I. And perhaps they love you as well as I—almost."

"O Tessy!"

There were signs that it was an exquisite relief to her to hear the impatient exclamation, though she had resolved so intrepidly to let generosity make one bid against herself. That was now done, and she had not the power to attempt self-immolation a second time then. They were joined by a milker from one of the cottages, and no more was said on that which concerned them so deeply. But Tess knew that this day would decide it.

In the afternoon several of the dairyman's household and assistants went down to the meads as usual, a long way from the dairy, where many of the cows were milked without being driven home. The supply was getting less as the animals advanced in calf, and the supernumerary milkers of the lush green season had been dismissed.

The work progressed leisurely. Each pailful was poured into tall cans that stood in a large spring-waggon which had been brought upon the scene; and when they were milked the cows trailed away.

Dairyman Crick, who was there with the rest, his wrapper gleaming miraculously white against a leaden evening sky, suddenly looked at his heavy watch.

"Why, 'tis later than I thought," he said. "Begad—we shan't be soon enough with this milk at the station, if we don't mind! There's no time to-day to take it home and mix it with the bulk afore sending off. It must go to station straight from here. Who'll drive it across?"

Mr Clare volunteered to do so, though it was none of his business, asking Tess to accompany him. The evening though sunless, had been warm and muggy for the season, and Tess had come out with her milking-hood only, naked-armed and jacketless; certainly not dressed for a drive. She therefore replied by glancing over her scant habiliments; but Clare gently urged her. She assented by relinquishing her pail and stool to the dairyman to take home; and mounted the spring-waggon beside Clare.

XXX

In the diminishing daylight they went along the level roadway through the meads, which stretched away into grey miles, and were backed in the extreme edge of distance by the swarthy and abrupt slopes of Egdon Heath. On its summits stood clumps and stretches of fir-trees, whose notched tips appeared like battlemented towers crowning black-fronted castles of enchantment.

They were so absorbed in the sense of being close to each other that they did not begin talking for a long while, the silence being broken only by the clucking of the milk in the tall cans behind them. The lane they followed was so solitary that the hazel nuts had remained on the boughs till they slipped from their shells, and the blackberries hung in heavy clusters. Every now and then Angel would fling the lash of his whip round one of these, pluck it off, and give it to his companion.

The dull sky soon began to tell its meaning by sending down herald-drops of rain, and the stagnant air of the day changed into a fitful breeze which played about their faces. The quicksilvery glaze on the rivers and pools vanished; from broad mirrors of light they changed to lustreless sheets of lead, with a surface like a rasp. But that spectacle did not affect her preoccupation. Her countenance, a natural carnation slightly embrowned by the season, had deepened its tinge with the beating of the rain-drops, and her hair, which the pressure of the cows' flanks had as usual caused to tumble down from its fastenings and stray beyond the curtain of her calico bonnet, was made clammy by the moisture, till it hardly was better than seaweed.

"I ought not to have come, I suppose," she murmured looking at the sky.

"I am sorry for the rain," said he. "But how glad I am to have you here!"

Remote Egdon disappeared by degrees behind the liquid gauze. The evening grew darker, and the roads being crossed by gates it was not safe to drive faster than at a walking pace. The air was rather chill.

"I am so afraid you will get cold, with nothing upon your arms and shoulders," he said. "Creep close to me, and perhaps the drizzle won't hurt you much. I should be sorrier still if I did not think that the rain might be helping me."

She imperceptibly crept closer, and he wrapped round them both a large piece of sail-cloth which was sometimes used to keep the sun off the milk-cans. Tess held it from slipping off him as well as herself, Clare's hands being occupied.

"Now we are all right again. Ah—no we are not! It runs down into my neck a little, and it must still more into yours. . . . That's better. Your arms are like wet marble, Tess. Wipe them in the cloth. Now if you stay quiet you will not get another drop. Well, dear—about that question of mine—that long-standing question?"

The only reply that he could hear for a little while was the smack of the horse's hoofs on the moistening road, and the cluck of the milk in the cans behind them.

"Do you remember what you said?"

"I do," she replied.

"Before we get home, mind."

"I'll try."

He said no more then. As they drove on the fragment of an old manor-house of Caroline date* rose against the sky: and was in due course passed and left behind.

"That," he observed, to entertain her, "is an interesting old place—one of the several seats which belonged to an ancient Norman family, formerly of great influence in the county—the d'Urbervilles. I never pass one of their residences without thinking of them. There is something very sad in the extinction of a family of renown—even if it was fierce, domineering, feudal renown."

"Yes," said Tess.

They crept along towards a point in the expanse of shade just at hand at which a feeble light was beginning to assert its presence; a spot where, by day, a fitful white streak of steam at intervals upon the dark green background denoted intermittent moments of contact between their secluded world and modern life. Modern life stretched out its steam feeler to this point three or four times a day, touched the native existences, and quickly withdrew its feeler again, as if what it touched had been uncongenial.

They reached the feeble light, which came from the smoky lamp of a little railway-station; a poor enough terrestrial star, yet in one sense of more importance to Talbothays Dairy and mankind than the celestial ones to which it stood in such humiliating contrast. The cans of new milk were unladen in the rain, Tess getting a little shelter from a neighbouring holly-tree.

Then there was the hissing of a train which drew up almost silently upon the wet rails, and the milk was rapidly swung can by can into the truck. The light of the engine flashed for a second upon Tess Durbeyfield's figure, motionless under the great holly-tree. No object could have looked more foreign to the gleaming cranks and wheels than this unsophisticated girl with the round bare arms, the rainy face and hair, the suspended attitude of a friendly leopard at pause, the print gown of no date or fashion, and the cotton bonnet drooping on her brow.

She mounted again beside her lover with a mute obedience characteristic of impassioned natures at times, and when they had wrapped themselves up, over head and ears, in the sail-cloth again, they plunged back into the now thick night. Tess was so receptive that the few minutes of contact with the whirl of material progress lingered in her thought.

"Londoners will drink it at their breakfasts to-morrow, won't they?" she asked. "Strange people, that we have never seen."

"Yes—I suppose they will. Though not as we send it. When its strength has been lowered so that it may not get up into their heads."

"Noble men and noble women—ambassadors and centurions— ladies and tradeswomen—and babies who have never seen a cow."

"Well, yes; perhaps; particularly centurions."

"Who don't know anything of us, and of where it comes from; or think how we two drove miles across the moor to-night in the rain that it might reach 'em in time."

"We did not drive entirely on account of these precious Londoners: we drove a little on our own—on account of that anxious matter which you will I am sure set at rest, dear Tess. Now, permit me to put it in this way: you belong to me already, you know; your heart I mean. Does it not?"

"You know as well as I. O yes, yes!"

"Then if your heart does, why not your hand?"

"My only reason was—on account of you—on account of a question—I have something to tell you—"

"But suppose it to be entirely for my happiness, and my worldly convenience also?"

"O yes—if it is for your happiness, and worldly convenience.—But my life before I came here—I want—"

"Well, it is for my convenience as well as my happiness. If I have a very large farm, either English or colonial, you will be invaluable as a wife to me; better than a woman out of the largest mansion in the county. So please, please dear Tessy disabuse your mind of the feeling that you will stand in my way."

"But my history. I want you to know it—you must let me tell—you will not like me so well!"

"Tell it if you wish to, dearest. This precious history then. Yes: I was born at so and so, Anno Domini—"

"I was born at Marlott," she said, catching at his words as a help, lightly as they were spoken. "And I grew up there. And I was in the sixth standard* when I left school, and they said I had great aptness, and should make a good teacher, so it was settled that I should be one. But there was trouble in my family: father was not very industrious, and he drank a little."

"Yes—yes. Poor child! Nothing new." He pressed her more closely to his side.

"And then—there is something very unusual about it—about me. I—I was—" Tess's breath quickened.

"Yes, dearest. Never mind."

"I—I.... am not a Durbeyfield, but a d'Urberville—a descendant of the same family as those that owned the old house we passed. And—we are all gone to nothing!"

"A d'Urberville.... Indeed! And is that all the trouble, dear Tess?"

"Yes," she answered faintly.

"Well—why should I love you less after knowing this?"

"I was told by the dairyman that you hated old families."

He laughed. "Well, it is true, in one sense. I do hate the aristocratic principle of blood before everything, and do think that as reasoners the only pedigrees we ought to respect are those spiritual ones of the wise and virtuous, without regard to corporeal paternity. But I am extremely interested in this news—you can have no idea how interested I am. Are you not interested yourself in being one of that well-known line?"

"No. I have thought it sad—especially since coming here, and knowing that many of the hills and fields I see once belonged to my father's people. But other hills and fields belonged to Retty's people, and perhaps others to Marian's, so that I don't value it particularly."

"Yes—it is surprising how many of the present tillers of the soil were once owners of it, and I sometimes wonder that a certain school of politicians don't make capital of the circumstance; but they don't seem to know it. . . . I wonder that I did not see the resemblance of your name to d'Urberville, and trace the manifest corruption. And this was the carking secret!"

She had not told. At the last moment her courage had failed her, she feared his blame for not telling him sooner; and her instinct of self-preservation was stronger than her candour.

"Of course," continued the unwitting Clare, "I should have been glad to know you to be descended exclusively from the long-suffering, dumb, unrecorded rank-and-file of the English nation, and not from the self-seeking few who made themselves powerful at the expense of the rest. But I am corrupted away from that by my affection for you, Tess, [he laughed as he spoke] and made selfish likewise. For your own sake I rejoice in your descent. Society is hopelessly snobbish, and this fact of your extraction may make an appreciable difference to its acceptance of you as my wife, after I have made you the well-read woman that I mean to make you. My mother, too, poor soul, will think so much better of you on account of it. Tess, you must spell your name correctly—d'Urberville—from this very day."

"I like the other way, rather best."

"But you *must*, dearest! Good heavens, why dozens of mushroom-millionaires would jump at such a possession! By the by, there's one of that kidney who has taken the name—where have I heard of him?—Up in the neighbourhood of The Chase, I think. Why, he is the very man who had that rumpus with my father I told you of. What an odd coincidence!"

"Angel, I think I would rather not take—the name! It is unlucky, perhaps." She was agitated.

"Now then, Mistress Teresa d'Urberville, I have you. Take my name, and so you will escape yours! The secret is out, so why should you any longer refuse me?"

"If it is *sure* to make you happy to have me as your wife, and you feel that you do wish to marry me, *very very* much—"

"I do dearest, of course!"

"I mean, that it is only your wanting me very much, and being hardly able to keep alive without me, whatever my offences, that would make me feel I ought to say I will."

"You will—you do say it, I know. You will be mine for ever and ever." He clasped her close and kissed her.

"Yes." She had no sooner said it than she burst into a dry hard sobbing, so violent that it seemed to rend her. Tess was not a hysterical girl by any means, and he was surprised.

"Why do you cry dearest?"

"I can't tell—quite!—I am so glad to think—of being yours, and making you happy."

"But this does not seem very much like gladness, my Tessy."

"I mean—I cry because I have broken down in my vow! I said I would die unmarried."

"But if you love me, you would like me to be your husband?"

"Yes, yes, yes! But O, I sometimes wish I had never been born!"

"Now, my dear Tess, if I did not know that you are very much excited, and very inexperienced, I should say that remark was not very complimentary. How came you to wish that if you care for me? Do you care for me? I wish you would prove it in some way."

"How can I prove it more than I have done?" She cried in a distraction of tenderness. "Will this prove it more?" She clasped his neck, and for the first time Clare learnt what an impassioned woman's kisses were like upon the lips of one whom she loved with all her heart and soul, as Tess loved him. "There—now do you believe?" she asked, flushed, and wiping her eyes.

"Yes. I never really doubted—never, never!"

So they drove on through the gloom, forming one bundle inside the sail-cloth, the horse going as he would, and the rain driving against them. She had consented. She might as well have agreed at first. The "appetite for joy", which pervades all creation; that tremendous force which sways humanity to its purpose, as the tide sways the helpless weed, was not to be controlled by vague lucubrations over the social rubric.

"I must write to my mother," she said. "You don't mind my doing that?"

"Of course not, dear child. You are a child to me, Tess, not to know how very proper it is to write to your mother at such a time, and how wrong it would be in me to object. Where does she live?"

"At the same place—Marlott. On the further side of Blackmoor Vale."

"Ah—then I *have* seen you before this summer—"

"Yes; at that dance on the green. But you would not dance with me. O I hope that is of no ill-omen for us now!"

XXXI

TESS wrote a most touching and urgent letter to her mother the very next day; and by the end of the week a response to her communication arrived, in Joan Durbeyfield's wandering, last-century hand.

Dear Tess,

J write these few lines hoping they will find you well, as they leave me at present thank God for it. Dear Tess we are all glad to hear that you are going really to be married soon. But with respect to your question Tess J say between ourselves quite private, but very strong, that on no account do you say a word of your bygone Trouble to him. J did not tell everything to your father, he being so proud on account of his respectability, which perhaps your Intended is the same. Many a woman, some of the Highest in the Land, have had a Trouble in their time; and why should you Trumpet yours when others don't Trumpet theirs? No girl would be such a fool, specially as it is so long ago, and not your Fault at all. J shall answer the same if you ask me Fifty Times. Besides, you must bear in mind that knowing it to be your childish nature to tell all that's in your Heart, so simple, J made you promise me never to let it out by Word or Deed, having your welfare in my mind, and you most solemnly did promise it going from this Door. J have not named either that question of your coming marriage to your father, as he would blab it everywhere, poor Simple Man.

Dear Tess keep up your Spirits and we mean to send you a Hogshead of Cyder* for your wedding knowing there is not much in your parts and thin Sour Stuff what there is. So no more at present and with kind love to your Young Man

From your affectte. mother
J. Durbeyfield.

"O mother mother!" murmured Tess.

She was recognizing how light was the touch of events the most oppressive upon Mrs Durbeyfield's elastic spirit. Her mother did not see life as Tess saw it. That haunting episode of bygone days was to her mother but a passing accident. But perhaps her mother was right as to the course to be followed, whatever she might be in her reasons. Silence seemed, on the face of it, best for her adored one's happiness: silence it should be.

Thus steadied by a command from the only person in the world who had any shadow of right to control her action, Tess grew calmer. The responsibility was shifted; and her heart was lighter than it had been for weeks. The days of declining autumn which followed her assent, beginning with the month of October, formed a season through which she lived in spiritual altitudes more nearly approaching ecstasy than any other period of her life.

There was hardly a touch of earth in her love for Clare. To her sublime trustfulness he was all that goodness could be, knew all that a guide, philosopher, and friend should know. She thought every line in the contour of his person the perfection of masculine beauty; his soul the soul of a saint; his intellect that of a seer. The wisdom of her love for him, as love, sustained her dignity; she seemed to be wearing a crown. The compassion of his love for her, as she saw it, made her lift up her heart to him in devotion. He would sometimes catch her large worshipful eyes, that had no bottom to them, looking at him from their depths, as if she saw something immortal before her.

She dismissed the past; trod upon it and put it out, as one treads on a coal that is smouldering and dangerous.

She had not known that men could be so disinterested, chivalrous, protective, in their love for women as he. Angel Clare was far from all that she thought him in this respect; absurdly far, indeed; but he was in truth more spiritual than animal; he had himself well in hand, and was singularly free from grossness. Though not cold-natured he was rather bright than hot; less Byronic than Shelleyan.* He could love desperately, but with a love more especially inclined to the imaginative and ethereal; it was a fastidious emotion which could jealously guard the loved one against his very self. This amazed and enraptured Tess, whose slight experiences had been so infelicitous till now; and in her reaction from indignation against the male sex she swerved to excess of honour for Clare.

They unaffectedly sought each other's company; in her honest faith she did not disguise her desire to be with him. The sum of her instincts on this matter, if clearly stated, would have been that the elusive quality in her sex which attracts men in general might be distasteful to so perfect a man after an avowal of love, since it must in its very nature carry with it a suspicion of art.

The country custom of unreserved comradeship out-of-doors during betrothal was the only custom she knew, and to her it had no strangeness; though it seemed oddly anticipative to Clare, till he saw how normal a thing she, in common with all the other dairy-folk, regarded it. Thus during this October month of wonderful afternoons they roved along the meads by creeping paths which followed the brinks of trickling tributary brooks, hopping across by little wooden bridges to the other side and back again. They were never out of the sound of some purling weir, whose buzz accompanied their own murmuring, while the beams of the sun, almost as horizontal as the mead itself, formed a pollen of radiance over the landscape. They saw tiny blue fogs in the shadows of trees and hedges, all the time that there was bright sunshine elsewhere. The sun was so near the ground, and the sward so flat, that the shadows of Clare and Tess would stretch a quarter of a mile ahead of them, like two long fingers pointing afar to where the green alluvial reaches abutted against the sloping sides of the vale.

Men were at work here and there—for it was the season for "taking up" the meadows, or digging the little waterways clear for the winter irrigation, and mending their banks where trodden down by the cows. The shovelfuls of loam, black as jet, brought there by the river when it was as wide as the whole valley were an essence of soils; pounded champaigns* of the past, steeped, refined and subtilized, to extraordinary richness, out of which came all the fertility of the mead, and of the cattle grazing there.

Clare hardily kept his arm round her waist in sight of these watermen, with the air of a man who was accustomed to public dalliance, though actually as shy as she who, with lips parted, and eyes askance on the labourers, wore the look of a wary animal the while.

"You are not ashamed of owning me as yours before them!" she said gladly.

"O no!"

"But if it should reach the ears of your friends at Emminster that you are walking about like this with me, a milkmaid—"

"The most bewitching milkmaid ever seen."

"—They might feel it a hurt to their dignity."

"My dear girl. A d'Urberville hurt the dignity of a Clare! It is a grand card to play—that of your belonging to such a family, and I am reserving it for a grand effect when we are married, and have the proofs of your descent, from Parson Tringham. Apart from that my future is to be totally foreign to my family—it will not affect even the surface of their lives. We shall leave this part of England—perhaps England itself—and what does it matter how people regard us here? You will like going, will you not?"

She could answer no more than a bare affirmative, so great was the emotion aroused in her at the thought of going through the world with him as his own familiar friend. Her feelings almost filled her ears like a babble of waves, and surged up to her eyes. She put her hand in his, and thus they went on, to a place where the reflected sun glared up from the river under a bridge, with a molten-metallic glow that dazzled their eyes, though the sun itself was hidden by the bridge. They stood still, whereupon little furred and feathered heads popped up from the smooth surface of the water; but, finding that the disturbing presences had paused, and not passed by, they disappeared again. Upon this river-brink they lingered till the fog began to close round them—which was very early in the evening at this time of the year—settling on the lashes of her eyes, where it rested like crystals, and on his brows and hair.

They walked later on Sundays, when it was quite dusk. Some of the dairy-people, who were also out of doors on the first Sunday evening after their engagement, heard her impulsive speeches, ecstasized to fragments, though they were too far off to hear the words discoursed; noted the spasmodic catch in her remarks, broken into syllables by the leapings of her heart, as she walked leaning on his arm; her contented pauses, the occasional little laugh, upon which her soul seemed to ride—the laugh of a woman in company with the man she loves and has won from all other women—unlike anything else in nature. They marked the buoyancy of her tread, like the skim of a bird which has not quite alighted.

Her affection for him was now the breath and light of Tess's being: it enveloped her as a photosphere, irradiated her into forget-fulness of her past sorrows, keeping back the gloomy spectres that would persist in their attempts to touch her—doubt, fear, moodiness, care, shame. She knew that they were waiting like wolves just outside the circumscribing light, but she had long spells of power to keep them in hungry subjection there.

A spiritual forgetfulness coexisted with an intellectual remem-brance. She walked in brightness, but she knew that in the back-ground those shapes of darkness were always spread. They might be receding, or they might be approaching, one or the other, a little every day.

One evening Tess and Clare were obliged to sit indoors keeping house, all the other occupants of the domicile being away. As they talked she looked thoughtfully up at him, and met his two appreciative eyes.

"I am not worthy of you—no, I am not!" she burst out, jumping up from her low stool as though appalled at his homage, and the fulness of her own joy thereat.

Clare, deeming the whole basis of her excitement to be that which was only the smaller part of it, said, "I won't have you speak like it, dear Tess! Distinction does not consist in the facile use of a contemptible set of conventions, but in being numbered among those who are true, and honest, and just, and pure, and lovely, and of good report*—as you are, my Tess."

She struggled with the sob in her throat. How often had that string of excellences made her young heart ache in church of late years, and how strange that he should have cited them now. "Why didn't you stay and love me when I—was sixteen; living with my little sisters and brothers, and you danced on the green—O why didn't you, why didn't you!" she said, impetuously clasping her hands.

Angel began to comfort and reassure her, thinking to himself, truly enough, what a creature of moods she was, and how careful he would have to be of her when she depended for her happiness entirely on him. "Ah—why didn't I stay!" he said. "That is just what I feel. If I had only known! But you must not be so bitter in your regret—why should you be?"

With the woman's instinct to hide she diverged hastily: "I should have had four years more of your heart than I can ever have now. Then I should not have wasted my time as I have done—I should have had so much longer happiness."

It was no mature woman with a long dark vista of intrigue behind her who was tormented thus; but a girl of simple life, not yet one-and-twenty, who had been caught during her days of immaturity like a bird in a springe. To calm herself the more completely she rose from her little stool and left the room, overturning the stool with her skirts as she went.

He sat on by the cheerful firelight thrown from a bundle of green ash sticks laid across the dogs; the sticks snapped pleasantly, and hissed out bubbles of sap from their ends. When she came back she was herself again.

"Do you not think you are just a wee bit capricious, fitful, Tess?" he said good-humouredly, as he spread a cushion for her on the stool, and seated himself in the settle beside her. "I wanted to ask you something, and just then you ran away."

"Yes—perhaps I am capricious," she murmured. She suddenly approached him and put a hand upon each of his arms. "No, Angel—I am not really so—by nature I mean!" The more particularly to assure him that she was not, she placed herself close to him in the settle, and allowed her head to find a resting-place against Clare's shoulder. "What did you want to ask me—I am sure I will answer it," she continued humbly.

"Well—you love me, and have agreed to marry me, and hence there follows a thirdly. 'When shall the day be.'"

"I like living like this."

"But I must think of starting in business on my own hook* with the new year, or a little later. And before I get involved in the multifarious details of my new position I should like to have secured my partner."

"But," she timidly answered, "to talk quite practically, wouldn't it be best not to marry till after all that?—though I can't bear the thought o' your going away and leaving me here!"

"Of course you cannot—and it is not best in this case. I want you to help me in many ways in making my start. When shall it be? Why not a fortnight from now?"

"No," she said becoming grave; "I have so many things to think of first."

"But—" He drew her gently nearer to him.

The reality of marriage was startling when it loomed so near. Before discussion of the question had proceeded further there walked round the corner of the settle into the full firelight of the apartment Mr Dairyman Crick, Mrs Crick, and two of the milkmaids.

Tess sprang like an elastic ball from his side to her feet, while her face flushed and her eyes shone in the firelight; "I knew how it would be if I sat so close to him!" she cried with vexation. "I said to myself they are sure to come and catch us! But I wasn't really sitting on his knee, though it might ha' seemed as if I was, almost!"

"Well—if so be you hadn't told us, I am sure we shouldn't ha' noticed that ye had been sitting anywhere at all, in this light," replied the dairyman. He continued to his wife, with the stolid mien of a man who understood nothing of the emotions relating to matrimony: "Now, Christianer, that shows that folks should never fancy other folks be supposing things when they bain't. O no—I should never ha' thought a word of where she was a sitting to, if she hadn't told me—not I."

"We are going to be married soon," said Clare, with improvised phlegm.

"Ah—and be ye! Well, I am truly glad to hear it, sir. I've thought you mid do such a thing for some time. She's too good for a dairy-maid—I said so the very first day I zid her—and a prize for any man; and what's more, a wonderful woman for a gentleman-farmer's wife; he won't be at the mercy of his baily wi' her at his side."

Somehow Tess disappeared. She had been even more struck with the look of the girls who followed Crick than abashed by Crick's blunt praise.

After supper, when she reached her bedroom, they were all present. A light was burning, and each damsel was sitting up whitely in her bed, awaiting Tess, the whole like a row of avenging ghosts.

But she saw in a few moments that there was no malice in their mood. They could scarcely feel as a loss what they had never expected to have. Their condition was objective, contemplative.

"He's going to marry her!" murmured Retty, never taking her eyes off Tess. "How her face do show it!"

"You *be* going to marry him?" asked Marian.

"Yes," said Tess.

"When?"

"Some day."

They thought that this was evasiveness only. "*Yes*—going to *marry* him—a gentleman!" repeated Izz Huett. And by a sort of fascination the three girls one after another crept out of their beds, and came and stood barefooted round Tess. Retty put her hands upon Tess's shoulders, as if to realize her friend's corporeality after such a miracle, and the other two laid their arms round her waist, all looking into her face.

"How it do seem! Almost more than I can think of!" said Izz Huett.

Marian kissed Tess. "Yes," she murmured as she withdrew her lips.

"Was that because of love for her, or because other lips have touched there by now?" continued Izz drily to Marian.

"I wasn't thinking o' that," said Marian simply. "I was on'y feeling all the strangeness o't—that she is to be his wife, and nobody else. I don't say nay to it, nor either of us, because we did not think of it—only loved him. Still nobody else is to marry'n in the world—no fine lady, nobody in silks and satins; but she who do live like we."

"Are you sure you don't dislike me for it?" said Tess in a low voice.

They hung about her in their white night-gowns, before replying, as if they considered their answer might lie in her look. "I don't know—I don't know," murmured Retty Priddle. "I want to hate 'ee; but I cannot!"

"That's how I feel," echoed Izz and Marian. "I can't hate her. Somehow she hinders me!"

"He ought to marry one of you," murmured Tess.

"Why?"

"You are all better than I."

"We better than you?" said the girls in a low slow whisper. "No, no, dear Tess!"

"You are!" she contradicted impetuously. And suddenly tearing away from their clinging arms she burst into a hysterical fit of tears, bowing herself on the chest of drawers, and repeating incessantly, "O yes, yes, yes!"

Having once given way she could not stop her weeping. "He ought to have had one of you!" she cried. "I think I ought to make him even now!—You would be better for him than—I don't know what I'm saying—O, O!"

They went up to her and clasped her round, but still her sobs tore her. "Get some water," said Marian. "She's upset by us. Poor thing—poor thing!"

They gently led her back to the side of her bed, where they kissed her warmly. "You are best for'n," said Marian. "More ladylike, and a better scholar than we, especially since he has taught 'ee so much. But even you ought to be proud. You *be* proud, I'm sure?"

"Yes—I am," she said. "And I am ashamed at so breaking down!"

When they were all in bed, and the light was out, Marian whispered across to her: "You will think of us when you be his wife, Tess, and of how we told 'ee that we loved him, and how we tried not to hate you, and did not hate you, and could not hate you, because you was his choice, and we never hoped to be chose by him."

They were not aware that at these words salt stinging tears trickled down upon Tess's pillow anew; and how she resolved with a bursting heart to tell all her history to Angel Clare, despite her mother's command; to let him for whom she lived and breathed* despise her if he would, and her mother regard her as a fool, rather than preserve a silence which might be deemed a treachery to him, and which somehow seemed a wrong to these.

XXXII

THIS penitential mood kept her from naming the wedding-day. The beginning of November found its date still in abeyance, though he asked her at the most tempting times. But Tess's desire seemed to be for a perpetual betrothal, in which everything should remain as it was then.

The meads were changing now; but it was still warm enough in early afternoons before milking to idle there awhile, and the state of dairy-work at this time of year allowed a spare hour for idling. Looking over the damp sod in the direction of the sun a glistening ripple of gossamer-webs was visible to their eyes under the luminary, like the track of moonlight on the sea. Gnats, knowing nothing of their brief glorification, wandered across the shimmer of this pathway, irradiated as if they bore fire within them; then passed out of its line, and were quite extinct. In the presence of these things he would remind her that the date was still the question.

Or he would ask her at night, when he accompanied her on some mission invented by Mrs Crick to give him the opportunity. This was mostly a journey to the farm-house on the slopes above the vale, to inquire how the advanced cows were getting on in the straw-barton to which they were relegated. For it was a time of the year that brought great changes to the world of kine. Batches of the animals were sent away daily to this lying-in hospital, where they lived on straw till their calves were born, after which event, and as soon as the calf could walk, mother and offspring were driven back to the dairy. In the interval which elapsed before the calves were sold there was, of course, little milking to be done, but as soon as the calf had been taken away the milkmaids would have to set to work as usual.

Returning from one of these dark walks they reached a great gravel cliff immediately over the levels, where they stood still and listened. The water was now high in the streams, squirting through the weirs and tinkling under culverts; the smallest gulleys were all full; there was no taking short cuts anywhere, and foot-passengers were compelled to follow the permanent ways. From the whole extent of the invisible vale came a multitudinous intonation; it forced upon their fancy that a great city lay below them, and that the murmur was the vociferation of its populace.

"It seems like tens of thousands of them," said Tess; "holding public meetings in their market-places, arguing, preaching, quarrelling, sobbing, groaning, praying, and cursing." Clare was not particularly heeding.

"Did Crick speak to you to-day, dear, about his not wanting much assistance during the winter months?"

"No."

"The cows are going dry* rapidly."

"Yes. Six or seven went to the straw-barton yesterday; and three the day before, making nearly twenty in the straw already. Ah—is it that the farmer don't want my help for the calving? O I am not wanted here any more! And I have tried so hard to—"

"Crick didn't exactly say that he would no longer require you. But knowing what our relations were he said in the most good-natured and respectful manner possible that he supposed on my leaving at Christmas I should take you with me, and on my asking what he would do without you he merely observed that, as a matter of fact, it was a time of year when he could do with a very little female help. I am afraid I was sinner enough to feel rather glad that he was in this way forcing your hand."

"I don't think you ought to have felt glad, Angel. Because 'tis always mournful not to be wanted, even if at the same time 'tis convenient."

"Well, it is convenient—you have admitted that." He put his finger upon her cheek. "Ah!" he said.

"What?"

"I feel the red rising up at her having been caught! . . . But why should I trifle so! We will not trifle—life is too serious."

"It is. Perhaps I saw that before you did."

She was seeing it then. To decline to marry him after all—in obedience to her emotion of last night—and leave the dairy, meant to go to some strange place, not a dairy; for milkmaids were not in request now calving-time was coming on; to go to some arable farm, where no divine being like Angel Clare was. She hated the thought; and she hated more the thought of going home.

"So that, seriously, dearest Tess," he continued, "since you will probably have to leave at Christmas, it is in every way desirable and convenient that I should carry you off then as my property. Besides,

if you were not the most uncalculating girl in the world you would
know that we could not go on like this for ever."

"I wish we could. That it would always be summer and autumn,
and you always courting me, and always thinking as much of me as
you have done through the past summer-time!"

"I always shall."

"O I know you will!" she cried with a sudden fervour of faith in
him. "Angel, I will fix the day when I will become yours for
always."

Thus at last it was arranged between them, during that dark
walk home, amid the myriads of liquid voices on the right hand
and left.

When they reached the dairy Mr and Mrs Crick were promptly
told—with injunctions to secrecy; for each of the lovers was desirous
that the marriage should be kept as private as possible. The dairyman, though he had thought of dismissing her soon, now made a
great concern about losing her. What should he do about his
skimming? Who would make the ornamental butter-pats for the
Anglebury and Sandbourne ladies? Mrs Crick congratulated Tess
on the shilly-shallying having at last come to an end, and said that
directly she set eyes on Tess she divined that she was to be the
chosen one of somebody who was no common outdoor man: Tess
had looked so superior as she walked across the barton on that
afternoon of her arrival: that she was of a good family she could
have sworn. In point of fact Mrs Crick did remember thinking that
Tess was graceful and good-looking as she approached; but the
superiority might have been a growth of the imagination aided by
subsequent knowledge.

Tess was now carried along upon the wings of the hours, without
the sense of a will. The word had been given; the number of the
day written down. Her naturally bright intelligence had begun to
admit the fatalistic convictions common to field-folk and those who
associate more extensively with natural phenomena than with their
fellow-creatures; and she accordingly drifted into that passive
responsiveness to all things her lover suggested, characteristic of the
frame of mind.

But she wrote anew to her mother, ostensibly to notify the
wedding-day; really to again implore her advice. It was a gentleman
who had chosen her, which perhaps her mother had not sufficiently

considered. A post-nuptial explanation, which might be accepted with a light heart by a rougher man, might not be received with the same feeling by him. But this communication brought no reply from Mrs Durbeyfield.

Despite Angel Clare's plausible representations to himself and to Tess of the practical need for their immediate marriage, there was, in truth, an element of precipitancy in the step, as became apparent at a later date. He loved her dearly, though perhaps rather ideally and fancifully than with the impassioned thoroughness of her feeling for him. He had entertained no notion, when doomed as he had thought to an unintellectual bucolic life, that such charms as he beheld in this idyllic creature would be found behind the scenes. Unsophistication was a thing to talk of; he had not known how it really struck one till he came here. Yet he was very far from seeing his future track clearly; and it might be a year or two before he would be able to consider himself fairly started in life. The secret lay in the tinge of recklessness imparted to his career and character by the sense that he had been made to miss his true destiny through the prejudices of his family.

"Don't you think 'twould have been better for us to wait till you were quite settled in your midland farm?" she once asked timidly. (A midland farm was the idea just then.)

"To tell the truth, my Tess, I don't like you to be left anywhere away from my protection and sympathy."

The reason was a good one, so far as it went. His influence over her had been so marked that she had caught his manner and habits, his speech and phrases, his likings and his aversions. And to leave her in farm-land would be to let her slip back again out of accord with him. He wished to have her under his charge for another reason. His parents had naturally desired to see her once at least before he carried her off to a distant settlement, English or colonial; and as no opinion of theirs was to be allowed to change his intention he judged that a couple of months' life with him in lodgings whilst seeking for an advantageous opening would be of some social assistance to her at what she might feel to be a trying ordeal, her presentation to his mother at the vicarage.

Next, he wished to see a little of the working of a flour-mill, having an idea that he might combine the use of one with corn-growing. The proprietor of a large old water-mill at Wellbridge— once the mill of an Abbey—had offered him the inspection of his time-honoured mode of procedure, and a hand in the operations for a few days, whenever he should choose to come. Clare paid a visit to the place, some few miles distant, one day at this time, to inquire particulars, and returned to Talbothays in the evening. She found him determined to spend a short time at the Wellbridge flour-mills; and what had determined him? Less the opportunity of an insight into grinding and bolting* than the casual fact that lodgings were to be obtained in that very farm-house which, before its mutilation, had been the mansion of a branch of the d'Urberville family. This was always how Clare settled practical questions; by a sentiment which had nothing to do with them. They decided to go immediately after the wedding, and remain for a fortnight, instead of journeying to towns and inns. "Then we will start off to examine some farms on the other side of London that I have heard of," he said, "and by March or April we will pay a visit to my father and mother."

Questions of procedure such as these arose and passed, and the day, the incredible day, on which she was to become his, loomed large in the near future. The thirty-first of December, New Year's Eve, was the date. His wife, she said to herself. Could it ever be? Their two selves together, nothing to divide them, every incident shared by them: why not? And yet why?

One Sunday morning Izz Huett returned from church, and spoke privately to Tess.

"You was not called home[1] this morning."

"What?"

"It should ha' been the first time of asking to-day," she answered looking quietly at Tess. "You meant to be married New Year's Eve, deary?"

The other returned a quick affirmative.

"And there must be three times of asking. And now there be only two Sundays left between."

Tess felt her cheek paling. Izz was right: of course there must be three. Perhaps he had forgotten? If so, there must be a week's postponement, and that was unlucky. How could she remind her lover? She who had been so backward was suddenly fired with impatience and alarm lest she should lose her dear prize.

---

[1]"called home"—local phrase for publication of banns.

A natural incident relieved her anxiety. Izz mentioned the omission of the banns to Mrs Crick, and Mrs Crick assumed a matron's privilege of speaking to Angel on the point. "Have ye forgot 'em, Mr Clare? The banns I mean."

"No, I have not forgot 'em," says Clare.

As soon as he caught Tess alone he assured her. "Don't let them tease you about the banns. A licence* will be quieter for us, and I have decided on a licence without consulting you. So if you go to church on Sunday morning you will not hear your own name, if you wished to."

"I didn't wish to hear it, dearest," she said proudly.

But to know that things were in train was an immense relief to Tess notwithstanding, who had well-nigh feared that somebody would stand up and forbid the banns on the ground of her history. How events were favouring her!

"I don't quite feel easy," she said to herself. "All this good fortune may be scourged out of me afterwards by a lot of ill. That's how Heaven mostly does. I wish I could have had common banns!"

But everything went smoothly. She wondered whether he would like her to be married in her present best white frock, or if she ought to buy a new one. The question was set at rest by his forethought, disclosed by the arrival of some large packages addressed to her. Inside them she found a whole stock of clothing, from bonnet to shoes, including a perfect morning costume such as would well suit the simple wedding they planned. He entered the house shortly after the arrival of the packages, and heard her upstairs undoing them.

A minute later she came down with a flush on her face and tears in her eyes.

"How thoughtful you've been!" she murmured, her cheek upon his shoulder. "Even to the gloves and handkerchief! My own love— how good, how kind!"

"No, no, Tess; just an order to a tradeswoman in London—nothing more."

And to divert her from thinking too highly of him he told her to go upstairs, and take her time, and see if it all fitted; and, if not, to get the village sempstress to make a few alterations.

She did return upstairs and put on the gown. Alone, she stood for a moment before the glass looking at the effect of her silk attire; and then there came into her head her mother's ballad of the mystic robe,

That never would become that wife
That had once done amiss,*

which Mrs Durbeyfield had used to sing to her as a child, so blithely and so archly, her foot on the cradle, which she rocked to the tune. Suppose this robe should betray her by changing colour as her robe had betrayed Queen Guénever. Since she had been at the dairy she had not once thought of the lines till now.

XXXIII

ANGEL felt that he would like to spend a day with her before the wedding, somewhere away from the dairy, as a last jaunt in her company while they were yet mere lover and mistress; a romantic day, in circumstances that would never be repeated; with that other and greater day beaming close ahead of them. During the preceding week, therefore, he suggested making a few purchases in the nearest town, and they started together.

Clare's life at the dairy had been that of a recluse in respect to the world of his own class. For months he had never gone near a town, and requiring no vehicle had never kept one, hiring the dairyman's cob or gig if he rode or drove. They went in the gig that day.

And then for the first time in their lives they shopped as partners in one concern. It was Christmas Eve, with its loads of holly and mistletoe, and the town was very full of strangers who had come in from all parts of the county on account of the day. Tess paid the penalty of walking about with happiness superadded to beauty on her countenance, by being much stared at as she moved amid them on his arm.

In the evening they returned to the inn at which they had put up, and Tess waited in the entry while Angel went to see the horse and gig brought to the door. The general sitting-room was full of guests, who were continually going in and out. As the door opened and shut each time for the passage of these the light within the parlour fell full upon Tess's face. Two men came out and passed by her among the rest. One of them had stared her up and down in surprise, and she fancied he was a Trantridge man, though that village lay so many miles off that Trantridge folk were rarities here.

"A comely maid, that," said the other.

"True—comely enough. But, unless I make a great mistake—" And he negatived the remainder of the definition forthwith.

Clare had just returned from the stable-yard, and confronting the man on the threshold heard the words, and saw the shrinking of Tess. The insult to her stung him to the quick, and before he had considered anything at all he struck the man on the chin with the full force of his fist, sending him staggering backwards into the passage.

The man recovered himself, and seemed inclined to come on, and Clare, stepping outside the door, put himself in a posture of defence. But his opponent began to think better of the matter. He looked anew at Tess as he passed her; and said to Clare, "I beg pardon, sir: 'twas a complete mistake: I thought she was another woman, forty miles from here."

Clare, feeling then that he had been too hasty, and that he was moreover to blame for leaving her standing in an inn passage, did what he usually did in such cases; gave the man five shillings to plaster the blow; and thus they parted, bidding each other a pacific good-night. As soon as Clare had taken the reins from the ostler, and the young couple had driven off, the two men went in the other direction:

"And was it a mistake?" said the second one.

"Not a bit of it. But I didn't want to hurt the gentleman's feelings—not I."

In the meantime the lovers were driving onward. "Could we—put off our wedding till a little later?" Tess asked in a dry dull voice. "I mean, if we wished?"

"No, my love. Calm yourself. Do you mean that the fellow may have time to summon me for assault?" he asked good-humouredly.

"No—I only meant—if it should have to be put off."

What she meant was not very clear, and he directed her to dismiss such fancies from her mind, which she obediently did as well as she could. But she was grave, very grave, all the way home; till she thought, "We shall go away, a very long distance, hundreds of miles from these parts, and such as this can never happen again, and no ghost of the past reach there."

They parted tenderly that night on the landing, and Clare ascended to his attic. Tess sat up getting on with some little requisites, lest the few remaining days should not afford sufficient time. While she sat she heard a noise in Angel's room overhead, a sound of thumping and struggling. Everybody else in the house was asleep and in her anxiety lest Clare should be ill she ran up and knocked at his door, and asked him what was the matter.

"O, nothing dear," he said from within. "I am so sorry I disturbed you! But the reason is rather an amusing one: I fell asleep and dreamt that I was fighting that fellow again who insulted you, and the noise you heard was my pummelling away with my fists at my portmanteau which I pulled out to-day for packing. I am occasionally liable to these freaks in my sleep. Go to bed and think of it no more."

This was the last drachm required to turn the scale of her indecision. Declare the past to him by word of mouth she could not, but there was another way. She sat down and wrote on the four pages of a note-sheet a succinct narrative of those events of three or four years ago, put it into an envelope, and directed it to Clare. Then, lest the flesh should again be weak, she crept upstairs without any shoes, and slipped the note under his door.

Her night was a broken one, as it well might be, and she listened for the first faint noise overhead. It came, as usual; he descended, as usual. She descended. He met her at the bottom of the stairs, and kissed her. Surely it was as warmly as ever?

He looked a little disturbed and worn, she thought. But he said not a word to her about her revelation, even when they were alone. Could he have had it? Unless he began the subject she felt that she could say nothing. So the day passed, and it was evident that whatever he thought he meant to keep to himself. Yet he was frank and affectionate as before. Could it be that her doubts were childish? that he forgave her; that he loved her for what she was; just as she was; and smiled at her disquiet as at a foolish nightmare? Had he really received her note? She glanced into his room, and could see nothing of it. It might be that he forgave her. But even if he had not received it she had a sudden enthusiastic trust that he surely would forgive her.

Every morning and night he was the same, and thus New Year's Eve broke—the wedding-day.

The lovers did not rise at milking-time, having through the whole of this last week of their sojourn at the dairy been accorded something of the position of guests, Tess being honoured with a room of her own. When they arrived downstairs at breakfast-time they were surprised to see what effects had been produced in the large kitchen for their glory since they had last beheld it. At some unnatural hour of the morning the dairyman had caused the yawning chimney-corner to be whitened, and the brick hearth reddened, and a blazing yellow damask blower to be hung across the arch, in place of the old grimy blue cotton one with a black sprig pattern which had formerly done duty here. This renovated aspect of what was the focus indeed of the room on a dull winter morning, threw a smiling demeanour over the whole apartment.

"I was determined to do summat in honour o't," said the dairyman. "And as you wouldn't hear of my gieing a rattling good randy wi' fiddles and bass-viols complete, as we should ha' done in old times, this was all I could think o', as a noiseless thing."

Tess's friends lived so far off that none could conveniently have been present at the ceremony, even had any been asked; but as a fact nobody was invited from Marlott. As for Angel's family, he had written and duly informed them of the time, and assured them that he would be glad to see one at least of them there for the day, if he would like to come. His brothers had not replied at all, seeming to be indignant with him; while his father and mother had written a rather sad letter, deploring his precipitancy in rushing into marriage, but making the best of the matter by saying that, though a dairywoman was the last daughter-in-law they could have expected, their son had arrived at an age at which he might be supposed to be the best judge.

This coolness in his relatives distressed Clare less than it would have done had he been without the grand card with which he meant to surprise them ere long. To produce Tess fresh from the dairy as a d'Urberville and a lady he had felt to be temerarious and risky: hence he had concealed her lineage till such time as, familiarized with worldly ways by a few months' travel and reading with him, he could take her on a visit to his parents and impart the knowledge while triumphantly producing her as worthy of such an ancient line. It was a pretty lover's dream, if no more. Perhaps Tess's lineage had more value for himself than for anybody in the world besides.

Her perception that Angel's bearing towards her still remained in no whit altered by her own communication, rendered Tess guiltily doubtful if he could have received it. She rose from breakfast before he had finished and hastened upstairs. It had occurred to her to look once more into the queer gaunt room which had been Clare's den, or rather eyrie, for so long, and climbing the ladder she stood at the open door of the apartment, regarding, and pondering. She stooped to the threshold of the doorway, where she had pushed in the note two or three days earlier, in such excitement. The carpet reached close to the sill, and under the edge of the carpet she discerned the faint white margin of the envelope containing her letter to him, which he obviously never had seen, owing to her having in her haste thrust it beneath the carpet as well as beneath the door.

With a feeling of faintness she withdrew the letter. There it was—sealed up, just as it had left her hands. The mountain had not yet been removed. She could not let him read it now, the house being in full bustle of preparation; and descending to her own room she destroyed the letter there.

She was so pale when he saw her again that he felt quite anxious. The incident of the misplaced letter she had jumped at as if it prevented a confession; but she knew in her conscience that it need not; there was still time. Yet everything was in a stir: there was coming and going; all had to dress, the Dairyman and Mrs Crick having been asked to accompany them as witnesses; and reflection, or deliberate talk, was well-nigh impossible. The only minute Tess could get to be alone with Clare was when they met upon the landing.

"I am so anxious to talk to you—I want to confess all my faults and blunders!" she said with attempted lightness.

"No, no—we can't have faults talked of—you must be deemed perfect to-day at least, my sweet," he cried. "We shall have plenty of time hereafter I hope to talk over our failings. I will confess mine at the same time."

"But it would be better for me to do it now I think, so that you could not say—"

"Well, my quixotic one, you shall tell me anything—say, as soon as we are settled in our lodging: not now. I too will tell you my faults then. But do not let us spoil the day with them: they will be excellent matter for a dull time."

"Then you don't wish me to, dearest?"

"I do not, Tessy, really."

The hurry of dressing and starting left no time for more than this. Those words of his seemed to reassure her on further reflection. She was whirled onward through the next couple of critical hours by the mastering tide of her devotion to him, which closed up further meditation. Her one desire, so long resisted, to make herself his, to call him her lord, her own—then, if necessary, to die—had at last lifted her up from her plodding reflective pathway. In dressing she moved about in a mental cloud of many-coloured idealities, which eclipsed all sinister contingencies by its brightness.

The church was a long way off, and they were obliged to drive, particularly as it was winter. A close carriage was ordered from a roadside inn, a vehicle which had been kept there ever since the old days of post-chaise travelling. It had stout wheel-spokes and heavy felloes,* a great curved bed, immense straps and springs, and a pole like a battering-ram. The postilion was a venerable "boy" of sixty— a martyr to rheumatic gout, the result of excessive exposure in youth, counteracted by strong liquors—who had stood at inn-doors doing nothing for the whole five-and-twenty years that had elapsed since he had no longer been required to ride professionally, as if expecting the old times to come back again. He had a permanent running wound on the outside of his right leg, originated by the constant bruisings of aristocratic carriage-poles during the many years that he had been in regular employ at the King's Arms, Casterbridge.

Inside this cumbrous and creaking structure, and behind this decayed conductor, the *partie carrée** took their seats; the bride and bridegroom, and Mr and Mrs Crick. Angel would have liked one at least of his brothers to be present as groomsman; but their silence after his gentle hint to that effect by letter had signified that they did not care to come. They disapproved of the marriage, and could not be expected to countenance it. Perhaps it was as well that they could not be present: they were not worldly young fellows; but fraternizing with dairy-folk would have struck unpleasantly upon their biassed niceness, apart from their views of the match.

Upheld by the momentum of the time Tess knew nothing of this; did not see anything; did not know the road they were taking to the church. She knew that Angel was close to her; all the rest was a luminous mist. She was a sort of celestial person, who owed her being to poetry; one of those classical divinities Clare was accustomed to talk to her about when they took their walks together.

The marriage being by licence there were only a dozen or so of people in the church: had there been a thousand they would have produced no more effect upon her. They were at stellar distances from her present world. In the ecstatic solemnity with which she swore her faith to him the ordinary sensibilities of sex seemed a flippancy. At a pause in the service, while they were kneeling together, she unconsciously inclined herself towards him, so that her shoulder touched his arm: she had been frightened by a passing thought, and the movement had been automatic, to assure herself that he was really there, and to fortify her belief that his fidelity would be proof against all things.

Clare knew that she loved him: every curve of her form showed that; but he did not know at that time the full depth of her devotion, its single-mindedness, its meekness; what long-suffering it guaranteed, what honesty, what endurance, what good-faith.

As they came out of church the ringers swung the bells off their rests, and a modest peal of three notes broke forth—that limited amount of expression having been deemed sufficient by the church builders for the joys of such a small parish. Passing by the tower with her husband on the path to the gate she could feel the vibrant air humming round them from the louvred belfry in a circle of sound; and it matched the highly charged mental atmosphere in which she was living.

This condition of mind, wherein she felt glorified by an irradiation not her own, like the Angel whom St John saw in the sun, lasted till the sound of the church bells had died away, and the emotions of the wedding-service had calmed down. Her eyes could dwell upon details more clearly now, and Mr and Mrs Crick having directed their own gig to be sent for them, to leave the carriage to the young couple, she observed the build and character of that conveyance for the first time. Sitting in silence she regarded it long.

"I fancy you seem oppressed, Tessy," said Clare.

"Yes," she answered putting her hand to her brow. "I tremble at many things. It is all so serious, Angel. . . . Among other things I seem to have seen this carriage before, to be very well acquainted with it. It is very odd—I must have seen it in a dream."

"Oh—you have heard the legend of the d'Urberville Coach—that well-known superstition of this county about your family when they were very powerful here; and this lumbering old thing reminds you of it."

"I have never heard of it to my knowledge," said she. "What is the legend—may I know it?"

"Well—I would rather not tell it in detail just now. A certain d'Urberville of the sixteenth or seventeenth century committed a dreadful crime in his family coach; and since that time members of the family see or hear the old coach whenever—. But I'll tell you another day—it is rather gloomy. Evidently some dim knowledge of it has been brought back to your mind by the sight of this venerable caravan."

"I don't remember hearing it before," she murmured. "Is it when we are going to die, Angel, that members of my family see it? Or is it when we have committed a crime?"

"Now Tess!" He silenced her by a kiss.

By the time they reached home she was contrite and spiritless. She was Mrs Angel Clare, indeed; but had she any moral right to the name? Was she not more truly Mrs Alexander d'Urberville? Could intensity of love justify what might be considered in upright souls as culpable reticence? She knew not what was expected of women in such cases; and she had no counsellor.

However, when she found herself alone in her room for a few minutes—the last day this on which she was ever to enter it—she knelt down and prayed. She tried to pray to God, but it was her husband who really had her supplication. Her idolatry of this man was such that she herself almost feared it to be ill-omened.* She was conscious of the notion expressed by Friar Laurence: "these violent delights have violent ends."* It might be too desperate for human conditions, too rank, too wild, too deadly. "O my love, my love, why do I love you so!" she whispered there alone; "for she you love is not my real self, but one in my image; the one I might have been."

Afternoon came and with it the hour for departure. They had decided to fulfil the plan of going for a few days to the lodgings in the old farm-house near Wellbridge Mill, at which he meant to reside during his investigation of flour-processes. At two o'clock there was nothing left to do but to start. All the servantry of the dairy were standing in the red-brick entry to see them go out, the dairyman and his wife following to the door. Tess saw her three chamber-mates in a row against the wall, pensively inclining their heads. She had much questioned if they would appear at the parting moment; but there they were, stoical and staunch to the last. She knew why the delicate Retty looked so fragile, and Izz so tragically sorrowful, and Marian so blank; and she forgot her own dogging shadow for a moment in contemplating theirs.

She impulsively whispered to him: "Will you kiss 'em all, once, poor things, for the first and last time?"

Clare had not the least objection to such a farewell formality—which was all that it was to him—and as he passed them he kissed them in succession where they stood, saying "Good-bye" to each as he did so. When they reached the door Tess femininely glanced back to discern the effect of that kiss of charity; there was no triumph in her glance, as there might have been. If there had it would have disappeared when she saw how moved the girls all were. The kiss had obviously done harm by awakening feelings they were trying to subdue.

Of all this Clare was unconscious. Passing on to the wicket-gate he shook hands with the dairyman and his wife, and expressed his last thanks to them for their attentions; after which there was a moment of silence before they had moved off. It was interrupted by the crowing of a cock. The white one with the rose comb had come and settled on the palings in front of the house, within a few yards of them, and his notes thrilled their ears through, dwindling away like echoes down a valley of rocks.

"Oh?" said Mrs Crick. "An afternoon crow?"

Two men were standing by the yard gate, holding it open. "That's bad,"* one murmured to the other, not thinking that the words could be heard by the group at the wicket.

The cock crew again—straight towards Clare.

"Well!" said the dairyman.

"I don't like to hear him!" said Tess to her husband. "Tell the man to drive on. Good-bye, good-bye!"

The cock crew again.

"Hoosh! Just you be off, sir, or I'll twist your neck!" said the dairyman with some irritation, turning to the bird and driving him away. And to his wife as they went indoors: "Now, to think o' that— just to-day! I've not heard his crow of an afternoon all the year afore."

"It only means a change in the weather," said she; "not what you think: 'tis impossible!"

XXXIV

THEY drove by the level road along the valley to a distance of a few miles, and reaching Wellbridge turned away from the village to the left, and over the great Elizabethan bridge which gives the place half its name. Immediately behind it stood the house wherein they had engaged lodgings, whose exterior features are so well known to all travellers through the Froom Valley; once portion of a fine manorial residence, and the property and seat of a d'Urberville, but since its partial demolition a farm-house.

"Welcome to one of your ancestral mansions!" said Clare as he handed her down. But he regretted the pleasantry; it was too near a satire.

On entering they found that, though they had only engaged a couple of rooms, the farmer had taken advantage of their proposed presence during the coming days to pay a New Year's visit to some friends; leaving a woman from a neighbouring cottage to minister to their few wants. The absoluteness of possession pleased them, and they realized it as the first moment of their experience under their own exclusive roof-tree.*

But he found that the mouldy old habitation somewhat depressed his bride. When the carriage was gone they ascended the stairs to wash their hands, the charwoman showing the way. On the landing Tess stopped and started.

"What's the matter?" said he.

"Those horried women!" she answered, with a smile. "How they frightened me."

He looked up, and perceived two life-size portraits on panels built into the masonry. As all visitors to the mansion are aware, these paintings represent women of middle age, of a date some two hundred years ago, whose lineaments once seen can never be forgotten. The long pointed features, narrow eye, and smirk of the one, so suggestive of merciless treachery; the bill-hook nose, large teeth, and bold eye of the other, suggesting arrogance to the point of ferocity, haunt the beholder afterwards in his dreams.

"Whose portraits are those?" asked Clare of the charwoman.

"I have been told by old folk that they were ladies of the

d'Urberville family, the ancient lords of this manor," she said. "Owing to their being builded into the wall they can't be moved away."

The unpleasantness of the matter was that, in addition to their effect upon Tess, her fine features were unquestionably traceable in these exaggerated forms. He said nothing of this, however, and regretting that he had gone out of his way to choose the house for their bridal time, went on into the adjoining room. The place having been rather hastily prepared for them they washed their hands in one basin. Clare touched hers under the water.

"Which are my fingers and which are yours?" he said, looking up. "They are very much mixed."

"They are all yours," said she, very prettily; and endeavoured to be gayer than she was. He had not been displeased with her thoughtfulness, on such an occasion; it was what every sensible woman would show: but Tess knew that she had been thoughtful to excess, and struggled against it.

The sun was so low on that short last afternoon of the year that it shone in through a small opening and formed a golden staff which stretched across to her skirt, where it made a spot like a paint-mark set upon her. They went into the ancient parlour to tea, and here they shared their first common meal alone. Such was their childishness, or rather his, that he found it interesting to use the same bread-and-butter plate as herself, and to brush crumbs from her lips with his own. He wondered a little that she did not enter into these frivolities with his own zest.

Looking at her silently for a long time: "She is a dear, dear Tess," he thought to himself, as one deciding on the true construction of a difficult passage. "Do I realize solemnly enough how utterly and irretrievably this little womanly thing is the creature of my good or bad faith and fortune? I think not. I think I could not, unless I were a woman myself. What I am in worldly estate, she is. What I become she must become. What I cannot be she cannot be. And shall I ever neglect her, or hurt her, or even forget to consider her? God forbid such a crime!"

They sat on over the tea-table waiting for their luggage, which the dairyman had promised to send before it grew dark. But evening began to close in and the luggage did not arrive, and they had brought nothing more than they stood in. With the departure of the sun the calm mood of the winter day changed. Out of doors there began noises as of silk smartly rubbed; the restful dead leaves of the preceding autumn were stirred to irritated resurrection, and whirled about unwillingly, and tapped against the shutters. It soon began to rain.

"That cock knew the weather was going to change," said Clare.

The woman who had attended upon them had gone home for the night; but she had placed candles upon the table, and now they lit them. Each candle-flame drew towards the fireplace.

"These old houses are so draughty," continued Angel, looking at the flames, and at the grease guttering down the sides. "I wonder where that luggage is? We haven't even a brush-and-comb."

"I don't know," she answered, absent-minded.

"Tess, you are not a bit cheerful this evening—not at all as you used to be. Those harridans on the panels upstairs have unsettled you. I am sorry I brought you here. I wonder if you really love me after all?"

He knew that she did, and the words had no serious intent; but she was surcharged with emotion, and winced like a wounded animal. Though she tried not to shed tears she could not help showing one or two.

"I did not mean it," said he, sorry. "You are worried at not having your things, I know. I cannot think why old Jonathan has not come with them. Why, it is seven o'clock. . . . Ah, there he is!"

A knock had come to the door; and there being nobody else to answer it Clare went out. He returned to the room with a small package in his hand.

"It is not Jonathan, after all," he said.

"How vexing," said Tess.

The packet had been brought by a special messenger, who had arrived at Talbothays from Emminster Vicarage, immediately after the departure of the married couple, and had followed them hither, being under injunction to deliver it into nobody's hands but theirs. Clare brought it to the light. It was less than a foot long, sewed up in canvas, sealed in red wax with his father's seal, and directed in his father's hand to "Mrs Angel Clare."

"It is a little wedding-present for you, Tess," said he, handing it to her. "How thoughtful they are!"

Tess looked a little flustered as she took it. "I think I would rather have you open it, dearest," said she turning over the parcel. "I don't

like to break those great seals. They look so serious. Please open it
for me!"

He undid the parcel. Inside was a case of morocco leather, on the
top of which lay a note and a key.

The note was for Clare, in the following words:

My dear son,
    Possibly you have forgotten that on the death of your godmother Mrs
Pitney when you were a lad, she—vain, kind woman that she was—left to
me a portion of the contents of her jewel-case in trust for your wife, if you
should ever have one, as a mark of her affection for you and whomsoever
you should choose. This trust I have fulfilled, and the diamonds have been
locked up at my banker's ever since. Though I feel it to be a somewhat
incongruous act in the circumstances I am as you will see bound to hand
over the articles to the woman to whom the use of them for her lifetime
will now rightly belong: and they are therefore promptly sent. They
become, I believe, heirlooms, strictly speaking, according to the terms of
your godmother's will. The precise words of the clause that refers to this
matter are enclosed.

"I do remember," said Clare. "But I had quite forgotten."

Unlocking the case they found it to contain a necklace with
pendant, bracelets, and earrings; and also some other small
ornaments.

Tess seemed afraid to touch them at first, but her eyes sparkled for
a moment as much as the stones when Clare spread out the set. "Are
they mine?" she asked incredulously.

"They are, certainly," said he.

He looked into the fire. He remembered how, when he was a lad of
fifteen, his godmother the Squire's wife—the only rich person with
whom he had ever come in contact—had pinned her faith to his
success; had prophesied a wondrous career for him. There had
seemed nothing at all out of keeping with such a conjectured career
in the storing up of these showy ornaments for his wife and the wives
of her descendants. They gleamed somewhat ironically now. "Yet
why?" he asked himself. It was but a question of vanity throughout:
and if that were admitted into one side of the equation it should be
admitted into the other. His wife was a d'Urberville: whom could
they become better than her?

Suddenly he said with enthusiasm, "Tess, put them on; put them
on!" And he turned from the fire to help her.

But as if by magic she had already donned them—necklace, earrings, bracelets and all.

"But the gown isn't right, Tess," said Clare. "It ought to be a low one for a set of brilliants like that."

"Ought it?" said Tess.

"Yes," said he. He suggested to her how to tuck in the upper edge of her bodice, so as to make it roughly approximate to the cut for evening wear; and when she had done this, and the pendant to the necklace hung isolated amid the whiteness of her throat as it was designed to do, he stepped back to survey her.

"My heavens," said Clare, "how beautiful you are!"

As everybody knows, fine feathers make fine birds: a peasant girl but very moderately prepossessing to the casual observer in her simple condition and attire, will bloom as an amazing beauty if clothed as a woman of fashion with the aids that art can render; while the beauty of the midnight crush would often cut but a sorry figure if placed inside the field-woman's wrapper, upon a monotonous acreage of turnips on a dull day. He had never till now estimated the artistic excellence of Tess's limbs and features.

"If you were only to appear in a ball-room!" he said. "But no, no, dearest; I think I love you best in the wing bonnet* and cotton frock—yes, better than in this, well as you support these dignities."

Tess's sense of her striking appearance had given her a flush of excitement, which was yet not happiness. "I'll take them off," she said, "in case Jonathan should see me. They are not fit for me are they? They must be sold I suppose?"

"Let them stay a few minutes longer. Sell them? Never. It would be a breach of faith."

Influenced by a second thought she readily obeyed: she had something to tell, and there might be help in these. She sat down with the jewels upon her; and again they indulged in conjectures as to where Jonathan could possibly be with their baggage. The ale they had poured out for his consumption when he came had gone flat with long standing.

Shortly after this they began supper, which was already laid on a side-table. Ere they had finished there was a jerk in the fire-smoke, the rising skein of which bulged out into the room, as if some giant had laid his hand on the chimney-top for a moment. It had been caused by the opening of the outer door. A heavy step was now heard in the passage, and Angel went out.

"I couldn't make nobody hear at all by knocking," apologized Jonathan Kail, for it was he at last. "And as 'twas raining out I opened the door. I've brought the things sir."

"I am very glad to see them. But you are very late."

"Well, yes, sir." There was something subdued in Jonathan Kail's tone, which had not been there in the day, and lines of concern were ploughed upon his forehead in addition to the lines of years. He continued: "We've all been gallied at the dairy at what might ha' been a most terrible affliction, since you and your mis'ess (so to name her now) left us this a'ternoon. Perhaps you ha'nt forgot the cock's afternoon crow?"

"Dear me—what—"

"Well, some says it do mane one thing, and some another, but what's happened is that poor little Retty Priddle hev tried to drown herself."

"No! Really? Why she bade us good-bye with the rest—"

"Yes. Well sir; when you and your mis'ess—so to name what she lawful is—when you two drove away, as I say, Retty and Marian put on their bonnets and went out; and as there is not much doing now, being New Year's Eve, and folks mops and brooms from what's inside 'em,* nobody took much notice. They went on to Lew-Everard, where they had summat to drink, and then on they vamped to Dree-armed Cross; and there they seem to have parted, Retty striking across the water-meads as if for home, and Marian going on to the next village, where there's another public-house. Nothing more was zeed or heard o' Retty till the waterman on his way home noticed something by the Great Pool; 'twas her bonnet and shawl packed up: in the water he found her. He and another man brought her home, thinking 'a was dead; but she fetched round by degrees."

Angel, suddenly recollecting that Tess was overhearing this gloomy tale, went to shut the door between the passage and the ante-room to the inner parlour where she was; but his wife, flinging a shawl round her, had come to the outer room and was listening to the man's narrative, her eyes resting absently on the luggage, and the drops of rain glistening upon it.

"And, more than this, there's Marian—she's been found dead drunk by the withy-bed.* A girl who hev never been known to touch anything before except shilling ale—though to be sure 'a was always a good trencher-woman,* as her face showed. It seems as if the maids had all gone out o' their minds!"

"And Izz?" asked Tess.

"Izz is about house as usual; but 'a do say 'a can guess how it happened; and she seems to be very low in mind about it, poor maid, as well she mid be. And so you see, sir, as all this happened just when we was packing your few traps and your mis'ess's night-rail and dressing things into the cart, why, it belated me."

"Yes. Well Jonathan, will you get the trunks upstairs, and drink a cup of ale, and hasten back as soon as you can, in case you should be wanted."

Tess had gone back to the inner parlour, and sat down by the fire, looking wistfully into it. She heard Jonathan Kail's heavy footsteps up and down the stairs till he had done placing the luggage, and heard him express his thanks for the ale her husband took out to him and for the gratuity he received. Jonathan's footsteps then died from the door, and his cart creaked away.

Angel slid forward the massive oak bar which secured the door, and coming in to where she sat over the hearth, pressed her cheeks between his hands from behind. He expected her to jump up gaily and unpack the toilet-gear that she had been so anxious about, but as she did not rise he sat down with her in the firelight, the candles on the supper-table being too thin and glimmering to interfere with its glow.

"I am so sorry you should have heard this sad story about the girls," he said. "Still, don't let it depress you. Retty was naturally morbid, you know."

"Without the least cause," said Tess. "While they who have cause to be, hide it, and pretend they are not."

This incident had turned the scale for her. They were simple and innocent girls on whom the unhappiness of unrequited love had fallen: they had deserved better at the hands of fate. She had deserved worse; yet she was the chosen one. It was wicked of her to take all without paying. She would pay to the uttermost farthing: she would tell, there and then. This final determination she came to while she looked into the fire, he holding her hand.

A steady glare from the now flameless embers painted the sides and back of the fireplace with its colour, and the well-polished andirons, and the old brass tongs that would not meet. The underside of the mantel-shelf was flushed with the high-coloured light, and the legs of the table nearest the fire. Tess's face and neck reflected the same warmth, which each gem turned into an Aldebaran or a Sirius*—a constellation of white, red, and green flashes, that interchanged their hues with her every pulsation.

"Do you remember what we said to each other this morning about telling our faults?" he asked abruptly, finding that she still remained immoveable. "We spoke lightly perhaps, and you may well have done so. But for me—it was no light promise. I want to make a confession to you, love."

This, from him, so unexpectedly apposite, had the effect upon her of a Providential interposition. "You have to confess something?" she said quickly, and even with gladness and relief.

"You did not expect it? Ah—you thought too highly of me. Now listen: put your head there; because I want you to forgive me, and not to be indignant with me for not telling you before, as perhaps I ought to have done."

How strange it was! He seemed to be her double. She did not speak, and Clare went on:

"I did not mention it because I was afraid of endangering my chance of you, darling, the great prize of my life—my fellowship, I call you. My brother's fellowship was won at his College; mine at Talbothays Dairy. Well, I would not risk it. I was going to tell you a month ago—at the time you agreed to be mine; but I could not; I thought it might frighten you away from me. I put it off; then I thought I would tell you yesterday, to give you a chance at least of escaping me. But I did not. And I did not this morning, when you proposed our confessing our faults on the landing—the sinner that I was! But I must now I see you sitting there so solemnly. I wonder if you will forgive me?"

"O yes! I am sure that—"

"Well, I hope so. But wait a minute: you don't know. To begin at the beginning. Though I imagine my poor father fears that I am one of the eternally lost for my doctrines, I am, of course, a believer in good morals, Tess, as much as you. I used to wish to be a teacher of men, and it was a great disappointment to me when I found I could not enter the Church. I admired spotlessness, even though I could lay no claim to it, and hated impurity, as I hope I do now. Whatever one may think of plenary inspiration one must heartily subscribe to these words of Paul: 'Be thou an example—in word, in conversation, in charity, in spirit, in faith, in purity.'* It is the only safeguard for us poor human beings: 'Integer vitæ', says a Roman poet who is strange company for St Paul:

> The man of upright life, from frailties free,
> Stands not in need of Moorish spear or bow.*

Well, a certain place is paved with good intentions, and having felt all that so strongly you will see what a terrible remorse it bred in me when, in the midst of my fine aims for other people, I myself fell."

He then told her of that time of his life to which allusion has been made when, tossed about by doubts and difficulties in London, like a cork on the waves, he plunged into eight-and-forty hours' dissipation with a stranger.

"Happily I awoke almost immediately to a sense of my folly," he continued. "I would have no more to say to her, and I came home. I have never repeated the offence. But I felt I should like to treat you with perfect frankness and honour, and I could not do so without telling this. Do you forgive me?"

She pressed his hand tightly for an answer.

"Then we will dismiss it at once and for ever—too painful as it is for the occasion—and talk of something lighter—"

"O Angel—I am almost glad—because now *you* can forgive *me*! I have not made my confession. I have a confession, too—remember, I said so."

"Ah, to be sure! Now then for it, wicked little one."

"Perhaps, although you smile, it is as serious as yours, or more so."

"It can hardly be more serious, dearest."

"It cannot—O no, it cannot!" She jumped up joyfully at the hope. "No, it cannot be more serious, certainly," she cried, "because 'tis just the same! I will tell you now."

She sat down again.

Their hands were still joined. The ashes under the grate were lit by the fire vertically, like a torrid waste. Imagination might have beheld a Last-Day luridness in this red-coaled glow, which fell on his face and hand, and on hers, peering into the loose hair about her brow, and firing the delicate skin underneath. A large shadow of her shape rose upon the wall and ceiling. She bent forward, at which each diamond on her neck gave a sinister wink like a toad's; and pressing her forehead against his temple she entered on her story of her acquaintance with Alec d'Urberville and its results, murmuring the words without flinching, and with her eyelids drooping down.

END OF PHASE THE FOURTH

PHASE THE FIFTH

THE WOMAN PAYS

PHASE THE FIFTH

THE WOMAN PAYS

XXXV

HER narrative ended: even its reassertions and secondary explanations were done. Tess's voice throughout had hardly risen higher than its opening tone; there had been no exculpatory phrase of any kind, and she had not wept.

But the complexion even of external things seemed to suffer transmutation as her announcement progressed. The fire in the grate looked impish, demoniacally funny, as if it did not care in the least about her strait. The fender grinned idly, as if it, too, did not care. The light from the water-bottle was merely engaged in a chromatic problem. All material objects around announced their irresponsibility with terrible iteration. And yet nothing had changed since the moments when he had been kissing her; or rather nothing in the substance of things. But the essence of things had changed.

When she ceased the auricular impressions from their previous endearments seemed to hustle away into the corners of their brains, repeating themselves as echoes from a time of supremely purblind foolishness.

Clare performed the irrelevant act of stirring the fire: the intelligence had not even yet got to the bottom of him. After stirring the embers he rose to his feet: all the force of her disclosure had imparted itself now. His face had withered. In the strenuousness of his concentration he treadled fitfully on the floor. He could not, by any contrivance, think closely enough; that was the meaning of his vague movement. When he spoke it was in the most inadequate, commonplace voice of the many varied tones she had heard from him.

"Tess!"

"Yes, dearest."

"Am I to believe this? From your manner I am to take it as true. O you cannot be out of your mind! You ought to be! Yet you are not.

. . . My wife, my Tess—nothing in you warrants such a supposition as that?"

"I am not out of my mind," she said.

"And yet—" He looked vacantly at her, to resume with dazed senses: "Why didn't you tell me before? Ah yes—you would have told me—in a way; but I hindered you. I remember!"

These, and other of his words, were nothing but the perfunctory babble of the surface while the depths remained paralyzed. He turned away, and bent over a chair. Tess followed him to the middle of the room where he was, and stood there staring at him with eyes that did not weep. Presently she slid down upon her knees beside his foot, and from this position she crouched in a heap. "In the name of our love, forgive me," she whispered with a dry mouth. "I have forgiven you for the same." And as he did not answer she said again, "forgive me, as you are forgiven. *I* forgive *you*, Angel."

"You,—yes, you do."

"But you do not forgive me?"

"O Tess, forgiveness does not apply to the case. You were one person: now you are another. My God—how can forgiveness meet such a grotesque—prestidigitation as that!"

He paused, contemplating this definition; then suddenly broke into horrible laughter—as unnatural and ghastly as a laugh in hell.

"Don't—don't! It kills me quite, that!" she shrieked. "O have mercy upon me—have mercy!"

He did not answer; and, sickly white, she jumped up. "Angel, Angel? What do you mean by that laugh?" she cried out. "Do you know—what this is to me?"

He shook his head.

"I have been hoping, longing, praying, to make you happy. I have thought, what joy it will be to do it, what an unworthy wife I shall be if I do not! That's what I have felt, Angel?"

"I know that."

"I thought, Angel, that you loved me—me, my very self! If it is I you do love, O how can it be that you look and speak so? It frightens me! Having begun to love you, I love you for ever—in all changes, in all disgraces, because you are yourself. I ask no more. Then how can you, O my own husband, stop loving me?"

"I repeat, the woman I have been loving is not you."

"But who?"

"Another woman in your shape."

She perceived in his words the realization of her own apprehensive foreboding in former times. He looked upon her as a species of impostor; a guilty woman in the guise of an innocent one. Terror was upon her white face as she saw it; her cheek was flaccid, and her mouth had almost the aspect of a round little hole. The horrible sense of his view of her so deadened her that she staggered; and he stepped forward, thinking she was going to fall.

"Sit down, sit down," he said gently. "You are ill: and it is natural that you should be."

She did sit down, without knowing where she was, that strained look still upon her face, and her eyes such as to make his flesh creep. "I don't belong to you any more, then; do I Angel?" she asked helplessly. "It is not me, but another woman like me that he loved, he says." The image raised caused her to take pity upon herself as one who was ill-used. Her eyes filled as she regarded her position further; she turned round and burst into a flood of self-sympathetic tears.

Clare was relieved at this change, for the effect on her of what had happened was beginning to be a trouble to him only less than the woe of the disclosure itself. He waited patiently, apathetically—till the violence of her grief had worn itself out, and her rush of weeping had lessened to a catching gasp at intervals.

"Angel," she said suddenly in her natural tones, the insane dry voice of terror having left her now. "Angel, am I too wicked for you and me to live together?"

"I have not been able to think what we can do."

"I shan't ask you to let me live with you, Angel; because I have no right to. I shall not write to mother and sisters to say we be married, as I said I would do. And I shan't finish the good-hussif'* I cut out and meant to make while we were in lodgings."

"Shan't you?"

"No. I shan't do anything, unless you order me to. And if you go away from me I shall not follow 'ee; and if you never speak to me any more I shall not ask why, unless you tell me I may."

"And if I do order you to do anything?"

"I will obey you, like your wretched slave, even if it is to lie down and die."

"You are very good. But it strikes me that there is a want of harmony between your present mood of self-sacrifice and your past mood of self-preservation."

These were the first words of antagonism. To fling elaborate sarcasms at Tess, however, was much like flinging them at a dog or cat. The charms of their subtlety passed by her unappreciated, and she only received them as inimical sounds which meant that anger ruled. She remained mute, not knowing that he was smothering his affection for her; she hardly observed that a tear descended slowly upon his cheek, a tear so large that it magnified the pores of the skin over which it rolled, like the object-lens of a microscope. Meanwhile reillumination as to the terrible and total change that her confession had wrought in his life, in his universe, returned to him, and he tried desperately to advance among the new conditions in which he stood. Some consequent action was necessary; yet what?

"Tess," he said, as gently as he could speak. "I cannot stay—in this room—just now. I will walk out a little way." He quietly left the room; and the two glasses of wine that he had poured out for their supper, one for her, one for him, remained on the table untasted. This was what their *Agape** had come to. At tea, two or three hours earlier, they had, in the freakishness of affection, drunk from one cup.

The closing of the door behind him, gently as it had been pulled to, roused Tess from her stupor. He was gone; she could not stay. Hastily flinging her cloak around her she opened the door and followed, putting out the candles as if she were never coming back. The rain was over, and the night was now clear.

She was soon close at his heels, for Clare walked slowly, and without purpose. His form beside her light grey figure looked black, sinister, and forbidding, and she felt as sarcasm the touch of the jewels of which she had been momentarily so proud. Clare turned at hearing her footsteps, but his recognition of her presence seemed to make no difference in him, and he went on over the five yawning arches of the great bridge in front of the house.

The cow and horse tracks in the road were full of water, the rain having been enough to charge them, but not enough to wash them away. Across these minute pools the reflected stars flitted in a quick transit as she passed; she would not have known they were shining overhead if she had not seen them there—the vastest things of the universe imaged in objects so mean.

The place to which they had travelled to-day was in the same valley as Talbothays, but some miles lower down the river; and the surroundings being open she kept easily in sight of him. Away from the house the road wound through the meads, and along these she followed Clare, without any attempt to come up with him or to attract him, but with dumb and vacant fidelity.

At last, however, her listless walk brought her up alongside him, and still he said nothing. The cruelty of fooled honesty is often great after enlightenment, and it was mighty in Clare now. The outdoor air had apparently taken away from him all tendency to act on impulse; she knew that he saw her without irradiation—in all her bareness; that Time was chanting his satiric psalm at her then:

> Behold, when thy face is made bare, he that loved thee shall hate;
> Thy face shall be no more fair at the fall of thy fate.
> For thy life shall fall as a leaf and be shed as the rain;
> And the veil of thine head shall be grief; and the crown shall be pain.*

He was still intently thinking, and her companionship had now insufficient power to break or divert the strain of thought. What a weak thing her presence must have become to him! She could not help addressing Clare:

"What have I done, what *have* I done? I have not told of anything that interferes with or belies my love for you. You don't think I planned it, do you? It is in your own mind, what you are angry at, Angel; it is not in me. O it is not in me, and I am not that deceitful woman you think me!"

"H'm—well. Not deceitful, my wife; but not the same. No: not the same. But do not make me reproach you: I have sworn that I will not; and I will do everything to avoid it."

But she went on pleading in her distraction; and perhaps said things that would have been better left to silence. "Angel, Angel: I was a child—a child when it happened! I knew nothing of men."

"You were more sinned against than sinning, that I admit."

"Then will you not forgive me?"

"I do forgive you. But forgiveness is not all."

"And love me?"

To this question he did not answer.

"O Angel—my mother says that it sometimes happens so—she knows several cases when they were worse than I, and the husband has not minded it much—has got over it, at least. And yet the woman has not loved him as I do you."

"Don't, Tess; don't argue. Different societies different manners. You almost make me say you are an unapprehending peasant woman, who have never been initiated into the proportions of social things. You don't know what you say."

"I am only a peasant by position, not by nature."

She spoke with an impulse to anger, but it went as it came.

"So much the worse for you. I think that parson who unearthed your pedigree would have done better if he had held his tongue. I cannot help associating your decline as a family with this other fact—of your want of firmness. Decrepit families imply decrepit wills, decrepit conduct. Heaven, why did you give me a handle for despising you more by informing me of your descent! Here was I thinking you a new-sprung child of nature: there were you, the belated seedling of an effete aristocracy!"

"Lots of families are as bad as mine in that. Retty's family were once large landowners, and so were Dairyman Billett's, and the Debbyhouses who now are carters were once the De Bayeux family. You find such as I everywhere; 'tis a feature of our county, and I can't help it."

"So much the worse for the county."

She took these reproaches in their bulk simply, not in their particulars: he did not love her as he had loved her hitherto, and to all else she was indifferent.

They wandered on again in silence. It was said afterwards that a cottager of Wellbridge, who went out late that night for a doctor, met two lovers in the pastures, walking very slowly, without converse, one behind the other, as in a funeral procession; and the glimpse that he obtained of their faces seemed to denote that they were anxious and sad. Returning later he passed them again in the same field, progressing just as slowly, and as regardless of the hour and of the cheerless night as before. It was only on account of his preoccupation with his own affairs, and the illness in his house, that he did not bear in mind the curious incident, which however he recalled a long while after.

During the interval of the cottager's going and coming she had said to her husband, "I don't see how I can help being the cause of much misery to you all your life. The river is down there: I can put an end to myself in it. I am not afraid."

"I don't wish to add murder to my other follies," he said.

"I will leave something to show that I did it myself—on account of my shame. They will not blame you then."

"Don't speak so absurdly—I wish not to hear it. It is nonsense to have such thoughts in this kind of case, which is rather one for satirical laughter than for tragedy. You don't in the least understand the quality of the mishap. It would be viewed in the light of a joke by nine-tenths of the world, if it were known. Please oblige me by returning to the house and going to bed."

"I will," said she dutifully.

They had rambled round by a road which led to the well-known ruins of the Cistercian abbey* behind the mill, the latter having, in centuries past, been attached to the monastic establishment. The mill still worked on, food being a perennial necessity; the abbey had perished, creeds being transient. One continually sees the ministration of the temporary outlasting the ministration of the eternal. Their walk having been circuitous they were still not far from the house, and in obeying his direction she only had to reach the large stone bridge across the main river, and follow the road for a few yards. When she got back everything remained as she had left it, the fire being still burning. She did not stay downstairs for more than a minute, but proceeded to her chamber, whither the luggage had been taken. Here she sat down on the edge of the bed, looking blankly around, and presently began to undress. In removing the light towards the bedstead its rays fell upon the tester of white dimity:* something was hanging beneath it, and she lifted the candle to see what it was. A bough of mistletoe: Angel had put it there; she knew that in an instant. This was the explanation of that mysterious parcel which it had been so difficult to pack and bring; whose contents he would not explain to her, saying that time would soon show her the purpose thereof. In his zest and his gaiety he had hung it there. How foolish and inopportune that mistletoe looked now.

Having nothing more to fear, having scarce anything to hope, for that he would relent there seemed no promise whatever, she lay down dully. When sorrow ceases to be speculative sleep sees her opportunity. Among so many happier moods which forbid repose this was a mood which welcomed it, and in a few minutes the lonely Tess forget existence, surrounded by the aromatic stillness of the chamber that had once, possibly, been the bride-chamber of her own ancestry.

Later on that night Clare also retraced his steps to the house. Entering softly to the sitting-room he obtained a light, and with the manner of one who had considered his course he spread his rugs upon the old horse-hair sofa which stood there, and roughly shaped it to a sleeping-couch. Before lying down he crept shoeless upstairs, and listened at the door of her apartment. Her measured breathing told that she was sleeping profoundly.

"Thank God!" murmured Clare; and yet he was conscious of a pang of bitterness at the thought—approximately true, though not wholly so—that having shifted the burden of her life to his shoulders she was now reposing without care.

He turned away to descend; then, irresolute, faced round to her door again. In the act he caught sight of one of the d'Urberville dames, whose portrait was immediately over the entrance to Tess's bedchamber. In the candlelight the painting was more than unpleasant. Sinister design lurked in the woman's features, a concentrated purpose of revenge on the other sex—so it seemed to him then. The Caroline bodice of the portrait was low—precisely as Tess's had been when he tucked it in to show the necklace; and again he experienced the distressing sensation of a resemblance between them.

The check was sufficient. He resumed his retreat and descended.

His air remained calm and cold, his small compressed mouth indexing his powers of self-control; his face wearing still that terribly sterile expression which had spread thereon since her disclosure. It was the face of a man who was no longer passion's slave, yet who found no advantage in his enfranchisement. He was simply regarding the harrowing contingencies of human experience, the unexpectedness of things. Nothing so pure, so sweet, so virginal as Tess had seemed possible all the long while that he had adored her, up to an hour ago; but

The little less, and what worlds away!*

He argued erroneously when he said to himself that her heart was not indexed in the honest freshness of her face; but Tess had no advocate to set him right. Could it be possible he continued, that eyes which as they gazed never expressed any divergence from what the tongue was telling, were yet ever seeing another world behind her ostensible one, discordant and contrasting?

He reclined on his couch in the sitting-room, and extinguished the light. The night came in, and took up its place there, unconcerned and indifferent; the night which had already swallowed up his happiness, and was now digesting it listlessly; and was ready to swallow up the happiness of a thousand other people with as little disturbance or change of mien.

XXXVI

CLARE arose in the light of a dawn that was ashy and furtive, as though associated with crime. The fireplace confronted him with its extinct embers; the spread supper-table, whereon stood the two full glasses of untasted wine, now flat and filmy; her vacated seat and his own; the other articles of furniture, with their eternal look of not being able to help it, their intolerable inquiry what was to be done? From above there was no sound; but in a few minutes there came a knock at the door. He remembered that it would be the neighbouring cottager's wife, who was to minister to their wants while they remained here.

The presence of a third person in the house would be extremely awkward just now, and, being already dressed, he opened the window and informed her that they could manage to shift for themselves that morning. She had a milk-can in her hand, which he told her to leave at the door. When the dame had gone away he searched in the back quarters of the house for fuel and speedily lit a fire. There was plenty of eggs, butter, bread, and so on, in the larder, and Clare soon had breakfast laid, his experiences at the dairy having rendered him facile in domestic preparations. The smoke of the kindled wood rose from the chimney without like a lotus-headed column; local people who were passing by saw it, and thought of the newly-married couple, and envied their happiness.

Angel cast a final glance round, and then going to the foot of the stairs called in a conventional voice, "Breakfast is ready!"

He opened the front door and took a few steps in the morning air. When, after a short space, he came back, she was already in the sitting-room, mechanically readjusting the breakfast things. As she was fully attired, and the interval since his calling her had been but two or three minutes, she must have been dressed or nearly so before he went to summon her. Her hair was twisted up in a large round mass at the back of her head, and she had put on one of the new frocks—a pale blue woollen garment with neck-frillings of white. Her hands and face appeared to be cold, and she had possibly been sitting dressed in the bedroom a long time without any fire. The marked civility of Clare's tone in calling her seemed to have inspired her, for the moment, with a new glimmer of hope. But it soon died when she looked at him.

The pair were, in truth, but the ashes of their former fires. To the hot sorrow of the previous night had succeeded heaviness: it seemed as if nothing could kindle either of them to fervour of sensation any more.

He spoke gently to her; and she replied with a like undemonstrativeness. At last she came up to him, looking in his sharply defined face as one who had no consciousness that her own formed a visible object also.

"Angel?" she said, and paused, touching him with her fingers lightly as a breeze, as though she could hardly believe to be there in the flesh the man who was once her lover. Her eyes were bright: her pale cheek still showed its wonted roundness, though half-dried tears had left glistening traces thereon; and the usually ripe red mouth was almost as pale as her cheek. Throbbingly alive as she was still, under the stress of her mental grief the life beat so brokenly that a little further pull upon it would cause real illness, dull her characteristic eyes, and make her mouth thin.

She looked absolutely pure. Nature, in her fantastic trickery, had set such a seal of maidenhood upon Tess's countenance that he gazed at her with a stupefied air:

"Tess—say it is not true! No, it is not true!"

"It is true."

"Every word?"

"Every word."

He looked at her imploringly, as if he would willingly have taken a lie from her lips, knowing it to be one, and have made of it, by some sort of sophistry, a valid denial. However she only repeated, "It is true."

"Is he living?" Angel then asked.

"The baby died."

"But the man?"

"He is alive."

A last despair passed over Clare's face. "Is he in England?"

"Yes."

He took a few vague steps. "My position—is this," he said abruptly. "I thought—any man would have thought—that by giving up all ambition to win a wife with social standing, with fortune, with knowledge of the world, I should secure rustic innocence, as surely as I should secure pink cheeks; but—However, I am no man to reproach you, and I will not."

Tess felt his position so entirely that the reminder had not been needed. Therein lay just the distress of it; she saw that he had lost all round.

"Angel—I should not have let it go on to marriage with you if I had not known that, after all, there was a last way out of it for you; though I hoped you would never—" Her voice grew husky.

"A last way?"

"I mean to get rid of me. You *can* get rid of me."

"How?"

"By divorcing me."

"Good heavens—how can you be so simple! How can I divorce you!"

"Can't you—now that I have told you? I thought my confession would give you grounds for that."

"O Tess—you are too, too—childish—unformed—crude, I suppose! I don't know what you are. You don't understand the law— you don't understand!"

"What—you cannot?"

"Indeed I cannot."

A quick shame mixed with the misery upon his listener's face. "I thought—I thought—" she whispered . . . . "O, now I see how wicked I seem to you. Believe me, believe me, on my soul, I never thought but that you could! I hoped you would not, yet I believed without a doubt that you could cast me off if you were determined, and didn't love me at—at—all!"

"You were mistaken," he said.

"O then I ought to have done it, to have done it last night! But I hadn't the courage. That's just like me!"

"The courage to do what?"

As she did not answer he took her by the hand. "What were you thinking of doing?" he inquired.

"Of putting an end to myself."

"When?"

She writhed under this inquisitorial manner of his. "Last night," she answered.

"Where?"

"Under your mistletoe."

"My good—! how?" he asked sternly.

"I'll tell you, if you won't be angry with me!" she said shrinking. "It was with the cord of my box. But I could not—do the last thing! I was afraid that it might cause a scandal to your name."

The unexpected quality of this confession, wrung from her, and not volunteered, shook him perceptibly. But he still held her, and letting his glance fall from her face downwards he said "Now, listen to this. You must not dare to think of such a horrible thing! How could you! You will promise me as your husband to attempt that no more."

"I am ready to promise. I saw how wicked it was."

"Wicked! The idea was unworthy of you beyond description."

"But Angel," she pleaded, enlarging her eyes in calm unconcern upon him. "It was thought of entirely on your account—to set you free without the scandal of the divorce that I thought you would have to get. I should never have dreamt of doing it on mine. However to do it with my own hand is too good for me, after all. It is you, my ruined husband, who ought to strike the blow. I think I should love you more, if that were possible, if you could bring yourself to do it, since there's no other way of escape for 'ee. I feel I am so utterly worthless. So very greatly in the way!"

"Ssh!"

"Well, since you say no, I won't. I have no wish opposed to yours."

He knew this to be true enough. Since the desperation of the night her activities had dropped to zero, and there was no further rashness to be feared.

Tess tried to busy herself again over the breakfast-table, with more or less success, and they sat down both on the same side, so that their glances did not meet. There was at first something awkward in hearing each other eat and drink, but this could not be escaped; moreover the amount of eating done was small on both sides. Breakfast over he rose, and, telling her the hour at which he might be expected to dinner, went off to the miller's, in a mechanical pursuance of the plan of studying that business, which had been his only practical reason for coming here.

When he was gone Tess stood at the window, and presently saw his form crossing the great stone bridge which conducted to the mill premises. He sank behind it, crossed the railway beyond, and disappeared. Then without a sigh she turned her attention to the room, and began clearing the table and setting it in order.

The charwoman soon came; her presence was at first a strain upon Tess; but afterwards an alleviation. At half-past twelve she left her assistant alone in the kitchen, and returning to the sitting-room waited for the reappearance of Angel's form behind the bridge.

About one he showed himself. Her face flushed, although he was a quarter of a mile off. She ran to the kitchen to get the dinner served by the time he should enter. He went first to the room where they had washed their hands together the day before; and as he entered the sitting-room the dish-covers rose from the dishes as if by his own motion.

"How punctual," he said.

"Yes—I saw you coming over the bridge," said she.

The meal was passed in commonplace talk of what he had been doing during the morning at the Abbey mill; of the methods of bolting and the old-fashioned machinery, which he feared would not enlighten him greatly on modern improved methods, some of it seeming to have been in use ever since the days it ground for the monks in the adjoining conventual buildings, now a heap of ruins. He left the house again in the course of an hour, coming home at dusk, and occupying himself through the evening with his papers. She feared she was in the way, and when the old woman was gone retired to the kitchen, where she made herself busy as well as she could for more than an hour.

Clare's shape appeared at the door. "You must not work like this," he said. "You are not my servant; you are my wife."

She raised her eyes, and brightened somewhat. "I may think myself that—indeed?" she murmured, in piteous raillery. "You mean in name! Well, I don't want to be anything more."

"You *may* think so, Tess? You are. What do you mean?"

"I don't know," she said hastily, with tears in her accents. "I thought I—because I am not respectable, I mean. . . . I told you I thought I was not respectable enough, long ago—and on that account I didn't want to marry you, only—only you urged me!" She broke into sobs and turned her back to him.

It would almost have won round any man but Angel Clare. Within the remoter depths of his constitution, so gentle and affectionate as he was in general, there lay hidden a hard logical deposit, like a vein of metal in a soft loam, which turned the edge of everything that attempted to traverse it. It had blocked his acceptance of the Church; it blocked his acceptance of Tess. Moreover his affection itself was less fire than radiance, and, with regard to the other sex, when he ceased to believe he ceased to follow; contrasting in this with many impressionable natures, who remain sensuously infatuated with what they intellectually despise. He waited till her sobbing ceased.

"I wish half the women in England were as respectable as you," he said, in an ebullition of bitterness against womankind in general. "It isn't a question of respectability, but one of principle."

He spoke such things as these and more of a kindred sort to her, being still swayed by the antipathetic wave which warps direct souls with such persistence when once their vision finds itself mocked by appearances. There was, it is true, underneath, a back-current of sympathy through which a woman of the world might have conquered him. But Tess did not think of this; she took everything as her deserts, and hardly opened her mouth. The firmness of her devotion to him was indeed almost pitiful: quick-tempered as she naturally was, nothing that he could say made her unseemly; she sought not her own; was not provoked; thought no evil of his treatment of her. She might just now have been Apostolic Charity* herself returned to a self-seeking modern world.

This evening, night, and morning, were passed precisely as the preceding ones had been passed. On one, and only one, occasion did she—the formerly free and independent Tess—venture to make any advances. It was on the third occasion of his starting after a meal to go out to the flour-mill. As he was leaving the table he said "Good-bye", and she replied in the same words, at the same time inclining her mouth in the way of his. He did not avail himself of the invitation, saying as he turned hastily aside, "I shall be home punctually."

Tess shrank into herself as if she had been struck. Often enough had he tried to reach those lips against her consent: often had he said gaily that her mouth and breath tasted of the butter and eggs and milk and honey on which she mainly lived, that he drew sustenance from them, and other follies of that sort. But he did not care for them now. He observed her sudden shrinking, and said gently: "You know, I have to think of a course. . . . It was imperative that we should stay together a little while, to avoid the scandal to you that would have resulted from our immediate parting. But you must see it is only for form's sake."

"Yes," said Tess absently.

He went out, and on his way to the mill stood still, and wished for a moment that he had responded yet more kindly, and kissed her once at least.

Thus they lived through this despairing day or two; in the same house, truly; but more widely apart than before they were lovers. It was evident to her that he was, as he had said, living with paralyzed activities, in his endeavour to think of a plan of procedure. She was awestricken to discover such determination under such apparent flexibility. His consistency was, indeed, too cruel. She no longer expected forgiveness now. More than once she thought of going away from him during his absence at the mill; but she feared that this, instead of benefiting him, might be the means of hampering and humiliating him yet more, if it should become known.

Meanwhile Clare was meditating verily. His thought had been unsuspended; he was becoming ill with thinking, eaten out with thinking, withered by thinking: scourged out of all his former pulsating, flexuous domesticity. He walked about saying to himself, "What's to be done—what's to be done!" and by chance she overheard him. It caused her to break the reserve about their future which had hitherto prevailed.

"I suppose—you are not going to live with me—long, are you, Angel?" she asked, the sunk corners of her mouth betraying how purely mechanical were the means by which she retained that expression of chastened calm upon her face.

"I cannot," he said, "without despising myself, and what is worse, perhaps despising you. I mean, of course, cannot live with you in the ordinary sense. At present, whatever I feel, I do not despise you. And let me speak plainly, or you may not see all my difficulties. How can we live together while that man lives?—he being your husband in Nature, and not I. If he were dead it might be different. . . . Besides, that's not all the difficulty; it lies in another consideration—one bearing upon the future of other people than ourselves. Think of the years to come, and children being born to us, and this past matter getting known—for it must get known. There is not an uttermost part of the earth but somebody comes from it or goes to it from elsewhere. Well, think of wretches of our flesh and blood growing up

under a taunt which they will gradually get to feel the full force of
with their expanding years. What an awakening for them! What a
prospect! Can you honestly say, remain, after contemplating this
contingency? Don't you think we had better endure the ills we have
than fly to others?"

Her eyelids, weighted with trouble, continued drooping as before.
"I cannot say remain," she answered. "I cannot. I had not thought
so far."

Tess's feminine hope—shall we confess it?—had been so obstin-
ately recuperative as to revive in her surreptitious visions of a
domiciliary intimacy continued long enough to break down his coldness even against his judgment. Though unsophisticated in the usual
sense she was not incomplete; and it would have denoted deficiency
of womanhood if she had not instinctively known what an argument
lies in propinquity. Nothing else would serve her, she knew, if this
failed. It was wrong to hope in what was of the nature of strategy, she
said to herself: yet that sort of hope she could not extinguish. His last
representation had now been made, and it was, as she had said, a new
view. She had truly never thought so far as that, and his lucid picture
of possible offspring who would scorn her was one that brought
deadly conviction to an honest heart which was humanitarian to its
centre. Sheer experience had already taught her that in some circumstances there was one thing better than to lead a good life, and that
was to be saved from leading any life whatever. Like all who have
been previsioned by suffering she could, in the words of M. Sully-
Prudhomme, hear a penal sentence in the fiat, "You shall be born,"*
particularly if addressed to potential issue of hers.

Yet such is the vulpine slyness of Dame Nature that till now Tess
had been hoodwinked by her love for Clare into forgetting it might
result in vitalizations that would inflict upon others what she had
bewailed as a misfortune to herself.

She therefore could not withstand his argument. But with the
self-combating proclivity of the supersensitive an answer thereto
arose in Clare's own mind, and he almost feared it. It was based
on her exceptional physical nature; and she might have used it
promisingly. She might have added besides: "On an Australian
upland or Texan plain who is to know or care about my misfortunes,
or to reproach me or you?" Yet like the majority of women, she
accepted the momentary presentment as if it were the inevitable.

And she may have been right. The intuitive heart of woman knoweth not only its own bitterness, but its husband's, and even if these assumed reproaches were not likely to be addressed to him or to his by strangers, they might have reached his ears from his own fastidious brain.

It was the third day of the estrangement. Some might risk the odd paradox that with more animalism he would have been the nobler man. We do not say it. Yet Clare's love was doubtless ethereal to a fault, imaginative to impracticability. With these natures corporeal presence is sometimes less appealing than corporeal absence, the latter creating an ideal presence that conveniently drops the defects of the real. She found that her personality did not plead her cause so forcibly as she had anticipated. The figurative phrase was true: she was another woman than the one who had excited his desire.

"I have thought over what you say," she remarked to him, moving her forefinger over the tablecloth, her other hand, which bore the ring that mocked them both, supporting her forehead. "It is quite true, all of it: it must be. You must go away from me."

"But what can you do?"

"I can go home."

Clare had not thought of that. "Are you sure?" he inquired.

"Quite sure. We ought to part: and we may as well get it past and done. You once said that I was apt to win men against their better judgment: and if I am constantly before your eyes I may cause you to change your plans in opposition to your reason and wish; and afterwards your repentance and my sorrow will be terrible."

"And you would like to go home?" he asked.

"I want to leave you, and go home."

"Then it shall be so."

Though she did not look up at him she started. There was a difference between the proposition and the covenant, which she had felt only too quickly.

"I feared it would come to this," she murmured, her countenance meekly fixed. "I don't complain, Angel. I—I think it best. What you said has quite convinced me. Yes, though nobody else should reproach me, if we should stay together, yet somewhen, years hence, you might get angry with me for any ordinary matter, and knowing what you do of my bygones, you yourself might be tempted to say words, and they might be overheard, perhaps by my own children.

O, what only hurts me now would torture and kill me then! I will go—to-morrow."

"And I shall not stay here. Though I didn't like to initiate it, I have seen that it was advisable we should part—at least for a while, till I can better see the shape that things have taken, and can write to you."

Tess stole a glance at her husband. He was pale, even tremulous; but, as before, she was appalled by the determination revealed in the depths of this gentle being she had married—the will to subdue the grosser to the subtler emotion, the substance to the conception, the flesh to the spirit. Propensities, tendencies, habits, were as dead leaves upon the tyrannous wind of his imaginative ascendency.

He may have observed her look, for he explained: "I think of people more kindly when I am away from them;" adding cynically, "God knows; perhaps we shall shake down together some day, for weariness; thousands have done it!"

That day he began to pack up, and she went upstairs and began to pack also. Both knew that it was in their two minds that they might part the next morning for ever, despite the gloss of assuaging conjectures thrown over their proceedings because they were of the sort to whom any parting which has an air of finality is a torture. He knew, and she knew, that though the fascination which each had exercised over the other—on her part independently of accomplishments—would probably in the first days of their separation be even more potent than ever, time must attenuate the effect; the practical arguments against accepting her as a housemate might pronounce themselves more strongly in the boreal light of a remoter view. Moreover when two people are once parted, have abandoned a common domicile and a common environment, new growths insensibly bud upward to fill each vacated place; unforeseen accidents hinder intentions, and old plans are forgotten.

XXXVII

MIDNIGHT came and passed silently, for there was nothing to announce it in the Valley of the Froom.

Not long after one o'clock there was a slight creak in the darkened farm-house once the mansion of the d'Urbervilles. Tess, who used the upper chamber, heard it, and awoke. It had come from the corner step of the staircase, which, as usual, was loosely nailed. She saw the door of her bedroom open; and the figure of her husband crossed the stream of moonlight with a curiously careful tread. He was in his shirt and trousers only, and her first flush of joy died when she perceived that his eyes were fixed in an unnatural stare on vacancy. When he reached the middle of the room he stood still, and murmured in tones of indescribable sadness, "Dead; dead; dead!"

Under the influence of any strongly disturbing force Clare would occasionally walk in his sleep, and even perform strange feats, such as he had done on the night of their return from market just before their marriage, when he re-enacted in his bedroom his combat with the man who had insulted her. Tess saw that continued mental distress had wrought him into that somnambulistic state now.

Her loyal confidence in him lay so deep down in her heart that awake or asleep he inspired her with no sort of personal fear: if he had entered with a pistol in his hand he would scarcely have disturbed her trust in his protectiveness.

Clare came close, and bent over her. "Dead, dead, dead!" he murmured.

After fixedly regarding her for some moments with the same gaze of unmeasurable woe he bent lower, enclosed her in his arms, and rolled her in the sheet as in a shroud. Then lifting her from the bed with as much respect as one would show to a dead body, he carried her across the room, murmuring, "My poor poor Tess, my dearest darling Tess! So sweet, so good, so true!"

The words of endearment, withheld so severely in his waking hours, were inexpressibly sweet to her forlorn and hungry heart. If it had been to save her weary life she would not, by moving or struggling, have put an end to the position she found herself in. Thus she lay in absolute stillness, scarcely venturing to breathe, and, wondering what he was going to do with her, suffered herself to be borne out upon the landing. "My wife—dead, dead!" he said.

He paused in his labours for a moment to lean with her against the bannister. Was he going to throw her down? Self-solicitude was near extinction in her, and in the knowledge that he had planned to depart on the morrow, possibly for always, she lay in his arms in this precarious position with a sense rather of luxury than of terror. If they could only fall together, and both be dashed to pieces, how fit, how desirable.

However he did not let her fall; but took advantage of the support of the handrail to imprint a kiss upon her lips—lips in the daytime scorned. Then he clasped her with a renewed firmness of hold, and descended the staircase. The creak of the loose stair did not awaken him, and they reached the ground-floor safely. Freeing one of his hands from his grasp of her for a moment, he slid back the door-bar, and passed out, slightly striking his stockinged toe against the edge of the door. But this he seemed not to mind, and, having room for extension in the open air, he lifted her against his shoulder, so that he could carry her with ease, the absence of clothes taking much from his burden. Thus he bore her off the premises in the direction of the river a few yards distant.

His ultimate intention if he had any, she had not yet divined; and she found herself conjecturing on the matter as a third person might have done. So easefully had she delivered her whole being up to him that it pleased her to think he was regarding her as his absolute possession, to dispose of as he should choose. It was consoling, under the hovering terror of to-morrow's separation, to feel that he really recognized her now as his wife Tess, and did not cast her off, even if in that recognition he went so far as to arrogate to himself the right of harming her.

Ah—now she knew what he was dreaming of; that Sunday morning when he had borne her along through the water with the other dairy-maids, who had loved him nearly as much as she, if that were possible, which Tess could hardly admit. Clare did not cross the bridge with her, but proceeding several paces on the same side towards the adjoining mill, at length stood still on the brink of the river.

Its waters, in creeping down these miles of meadow-land, frequently divided, serpentining in purposeless curves, looping themselves around little islands that had no name, returning, and re-embodying themselves as a broad main stream further on. Opposite the spot to which he had brought her was such a general confluence, and the river there was proportionately voluminous and deep. Across it was a narrow footbridge; but now the autumn flood had washed the handrail away, leaving the bare plank only, which, lying a few inches above the speeding current, formed a giddy pathway for even steady heads; and Tess had noticed from the window of the house in the daytime young men walking across upon it as a feat in balancing. Her husband had possibly observed the same performance; anyhow he now mounted the plank, and sliding one foot forward advanced along it.

Was he going to drown her? Probably he was. The spot was lonely; the river deep and wide enough to make such a purpose easy of accomplishment. He might drown her if he would: it would be better than parting to-morrow to lead severed lives.

The swift stream raced and gyrated under them, tossing, distorting, and splitting the moon's reflected face. Spots of froth travelled past, and intercepted weeds waved behind the piles. If they could both fall together into the current now, their arms would be so tightly clasped together that they could not be saved: they would go out of the world almost painlessly, and there would be no more reproach to her, or to him for marrying her. His last half-hour with her would have been a loving one; while if they lived till he awoke his daytime aversion would return, and this hour would remain to be contemplated only as a transient dream.

The impulse stirred in her, yet she dared not indulge it, to make a movement that would have precipitated them both into the gulf. How she valued her own life had been proved; but his—she had no right to tamper with it. He reached the other side with her in safety.

Here they were within a plantation which formed the Abbey grounds, and taking a new hold of her he went onward a few steps till they reached the ruined choir of the Abbey-church. Against the north wall was the empty stone coffin of an abbot, in which every tourist with a turn for grim humour was accustomed to stretch himself. In this Clare carefully laid Tess. Having kissed her lips a second time he breathed deeply, as if a greatly desired end were attained. Clare then lay down on the ground alongside, when he immediately fell into the deep dead slumber of exhaustion, and remained motionless as a log. The spurt of mental excitement which had produced the effort was now over.

Tess sat up in the coffin. The night, though dry and mild for the season, was more than sufficiently cold to make it dangerous for him to remain here long, in his half-clothed state. If he were left to himself he would in all probability stay there till the morning, and be chilled to certain death. She had heard of such deaths after sleep-walking. But how could she dare to awaken him, and let him know what he had been doing, when it would mortify him to discover his folly in respect of her? Tess, however, stepping out of her stone confine, shook him slightly, but was unable to arouse him without being violent. It was indispensable to do something, for she was beginning to shiver, the sheet being but a poor protection. Her excitement had in a measure kept her warm during the few minutes' adventure; but that beatific interval was over.

It suddenly occurred to her to try persuasion; and accordingly she whispered in his ear, with as much firmness and decision as she could summon: "Let us walk on, darling," at the same time taking him suggestively by the arm. To her relief he unresistingly acqui-esced; her words had apparently thrown him back into his dream, which thenceforward seemed to enter on a new phase, wherein he fancied she had risen as a spirit, and was leading him to heaven. Thus she conducted him by the arm to the stone bridge in front of their residence, crossing which they stood at the manor-house door. Tess's feet were quite bare, and the stones hurt her, and chilled her to the bone; but Clare was in his woollen stockings, and appeared to feel no discomfort.

There was no further difficulty. She induced him to lie down on his own sofa bed, and covered him up warmly, lighting a temporary fire of wood, to dry any dampness out of him. The noise of these attentions she thought might awaken him, and secretly wished that they might. But the exhaustion of his mind and body was such that he remained undisturbed.

As soon as they met the next morning Tess divined that Angel knew little or nothing of how far she had been concerned in the night's excursion, though as regarded himself he may have been aware that he had not lain still. In truth he had awakened that morning from a sleep deep as annihilation, and, during those first few moments in which the brain, like a Samson shaking himself, is trying its strength, he had some dim notion of an unusual nocturnal proceeding. But the realities of his situation soon displaced conjecture on the other subject.

He waited in expectancy to discern some mental pointing: he knew that if any intention of his, concluded over-night, did not vanish in the light of morning, it stood on a basis approximating to one of pure reason, even if initiated by impulse of feeling; that it was so far, therefore, to be trusted. He thus beheld in the pale morning light the resolve to separate from her; not as a hot and indignant instinct, but denuded of the passionateness which had made it scorch and burn: standing in its bones; nothing but a skeleton, but none the less there. Clare no longer hesitated.

At breakfast, and while they were packing the few remaining articles, he showed his weariness from the night's effort so unmistak- ably that Tess was on the point of revealing all that had happened; but the reflection that it would anger him, grieve him, stultify him, to know that he had instinctively manifested a fondness for her of which his commonsense did not approve; that his inclination had compromised his dignity when reason slept, again deterred her. It was too much like laughing at a man when sober for his erratic deeds during intoxication.

It just crossed her mind, too, that he might have a faint recollection of his tender vagary, and was disinclined to allude to it from a conviction that she would take amatory advantage of the opportunity it gave her of appealing to him anew not to go.

He had ordered by letter a vehicle from the nearest town, and soon after breakfast it arrived. She saw in it the beginning of the end—the temporary end, at least, for the revelation of his tenderness by the incident of the night raised dreams of a possible future with him. The luggage was put on the top, and the man drove them off, the miller and the old waiting-woman expressing some surprise at their precipitate departure, which Clare attributed to his discovery that the mill-work was not of the modern kind which he wished to investigate, a statement that was true so far as it went. Beyond this there was nothing in the manner of their leaving to suggest a *fiasco*, or that they were not going together to visit friends.

Their route lay near the dairy from which they had started with such solemn joy in each other a few days back, and as Clare wished to wind up his business with Mr Crick Tess could hardly avoid paying

Mrs Crick a call at the same time, unless she would excite suspicion of their unhappy state.

To make the call as unobtrusive as possible they left the carriage by the wicket leading down from the high-road to the dairyhouse, and descended the track on foot, side by side. The withy-bed had been cut, and they could see over the stumps the spot to which Clare had followed her when he pressed her to be his wife: to the left the enclosure in which she had been fascinated by his harp; and far away, behind the cowstalls, the mead which had been the scene of their first embrace. The gold of the summer picture was now grey, the colours mean, the rich soil mud, and the river cold.

Over the barton-gate the dairyman saw them, and came forward, throwing into his face the kind of jocularity deemed appropriate in Talbothays and its vicinity on the reappearance of the newly-married. Then Mrs Crick emerged from the house, and several others of their old acquaintance; though Marian and Retty did not seem to be there.

Tess valiantly bore their sly attacks and friendly humours, which affected her far otherwise than they supposed. In the tacit agreement of husband and wife to keep their estrangement a secret they behaved as would have been ordinary. And then, although she would rather there had been no word spoken on the subject, Tess had to hear in detail the story of Marian and Retty. The latter had gone home to her father's; and Marian had left to look for employment elsewhere. They feared she would come to no good.

To dissipate the sadness of this recital Tess went and bade all her favourite cows good-bye, touching each of them with her hand: and as she and Clare stood side by side at leaving, as if united body and soul, there would have been something peculiarly sorry in their aspect to one who should have seen it truly: two limbs of one life, as they outwardly were, his arm touching hers, her skirts touching him, facing one way, as against all the dairy facing the other, speaking in their adieux as "we"; and yet sundered like the poles. Perhaps something unusually stiff and embarrassed in their attitude, some awkwardness in acting up to their profession of unity, different from the natural shyness of young couples, may have been apparent; for when they were gone Mrs Crick said to her husband, "How onnatural the brightness of her eyes did seem, and how they stood like waxen images and talked as if they were in a dream! Didn't it strike 'ee that 'twas so? Tess had always sommat strange in her; and she's not now quite like the proud young bride of a well-be-doing man."

They re-entered the vehicle, and were driven along the roads towards Weatherbury and Stagfoot Lane, till they reached the Lane inn, where Clare dismissed the fly* and man. They rested here awhile, and entering the Vale were next driven onward towards her home by a stranger who did not know their relations. At a midway point, when Nuttlebury had been passed, and where there were cross-roads, Clare stopped the conveyance, and said to Tess that if she meant to return to her mother's house it was here that he would leave her. As they could not talk with freedom in the driver's presence he asked her to accompany him for a few steps on foot along one of the branch roads; she assented, and directing the man to wait a few minutes they strolled away.

"Now, let us understand each other," he said gently. "There is no anger between us, though there is that which I cannot endure at present. I will try to bring myself to endure it. I will let you know where I go to, as soon as I know myself. And if I can bring myself to bear it—if it is desirable, possible—I will come to you. But until I come to you it will be better that you should not try to come to me."

The severity of the decree seemed deadly to Tess: she saw his view of her clearly enough: he could regard her in no other light than that of one who had practised gross deceit upon him. Yet could a woman who had done even what she had done deserve all this? But she could contest the point with him no further. She simply repeated after him his own words.

"Until you come to me I must not try to come to you."

"Just so."

"May I write to you?"

"O yes—if you are ill, or want anything at all. I hope that will not be the case; so that it may happen that I write first to you."

"I agree to the conditions, Angel; because you know best what my punishment ought to be; only—only—don't make it more than I can bear!"

That was all she said on the matter. If Tess had been artful; had she made a scene, fainted, wept hysterically, in that lonely lane, notwithstanding the fury of fastidiousness with which he was possessed he would probably not have withstood her. But her mood of long-suffering made his way easy for him, and she herself was his best advocate, Pride, too, entered into her submission—which perhaps was a symptom of that reckless acquiescence in chance too apparent in the whole d'Urberville family—and the many effective chords which she could have stirred by an appeal were left untouched.

The remainder of their discourse was on practical matters only. He now handed her a packet containing a fairly good sum of money, which he had obtained from his bankers for the purpose. The brilliants, the interest in which seemed to be Tess's for her life only (if he understood the wording of the will), he advised her to let him send to a bank for safety; and to this she readily agreed.

These things arranged he walked with Tess back to the carriage, and handed her in. The coachman was paid and told where to drive her. Taking next his own bag and umbrella—the sole articles he had brought with him hitherward—he bade her good-bye; and they parted there and then.

The fly moved creepingly up a hill, and Clare watched it go, with an unpremeditated hope that Tess would look out of the window for one moment. But that she never though of doing, would not have ventured to do, lying in a half-dead faint inside. Thus he beheld her recede, and in the anguish of his heart quoted a line from a poet, with peculiar emendations of his own:—

God's *not* in his heaven: all's *wrong* with the world!*

When Tess had passed over the crest of the hill he turned to go his own way, and hardly knew that he loved her still.

XXXVIII

As she drove on through Blackmoor Vale, and the landscape of her youth began to open around her, Tess aroused herself from her stupor. Her first thought was, how would she be able to face her parents?

She reached a turnpike-gate which stood upon the highway to the village. It was thrown open by a stranger, not by the old man who had kept it for many years, and to whom she had been known: he had probably left on New Year's Day, the date when such changes were made. Having received no intelligence lately from her home she asked the turnpike-keeper for news.

"Oh—nothing, miss," he answered. "Marlott is Marlott still. Folks have died, and that. John Durbeyfield, too, hev had a daughter married this week to a gentleman-farmer; not from John's own house, you know: they was married elsewhere; the gentleman being of that high standing that John's own folk was not considered well-be-doing enough to have any part in it, the bridegroom seeming not to know how't have been discovered that John is a old and ancient nobleman himself by blood, with family skillentons in their own vaults to this day, but done out of his property in the time o' the Romans. However Sir John, as we call 'n now, kept up the wedding-day as well as he could, and stood treat to everybody in the parish; and John's wife sung songs at The Pure Drop till past eleven o'clock."

Hearing this Tess felt so sick at heart that she could not decide to go home publicly in the fly, with her luggage and belongings. She asked the turnpike-keeper if she might deposit her things at his house for a while, and on his offering no objection she dismissed her carriage, and went on to the village alone, by a back lane.

At sight of her father's chimney she asked herself how she could possibly enter the house? Inside that cottage her relations were calmly supposing her far away on a wedding tour with a comparatively rich man who was to conduct her to bouncing prosperity; while here she was, friendless, creeping up to the old door quite by herself, with no better place to go to in the world.

She did not reach the house unobserved. Just by the garden-hedge she was met by a girl who knew her—one of the two or three with whom she had been intimate at school. After making a few inquiries as to how Tess came there her friend, unheeding her tragic look, interrupted with, "But where's thy gentleman, Tess?"

Tess hastily explained that he had been called away on business, and leaving her interlocutor clambered over the garden-hedge, and thus made her way to the house.

As she went up the garden-path she heard her mother singing by the back door, coming in sight of which she perceived Mrs Durbeyfield on the doorstep in the act of wringing a sheet. Having performed this without observing Tess she went indoors, and her daughter followed her.

The washing-tub stood in the same old place on the same old quarter-hogshead, and her mother, having thrown the sheet aside, was about to plunge in her arms anew.

"Why—Tess—my chil'—I thought you was married—married really and truly this time—we sent the cider—"

"Yes, mother; so I am."

"Going to be?"

"No—I am married."

"Married? Then where's thy husband?"

"Oh—he's gone away for a time."

"Gone away? When was you married then? The day you said?"

"Yes, Tuesday, mother."

"And now 'tis on'y Saturday, and he gone away?"

"Yes. He's gone."

"What's the meaning o' that? 'Nation seize such husbands as you seem to get, say I!"

"Mother—" Tess went across to Joan Durbeyfield, laid her face upon the matron's bosom, and burst into sobs. "I don't know how to tell 'ee, mother! . . . You said to me, and wrote to me, that I was not to tell him. But I did tell him—I couldn't help it—and he went away!"

"O you little fool—you little fool!" burst out Mrs Durbeyfield, splashing Tess and herself in her agitation. "My good God, that ever I should ha' lived to say it—but I say it again, you little fool!"

Tess was convulsed with weeping, the tension of so many days having relaxed at last. "I know it—I know, I know!" she gasped through her sobs. "But O my mother, I could not help it; he was so good—and I felt the wickedness of trying to blind him as to what had happened. If—if—it were to be done again—I should do the same. I could not—I dared not—so sin—against him!"

"But you sinned enough to marry him first."

"Yes, yes: that's where my misery do lie. But I thought he could get rid o' me by law, if he were determined not to overlook it. And O if you knew—if you could only half know how I loved him— how anxious I was to have him—and how wrung I was between caring so much for him and my wish to be fair to him!" Tess was so shaken that she could get no further, and sank a helpless thing into a chair.

"Well well; what's done can't be undone. I'm sure I don't know why children o' my bringing forth should all be bigger simpletons than other people's;—not to know better than to blab such a thing as that, when he couldn't ha' found it out till too late!" Here Mrs Durbeyfield began shedding tears on her own account, as a mother to be pitied. "What your father will say, I don't know!" she continued; "for he's been talking about the wedding up at Rolliver's, and The Pure Drop, every day since, and about his family getting back to their rightful position through you—poor silly man—and now you've made this mess of it! The Lord-a-Lord!"

As if to bring matters to a focus, Tess's father was heard approaching at that moment. He did not, however, enter immediately, and Mrs Durbeyfield said that she would break the bad news to him herself, Tess keeping out of sight for the present. After her first burst of disappointment Joan began to take the mishap as she had taken Tess's original trouble, as she would have taken a wet holiday or failure in the potato-crop; as a thing which had come upon them irrespective of desert or folly; a chance external impingement to be borne with; not a lesson.

Tess retreated upstairs, and beheld casually that the beds had been shifted, and new arrangements made. Her old bed had been adapted for two younger children. There was no place here for her now.

The room below being unceiled she could hear most of what went on there. Presently her father entered, apparently carrying a live hen. He was a foot-haggler now, having been obliged to sell his second horse, and he travelled with his basket on his arm. The hen had been carried about this morning as it was often carried, to show people that he was in his work, though it had lain, with its legs tied, under the table at Rolliver's for more than an hour.

"We've just had up a story about—" Durbeyfield began, and thereupon related in detail to his wife a discussion which had arisen at the inn about the clergy, originated by the fact of his daughter having married into a clerical family. "They was formerly styled 'sir', like my own ancestry," he said; "though nowadays their true style, strictly speaking, is 'clerk' only." As Tess had wished that no great publicity should be given to the event he had mentioned no particulars. He hoped she would remove that prohibition soon. He proposed that the couple should take Tess's own name, d'Urberville, as uncorrupted. It was better than her husband's. He asked if any letter had come from her that day.

Then Mrs Durbeyfield informed him that no letter had come, but Tess unfortunately had come herself.

When at length the collapse was explained to him a sullen mortification, not usual with Durbeyfield, overpowered the influence of the cheering glass. Yet the intrinsic quality of the event moved his touchy sensitiveness less than its conjectured effect upon the minds of others.

"To think, now, that this was to be the end o't," said Sir John. "And I with a family vault under that there church of Kingsbere as big as Squire Jollard's ale-cellar, and my folk lying there in sixes and sevens, as genuine county bones and marrow as any recorded in history. And now to be sure what they fellers at Rolliver's and The Pure Drop will say to me; how they'll squint and glane, and say 'This is yer mighty match is it; this is yer getting back to the true level of yer forefathers in King Norman's time!' I feel this is too much, Joan: I shall put an end to myself, title and all—I can bear it no longer! . . . But she can make him keep her if he's married her?"

"Why yes. But she won't think o' doing that."

"D'ye think he really have married her?—or is it like the first—"

Poor Tess, who had heard as far as this, could not bear to hear more. The perception that her word could be doubted even here, in her own parental house, set her mind against the spot as nothing else could have done. How unexpected were the attacks of destiny. And if her father doubted her a little, would not neighbours and acquaintance doubt her much? O, she could not live long at home.

A few days, accordingly, were all that she allowed herself here, at the end of which time she received a short note from Clare, informing her that he had gone to the North of England to look at a farm. In her craving for the lustre of her true position as his wife, and to hide from her parents the vast extent of the division between them, she made use of this letter as her reason for again departing, leaving them under the impression that she was setting out to join him. Still further to screen her husband from any imputation of unkindness to her, she took twenty-five of the fifty pounds Clare had given her, and handed the sum over to her mother, as if the wife of a man like Angel Clare could well afford it, saying that it was a slight return for the trouble and humiliation she had brought upon them in years past. With this assertion of her dignity she bade them farewell; and after that there were lively doings in the Durbeyfield household for some time, on the strength of Tess's bounty; her mother saying, and indeed believing, that the rupture which had arisen between the young husband and wife had adjusted itself under their strong feeling that they could not live apart from each other.

XXXIX

IT was three weeks after the marriage that Clare found himself descending the hill which led to the well-known parsonage of his father. With his downward course the tower of the church rose into the evening sky in a manner of inquiry as to why he had come, and no living person in the twilighted town seemed to notice him, still less to expect him. He was arriving like a ghost, and the sound of his own footsteps was almost an encumbrance to be got rid of.

The picture of life had changed for him. Before this time he had known it but speculatively; now he thought he knew it as a practical man; though perhaps he did not, even yet. Nevertheless, humanity stood before him no longer in the pensive sweetness of Italian art, but in the staring and ghastly attitudes of a Wiertz Museum, and with the leer of a study by Van Beers.*

His conduct during these first weeks had been desultory, beyond description. After mechanically attempting to pursue his agricultural plans as though nothing unusual had happened, in the manner recommended by the great and wise men of all ages, he concluded that very few of those great and wise men had ever gone so far outside themselves as to test the feasibility of their counsel. "This is the chief thing: be not perturbed", said the Pagan moralist.* That was just Clare's own opinion. But he was perturbed. "Let not your heart be troubled, neither let it be afraid", said the Nazarene.* Clare chimed in cordially; but his heart was troubled all the same. How he would have liked to confront those two great thinkers, and earnestly appeal to them as fellow-man to fellow-men, and ask them to tell him their method.

His mood transmuted itself into a dogged indifference, till at length he fancied he was looking on his own existence with the passive interest of an outsider.

He was embittered by the conviction that all this desolation had been brought about by the accident of her being a d'Urberville. When he found that Tess came of that exhausted ancient line, and was not of the new tribes from below, as he had fondly dreamed, why had he not stoically abandoned her, in fidelity to his principles? This was what he had got by apostacy, and his punishment was deserved.

Then he became weary and anxious; and his anxiety increased. He wondered if he had treated her unfairly. He ate without knowing that he ate, and drank without tasting. As the hours dropped past, as the motive of each act in the long series of bygone days presented itself to his view, he perceived how intimately the notion of having Tess as a dear possession was mixed up with all his schemes and words and ways.

In going hither and thither he observed in the outskirts of a small town a red and blue placard setting forth the great advantages of the Empire of Brazil as a field for the emigrating agriculturist. Land was offered there on exceptionally advantageous terms. Brazil somewhat attracted him as a new idea. Tess could eventually join him there, and perhaps in that country of contrasting scenes and notions and habits the conventions would not be so operative which made life with her seem impracticable to him here. In brief, he was strongly inclined to try Brazil, especially as the season for going thither was just at hand.

With this view he was returning to Emminster to disclose his plan to his parents, and to make the best explanation he could make of arriving without Tess, short of revealing what had actually separated them. As he reached the door the new moon shone upon his face, just as the old one had done in the small hours of that morning when he had carried his wife in his arms across the river to the graveyard of the monks; but his face was thinner now.

Clare had given his parents no warning of his visit, and his arrival stirred the atmosphere of the vicarage as the dive of a kingfisher stirs a quiet pool. His father and mother were both in the drawing-room, but neither of his brothers was now at home. Angel entered and closed the door quietly behind him.

"But—where's your wife, dear Angel?" cried his mother. "How you surprise us!"

"She is at her mother's—temporarily. I have come home rather in a hurry, because I've decided to go to Brazil."

"Brazil! Why they are all Roman Catholics there, surely!"

"Are they? I hadn't thought of that."

But even the novelty and painfulness of his going to a Papistical land could not displace for long Mr and Mrs Clare's natural interest in their son's marriage. "We had your brief note three weeks ago announcing that it had taken place," said Mrs Clare, "and your father sent your godmother's gift to her, as you know. Of course it was best that none of us should be present, especially as you preferred to marry her from the dairy, and not at her home, wherever that may be. It would have embarrassed you, and given us no pleasure. Your brothers felt that very strongly. Now it is done we do not complain, particularly if she suits you for the business you have chosen to follow, instead of the ministry of the gospel. . . . Yet I wish I could have seen her first, Angel, or have known a little more about her. We sent her no present of our own, not knowing what would best give her pleasure, but you must suppose it only delayed. Angel, there is no irritation in my mind or your father's against you for this marriage; but we have thought it much better to reserve our liking for your wife till we could see her. And now you have not brought her. It seems strange. What has happened?"

He replied that it had been thought best by them that she should go to her parents' home for the present, whilst he came there.

"I don't mind telling you, dear mother," he said, "that I always meant to keep her away from this house till I should feel she could come with credit to you. But this idea of Brazil is quite a recent one. If I do go it will be unadvisable for me to take her on this my first journey. She will remain at her mother's till I come back."

"And I shall not see her before you start?"

He was afraid they would not. His original plan had been, as he had said, to refrain from bringing her there for some little while—not to wound their prejudices—feelings—in any way; and for other reasons he had adhered to it. He would have to visit home in the course of a year, if he went out at once; and it would be possible for them to see her before he started a second time—with her.

A hastily prepared supper was brought in, and Clare made further exposition of his plans. His mother's disappointment at not seeing the bride still remained with her. Clare's late enthusiasm for Tess had infected her through her maternal sympathies, till she had almost fancied that a good thing could come out of Nazareth*—a charming woman out of Talbothays Dairy. She watched her son as he ate.

"Cannot you describe her? I am sure she is very pretty, Angel."

"Of that there can be no question!" he said with a zest which covered its bitterness.

"And that she is pure and virtuous goes without question."

"Pure and virtuous: of course she is."

"I can see her quite distinctly. You said the other day that she was fine in figure; roundly built; had deep red lips like Cupid's bow; dark eyelashes and brows, an immense rope of hair like a ship's cable, and large eyes violety-bluey-blackish."

"I did, mother."

"I quite see her. And living in such seclusion she naturally had scarce ever seen any young man from the world without till she saw you."

"Scarcely."

"You were her first love?"

"Of course."

"There are worse wives than these simple, rosy-mouthed, robust girls of the farm. Certainly I could have wished—well, since my son is to be an agriculturist it is perhaps but proper that his wife should have been accustomed to an outdoor life."

His father was less inquisitive; but when the time came for the chapter from the bible which was always read before evening prayers, the vicar observed to Mrs Clare, "I think, since Angel has come, that it will be more appropriate to read the thirty-first of Proverbs than the chapter which we should have had in the usual course of our reading?"

"Yes: certainly," said Mrs Clare. "The words of King Lemuel" (she could cite chapter and verse as well as her husband). "My dear son, your father has decided to read us the chapter in Proverbs in praise of a virtuous wife.* We shall not need to be reminded to apply the words to the absent one. May heaven shield her in all her ways."

A lump rose in Clare's throat. The portable lectern was taken out from the corner and set in the middle of the fireplace, the two old servants came in, and Angel's father began to read at the tenth verse of the aforesaid chapter:

" 'Who can find a virtuous woman? for her price is far above rubies. She riseth while it is yet night, and giveth meat to her household. . . . She girdeth her loins with strength, and strengtheneth her arms. She perceiveth that her merchandise is good: her candle goeth not out by night. She looketh well to the ways of her household and eateth not the bread of idleness. Her children arise up and call her blessed; her husband also, and he praiseth her. Many daughters have done virtuously, but thou excellest them all.' "

When prayers were over his mother said: "I could not help thinking how very aptly that chapter your dear father read, applied, in some of its particulars, to the woman you have chosen. The perfect woman, you see, was a working woman; not an idler, not a fine lady; but one who used her hands and her head and her heart for the good of others. 'Her children arise up and call her blessed: her husband also, and he praiseth her. Many daughters have done virtuously, but she excelleth them all.' . . . Well, I wish I could have seen her, Angel. Since she is pure and chaste she would have been refined enough for me."

Clare could bear this no longer. His eyes were full of tears which seemed like drops of molten lead. He bade a quick good-night to these sincere and simple souls whom he loved so well; who knew neither the world the flesh nor the devil in their own hearts;* only as something vague and external to themselves. He went to his own chamber.

His mother followed him and tapped at his door. Clare opened it to discover her standing without, with anxious eyes.

"Angel," she asked, "is there something wrong that you go away so soon? I am quite sure you are not yourself!"

"I am not, quite, mother," said he.

"About her? Now my son, I know it is that—I know it is about her. Have you quarrelled in these three weeks?"

"We have not exactly quarrelled," he said. "But we have had a difference—"

"Angel—is she a young woman whose history will bear investigation?" With a mother's instinct Mrs Clare had put her finger on the kind of trouble that would cause such a disquiet as seemed to agitate her son.

"She is spotless!" he replied; and felt that if it had sent him to eternal hell there and then he would have told that lie.

"Then never mind the rest. After all, there are few purer things in nature than an unsullied country maid. Any crudeness of manner which may offend your more educated sense at first, will, I am sure, disappear under the influence of your companionship and tuition."

Such terrible sarcasm of blind magnanimity brought home to Clare the secondary perception that he had utterly wrecked his career by this marriage, which had not been among his early thoughts after the disclosure. True, on his own account he cared very little about his career; but he had wished to make it at least a respectable one on account of his parents and brothers. And now as he looked into the candle its flame dumbly expressed to him that it was made to shine on sensible people, and that it abhorred lighting the face of a dupe and a failure.

When his agitation had cooled he would be at moments incensed with his poor wife for causing a situation in which he was obliged to practise deception on his parents. He almost talked to her in his anger, as if she had been in the room. And then her cooing voice, plaintive in expostulation, disturbed the darkness, the velvet touch of her lips passed over his brow, and he could distinguish in the air the warmth of her breath.

This night the woman of his belittling deprecations was thinking how great and good her husband was. But over them both there hung a deeper shade than the shade which Angel Clare perceived, namely, the shade of his own limitations. With all his attempted independence of judgement this advanced and well-meaning young man, a sample product of the last five-and-twenty years, was yet the slave to custom and conventionality when surprised back into his early teachings. No prophet had told him, and he was not prophet enough to tell himself, that essentially this young wife of his was as deserving of the praise of King Lemuel as any other woman endowed with the same dislike of evil, her moral value having to be reckoned not by achievement but by tendency. Moreover the figure near at hand suffers on such occasions, because it shows up its sorriness without shade; while vague figures afar off are honoured in that their distance makes artistic virtues of their stains. In considering what Tess was not he overlooked what she was, and forgot that the defective can be more than the entire.

XL

At breakfast Brazil was the topic, and all endeavoured to take a hopeful view of Clare's proposed experiment with that country's soil, notwithstanding the discouraging reports of some farm-labourers who had emigrated thither and returned home within the twelve months. After breakfast Clare went into the little town to wind up such trifling matters as he was concerned with there; and to get from the local bank all the money he possessed. On his way back he encountered Miss Mercy Chant by the church, from whose walls she seemed to be a sort of emanation. She was carrying an armful of bibles for her class, and such was her view of life that events which produced heartache in others wrought beatific smiles upon her; an enviable result although, in the opinion of Angel, it was obtained by a curiously unnatural sacrifice of humanity to mysticism.

She had learnt that he was about to leave England, and observed what an excellent and promising scheme it seemed to be.

"Yes; it is a likely scheme enough, in a commercial sense, no doubt," he replied. "But, my dear Mercy, it snaps the continuity of existence. Perhaps a cloister would be preferable."

"A cloister! O Angel Clare!"

"Well?"

"Why—you wicked man, a cloister implies a monk; and a monk Roman Catholicism!"

"And Roman Catholicism sin, and sin damnation. Thou art in a parlous state, Angel Clare!"

"*I* glory in my Protestantism," she said severely.

Then Clare, thrown by sheer misery into one of the demoniacal moods in which a man does despite to his true principles, called her close to him, and fiendishly whispered in her ear the most heterodox ideas he could think of. His momentary laughter at the horror which appeared on her fair face ceased when it merged in pain and anxiety for his welfare. "Dear Mercy," he said; "you must forgive me! I think I am going crazy!"

She thought that he was, and thus the interview ended, and Clare re-entered the vicarage. With the local banker he deposited the jewels till happier days should arise. He also paid into the bank thirty pounds—to be sent to Tess in a few months, as she might require; and wrote to her at her parents' home in Blackmoor Vale to inform her of what he had done. This amount, with the sum he had already placed in her hands—about fifty pounds—he hoped would be amply sufficient for her wants just at present, particularly as, in an emergency, she had been directed to apply to his father.

He deemed it best not to put his parents into communication with her by informing them of her address: and being unaware of what had really happened to estrange the two neither his father nor his mother suggested that he should do so. During the day he left the parsonage, for what he had to complete he wished to get done quickly.*

As the last duty before leaving this part of England it was necessary for him to call at the Wellbridge farm-house, in which he had spent with Tess the first three days of their marriage; the trifle of rent having to be paid, the key given up of the rooms they had occupied, and two or three small articles fetched away that they had left behind. It was under this roof that the deepest shadow ever thrown upon his life had stretched its gloom over him. Yet when he had unlocked the door of the sitting-room, and looked into it, the memory which returned first upon him was that of their happy arrival on a similar afternoon, the first fresh sense of sharing a habitation conjointly, the first meal together, the chatting by the fire with joined hands.

The farmer and his wife were in the fields at the moment of his visit, and Clare was in the rooms alone for some time. Inwardly swollen with a renewal of sentiments that he had not quite reckoned with he went upstairs to her chamber which had never been his. The bed was smooth as she had made it with her own hands on the morning of leaving. The mistletoe hung under the tester just as he had placed it. Having been there three or four weeks it was turning colour, and the leaves and berries were wrinkled. Angel took it down, and crushed it into the grate. Standing there he for the first time doubted whether his course in this conjuncture had been a wise, much less a generous one. But had he not been cruelly blinded? In the incoherent multitude of his emotions he knelt down at the bedside wet-eyed. "O Tess—if you had only told me sooner I would have forgiven you!" he mourned.

Hearing a footstep below he rose and went to the top of the stairs. At the bottom of the flight he saw a woman standing, and on her turning up her face recognized the pale dark-eyed Izz Huett.

"Mr Clare," she said, "I've called to see you and Mrs Clare, and to inquire if ye be well. I thought you might be back here again."

This was a girl whose secret he had guessed, but who had not yet guessed his: an honest girl who loved him: one who would have made as good or nearly as good a practical farmer's wife as Tess.

"I am here alone," he said. "We are not living here now." Explaining why he had come he asked "Which way are you going home, Izz?"

"I have no home at Talbothays Dairy now, sir," she said.

"Why is that?"

Izz looked down. "It was so dismal there that I left. I am staying out this way." She pointed in a contrary direction—the direction in which he was journeying.

"Well—are you going there now? I can take you if you wish for a lift."

Her olive complexion grew richer in hue. "Thank 'ee Mr Clare," she said.

He soon found the farmer, and settled the account for his rent and the few other items which had to be considered by reason of the sudden abandonment of the lodgings. On Clare's return to his horse and gig Izz jumped up beside him.

"I am going to leave England, Izz," he said, as they drove on. "Going to Brazil."

"And do Mrs Clare like the notion of such a journey?" she asked.

"She is not going at present—say for a year or so. I am going out to reconnoitre—to see what life there is like."

They sped along eastward for some considerable distance, Izz making no observation. "How are the others?" he inquired. "How is Retty?"

"She was in a sort of nervous state when I zid her last; and so thin and hollow-cheeked that 'a do seem in a decline. Nobody will ever fall in love wi' her any more," said Izz absently.

"And Marian?"

Izz lowered her voice. "Marian drinks."

"Indeed!"

"Yes—the dairyman has got rid of her."

"And you?"

"I don't drink: and I bain't in a decline. But—I am no great things at singing afore breakfast now!"

"How is that? Do you remember how neatly you used to turn ' 'Twas down in Cupid's Gardens', and 'The Tailor's Breeches',* at morning milking?"

"Ah—yes. When you first came, sir, that was. Not when you had been there a bit."

"Why was that falling-off?"

Her black eyes flashed up to his face for one moment by way of answer.

"Izz!—how weak of you—for such as I!" he said; and fell into reverie. "Then—suppose I had asked *you* to marry me?"

"If you had, I should have said yes; and you would have married a woman who loved 'ee."

"Really?"

"Down to the ground!" she whispered vehemently. "O my God! did you never guess it till now!"

By and by they reached a branch road to a village. "I must get down—I live out there," said Izz abruptly, never having spoken since her avowal.

Clare slowed the horse. He was incensed against his fate, bitterly disposed towards social ordinances; for they had cooped him up in a corner out of which there was no legitimate pathway. Why not be revenged on society by shaping his future domesticities loosely, instead of kissing the pedagogic rod of convention in this ensnaring manner?

"I am going to Brazil alone, Izz," said he. "I have separated from my wife for personal, not voyaging, reasons. I may never live with her again. I may not be able to love you; but—will you go with me instead of her?"

"You truly wish me to go?"

"I do. I have been badly used enough to wish for relief. And you at least love me disinterestedly."

"Yes—I will go," said Izz after a pause.

"You will? You know what it means, Izz?"

"It means that I shall live with you for the time you are over there—that's good enough for me."

"Remember, you are not to trust me in morals now. But I ought to

remind you that it will be wrong-doing in the eyes of civilization—
western civilization, that is to say."

"I don't mind that: no woman do when it comes to agony-point,
and there's no other way."

"Then don't get down, but sit where you are."

He drove past the cross-roads, one mile, two miles, without showing any signs of affection. "You love me very very much, Izz?" he
suddenly asked.

"I do—I have said I do. I loved you all the time we was at the dairy
together."

"More than Tess?"

She shook her head. "No," she murmured: "not more than she."

"How's that?"

"Because nobody could love 'ee more than Tess did! . . . She
would have laid down her life for 'ee. I could do no more!"

Like the prophet on the top of Peor* Izz Huett would fain have
spoken perversely at such a moment; but the fascination exercised
over her rougher nature by Tess's character compelled her to grace.

Clare was silent: his heart had risen at these straightforward words
from such an unexpected, unimpeachable quarter. In his throat was
something as if a sob had solidified there. His ears repeated: "*She
would have laid down her life for 'ee. I could do no more!*"

"Forget our idle talk, Izz," he said turning the horse's head
suddenly. "I don't know what I've been saying! I will now drive you
back to where your lane branches off."

"So much for honesty towards 'ee! O—how can I bear it—how
can I—how can I!" Izz Huett burst into wild tears and beat her
forehead as she saw what she had done.

"Do you regret that poor little act of justice to an absent one? O
Izz—don't spoil it by regret!"

She stilled herself by degrees. "Very well, sir. Perhaps I didn't
know what I was saying either, wh—when I agreed to go. I wish—
what cannot be."

"Because I have a loving wife already."

"Yes—yes. You have."

They reached the corner of the lane which they had passed half-an-
hour earlier; and she hopped down. "Izz—please, please forget my
momentary levity!" he cried. "It was so ill-considered, so ill-advised!"

"Forget it: never, never! O, it was no levity to me!"

He felt how richly he deserved the reproach that the wounded cry conveyed, and in a sorrow that was inexpressible leapt down and took her hand. "Well, but Izz—we'll part friends, anyhow? You don't know what I've had to bear!"

She was a really generous girl, and allowed no further bitterness to mar their adieux. "I forgive 'ee, sir," she said.

"Now Izz," he said, while she stood beside him there, forcing himself to the mentor's part he was far from feeling; "I want you to tell Marian when you see her that she is to be a good woman, and not to give way to folly. Promise that. And tell Retty that there are more worthy men than I in the world, that for my sake she is to act wisely and well—remember the words—wisely and well—for my sake. I send this message to them as a dying man to the dying; for I shall never see them again. And you Izzy—you have saved me by your honest words about my wife from an incredible impulse towards folly and treachery. Women may be bad, but they are not so bad as men in these things! On that one account I can never forget you. Be always the good and sincere girl you have hitherto been; and think of me as a worthless lover, but a faithful friend. Promise."

She gave the promise. "Heaven bless and keep you sir: good-bye!"

He drove on; but no sooner had Izz turned into the lane and Clare was out of sight than she flung herself down on the bank in a fit of racking anguish; and it was with a strained, unnatural face that she entered her mother's cottage late that night. Nobody ever was told how Izz spent the dark hours that intervened between Angel Clare's parting from her and her arrival home.

Clare too, after bidding the girl farewell, was wrought to aching thoughts and quivering lips. But his sorrow was not for Izz. That evening he was within a feather-weight's turn of abandoning this road to the nearest station, and driving across that elevated dorsal line of South Wessex which divided him from his Tess's home. It was neither a contempt for her nature, nor the probable state of her heart, which deterred him.

No: it was a sense that, despite her love as corroborated by Izz's admission, the facts had not changed. If he was right at first, he was right now. And the momentum of the course on which he had embarked tended to keep him going in it, unless diverted by a stronger, more sustained force than had played upon him this afternoon. He could soon come back to her. He took the train that night for London; and five days after shook hands in farewell of his brothers at the port of embarkation.

XLI

FROM the foregoing events of the winter-time let us press on to an October day, more than eight months subsequent to the parting of Clare and Tess. We discover the latter in changed conditions: instead of a bride with boxes and trunks which others bore, we see her a lonely woman with a basket and a bundle, in her own porterage, as at an earlier time when she was no bride; instead of the ample means that were projected by her husband for her comfort through this probationary period, she can produce only a flattened purse.

After leaving her Marlott home again, she had got through the spring and summer without any great stress upon her physical powers, the time being mainly spent in rendering light irregular service at dairy-work near Port-Bredy, to the west of the Blackmoor Valley, equally remote from her native place and from Talbothays. She preferred this to living on his allowance. Mentally she remained in utter stagnation, a condition which the mechanical occupation rather fostered than checked. Her consciousness was at that other dairy; at that other season; in the presence of the tender lover who had confronted her there; he who, the moment she had grasped him to keep for her own, had disappeared like a shape in a vision.

The dairy-work lasted only till the milk began to lessen, for she had not met with a second regular engagement as at Talbothays, but had done duty as a supernumerary only. However, as harvest was now beginning, she had simply to remove from the pasture to the stubble to find plenty of further occupation, and this continued till harvest was done.

Of the five-and-twenty pounds which had remained to her of Clare's allowance, after deducting the other half of the fifty as a contribution to her parents for the trouble and expense to which she had put them, she had as yet spent but little. But there now followed an unfortunate interval of wet weather, during which she was obliged to fall back upon her sovereigns.

She could not bear to let them go. Angel had put them into her hand, had obtained them bright and new from his bank for her: his touch had consecrated them to souvenirs of himself; they appeared to have had as yet no other history than such as was created by his and her own experiences; and to disperse them was like giving away relics.* But she had to do it, and one by one they left her hands.

She had been compelled to send her mother her address from time to time; but she concealed her circumstances. When her money had almost gone a letter from her mother reached her. Joan stated that they were in a dreadful difficulty: the autumn rains had gone through the thatch of the house, which required entire renewal; but this could not be done because the previous thatching had never been paid for. New rafters, and a new ceiling upstairs, also were required, which, with the previous bill, would amount to a sum of twenty pounds. As her husband was a man of means, and had doubtless returned by this time, could she not send them the money?

Tess had thirty pounds coming to her almost immediately from Angel's bankers; and the case being so deplorable, as soon as the sum was received she sent the twenty as requested. Part of the remainder she was obliged to expend in winter clothing; leaving only a nominal sum for the whole inclement season at hand. When the last pound had gone a remark of Angel's, that whenever she required further resources she was to apply to his father, remained to be considered.

But the more Tess thought of the step the more reluctant was she to take it. The same delicacy, pride, false shame, whatever it may be called, on Clare's account, which had led her to hide from her own parents the prolongation of the estrangement, hindered her in own-ing to his that she was in want after the fair allowance he had left her. They probably despised her already; how much more they would despise her in the character of a mendicant. The consequence was that by no effort could the parson's daughter-in-law bring herself to let him know her state.

Her reluctance to communicate with her husband's parents might, she thought, lessen with the lapse of time; but with her own the reverse obtained. On her leaving their house after the short visit subsequent to her marriage they were under the impression that she was ultimately going to join her husband, and from that time to the present she had done nothing to disturb their belief that she was awaiting his return in comfort, hoping against hope that his journey to Brazil would result in a short stay only, after which he would come to fetch her; or that he would write for her to join him: in any case that they would soon present a united front to their families and the world. This hope she still fostered. To let her parents know that she was a deserted wife, dependent, now that she had relieved their necessities, on her own hands for a living, after the *éclat** of a marriage which was to nullify the collapse of the first attempt, would be too much indeed.

The set of brilliants returned to her mind. Where Clare had deposited them she did not know, and it mattered little, if it were true that she could only use and not sell them. Even were they absolutely hers it would be passing mean to enrich herself by a legal title to them which was not essentially hers at all.

Meanwhile her husband's days had been by no means free from trial. At this moment he was lying ill of fever in the clay lands near Curitiba in Brazil, having been drenched with thunderstorms and persecuted by other hardships, in common with all the English farmers and farm labourers who, just at this time, were deluded into going thither by the promises of the Brazilian Government, and by the baseless assumption that those frames which, ploughing and sowing on English uplands, had resisted all the weathers to whose moods they had been born, could resist equally well all the weathers by which they were surprised on Brazilian plains.*

To return. Thus it happened that when the last of Tess's sovereigns had been spent she was unprovided with others to take their place, while on account of the season she found it increasingly difficult to get employment. Not being aware of the rarity of intelligence, energy, health, and willingness in any sphere of life, she refrained from seeking an indoor occupation; fearing towns, large houses, people of means and social sophistication, and of manners other than rural. From that direction of gentility black care had come. Society might be better than she supposed from her slight experience of it. But she had no proof of this; and her instinct in the circumstances was to avoid its purlieus.

The small dairies to the west, beyond Port-Bredy, in which she had served as supernumerary milkmaid during the spring and summer required no further aid. Room would probably have been made for her at Talbothays, if only out of sheer compassion; but comfortable as her life had been there she could not go back. The anti-climax would be too intolerable; and her return might bring reproach upon her idolized husband. She could not have borne their pity, and their whispered remarks to one another upon her strange situation; though she would almost have faced a knowledge of her circumstances by every individual there, so long as her story had remained isolated in the mind of each. It was the interchange of ideas about her that made her sensitiveness wince. Tess could not account for this distinction; she simply knew that she felt it.

She was now on her way to an upland farm in the centre of the county, to which she had been recommended by a wandering letter which had reached her from Marian. Marian had somehow heard that Tess was separated from her husband—probably through Izz Huett—and the good-natured and now tippling girl, deeming Tess in trouble, had hastened to notify to her former friend that she herself had gone to this upland spot after leaving the dairy, and would like to see her there, where there was room for other hands, if it was really true that she worked again as of old.

With the shortening of the days all hope of obtaining her husband's forgiveness began to leave her; and there was something of the habitude of the wild animal in the unreflecting instinct with which she rambled on—disconnecting herself by littles from her eventful past at every step, obliterating her identity, giving no thought to accidents or contingencies which might make a quick discovery of her whereabouts by others of importance to her own happiness, if not to theirs.

Among the difficulties of her lonely position not the least was the attention she excited by her appearance, a certain bearing of distinction which she had caught from Clare being superadded to her natural attractiveness. Whilst the clothes lasted which had been prepared for her marriage these casual glances of interest caused her no inconvenience, but as soon as she was compelled to don the wrapper of a fieldwoman rude words were addressed to her more than once; but nothing occurred to cause her bodily fear till a particular November afternoon.

She had preferred the country west of the River Brit to the upland farm for which she was now bound, because, for one thing, it was nearer to the home of her husband's father; and to hover about that region unrecognized, with the notion that she might decide to call at the vicarage some day, gave her pleasure. But having once decided to try the higher and drier levels she pressed back eastward, marching afoot towards the village of Chalk-Newton, where she meant to pass the night.

The lane was long and unvaried, and, owing to the rapid shortening of the days, dusk came upon her before she was aware. She had reached the top of a hill, down which the lane stretched its serpentine length in glimpses, when she heard footsteps behind her back, and in a few moments she was overtaken by a man. He stepped up alongside Tess, and said "Good-night, my pretty maid," to which she civilly replied.

The light still remaining in the sky lit up her face, though the landscape was nearly dark. The man turned and stared hard at her.

"Why, surely, it is the young wench who was at Trantridge awhile—young Squire d'Urberville's friend? I was there at that time, though I don't live there now."

She recognized in him the well-to-do boor whom Angel had knocked down at the inn for addressing her coarsely. A spasm of anguish shot through her; and she returned him no answer.

"Be honest enough to own it; and that what I said in the town was true, though your fancy-man* was so up about it—hey, my sly one? You ought to beg my pardon for that blow of his, considering."

Still no answer came from Tess. There seemed only one escape for her hunted soul. She suddenly took to her heels with the speed of the wind, and without looking behind her ran along the road till she came to a gate which opened directly into a plantation. Into this she plunged, and did not pause till she was deep enough in its shade to be safe against any possibility of discovery.

Under foot the leaves were dry, and the foliage of some holly bushes which grew among the deciduous trees was dense enough to keep off draughts. She scraped together the dead leaves till she had formed them into a large heap, making a sort of nest in the middle. Into this Tess crept.

Such sleep as she got was naturally fitful: she fancied she heard strange noises, but persuaded herself that they were caused by the breeze. She thought of her husband in some vague warm clime on the other side of the globe, while she was here in the cold. Was there another such a wretched being as she in the world, Tess asked herself; and thinking of her wasted life said "All is vanity."* She repeated the words mechanically, till she reflected that this was a most inadequate thought for modern days. Solomon had thought as far as that more than two thousand years ago: she herself, though not in the van of thinkers, had got much further. If all were only vanity who would mind it? All was, alas, worse than vanity—injustice, punishment, exaction, death. The wife of Angel Clare put her hand to her brow, and felt its curve, and the edges of her eye-sockets perceptible under the soft skin, and thought as she did so that a time would come when that bone would be bare. "I wish it were now," she said.

In the midst of these whimsical fancies she heard anew strange sounds among the leaves. It might be the wind; yet there was scarcely any wind. Sometimes it was a palpitation, sometimes a flutter; sometimes it was a sort of gasp or gurgle. Soon she was certain that the noises came from wild creatures of some kind, the more so when, originating in the boughs overhead, they were followed by the fall of a heavy body upon the ground. Had she been ensconced here under other and more pleasant conditions she would have become alarmed; but outside humanity she had at present no fear.

Day at length broke in the sky. When it had been day aloft for some little while it became day in the wood.

Directly the assuring and prosaic light of the world's active hours had grown strong, she crept from under her hillock of leaves and looked around boldly. Then she perceived what had been going on to disturb her. The plantation wherein she had taken shelter ran down at this spot into a peak which ended it hitherward, outside the hedge being arable ground. Under the trees several pheasants lay about, their rich plumage dabbled with blood; some were dead, some feebly twitching a wing, some staring up at the sky, some pulsating quickly, some contorted, some stretched out—all of them writhing in agony except the fortunate ones whose tortures had ended during the night by the inability of nature to bear more.

Tess guessed at once the meaning of this. The birds had been driven down into this corner the day before by some shooting party; and while those that had dropped dead under the shot, or had died before nightfall, had been searched for and carried off, many badly wounded birds had escaped and hidden themselves away, or risen among the thick boughs, where they had maintained their position till they grew weaker with loss of blood in the night-time, when they had fallen one by one as she had heard them.

She had occasionally caught glimpses of these men in her girlhood, looking over hedges or peering through bushes and pointing their guns, strangely accoutred, a bloodthirsty light in their eyes. She had been told that, rough and brutal as they seemed just then, they were not like this all the year round, but were, in fact, quite civil persons; save during certain weeks of autumn and winter when, like the inhabitants of the Malay Peninsula, they ran amuck,* and made it their purpose to destroy life—in this case harmless feathered creatures, brought into being by artificial means solely to gratify these propensities—at once so unmannerly and so unchivalrous towards their weaker fellows in nature's teeming family.

With the impulse of a soul who could feel for kindred sufferers as much as for herself, Tess's first thought was to put the still living birds out of their torture, and to this end with her own hands she broke the necks of as many as she could find, leaving them to lie where she had found them till the gamekeepers should come, as they probably would come, to look for them a second time.

"Poor darlings—to suppose myself the most miserable being on earth in the sight o' such misery as yours!" she exclaimed, her tears running down as she killed the birds tenderly. "And not a twinge of bodily pain about me! I be not mangled, and I be not bleeding, and I have two hands to feed and clothe me." She was ashamed of herself for her gloom of the night, based on nothing more tangible than a sense of condemnation under an arbitrary law of society which had no foundation in Nature.

XLII

IT was now broad day and she started again, emerging cautiously upon the highway. But there was no need for caution: not a soul was at hand, and Tess went onward with fortitude, her recollection of the birds' silent endurance of their night of agony impressing upon her the relativity of sorrows, and the tolerable nature of her own, if she could once rise high enough to despise opinion. But that she could not do, so long as it was held by Clare.

She reached Chalk-Newton and breakfasted at an inn, where several young men were troublesomely complimentary to her good looks. Somehow she felt hopeful, for was it not possible that her husband also might say these same things to her even yet? She was bound to take care of herself on the chance of it, and keep off these casual lovers. To this end Tess resolved to run no further risks from her appearance. As soon as she got out of the village she entered a thicket and took from her basket one of the oldest field-gowns, which she had never put on even at the dairy—never since she had worked among the stubble at Marlott. She also, by a felicitous thought, took a handkerchief from her bundle, and tied it round her face under her bonnet, covering her chin, and half her cheeks, and temples, as if she were suffering from toothache. Then with her little scissors, by the aid of a pocket looking-glass, she mercilessly snipped her eyebrows off; and thus insured against aggressive admiration she went on her uneven way.

"What a mommet of a maid!" said the next man who met her to a companion.

Tears came into her eyes for very pity of herself as she heard him.

"But I don't care!" she said. "O no—I don't care! I'll always be ugly now, because Angel is not here, and I have nobody to take care of me. My husband that was is gone away, and never will love me any more; but I love him just the same, and hate all other men, and like to make 'em think scornfully of me!"

Thus Tess walks on, a figure which is part of the landscape; a fieldwoman pure and simple, in winter guise: a grey serge cape, a red woollen cravat, a stuff skirt covered by a whitey-brown rough wrapper, and buff leather gloves. Every thread of that old attire has become faded and thin under the stroke of rain-drops, the burn of sunbeams, and the stress of winds. There is no sign of young passion in her now:

> The maiden's mouth is cold
> . . . . .
> Fold over simple fold
> Binding her head.*

Inside this exterior, over which the eye might have roved as over a thing scarcely percipient, almost inorganic, there was the record of a pulsing life which had learnt too well, for its years, of the dust and ashes of things, of the cruelty of lust and the fragility of love.

Next day the weather was bad, but she trudged on, the honesty, directness, and impartiality of elemental enmity disconcerting her but little. Her object being a winter's occupation and a winter's home there was no time to lose. Her experience of short hirings had been such that she was determined to accept no more.

Thus she went forward from farm to farm in the direction of the place whence Marian had written to her, which she determined to make use of as a last shift only, its rumoured stringencies being the reverse of tempting. First she inquired for the lighter kinds of employment, and, as acceptance in any variety of these grew hopeless, applied next for the less light, till, beginning with the dairy and poultry tendance that she liked best, she ended with the heavy and coarse pursuits which she liked least—work on arable land: work of such roughness, indeed, as she would never have deliberately volunteered for.

Towards the second evening she reached the irregular chalk tableland or plateau, bosomed with semi-globular tumuli—as if Cybele the Many-breasted* were supinely extended there—which stretched between the valley of her birth and the valley of her love. Here the air was dry and cold, and the long cart-roads were blown white and dusty within a few hours after rain. There were few trees, or none, those that would have grown in the hedges being mercilessly plashed down with the quickset by the tenant-farmers, the natural enemies of tree, bush, and brake. In the middle distance ahead of her she could see the summits of Bulbarrow and of Nettlecombe Tout, and they seemed friendly. They had a low and unassuming aspect from this upland, though as approached on the other side from Blackmoor in her childhood they were as lofty bastions against the sky. Southerly, at many miles' distance, and over the hills and ridges coastward, she could discern a surface like polished steel: it was the English Channel at a point far out towards France.

Before her, in a slight depression, were the remains of a village. She had, in fact, reached Flintcomb-Ash, the place of Marian's sojourn. There seemed to be no help for it; hither she was doomed to come. The stubborn soil around her showed plainly enough that the kind of labour in demand here was of the roughest kind; but it was time to rest from searching, and she resolved to stay, particularly as it began to rain. At the entrance to the village was a cottage whose gable jutted into the road, and before applying for a lodging she stood under its shelter, and watched the evening close in.

"Who would think I was Mrs Angel Clare!" she said.

The wall felt warm to her back and shoulders, and she found that immediately within the gable was the cottage fireplace, the heat of which came through the bricks. She warmed her hands upon them, and also put her cheek—red and moist with the drizzle—against their comforting surface. The wall seemed to be the only friend she had. She had so little wish to leave it that she could have stayed there all night.

Tess could hear the occupants of the cottage—gathered together after their day's labour—talking to each other within, and the rattle of their supper-plates was also audible. But in the village-street she had seen no soul as yet. The solitude was at last broken by the approach of one feminine figure, who, though the evening was cold, wore the print gown and tilt-bonnet of summer-time. Tess instinctively thought it might be Marian, and when she came near enough to be distinguishable in the gloom surely enough it was she. Marian was even stouter and redder in the face than formerly, and decidedly shabbier in attire. At any previous period of her existence Tess would hardly have cared to renew the acquaintance in such conditions; but her loneliness was excessive, and she responded readily to Marian's greeting.

Marian was quite respectful in her inquiries, but seemed much moved by the fact that Tess should still continue in no better condition than at first; though she had dimly heard of the separation.

"Tess—Mrs Clare—the dear wife of dear he!—and is it really so bad as this, my child? Why is your cwomely face tied up in such a way? Anybody been beating 'ee? Not *he*!"

"No, no, no! I merely did it not to be clipsed or colled, Marian." She pulled off in disgust a bandage which could suggest such wild thoughts.

"And you've got no collar on." (Tess had been accustomed to wear a little white collar at the dairy.)

"I know it, Marian."

"You've lost it travelling?"

"I've not lost it—the truth is I don't care anything about my looks; and so I didn't put it on."

"And you don't wear your wedding-ring?"

"Yes I do—but not in public. I wear it round my neck on a ribbon. I don't wish people to think who I am by marriage; or that I am married at all: it would be so awkward while I lead my present life."

Marian paused. "But you *be* a gentleman's wife; and it seems hardly fair that you should live like this?"

"O yes it is—quite fair—though I am very unhappy."

"Well, well. . . . *He* married you: and you can be unhappy!"

"Wives are unhappy sometimes; from no fault of their husbands: from their own."

"You've no faults, deary; that I'm sure of. And he's none. So it must be something outside ye both."

"Marian—dear Marian—will you do me a good turn without asking questions? My husband has gone abroad, and somehow I have overrun my allowance, so that I have to fall back upon my old work for a time. Do not call me Mrs Clare, but Tess as before. Do they want a hand here?"

"O yes—they'll take one always—because few care to come. 'Tis a starve-acre place. Corn and swedes are all they grow. Though I be here myself I feel 'tis a pity for such as you to come."

"But you used to be as good a dairywoman as I."

"Yes; but I've got out o' that since I took to drink. Lord, that's the only comfort I've got now. If you engage, you'll be set swede-hacking. That's what I be doing; but you won't like it."

"O—anything. Will you speak for me?"

"You will do better by speaking for yourself."

"Very well. Now, Marian, remember; nothing about *him*, if I get the place. I don't wish to bring his name down to the dirt."

Marian, who was really a trustworthy girl, though of coarser grain than Tess, promised anything she asked. "This is pay-night," she said; "and if you were to come with me you would know at once. I be real sorry that you are not happy; but 'tis because he's away I know. You couldn't be unhappy if he were here, even if he gie'd ye no money; even if he used you like a drudge."

"That's true. I could not!"

They walked on together, and soon reached the farm-house, which was almost sublime in its dreariness. There was not a tree within sight. There was not, at this season, a green pasture: nothing but fallow and turnips everywhere—in large fields divided by hedges plashed* to unrelieved levels.

Tess waited outside the door of the farm-house till the group of workfolk had received their wages, and then Marian introduced her. The farmer himself, it appeared, was not at home, but his wife, who represented him this evening, made no objection to hiring Tess, on her agreeing to remain till Old Lady-Day. Female field-labour was seldom offered now, and its cheapness made it profitable for tasks which women could perform as readily as men.

Having signed the agreement there was nothing more for Tess to do at present than to get a lodging, and she found one in the house at whose gable-wall she had warmed herself. It was a poor subsistence that she had ensured, but it would afford a shelter for the winter at any rate.

That night she wrote to inform her parents of her new address, in case a letter should arrive at Marlott from her husband. But she did not tell them of the sorriness of her situation: it might have brought reproach upon him.

XLIII

THERE was no exaggeration in Marian's definition of Flintcomb-Ash farm as a starve-acre place. The single fat thing on the soil was Marian herself; and she was an importation. Of the three classes of village, the village cared for by its lord, the village cared for by itself, and the village uncared for either by itself or by its lord—(in other words the village of a resident squire's tenantry, the village of free or copyholders, and the absentee-owner's village, farmed with the land)—this place Flintcomb-Ash was the third.

But Tess set to work. Patience, that blending of moral courage with physical timidity, was now no longer a minor feature in Mrs Angel Clare; and it sustained her.

The swede-field, in which she and her companion were set hacking, was a stretch of a hundred odd acres, in one patch, on the highest ground of the farm, rising above stony lanchets or lynchets—the outcrop of siliceous veins in the chalk formation, composed of myriads of loose white flints in bulbous, cusped, and phallic shapes. The upper half of each turnip had been eaten off by the live-stock, and it was the business of the two women to grub up the lower or earthy half of the root with a hooked fork called a hacker, that it might be eaten also. Every leaf of the vegetable having already been consumed the whole field was in colour a desolate drab; it was a complexion without features, as if a face from chin to brow should be only an expanse of skin. The sky wore, in another colour, the same likeness; a white vacuity of countenance with the lineaments gone. So these two upper and nether visages confronted each other, all day long the white face looking down on the brown face, and the brown face looking up at the white face, without anything standing between them but the two girls crawling over the surface of the former like flies.

Nobody came near them, and their movements showed a mechanical regularity—their forms standing enshrouded in hessian "wroppers"—sleeved brown pinafores, tied behind to the bottom, to keep their gowns from blowing about; scant skirts revealing boots that reached high up the ancles, and yellow sheepskin gloves with gauntlets. The pensive character which the curtained hood lent to their bent heads would have reminded the observer of some early Italian conception of the two Marys.*

They worked on hour after hour, unconscious of the forlorn aspect they bore in the landscape, not thinking of the justice or injustice of their lot. Even in such a position as theirs it was possible to exist in a dream. In the afternoon the rain came on again, and Marian said that they need not work any more. But if they did not work they would not be paid; so they worked on. It was so high a situation, this field, that the rain had no occasion to fall, but raced along horizontally upon the yelling wind, sticking into them like glass splinters, till they were wet through. Tess had not known till now what was really meant by that. There are degrees of dampness, and a very little is called being wet through in common talk. But to stand working slowly in a field, and feel the creep of rainwater, first in legs and shoulders, then on hips and head, then at back, front, and sides, and yet to work on till the leaden light diminishes and marks that the sun is down, demands a distinct modicum of stoicism, even of valour.

Yet they did not feel the wetness so much as might be supposed. They were both young, and they were talking of the time when they lived and loved together at Talbothays Dairy, that happy green tract of land where summer had been liberal in her gifts; in substance to all, emotionally to these. Tess would fain not have conversed with Marian of the man who was legally, if only nominally, her husband; but the irresistible fascination of the subject betrayed her into reciprocating Marian's remarks. And thus, as has been said, though the damp curtains of their bonnets flapped smartly into their faces, and their wrappers clung about them to wearisomeness, they lived all this afternoon in memories of green sunny romantic Talbothays.

"You can see a gleam of a hill within a few miles o' Froom Valley from here when 'tis fine," said Marian.

"Ah—can you?" said Tess, awake to the new value of this locality.

So the two forces were at work here as everywhere, the inherent will to enjoy, and the circumstantial will against enjoyment. Marian's will had a method of assisting itself by taking from her pocket as the afternoon wore on a pint bottle corked with white rag, from which she invited Tess to drink. Tess's unassisted power of dreaming, however, being enough for her sublimation at present, she declined except the merest sip, and then Marian took a pull herself from the spirits. "I've got used to it," she said, "and can't leave it off now. 'Tis my only comfort. . . . You see I lost him: you didn't: and you can do without it perhaps."

Tess thought her loss as great as Marian's, but upheld by the dignity of being Angel's wife in the letter at least, she accepted Marian's differentiation.

Amid this scene Tess slaved in the morning frosts and in the afternoon rains. When it was not swede-grubbing it was swede-trimming, in which process they sliced off the earth and fibres with a bill-hook* before storing the roots for future use. At this occupation they could shelter themselves by a thatched hurdle if it rained; but if it was frosty even their thick leather gloves could not prevent the frozen masses they handled from biting their fingers. Still Tess hoped. She had a conviction that sooner or later the magnanimity which she persisted in reckoning as a chief ingredient of Clare's character would lead him to rejoin her.

Marian, primed to a humorous mood, would discover the queer-shaped flints aforesaid, and shriek with laughter, Tess remaining severely obtuse. They often looked across the country to where the Var or Froom was known to stretch, even though they might not be able to see it; and fixing their eyes on the cloaking grey mist imagined the old times they had spent out there.

"Ah," said Marian, "how I should like another or two of our old set to come here! Then we could bring up Talbothays every day here a field, and talk of he, and of what nice times we had there, and o' the old things we used to know, and make it all come back again a'most, in seeming!" Marian's eyes softened, and her voice grew vague as the visions returned. "I'll write to Izz Huett," she said. "She's biding at home doing nothing now, I know, and I'll tell her we be here, and ask her to come. And perhaps Retty is well enough now."

Tess had nothing to say against the proposal, and the next she heard of this plan for importing old Talbothays joys was two or three days later when Marian informed her that Izz had replied to her inquiry, and had promised to come if she could.

There had not been such a winter for years. It came on in stealthy and measured glides like the moves of a chess-player. One morning the few lonely trees and the thorns of the hedgerows appeared as if they had put off a vegetable for an animal integument. Every twig was covered with a white nap as of fur grown from the rind during the night, giving it four times its usual stoutness; the whole bush or tree forming a staring sketch in white lines on the mournful grey of the sky and horizon. Cobwebs revealed their presence on sheds and walls where none had ever been observed till brought out into visibility by this crystallizing atmosphere, hanging like loops of white worsted from salient points of the outhouses, posts, and gates.

After this season of congealed dampness came a spell of dry frost, when strange birds from behind the north pole began to arrive silently on the upland of Flintcomb-Ash; gaunt spectral creatures with tragical eyes—eyes which had witnessed scenes of cataclysmal horror in inaccessible polar regions, of a magnitude such as no human being had ever conceived, in curdling temperatures that no man could endure; which had beheld the crash of icebergs and the slide of snow-hills by the shooting light of the Aurora; been half blinded by the whirl of colossal storms and terraqueous distortions; and retained the expression of feature that such scenes had engendered. These nameless birds came quite near to Tess and Marian; but of all they had seen which humanity would never see, they brought no account. The traveller's ambition to tell was not theirs; and with dumb impassivity they dismissed experiences which they did not value for the immediate incidents of this homely upland—the trivial movements of the two girls in disturbing the clods with their hackers so as to uncover something or other that these visitants relished as food.

Then one day a peculiar quality invaded the air of this open country. There came a moisture which was not of rain, and a cold which was not of frost. It chilled the eyeballs of the twain, made their brows ache, penetrated to their skeletons, affecting the surface of the body less than its core. They knew that it meant snow; and in the night the snow came. Tess, who continued to live at the cottage with the warm gable that cheered any lonely pedestrain who paused beside it, awoke in the night, and heard above the thatch noises which seemed to signify that the roof had turned itself into a gymnasium of all the winds. When she lit her lamp to get up in the morning she found that the snow had blown through a chink in the casement, forming a white cone of the finest powder against the inside, and had also come down the chimney, so that it lay sole-deep upon the floor, on which her shoes left tracks when she moved about. Without, the storm drove so fast as to create a snow-mist in the kitchen; but as yet is was too dark out-of-doors to see anything.

Tess knew that it was impossible to go on with the swedes; and by the time she had finished breakfast beside the solitary little lamp Marian arrived to tell her that they were to join the rest of the women at reed-drawing* in the barn till the weather changed. As soon therefore as the uniform cloak of darkness without began to turn to a disordered medley of greys they blew out the lamp, wrapped themselves up in their thickest pinners, tied their woollen cravats round their necks and across their chests, and started for the barn. The snow had followed the birds from the polar basin as a white pillar of a cloud, and individual flakes could not be seen. The blast smelt of icebergs, arctic seas, whales, and white bears, carrying the snow so that it licked the land but did not deepen on it. They trudged onwards with slanted bodies through the flossy fields, keeping as well as they could in the shelter of hedges, which, however, acted as strainers rather than screens. The air, afflicted to pallor with the hoary multitudes that infested it, twisted and spun them eccentrically, suggesting an achromatic chaos of things. But both the young women were fairly cheerful: such weather on a dry upland is not in itself dispiriting.

"Ha-ha! the cunning northern birds knew this was coming," said Marian. "Depend upon't, they keep just in front o't all the way from the North Star. . . . Your husband, my dear, is, I make no doubt, having scorching weather all this time. Lord, if he could only see his pretty wife now! Not that this weather hurts your beauty at all—in fact, it rather does it good."

"You mustn't talk about him to me, Marian," said Tess severely.

"Well but—surely you care for 'n! Do you?"

Instead of answering Tess, with tears in her eyes, impulsively faced in the direction in which she imagined South America to lie, and putting up her lips, blew out a passionate kiss upon the snowy wind.

"Well, well—I know you do. But 'pon my body, it is a rum life for a married couple! . . . There—I won't say another word! Well, as for the weather, it won't hurt us in the wheat-barn; but reed-drawing is fearful hard work—worse than swede-hacking. I can stand it because I'm stout; but you be slimmer than I. I can't think why maister should have set 'ee at it."

They reached the wheat-barn and entered it. One end of the long structure was full of corn: the middle was where the reed-drawing was carried on, and there had already been placed in the reed-press the evening before as many sheaves of wheat as would be sufficient for the women to draw from during the day.

"Why—here's Izz!" said Marian.

Izz it was, and she came forward. She had walked all the way from her mother's house on the previous afternoon, and not deeming the distance so great had been belated, arriving however just before the snow began, and sleeping at the ale-house. The farmer had agreed with her mother at market to take her on if she came to-day, and she had been afraid to disappoint him by delay.

In addition to Tess, Marian, and Izz there were two women from a neighbouring village; two Amazonian sisters, whom Tess with a start remembered as Dark Car the Queen of Spades and her junior the Queen of Diamonds—those who had tried to fight with her in the midnight quarrel at Trantridge. They showed no recognition of her, and possibly had none, for they had been under the influence of liquor on that occasion, and were only temporary sojourners there as here. They did all kinds of men's work by preference, including well-sinking, hedging, ditching, and excavating, without any sense of fatigue. Noted reed-drawers were they too, and looked round upon the other three with some superciliousness.

Putting on their gloves all set to work in a row in front of the press, an erection formed of two posts connected by a cross-beam, under which the sheaves to be drawn from were laid ears outward, the beam being pegged down by pins in the uprights, and lowered as the sheaves diminished.

The day hardened in colour, the light coming in at the barn-doors upwards from the snow instead of downwards from the sky. The girls pulled handful after handful from the press; but by reason of the presence of the strange women, who were recounting scandals, Marian and Izz could not at first talk of old times, as they wished to do. Presently they heard the muffled tread of a horse, and the farmer rode up to the barn-door. When he had dismounted he came close to Tess, and remained looking musingly at the side of her face. She had not turned at first, but his fixed attitude led her to look round, when she perceived that her employer was the native of Trantridge, from whom she had taken flight on the high-road, because of his allusion to her history.

He waited till she had carried the drawn bundles to the pile outside, when he said: "So you be the young woman who took my civility in such ill part? Be drowned if I didn't think you might be, as soon as I heard of your being hired. Well, you thought you had got the better of me the first time at the inn with your fancy-man, and the second time on the road when you bolted; but now I think I've got the better of you." He concluded with a hard laugh.

Tess, between the Amazons and the farmer like a bird caught in a clap-net,* returned no answer, continuing to pull the straw. She could read character sufficiently well to know by this time that she had nothing to fear from her employer's gallantry; it was rather the tyranny induced by his mortification at Clare's treatment of him. Upon the whole she preferred that sentiment in man, and felt brave enough to endure it.

"You thought I was in love with 'ee, I suppose? Some women are such fools, to take every look as serious earnest. But there's nothing like a winter afield for taking that nonsense out o' young wenches' heads; and you've signed and agreed till Lady-Day. Now, are you going to beg my pardon?"

"I think you ought to beg mine."

"Very well—as you like. But we'll see which is master here. Be they all the sheaves you've done to-day?"

"Yes sir."

" 'Tis a very poor show. Just see what they've done over there" (pointing to the two stalwart women). "The rest, too, have done better than you."

"They've all practised it before, and I have not. And I thought it made no difference to you as it is task-work, and we are only paid for what we do."

"O but it does. I want the barn cleared."

"I am going to work all the afternoon instead of leaving at two as the others will do."

He looked sullenly at her and went away. Tess felt that she could not have come to a much worse place; but anything was better than gallantry. When two o'clock arrived the professional reed-drawers tossed off the last half-pint in their flagon, put down their hooks, tied their last sheaves, and went away. Marian and Izz would have done likewise, but on hearing that Tess meant to stay, to make up by longer hours for her lack of skill, they would not leave her. Looking out at the the snow, which still fell, Marian exclaimed, "Now we've got it all to ourselves." And so at last the conversation turned to their old experiences at the dairy; and, of course, the incidents of their affection for Angel Clare.

"Izz and Marian," said Mrs Angel Clare, with a dignity which was extremely touching, seeing how very little of a wife she was: "I can't join in talk with you now, as I used to do, about Mr Clare; you will see that I cannot; because, although he is gone away from me for the present, he is my husband."

Izz was by nature the sauciest and most caustic of all the four girls who had loved Clare. "He was a very splendid lover, no doubt," she said. "But I don't think he is a too fond husband to go away from you so soon."

"He had to go, he was obliged to go, to see about the land over there," pleaded Tess.

"He might have tided 'ee over the winter."

"Ah—that's owing to an accident—a misunderstanding; and we won't argue it," Tess answered with tearfulness in her words. "Perhaps there's a good deal to be said for him. He did not go away, like some husbands, without telling me; and I can always find out where he is."

After this they continued for some long time in a reverie, as they went on seizing the ears of corn, drawing out the straw, gathering it under their arms, and cutting off the ears with their bill-hooks, nothing sounding in the barn but the swish of the straw, and the crunch of the hook. Then Tess suddenly flagged, and sank down upon the heap of wheat ears at her feet.

"I knew you wouldn't be able to stand it!" cried Marian. "It wants harder flesh than yours for this work."

Just then the farmer entered. "O that's how you get on when I am away," he said to her.

"But it is my own loss," she pleaded. "Not yours."

"I want it finished," he said doggedly, as he crossed the barn and went out at the other doors.

"Don't 'ee mind him, there's a dear," said Marian. "I've worked here before. Now you go and lie down there, and Izz and I will make up your number."

"I don't like to let you do that. I'm taller than you, too."

However she was so overcome that she consented to lie down

awhile, and reclined on a heap of pull-tails—the refuse after the straight straw had been drawn—thrown up at the further side of the barn. Her succumbing had been as largely owing to agitation at reopening the subject of her separation from her husband as to the hard work. She lay in a state of percipience without volition, and the rustle of the straw and the cutting of the ears by the others had the weight of bodily touches.

She could hear from her corner, in addition to these noises, the murmur of their voices. She felt certain that they were continuing the subject already broached, but their voices were so low that she could not catch the words. At last Tess grew more and more anxious to know what they were saying, and persuading herself that she felt better she got up and resumed work.

Then Izz Huett broke down. She had walked more than a dozen miles the previous evening, had gone to bed at midnight, and had risen again at five o'clock. Marian alone, thanks to her bottle of liquor and her stoutness of build, stood the strain upon back and arms without suffering. Tess urged Izz to leave off, agreeing, as she felt better, to finish the day without her, and make equal division of the number of sheaves.

Izz accepted the offer gratefully; and disappeared through the great door into the snowy track to her lodging. Marian, as was the case every afternoon at this time, on account of the bottle, began to feel in a romantic vein.

"I should not have thought it of him—never!" she said in a dreamy tone. "And I loved him so! I didn't mind his having *you*. But this about Izz is too bad!"

Tess, in her start at the words, narrowly missed cutting off a finger with the bill-hook.

"Is it about my husband?" she stammered.

"Well, yes. Izz said 'Don't 'ee tell her'; but I am sure I can't help it! It was what he wanted Izz to do. . . . He wanted her to go off to Brazil with him."

Tess's face faded as white as the scene without, and its curves straightened. "And did Izz refuse to go?" she asked.

"I don't know. Anyhow he changed his mind."

"Pooh—then he didn't mean it. 'Twas just a man's jest!"

"Yes he did; for he drove her a good-ways towards the station."

"He didn't take her!"

They pulled on in silence till Tess, without any premonitory symptoms, burst out crying.

"There!" said Marian. "Now I wish I hadn't told 'ee!"

"No. It is a very good thing that you have done! I have been living on in a thirtover, lackaday way, and have not seen what it may lead to! I ought to have sent him a letter oftener. He said I could not go to him, but he didn't say I was not to write as often as I liked. I won't dally like this any longer. I have been very wrong and neglectful in leaving everything to be done by him!"

The dim light in the barn grew dimmer, and they could see to work no longer. When Tess had reached home that evening and had entered into the privacy of her little whitewashed chamber she began impetuously writing a letter to Clare. But falling into doubt she could not finish it. Afterwards she took her ring from the ribbon on which she wore it next her heart, and retained it on her finger all night, as if to fortify herself in the sensation that she was really the wife of this elusive lover of hers, who could propose that Izz should go with him abroad, so shortly after he had left her. Knowing that, how could she write entreaties to him, or show that she cared for him any more?

XLIV

BY the disclosure in the barn her thoughts were led anew in the direction which they had taken more than once of late—to the distant Emminster Vicarage. It was through her husband's parents that she had been charged to send a letter to Clare, if she desired; and to write to them direct if in difficulty. But that sense of her having morally no claim upon him had always led Tess to suspend her impulse to send these notes; and to the family at the vicarage therefore, as to her own parents since her marriage, she was virtually non-existent. This self-effacement in both directions had been quite in consonance with her independent character of desiring nothing by way of favour or pity to which she was not entitled on a fair consideration of her deserts. She had set herself to stand or fall by her qualities, and to waive such merely technical claims upon a strange family as had been established for her by the flimsy fact of a member of that family, in a season of impulse, writing his name in a church-book beside hers.

But now that she was stung to a fever by Izz's tale there was a limit to her powers of renunciation. Why had her husband not written to her? He had distinctly implied that he would at least let her know of the locality to which he had journeyed; but he had not sent a line to notify his address. Was he really indifferent? But was he ill? Was it for her to make some advance? Surely she might summon the courage of solicitude, call at the vicarage for intelligence, and express her grief at his silence. If Angel's father were the good man she had heard him represented to be, he would be able to enter into her heart-starved situation. Her social hardships she could conceal.

To leave the farm on a week-day was not in her power; Sunday was her only possible opportunity. Flintcomb-Ash being in the middle of the cretaceous tableland* over which no railway had climbed as yet, it would be necessary to walk. And the distance being fifteen miles each way she would have to allow herself a long day for the undertaking, by rising early.

A fortnight later, when the snow had gone, and had been followed by a hard black frost, she took advantage of the state of the roads to try the experiment. At four o'clock that Sunday morning she came downstairs and stepped out into the starlight. The weather was still favourable, the ground ringing under her feet like an anvil.

Marian and Izz were much interested in her excursion, knowing that the journey concerned her husband. Their lodgings were in a cottage a little further along the lane, but they came and assisted Tess in her departure, and argued that she should dress up in her very prettiest guise to captivate the hearts of her parents-in-law; though she, knowing of the austere and Calvinistic tenets of old Mr Clare, was indifferent, and even doubtful. A year had now elapsed since her sad marriage, but she had preserved sufficient draperies from the wreck of her then full wardrobe to clothe her very charmingly as a simple country girl with no pretension to recent fashion; a soft grey woollen gown, with white crape quilling* against the pink skin of her face and neck; and a black velvet jacket and hat.

" 'Tis a thousand pities your husband can't see 'ee now—you do look a real beauty!" said Izz Huett, regarding Tess as she stood on the threshold, between the steely starlight without, and the yellow candlelight within. Izz spoke with a magnanimous abandonment of herself to the situation: she could not be—no woman with a heart bigger than a hazel-nut could be—antagonistic to Tess in her presence, the influence which she exercised over those of her own sex being of a warmth and strength quite unusual, curiously overpowering the less worthy feminine feelings of spite and rivalry.

With a final tug and touch here, and a slight brush there, they let her go; and she was absorbed into the pearly air of the fore-dawn. They heard her footsteps tap along the hard road as she stepped out to her full pace. Even Izz hoped she would win, and, though without any particular respect for her own virtue, felt glad that she had been prevented wronging her friend when momentarily tempted by Clare.

It was a year ago all but a day that Clare had married Tess, and only a few days less than a year that he had been absent from her. Still, to start on a brisk walk, and on such an errand as hers, on a dry clear wintry morning, through the rarified air of these chalky hogs'-backs,* was not depressing: and there is no doubt that her dream at starting was to win the heart of her mother-in-law, tell her whole history to that lady, enlist her on her side, and so gain back the truant.

In time she reached the edge of the vast escarpment below which stretched the loamy Vale of Blackmoor, now lying misty and still in the dawn. Instead of the colourless air of the uplands the atmosphere

down there was a deep blue. Instead of the great enclosures of a
hundred acres in which she was now accustomed to toil there were
little fields below her of less than half-a-dozen acres, so numerous
that they looked from this height like the meshes of a net. Here the
landscape was whitey-brown; down there, as in the Froom Valley, it
was always green. Yet it was in that vale that her sorrow had taken
shape, and she did not love it as formerly. Beauty to her, as to all who
have felt, lay not in the thing, but in what the thing symbolized.

Keeping the Vale on her right she steered steadily westward;
passing above the Hintocks, crossing at right-angles the high-road
from Sherton-Abbas to Casterbridge, and skirting Dogbury Hill
and High-Stoy, with the dell between them called "The Devil's
Kitchen." Still following the elevated way she reached Cross-in-
Hand, where the stone pillar stands desolate and silent, to mark the
site of a miracle or a murder, or both. Three miles further she cut
across the straight and deserted Roman road called Long-Ash Lane;
leaving which as soon as she reached it she dipped down a hill by a
transverse lane into the small town or village of Evershead, being
now about half-way over the distance. She made a halt here, and
breakfasted a second time heartily enough—not at the Sow-and-
Acorn, for she avoided inns, but at a cottage by the church.

The second half of her journey was through a more gentle country,
by way of Benvill Lane. But as the mileage lessened between her and
the spot of her pilgrimage so did Tess's confidence decrease, and her
enterprise loom out more formidably. She saw her purpose in such
staring lines, and the landscape so faintly, that she was sometimes in
danger of losing her way. However, about noon she paused by a gate
on the edge of the basin in which Emminster and its vicarage lay.

The square tower beneath which she knew that at that moment
the vicar and his congregation were gathered had a severe look in her
eyes. She wished that she had somehow contrived to come on a
week-day. Such a good man might be prejudiced against a woman
who had chosen Sunday, never realising the necessities of her case.
But it was incumbent upon her to go on now. She took off the thick
boots in which she had walked thus far, put on her pretty thin ones
of patent leather, and, stuffing the former into the hedge by the
gate-post where she might readily find them again, descended
the hill; the freshness of colour she had derived from the keen air
thinning away in spite of her as she drew near the parsonage.

Tess hoped for some accident that might favour her; but nothing favoured her. The shrubs on the vicarage lawn rustled uncomfortably in the frosty breeze; she could not feel, by any stretch of imagination, dressed to her highest as she was, that the house was the residence of near relations: and yet nothing essential, in nature or emotion, divided her from them: in pains, pleasures, thoughts, birth, death, and after death, they were the same.

She nerved herself by an effort, entered the swing-gate, and rang the door-bell. The thing was done: there could be no retreat. No: the thing was not done: nobody answered to her ringing. The effort had to be risen to and made again. She rang a second time; and the agitation of the act, coupled with her weariness after the fifteen miles' walk, led her to support herself while she waited by resting her hand on her hip, and her elbow against the wall of the porch. The wind was so nipping that the ivy-leaves had become wizened and grey, each tapping incessantly upon its neighbour with a disquieting stir of her nerves. A piece of blood-stained paper, caught up from some meat-buyer's dust-heap, beat up and down the road without the gate, too flimsy to rest, too heavy to fly away; and a few straws kept it company.

The second peal had been louder; and still nobody came. Then she walked out of the porch, opened the gate and passed through. And though she looked dubiously at the house-front as if inclined to return, it was with a breath of relief that she closed the gate. A feeling haunted her that she might have been recognized, (though how she could not tell), and orders been given not to admit her.

Tess went as far as the corner. She had done all she could do; but determined not to escape present trepidation at the expense of future distress, she walked back again quite past the house, looking up at all the windows.

Ah—the explanation was that they were all at church, every one. She remembered her husband saying that his father always insisted upon the household, servants included, going to morning service, and as a consequence eating cold food when they came home. It was therefore only necessary to wait till the service was over. She would not make herself conspicuous by waiting on the spot, and she started to get past the church into the lane. But as she reached the church-yard-gate the people began pouring out, and Tess found herself in the midst of them.

The Emminster congregation looked at her as only a congregation of small country-townsfolk walking home at its leisure can look at a woman out of the common whom it perceives to be a stranger. She quickened her pace and ascended the road by which she had come, to find a retreat between its hedges till the vicar's family should have lunched, and it might be convenient for them to receive her. She soon distanced the churchgoers, except two youngish men who, linked arm in arm, were beating up behind her at a quick step.

As they drew nearer she could hear their voices engaged in earnest discourse; and, with the natural quickness of a woman in her situation, did not fail to recognize in those voices the quality of her husband's tones. The pedestrians were his two brothers. Forgetting all her plans Tess's one dread was lest they should overtake her, now, in her disorganized condition, before she was prepared to confront them, for though she felt that they could not identify her she instinctively dreaded their scrutiny. The more briskly they walked the more briskly walked she. They were plainly bent upon taking a short quick stroll before going indoors to lunch or dinner, to restore warmth to limbs chilled with sitting through a long service.

Only one person had preceded Tess up the hill, a lady like young woman, somewhat interesting, though perhaps a trifle *guindée** and prudish. Tess had nearly overtaken her when the speed of her brothers-in-law brought them so nearly behind her back that she could hear every word of their conversation. They said nothing, however, which particularly interested her till, observing the young lady still further in front, one of them remarked "There is Mercy Chant. Let us overtake her."

Tess knew the name. It was the woman who had been destined for Angel's life-companion by his and her parents, and whom he probably would have married but for her intrusive self. She would have known as much without previous information if she had waited a moment, for one of the brothers proceeded to say: "Ah, poor Angel, poor Angel! I never see that nice girl without more and more regretting his precipitancy in throwing himself away upon a dairymaid, or whatever she may be. It is a queer business, apparently. Whether she has joined him yet or not I don't know; but she had not done so some months ago, when I heard from him."

"I can't say. He never tells me anything nowadays. His ill-considered marriage seems to have completed that estrangement from me which was begun by his extraordinary opinions."

Tess beat up the long hill still faster; but she could not outwalk them without exciting notice. At last they outsped her altogether and passed her by. The young lady still further ahead heard their footsteps and turned. Then there was a greeting and a shaking of hands; and the three went on together.

They soon reached the summit of the hill; and evidently intending this point to be the limit of their promenade slackened pace and turned all three aside to the gate whereat Tess had paused an hour before that time, to reconnoitre the town before descending into it. During their discourse one of the clerical brothers probed the hedge carelessly with his umbrella, and dragged something to light.

"Here's a pair of old boots," he said. "Thrown away I suppose by some tramp or other."

"Some imposter who wished to come into the town barefoot, perhaps, and so excite our sympathies," said Miss Chant. "Yes; it must have been; for they are excellent walking-boots—by no means worn out. What a wicked thing to do! I'll carry them home for some poor person."

Cuthbert Clare, who had been the one to find them, picked them up for her with the crook of his stick; and Tess's boots were appropriated. She, who had heard this, walked past under the screen of her woollen veil; till, presently looking back, she perceived that the church-party had left the gate with her boots, and retreated down the hill.

Thereupon our heroine resumed her walk. Tears, blinding tears, were running down her face. She knew that it was all sentiment, all baseless impressibility, which had caused her to read the scene as her own condemnation; nevertheless she could not get over it; she could not contravene in her own defenceless person all these untoward omens. It was impossible to think of returning to the vicarage. Angel's wife felt almost as if she had been hounded up that hill like a scorned thing by those, to her, superfine clerics. Innocently as the slight had been inflicted, it was somewhat unfortunate that she had encountered the sons and not the father, who, despite his narrowness, was far less starched and ironed than they, and had to the full the gift of charity. As she again thought of her dusty boots she almost pitied those habiliments for the quizzing to which they had been subjected, and felt how hopeless life was for their owner.

"Ah," she said, still sighing in pity of herself, "*they* didn't know that I wore those over the roughest part of the road to save these pretty ones *he* bought for me—no—they did not know it! And they didn't think that *he* chose the colour o' my pretty frock—no—how could they? If they had known perhaps they would not have cared; for they don't care much for him, poor thing!"

Then she grieved for the beloved man whose conventional standard of judgment had caused her all these latter sorrows; and she went her way without knowing that the greatest misfortune of her life was this feminine loss of courage at the last and critical moment, through her estimating her father-in-law by his sons. Her present condition was precisely one which would have enlisted the sympathies of old Mr and Mrs Clare. Their hearts went out of them at a bound towards extreme cases, when the subtle mental troubles of the less desperate among mankind failed to win their interest or regard. In jumping at publicans and sinners they would forget that a word might be said for the worries of scribes and pharisees; and this defect or limitation might have recommended their own daughter-in-law to them at this moment as a fairly choice sort of lost person for their love.

Thereupon she began to plod back along the road by which she had come not altogether full of hope, but full of a conviction that a crisis in her life was approaching. No crisis, apparently, had super- vened; and there was nothing left for her to do but to continue upon that starve-acre farm till she could again summon courage to face the vicarage. She did, indeed, take sufficient interest in herself to throw up her veil on this return journey, as if to let the world see that she could at least exhibit a face such as Mercy Chant could not show. But it was done with a sorry shake of the head. "It is nothing—it is nothing!" she said. "Nobody loves it; nobody sees it. Who cares about the looks of a castaway like me!"

Her journey back was rather a meander than a march. It had no sprightliness; no purpose; only a tendency. Along the tedious length of Benvill Lane she began to grow tired; and she leant upon gates, and paused by milestones.

She did not enter any house till at the seventh or eighth mile she descended the steep long hill below which lay the village or townlet of Evershead, where in the morning she had breakfasted with such contrasting expectations. The cottage by the church, in which she again sat down, was almost the first at that end of the village, and while the woman fetched her some milk from the pantry Tess, looking down the street, perceived that the place seemed quite deserted.

"The people are gone to afternoon service, I suppose?" she said.

"No my dear," said the old woman. " 'Tis too soon for that: the bells hain't strook out yet. They be all gone to hear the preaching in yonder barn: a ranter preaches there between the services—an excellent fiery Christian man, they say. But, Lord, I don't go to hear'n. What comes in the regular way over the pulpit is hot enough for I."

Tess soon went onward into the village, her footsteps echoing against the houses as though it were a place of the dead. Nearing the central part her echoes were intruded on by other sounds; and seeing the barn not far off the road, she guessed these to be the utterances of the preacher.

His voice became so distinct in the still clear air that she could soon catch his sentences, though she was on the closed side of the barn. The sermon, as might be expected, was of the extremest antinomian type; on justification by faith, as expounded in the theology of St Paul. This fixed idea of the rhapsodist was delivered with animated enthusiasm, in a manner entirely declamatory, for he had plainly no skill as a dialectician. Although Tess had not heard the beginning of the address she learnt what the text had been from its constant iteration:

*"O foolish Galatians, who hath bewitched you, that ye should not obey the truth, before whose eyes Jesus Christ hath been evidently set forth, crucified among you?"**

Tess was all the more interested, as she stood listening behind, in finding that the preacher's doctrine was a vehement form of the views of Angel's father; and her interest intensified when the speaker began to detail his own spiritual experiences of how he had come by these views. He had, he said, been the greatest of sinners. He had scoffed; he had wantonly associated with the reckless and the lewd. But a day of awakening had come; and, in a human sense, it had been brought about mainly by the influence of a certain clergyman, whom he had at first grossly insulted; but whose parting words had sunk into his heart, and had remained there, till by the grace of Heaven they had worked this change in him, and made him what they saw him.

But more startling to Tess than the doctrine had been the voice, which, impossible as it seemed, was precisely that of Alec d'Urberville. Her face fixed in painful suspense she came round to the front of the barn, and passed before it. The low winter sun beamed directly upon the great double-doored entrance on this side; one of the doors being open; so that the rays stretched far in over the threshing-floor to the preacher and his audience, all snugly sheltered from the northern breeze. The listeners were entirely villagers, among them being the man whom she had seen carrying the red paint-pot on a former memorable occasion. But her attention was given to the central figure, who stood upon some sacks of corn, facing the people and the door. The three o'clock sun shone full upon him, and the strange enervating conviction that her seducer confronted her, which had been gaining ground in Tess ever since she had heard his words distinctly, was at last established as a fact indeed.

END OF PHASE THE FIFTH

PHASE THE SIXTH

THE CONVERT

PHASE THE SIXTH

THE CONVERT

XLV

TILL this moment she had never seen or heard from d'Urberville since her departure from Trantridge.

The rencounter came at a heavy moment, one of all moments calculated to permit its impact with the least emotional shock. But such was unreasoning memory that, though he stood there openly and palpably a converted man, who was sorrowing for his past irregularities, a fear overcame her, paralyzing her movement so that she neither retreated nor advanced.

To think of what emanated from that countenance when she saw it last; and to behold it now.

There was the same handsome unpleasantness of mein; but now he wore neatly trimmed, old-fashioned whiskers, the sable moustache having disappeared; and his dress was half-clerical, a modification which had changed his expression sufficiently to abstract the dandyism from his features, and to hinder for a second her belief in his identity.

To Tess's sense there was, just at first, a ghastly *bizarrerie*, a grim incongruity, in the march of these solemn words of Scripture out of such a mouth. This too familiar intonation, less than four years earlier, had brought to her ears expressions of such divergent purpose that her heart became quite sick at the irony of the contrast.

It was less a reform than a transfiguration. The former curves of sensuousness were now modulated to lines of devotional passion. The lip-shapes that had meant seductiveness were now made to express supplication; the glow on the cheek that yesterday could be translated as riotousness was evangelized to-day into the splendour of pious rhetoric; animalism had become fanaticism; Paganism Paulinism; the bold rolling eye that had flashed upon her form in the old time with such mastery now beamed with the rude energy of a theolatry that was almost ferocious. Those black angularities which his face had used to put on when his wishes were thwarted now did duty in picturing the incorrigible backslider who would insist upon turning again to his wallowing in the mire.

The lineaments, as such, seemed to complain. They had been diverted from their hereditary connotation to signify impressions for which nature did not intend them. Strange that their very elevation was a misapplication; that to raise seemed to falsify.

Yet could it be so? She would admit the ungenerous sentiment no longer. D'Urberville was not the first wicked man who had turned away from his wickedness to save his soul alive, and why should she deem it unnatural in him? It was but the usage of thought which had been jarred in her at hearing good new words in bad old notes. The greater the sinner the greater the saint: it was not necessary to dive far into Christian history to discover that.

Such impressions as these moved her vaguely, and without strict definiteness. As soon as the nerveless pause of her surprise would allow her to stir, her impulse was to pass on out of his sight. He had obviously not discerned her yet in her position against the sun. But the moment that she moved again he recognized her.

The effect upon her old lover was electric, far stronger than the effect of his presence upon her. His fire, the tumultuous ring of his eloquence, seemed to go out of him. His lip struggled and trembled under the words that lay upon it; but deliver them it could not as long as she faced him. His eyes, after their first glance upon her face, hung confusedly in every other direction but hers, but came back in a desperate leap every few seconds. This paralysis lasted, however, but a short time; for Tess's energies returned with the atrophy of his, and she walked as fast as she was able past the barn and onward.

As soon as she could reflect it appalled her, this change in their relative platforms. He who had wrought her undoing was now on the side of the spirit, while she remained unregenerate. And, as in the legend, it had resulted that her Cyprian image had suddenly appeared upon his altar, whereby the fire of the priest had been well-nigh extinguished.*

She went on without turning her head. Her back seemed to be endowed with a sensitiveness to ocular beams—even her clothing— so alive was she to a fancied gaze which might be resting upon her from the outside of that barn. All the way along to this point her heart had been heavy with an inactive sorrow; now there was a change in the quality of its trouble. That hunger for affection too long withheld was for the time displaced by an almost physical sense of an implacable past which still engirdled her. It intensified her consciousness of error to a practical despair; the break of continuity between her earlier and present existence, which she had hoped for, had not after all taken place. Bygones would never be complete bygones till she was a bygone herself.

Thus absorbed she recrossed the northern part of Long-Ash Lane at right angles, and presently saw before her the road ascending whitely to the upland along whose margin the remainder of her journey lay. Its dry pale surface stretched severely onward, unbroken by a single figure, vehicle, or mark, save some occasional brown horse-droppings which dotted its cold aridity here and there. While slowly breasting this ascent Tess became conscious of footsteps behind her, and turning she saw approaching that well-known form, so strangely accoutred as the Methodist—the one personage in all the world whom she wished not to encounter alone on this side of the grave.

There was not much time, however, for thought or elusion, and she yielded as calmly as she could to the necessity of letting him overtake her. She saw that he was excited, less by the speed of his walk than by the feelings within him.

"Tess!" he said.

She slackened speed without looking round.

"Tess!" he repeated. "It is I—Alec d'Urberville."

She then looked back at him, and he came up. "I see it is," she answered coldly.

"Well—is that all? Yet I deserve no more! Of course," he added, with a slight laugh, "there is something of the ridiculous to your eyes in seeing me like this. But—I must put up with that. . . . I heard you had gone away, nobody knew where. Tess, you wonder why I have followed you?"

"I do, rather. And I would that you had not, with all my heart."

"Yes—you may well say it," he returned grimly as they moved onward together, she with unwilling tread. "But don't mistake me; I beg this because you may have been led to do so in noticing—if you did notice it—how your sudden appearance unnerved me down there. It was but a momentary faltering; and considering what—you had been to me, it was natural enough. But will helped me through it—though perhaps you think me a humbug for saying it—and immediately afterwards I felt that, of all persons in the world whom it was my duty and desire to save from the wrath to come—sneer if you like—the woman whom I had so grievously wronged was that person. I have come with that sole purpose in view—nothing more."

There was the smallest vein of scorn in her words of rejoinder: "Have you saved yourself? Charity begins at home, they say."

"*I* have done nothing!" said he indifferently. "Heaven, as I have been telling my hearers, has done all. No amount of contempt that you can pour upon me, Tess, will equal what I have poured upon myself—the old Adam, of my former years. Well, it is a strange story; believe it or not; but I can tell you the means by which my conversion was brought about, and I hope you will be interested enough at least to listen. Have you ever heard the name of the parson of Emminster—you must have done so?—old Mr Clare; one of the most earnest of his school; one of the few intense men left in the Church; not so intense as the extreme wing of Christian believers with which I have thrown in my lot, but quite an exception among the established clergy, the younger of whom are gradually attenuating the true doctrines by their sophistries till they are but the shadow of what they were. I only differ from him on the question of Church and State—the interpretation of the text, 'Come out from among them and be ye separate, saith the Lord'*—that's all. He is one who, I firmly believe, has been the humble means of saving more souls in this country than any other man you can name. You have heard of him?"

"I have," she said.

"He came to Trantridge two or three years ago, to preach on behalf of some Missionary Society; and I, wretched fellow that I was, insulted him when, in his disinterestedness, he tried to reason with me and show me the way. He did not resent my conduct. He simply said that some day I should receive the first-fruits of the Spirit—that those who came to scoff sometimes remained to pray.* There was a strange magic in his words. They sank into my mind. But the loss of my mother hit me most; and by degrees I was brought to see daylight. Since then my one desire has been to hand on the true view to others, and that is what I was trying to do to-day; though it is only lately that I have preached hereabout. The first months of my ministry have been spent in the north of England among strangers, where I preferred to make my earliest clumsy attempts, so as to acquire courage before undergoing that severest of all tests of one's sincerity, addressing those who have known one, and have been one's companions in the days of darkness. . . . If you could only know, Tess, the pleasure of having a good slap at yourself, I am sure—"

"Don't go on with it!" she cried passionately, as she turned away from him to a stile by the wayside, on which she bent herself. "I can't believe in such sudden things. I feel indignant with you for talking to me like this, when you know—when you know what harm you've done me! You, and those like you, take your fill of pleasure on earth by making the life of such as me bitter and black with sorrow; and then it is a fine thing, when you have had enough of that, to think of securing your pleasure in heaven by becoming converted. Out upon such—I don't believe in you—I hate it!"

"Tess," he insisted; "don't speak so! It came to me like a jolly new idea! And you don't believe me? What don't you believe?"

"Your conversion. Your scheme of religion."

"Why?"

She dropped her voice. "Because a better man than you does not believe in such."

"What a woman's reason! Who is this better man?"

"I cannot tell you."

"Well," he declared, a resentment beneath his words seeming ready to spring out at a moment's notice; "God forbid that I should say I am a good man—and you know I don't say any such thing. I am new to goodness, truly; but new comers see furthest sometimes."

"Yes," she replied sadly. "But I cannot believe in your conversion to a new spirit. Such flashes as you feel, Alec, I fear don't last."

Thus speaking she turned from the stile over which she had been learning, and faced him; whereupon his eyes, falling casually upon the familiar countenance and form, remained contemplating her. The inferior man was quiet in him now; but it was surely not extracted, nor even entirely subdued.

"Don't look at me like that!" he said abruptly.

Tess, who had been quite unconscious of her action and mien, instantly withdrew the large dark gaze of her eyes, stammering with a flush, "I beg your pardon." And there was revived in her the wretched sentiment which had often come to her before, that in inhabiting the fleshly tabernacle* with which Nature had endowed her, she was somehow doing wrong.

"No, no. Don't beg my pardon. But since you wear a veil to hide your good looks, why don't you keep it down?"

She pulled down the veil, saying hastily: "It was mostly to keep off the wind."

"It may seem harsh of me to dictate like this!" he went on. "But it is better that I should not look too often on you. It might be dangerous."

"Ssh!" said Tess.

"Well women's faces have had too much power over me already for me not to fear them. An evangelist has nothing to do with such as they: and it reminds me of the old times that I would forget."

After this their conversation dwindled to a casual remark now and then as they rambled onward, Tess inwardly wondering how far he was going with her, and not liking to send him back by positive mandate. Frequently when they came to a gate or stile they found painted theron in red or blue letters some text of Scripture, and she asked him if he knew who had been at the pains to blazon these announcements. He told her that the man was employed by himself and others who were working with him in that district, to paint these reminders that no means might be left untried which might move the hearts of a wicked generation.

At length the road touched the spot called "Cross-in-Hand". Of all spots on the bleached and desolate upland this was the most forlorn. It was so far removed from the charm which is sought in landscape by artists and view-lovers as to reach a new kind of beauty, a negative beauty of tragic tone. The place took its name from a stone pillar which stood there, a strange rude monolith, from a stratum unknown in any local quarry, on which was roughly carved a human hand. Differing accounts were given of its history and purport. Some authorities stated that a devotional cross had once formed the complete erection thereon, of which the present relic was but the stump; others that the stone as it stood was entire, and that it had been fixed there to mark a boundary, or place of meeting. Anyhow, whatever the origin of the relic, there was, and is, something sinister, or solemn, according to mood, in the scene amid which it stands: something tending to impress the most phlegmatic passer-by.

"I think I must leave you now," he remarked, as they drew near to this spot. "I have to preach at Abbot's-Cernel at six this evening, and my way lies across to the right from here. And you upset me somewhat too, Tessy—I cannot, will not say why. I must go away, and get strength. . . . How is it that you speak so fluently now; who has taught you such good English?"

"I have learnt things in my troubles," she said evasively.

"What troubles have you had?"

She told him of the first one—the only one that related to him.

D'Urberville was struck mute. "I knew nothing of this till now!" he next murmured. "Why didn't you write to me when you felt your trouble coming on?"

She did not reply; and he broke the silence by adding: "Well—you will see me again."

"No," she answered. "Don't come near me!"

"I will think. But before we part, come here." He stepped up to the pillar. "This was once a Holy Cross. Relics are not in my creed; but I fear you at moments—far more than you need fear me at present; and to lessen my fear, put your hand upon that stone hand, and swear that you will never tempt me—by your charms or ways."

"Good God—how can you ask what is so unnecessary! All that is furthest from my thought."

"Yes—but swear it."

Tess, half frightened, gave way to his importunity, placed her hand upon the stone, and swore.

"I am sorry you are not a believer," he continued; "that some unbeliever should have got hold of you, and unsettled your mind. But no more now. At home at least I can pray for you; and I will; and who knows what may not happen? I'm off. Good-bye!"

He turned to a hunting-gate in the hedge, and without letting his eyes again rest upon her, leapt over and struck out across the down in the direction of Abbot's-Cernel. As he walked his face showed perturbation, and by and by, as if instigated by a former thought, he drew from his pocket a small book, between the leaves of which was folded a letter, worn and soiled, as from much re-reading. D'Urberville opened the letter; it was dated several months before this time, and was signed by Parson Clare.

The letter began by expressing the writer's unfeigned joy at d'Urberville's conversion, and thanked him for his kindness in communicating with the parson on the subject. It expressed Mr Clare's warm assurance of forgiveness for d'Urberville's former conduct, and his interest in the young man's plans for the future. He,

Mr Clare, would much have liked to see d'Urberville in the Church to whose ministry he had devoted so many years of his own life, and would have helped him to enter a theological college to that end; but since his correspondent had possibly not cared to do this on account of the delay it would have entailed, he was not the man to insist upon its paramount importance. Every man must work as he could best work, and in the method towards which he felt impelled by the Spirit.

D'Urberville read and re-read this letter, and seemed to quiz himself cynically. He also read some passages from memoranda as he walked; till his face assumed a calm, and apparently the image of Tess no longer troubled his mind.

She meanwhile had kept along the edge of the hill by which lay her nearest way home. Within the distance of a mile she met a solitary shepherd.

"What is the meaning of that old stone I have passed?" she asked of him. "Was it ever a Holy Cross?"

"Cross—no; 'twer not a cross. 'Tis a thing of ill-omen, miss. It was put up in wuld times by the relations of a malefactor who was tortured there by nailing his hand to a post, and afterwards hung. The bones lie underneath. They say he sold his soul to the devil, and that he walks at times."

She felt the *petite mort** at this unexpectedly gruesome information, and left the solitary man behind her. It was dusk when she drew near to Flintcomb-Ash; and in the lane at the entrance to the hamlet she approached a girl and her lover without their observing her. They were talking no secrets, and the clear, unconcerned voice of the young woman, in response to the warmer accents of the man, spread into the chilly air as the one soothing thing within the dusky horizon, full of a stagnant obscurity upon which nothing else intruded. For a moment the voices cheered the heart of Tess, till she reasoned that this interview had its origin, on one side or the other, in the same attraction which had been the prelude to her own tribulation. When she came close the girl turned serenely and recognized her, the young man walking off in embarrassment. The woman was Izz Huett, whose interest in Tess's excursion immediately superseded her own proceedings. Tess did not explain very clearly its results, and Izz, who was a girl of tact, began to speak of her own little affair, a phase of which Tess had just witnessed.

"He is Amby Seedling, the chap who used to sometimes come and help at Talbothays," she explained indifferently. "He actually inquired and found out that I had come here, and has followed me. He says he's been in love wi' me these two years. But I've hardly answered him."

XLVI

SEVERAL days had passed since her futile journey, and Tess was afield. The dry winter wind still blew, but a screen of thatched hurdles erected in the eye of the blast kept its force away from her. On the sheltered side was a turnip-slicing machine, whose bright blue hue of new paint seemed almost vocal in the otherwise subdued scene. Opposite its front was a long mound or "grave", in which the roots had been preserved since early winter. Tess was standing at the uncovered end, chopping off with a bill-hook the fibres and earth from each root, and throwing it after the operation into the slicer. A man was turning the handle of the machine, and from its trough came the newly-cut swedes, the fresh smell of whose yellow chips was accompanied by the sounds of the snuffling wind, the smart swish of the slicing-blades, and the choppings of the hook in Tess's leather-gloved hand.

The wide acreage of blank agricultural brownness apparent where the swedes had been pulled, was beginning to be striped in wales of darker brown, gradually broadening to ribands. Along the edge of each of these something crept upon ten legs, moving without haste and without rest up and down the whole length of the field; it was two horses and a man, the plough going between them, turning up the cleared ground for a spring sowing.

For hours nothing relieved the joyless monotony of things. Then, far beyond the ploughing-teams, a black speck was seen; it had come from the corner of a fence, where there was a gap, and its tendency was up the incline, towards the swede-cutters. From the proportions of a mere point it advanced to the shape of a ninepin, and was soon perceived to be a man in black, arriving from the direction of Flintcomb-Ash. The man at the slicer, having nothing else to do with his eyes, continually observed the comer, but Tess, who was occupied, did not perceive him till her companion directed her attention to his approach.

It was not her hard taskmaster, Farmer Groby; it was one in a semi-clerical costume, who now represented what had once been the free-and-easy Alec d'Urberville. Not being hot at his preaching there was less enthusiasm about him now, and the presence of the grinder seemed to embarrass him. A pale distress was already on Tess's face, and she pulled her curtained hood further over it. D'Urberville came up and said quietly, "I want to speak to you, Tess."

"You have refused my last request, not to come near me." said she.

"Yes, but I have a good reason."

"Well—tell it."

"It is more serious than you may think." He glanced round, to see if he were overheard. They were at some distance from the man who turned the slicer, and the movement of the machine, too, sufficiently prevented Alec's words reaching other ears. D'Urberville placed himself so as to screen Tess from the labourer, turning his back to the latter. "It is this," he continued with capricious compunction. "In thinking of your soul and mine when we last met, I neglected to inquire as to your worldly condition. You were well-dressed, and I did not think of it. But I see now that it is hard, harder than it used to be when I—knew you; harder than you deserve. Perhaps a good deal of it is owing to me!"

She did not answer, and he watched her inquiringly, as, with bent head, her face completely screened by the hood, she resumed her trimming of the swedes. By going on with her work she felt better able to keep him outside her emotions.

"Tess," he added, with a sigh of discontent,—"yours was the very worst case I ever was concerned in. I had no idea of what had resulted till you told me. Scamp that I was, to foul that innocent life. The whole blame was mine; the whole unconventional business of our time at Trantridge. You, too, the real article of which I am but the plated imitation—ha, ha!—what a blind young thing you were as to possibilities! I say in all earnestness that it is a shame for parents to bring up their girls in such dangerous ignorance of the gins and nets that the wicked may set for them,* whether their motive be a good one, or the result of simple indifference."

Tess still did no more than listen, throwing down one globular root and taking up another with automatic regularity, the pensive contour of the mere fieldwoman alone marking her.

"But it is not that I came to say," d'Urberville went on. "My circumstances are these. I have lost my mother since you were at Trantridge, and the place is my own. But I intend to sell it, and try to devote myself to missionary work in Africa. A devil of a poor hand I shall make at the trade, no doubt. However, what I want to ask you is, will you put it in my power to make the only amends I can make for the trick I played you—that is, will you be my wife, and go with me? . . . I have already obtained this precious document, to save time. It was my old mother's dying wish."

He drew a piece of parchment from his pocket, with a slight fumbling of embarrassment.

"What is it?" said she.

"A marriage licence."

"O no, sir—no," she said quickly, starting back.

"You will not? Why is that?" And as he asked the question a disappointment which was not entirely a disappointment of thwarted duty crossed d'Urberville's face. It was unmistakably a symptom that something of his old passion for her had been revived; duty and desire ran hand in hand. "Surely," he began again, in more impetuous tones, and then looked round at the labourer who turned the slicer.

Tess, too, felt that the argument could not be ended there. Informing the man that a gentleman had come to see her, with whom she wished to walk a little way, she moved off with d'Urberville across the zebra-striped field. When they reached the first newly-ploughed section he held out his hand to help her over it; but she stepped forward on the summits of the earth-rolls as if she did not see him.

"You will not marry me, Tess, and make me a self-respecting man?" he repeated as soon as they were over the furrows.

"I cannot."

"But why?"

"You know I have no affection for you."

"But you would get to feel that in time, perhaps—as soon as you really could forgive me?"

"Never!"

"Why so positive?"

"I love somebody else."

The words seemed to astonish him. "You do?" he cried. "Somebody else? . . . But has not a sense of what is morally right and proper any weight with you?"

"No, no, no—don't say that!"

"Anyhow, then, your love for this other man may be only a passing feeling, which you will overcome—"

"No, no."

"Yes, yes! Why not?"

"I cannot tell you."

"You must in honour!"

"Well then . . . I have married him."

"Ah!" he exclaimed. And he stopped dead, and gazed at her.

"I did not wish to tell—I did not mean to!" she pleaded. "It is a secret here, or at any rate but dimly known. So will you, *please* will you, keep from questioning me? You must remember that we are now strangers."

"Strangers—are we? Strangers!" For a moment a flash of his old irony marked his face; but he determinedly chastened it down. "Is that man your husband?" he asked mechanically, denoting by a sign the labourer who turned the machine.

"That man!" she said proudly. "I should think not!"

"Who, then?"

"Do not ask what I do not wish to tell," she begged, and flashed her appeal to him from her upturned face and lash-shadowed eyes.

D'Urberville was disturbed. "But I only asked for your sake!" he retorted hotly. "Angels of heaven—God forgive me for such an expression—I came here, I swear, as I thought for your good. Tess—don't look at me so—I cannot stand your looks! There never were such eyes, surely, before Christianity or since! . . . There—I won't lose my head; I dare not. I own that the sight of you has waked up my love for you, which I believed was extinguished with all such feelings. But I thought that our marriage might be a sanctification for us both. 'The unbelieving husband is sanctified by the wife, and the unbelieving wife is sanctified by the husband,'* I said to myself. But my plan is dashed from me; and I must bear the disappointment." He moodily reflected, with his eyes on the ground. "Married. Married! . . . Well, that being so," he added quite calmly, tearing the licence slowly into halves and putting them in his pocket; "that being prevented, I should like to do some good to you and your husband, whoever he may be. There are many questions that I am tempted to ask, but I will not do so, of course, in opposition to your wishes. Though if I could know your husband I might more easily benefit him and you. Is he on this farm?"

"No," she murmured. "He is far away."

"Far away? From *you*? What sort of husband can he be?"

"O do not speak against him! It was through you. He found out—"

"Ah, is it so! . . . That's sad, Tess!"

"Yes."

"But to stay away from you—to leave you to work like this—"

"He does not leave me to work," she cried springing to the defence of the absent one with all her fervour. "He don't know it. It is by my own arrangement."

"Then does he write?"

"I—I cannot tell you. There are things which are private to ourselves."

"Of course that means that he does not. You are a deserted wife, my fair Tess!" In an impulse he turned suddenly to take her hand: the buff glove was on it, and he seized only the rough leather fingers which did not express the life or shape of those within.

"You must not, you must not!" she cried fearfully, slipping her hand from the glove as from a pocket, and leaving it in his grasp. "O will you go away—for the sake of me and my husband—go, in the name of your own Christianity!"

"Yes, yes; I will," he said abruptly, and thrusting the glove back to her turned to leave. Facing round, however, he said, "Tess, as God is my judge, I meant no humbug in taking your hand!"

A pattering of hoofs on the soil of the field, which they had not noticed in their preoccupation, ceased close behind them; and a voice reached her ear: "What the devil are you doing away from your work at this time o' day?"

Farmer Groby had espied the two figures from the distance, and had inquisitively ridden across to learn what was their business in his field.

"Don't speak like that to her!" said d'Urberville, his face blackening with something that was not Christianity.

"Indeed, Mister. And what mid Methodist pa'sons have to do with she?"

"Who is the fellow?" asked d'Urberville turning to Tess.

She went close up to him. "Go—I do beg you!" she said.

"What—and leave you to that tyrant? I can see in his face what a churl he is."

"He won't hurt me. *He's* not in love with me. I can leave at Lady-Day."

"Well—I have no right but to obey, I suppose. But,—well, good-bye."

Her defender, whom she dreaded more than her assailant, having reluctantly disappeared, the farmer continued his reprimand, which Tess took with the greatest coolness, that sort of attack being independent of sex. To have as a master this man of stone, who would have cuffed her if he had dared, was almost a relief, after her former experiences. She silently walked back towards the summit of the field that was the scene of her labour, so absorbed in the interview which had just taken place that she was hardly aware that the nose of Groby's horse almost touched her shoulders. "If so be you make an agreement to work for me till Lady-Day, I'll see that you carry it out," he growled. " 'Od rot the women—now 'tis one thing, and then 'tis another! But I'll put up with it no longer!"

Knowing very well that he did not harass the other women of the farm as he harassed her out of spite for the flooring he had once received she did for one moment picture what might have been the result if she had been free to accept the offer just made her of being the monied Alec's wife. It would have lifted her completely out of subjection, not only to her present oppressive employer, but to a whole world who seemed to despise her. "But no, no!" she said breathlessly. "I could not have married him now. He is so unpleasant to me."

That very night she began an appealing letter to Clare, concealing from him her hardships, and assuring him of her undying affection. Any one who had been in a position to read between the lines would have seen that at the back of her great love was some monstrous fear, almost a desperation, as to some secret contingencies which were not disclosed. But again she did not finish her effusion: he had asked Izz to go with him, and perhaps he did not care for her at all. She put the letter in her box; and wondered if it would ever reach Angel's hands.

After this her daily tasks were gone through heavily enough, and brought on the day which was of great import to agriculturists, the day of the Candlemas Fair.* It was at this fair that the new engagements were entered into for the twelvemonths following the ensuing Lady-Day, and those of the farming population who thought of changing their places duly attended at the county-town where the fair was held. Nearly all the labourers on Flintcomb-Ash Farm intended flight, and early in the morning there was a general exodus in the direction of the town, which lay at a distance of from ten to a dozen miles over hilly country. Though Tess also meant to leave at the quarter-day, she was one of the few who did not go to the fair; having a vaguely shaped hope that something would happen to render another outdoor engagement unnecessary.

It was a peaceful February day, of wonderful softness for the time, and one would almost have thought that winter was over. She had hardly finished her dinner when d'Urberville's figure darkened the window of the cottage wherein she was a lodger, which she had all to herself to-day.

Tess jumped up, but her visitor had knocked at the door, and she could hardly in reason run away. D'Urberville's knock, his walk up to the door, had some indescribable quality of difference from his air when she last saw him: they seemed to be acts of which the doer was ashamed. She thought that she would not open the door. But as there was no sense in that either, she arose, and having lifted the latch stepped back quickly. He came in, saw her, and flung himself down into a chair before speaking.

"Tess—I couldn't help it," he began desperately, as he wiped his heated face, which had also a superimposed flush of excitement. "I felt that I must call, at least to ask how you are. I assure you I had not been thinking of you at all till I saw you that Sunday: now I cannot get rid of your image, try how I may! It is hard that a good woman should do harm to a bad man; yet so it is. If you would only pray for me, Tess!"

The suppressed discontent of his manner was almost pitiable and yet Tess did not pity him. "How can I pray for you?" she said; "when I am forbidden to believe that the great Power who moves the world would alter his plans on my account."

"You really think that?"

"Yes. I have been cured of the presumption of thinking otherwise."

"Cured? By whom?"

"By my husband, if I must tell."

"Ah—your husband. . . . your husband. How strange it seems! I remember you hinted something of the sort the other day. What do you really believe in these matters, Tess?" he asked. "You seem to have no religion—perhaps owing to me."

"But I have. Though I don't believe in anything supernatural."

D'Urberville looked at her with misgiving. "Then do you think that the line I take is all wrong?"

"A good deal of it."

"H'm—and yet I've felt so sure about it," he said uneasily.

"I believe in the *spirit* of the Sermon on the Mount,* and so did my dear husband. . . . But I don't believe—"

Here she gave her negations.

"The fact is," said d'Urberville, drily; "whatever your dear husband believed you accept, and whatever he rejected you reject, without the least inquiry or reasoning on your own part. That's just like you women. Your mind is enslaved to his."

"Ah, because he knew everything!" said she with a triumphant simplicity of faith in Angel Clare that the most perfect man could hardly have deserved, much less her husband.

"Yes, but you should not take negative opinions wholesale from another person like that. A pretty fellow he must be, to teach you such scepticism."

"He never forced my judgment! He would never argue on the subject with me. But I looked at it in this way; what he believed after inquiring deep into doctrines was much more likely to be right than what I might believe who hadn't looked into doctrines at all."

"What used he to say? He must have said something."

She reflected; and with her acute memory for the letter of Angel Clare's remarks, even when she did not comprehend their spirit, she recalled a merciless polemical syllogism that she had heard him use when, as it occasionally happened, he indulged in a species of thinking aloud with her at his side. In delivering it she gave also Clare's accent and manner with reverential faithfulness.

"Say that again," asked d'Urberville, who had listened with the greatest attention.

She repeated the argument, and d'Urberville thoughtfully murmured the words after her. "Anything else?" he presently asked.

"He said at another time something like this"; and she gave another, which might possibly have been paralleled in many a work of the pedigree ranging from the *Dictionnaire Philosophique** to Huxley's *Essays*.*

"Ah. . . . ha. How do you remember them?"

"I wanted to believe what he believed, though he didn't wish me to; and I managed to coax him to tell me a few of his thoughts. I can't say I quite understand that one; but I know it is right."

"H'm. Fancy your being able to teach me what you don't know yourself." He fell into thought.

"And so I threw in my spiritual lot with his," she resumed. "I didn't wish it to be different. What's good enough for him is good enough for me."

"Does he know that you are as big an infidel as he?"

"No—I never told him—if I am an infidel."

"Well—you are better off to-day than I am, Tess, after all. You don't believe that you ought to preach my doctrine, and therefore do no despite to your conscience in abstaining. I do believe I ought to preach it, but like the devils I believe and tremble,* for I suddenly leave off preaching it, and give way to my passion for you."

"How?"

"Why," he said; "I have come all the way here to see you to-day. But I started from home to go to Casterbridge Fair, where I have undertaken to preach the Word from a waggon at half-past two this afternoon, and where all the brethren are expecting me this minute. Here's the announcement."

He drew from his breast-pocket a poster whereon was printed the day, hour, and place of the meeting, at which he, d'Urberville, would preach the Gospel as aforesaid.

"But how can you get there?" said Tess, looking at the clock.

"I cannot get there. I have come here."

"What, you have really arranged to preach, and—"

"I have arranged to preach and I shall not be there—by reason of my burning desire to see a woman whom I once despised!—No, by my word and truth, I never despised you: if I had I should not love you now. Why I did not think small of you was on account of your being unsmirched in spite of all: you took yourself off from me so quickly and resolutely when you saw the situation; you did not remain at my pleasure; so that there was one petticoat in the world for whom I had no contempt; and you are she. But you may well despise me now. I thought I worshipped on the mountain; but I find I still serve in the groves.* Ha-ha!"

"O Alec d'Urberville—what does this mean—what have I done?"

"Done? Nothing intentionally. But you have been the means—the innocent means—of my backsliding, as they call it. I ask myself am I indeed one of those 'servants of corruption' who, 'after they have escaped the pollutions of the world are again entangled therein and overcome,'—whose latter end is worse than their beginning?"* He laid his hand on her shoulder. "Tess, my girl, I was on the way to, at least, social salvation till I saw you again." He smiled, shaking her as if she were a child. "And why then have you tempted me? I was firm as a man could be till I saw those eyes and that mouth again— surely there never was such a maddening mouth since Eve's."* His voice sank, and a hot archness shot from his own black eyes. "You temptress, Tess; you dear damned witch of Babylon*—I could not resist you as soon as I met you again!"

"I couldn't help your seeing me again!" said Tess, recoiling.

"I know it—I repeat that I do not blame you. But the fact remains. When I saw you ill-used on the farm that day I was nearly mad to think that I had no legal right to protect you—that I could not have it; whilst he who has it seems to neglect you utterly."

"Don't speak against him—he is absent!" she cried in much excitement. "Treat him honourably—he has never wronged you! O leave his wife, before any scandal spreads that may do harm to his honest name!"

"I will—I will," he said, like a man irresolute. "I have broken my engagement to preach to those poor drunken boobies at the fair—it is the first time I have played such a practical joke. A month ago I should have been horrified at such a possibility. I'll go away—to swear—and—ah, can I!—to keep away." Then, suddenly: "One clasp, Tessy—one! Only for old friendship—"

"I am without defence, Alec—a good man's honour is in my keeping—think—be ashamed!"

"Pooh! Well yes—yes!" He clenched his lips, mortified with himself for his weaknesses. The corpses of those old fitful passions which had lain inanimate amid the lines of his face ever since his reformation seemed to wake and come together as in a resurrection. He went out indeterminately.

Though d'Urberville had declared that this breach of his engagement to-day was the simple backsliding of a believer, Tess's words, as echoed from Angel Clare, had made a deep impression upon him, and continued to do so after he had left her. He moved on in silence, as if his energies were benumbed by the hitherto undreamt-of possibility that his position was untenable. Reason had had nothing to do with his whimsical conversion, which was perhaps the mere freak of a careless man in search of a new sensation, and temporarily impressed by his mother's death.

The drops of logic Tess had let fall into the sea of his enthusiasm served to chill its effervescence to stagnation. He said to himself as he pondered again and again over the crystallized phrases that she had handed on to him: "That clever fellow little thought that by telling her those things he might be paving my way back to her!"

XLVII

IT is the threshing of the last wheat-rick at Flintcomb-Ash Farm. The dawn of the March morning is singularly inexpressive, and there is nothing to show where the eastern horizon lies. Against the twilight rises the trapezoidal top of the stack, which has stood forlornly here through the washing and bleaching of the wintry weather.

When Izz Huett and Tess arrived at the scene of operations only a rustling denoted that others had preceded them; to which, as the light increased, there were presently added the silhouettes of two men on the summit. They were busily "unhaling" the rick, that is, stripping off the thatch before beginning to throw down the sheaves; and while this was in progress Izz and Tess, with the other women-workers in their whitey-brown pinners, stood waiting and shivering, Farmer Groby having insisted upon their being upon the spot thus early, to get the job over if possible by the end of the day. Close under the eaves of the stack, and as yet barely visible was the red tyrant that the women had come to serve—a timber-framed construction, with straps and wheels appertaining—the threshing-machine, which, whilst it was going, kept up a despotic demand upon the endurance of their muscles and nerves.

A little way off there was another indistinct figure; this one black, with a sustained hiss that spoke of strength very much in reserve. The long chimney running up beside an ash-tree, and the warmth which radiated from the spot, explained without the necessity of much daylight that here was the engine which was to act as the *primum mobile** of this little world. By the engine stood a dark motion-less being, a sooty and grimy embodiment of tallness, in a sort of trance, with a heap of coals by his side: it was the engine-man. The isolation of his manner and colour lent him the appearance of a creature from Tophet, who had strayed into the pellucid smokeless-ness of this region of yellow grain and pale soil, with which he had nothing in common, to amaze and to discompose its aborigines.

What he looked he felt. He was in the agricultural world, but not of it. He served fire and smoke; these denizens of the fields served vegetation, weather, frost, and sun. He travelled with his engine from farm to farm, from county to county, for as yet the steam threshing-machine was itinerant in this part of Wessex. He spoke in a strange northern accent, his thoughts being turned inwards upon himself, his eye on his iron charge; hardly perceiving the scenes around him, and caring for them not at all; holding only strictly necessary intercourse with the natives, as if some ancient doom compelled him to wander here against his will in the service of his Plutonic* master. The long strap which ran from the driving-wheel of his engine to the red thresher under the rick was the sole tie-line between agriculture and him.

While they uncovered the sheaves he stood apathetic beside his portable repository of force, round whose hot blackness the morning air quivered. He had nothing to do with preparatory labour. His fire was waiting incandescent, his steam was at high-pressure, in a few seconds he could make the long strap move at an invisible velocity. Beyond its extent the environment might be corn, straw, or chaos; it was all the same to him. If any of the autochthonous idlers asked him what he called himself, he replied shortly "an engineer."

The rick was unhaled by full daylight; the men then took their places, the women mounted, and the work began. Farmer Groby— or, as they called him, "he"—had arrived ere this, and by his orders Tess was placed on the platform of the machine, close to the man who fed it; her business being to untie every sheaf of corn handed on to her by Izz Huett who stood next, but on the rick, so that the feeder could seize it and spread it over the revolving drum which whisked out every grain in one moment.

They were soon in full progress, after a preparatory hitch or two, which rejoiced the hearts of those who hated machinery. The work sped on till breakfast-time, when the thresher was stopped for half-an-hour; and on starting again after the meal the whole supplementary strength of the farm was thrown into the labour of constructing the straw-rick which began to grow beside the stack of corn. A hasty lunch was eaten as they stood, without leaving their positions; and then another couple of hours brought them near to dinner-time; the inexorable wheels continuing to spin, and the penetrating hum of the thresher to thrill to the very marrow all who were near the revolving wire cage.

The old men on the rising straw-rick talked of the past days when they had been accustomed to thresh with flails on the oaken barn-floor; when everything, even to the winnowing, was effected by hand-labour, which to their thinking, though slow, produced better results. Those, too, on the corn-rick, talked a little; but the perspiring ones at the machine, including Tess, could not lighten their duties by the exchange of many words. It was the ceaselessness of the work which tried her so severely, and began to make her wish that she had never come to Flintcomb-Ash. The women on the corn-rick, Marian, who was one of them, in particular, could stop to drink ale or cold tea from the flagon now and then, or to exchange a few gossiping remarks while they wiped their faces or cleared the fragments of straw and husk from their clothing; but for Tess there was no respite; for, as the drum never stopped, the man who fed it could not stop, and she, who had to supply the man with untied sheaves, could not stop either, unless Marian changed places with her, which she sometimes did for half an hour in spite of Groby's objection that she was too slow-handed for a feeder.

For some probably economical reason it was usually a woman who was chosen for this particular duty, and Groby gave as his motive in selecting Tess that she was one of those who best combined strength with quickness in untying, and both with staying power; and this may have been true. The hum of the thresher, which prevented speech, increased to a raving whenever the supply of corn fell short of the regular quantity. As Tess and the man who fed could never turn their heads, she did not know that just before the dinner-hour a person had come silently into the field by the gate, and had been standing under a second rick watching the scene, and Tess in particular. He was dressed in a tweed suit of fashionable pattern, and he twirled a gay walking-cane.

"Who is that?" said Izz Huett to Marian. She had at first addressed the inquiry to Tess, but the latter could not hear it.

"Somebody's fancy-man, I s'pose," said Marian laconically.

"I'll lay a guinea he's after Tess."

"O no. 'Tis a ranter pa'son who's been sniffing after her lately— not a dandy like this."

"Well—this is the same man."

"The same man as the preacher? But he's quite different?"

"He hev left off his black coat and white neckercher, and hev cut off his whiskers; but he's the same man for all that."

"D'ye really think so. Then I'll tell her," said Marian.

"Don't. She'll see him soon enough, good-now."

"Well, I don't think it at all right for him to join his preaching to courting a married woman, even though her husband mid be abroad, and she, in a sense, a widow."

"Oh—he can do her no harm," said Izz drily. "Her mind can no more be heaved from that one place where it do bide than a stooded waggon from the hole he's in. Lord love 'ee, neither court-paying, nor preaching, nor the seven thunders themselves, can wean a woman when 'twould be better for her that she should be weaned."

Dinner-time came, and the whirling ceased, whereupon Tess left her post, her knees trembling so wretchedly with the shaking of the machine that she could scarcely walk. "You ought to het a quart o' drink into 'ee, as I've done," said Marian. "You wouldn't look so white then. Why, souls above us, your face is as if you'd been hag-rode!"*

It occurred to the good-natured Marian that, as Tess was so tired, her discovery of her visitor's presence might have the bad effect of taking away her appetite; and Marian was thinking of inducing Tess to descend by a ladder on the further side of the stack when the gentleman came forward and looked up.

Tess uttered a short little "Oh!" and a moment after she said quickly, "I shall eat my dinner here—right on the rick."

Sometimes, when they were so far from their cottages, they all did this; but as there was rather a keen wind going to-day Marian and the rest descended, and sat under the straw-stack.

The new-comer was, indeed, Alec d'Urberville the late evangelist, despite his changed attire and aspect. It was obvious at a glance that the original *Weltlust* had come back; that he had restored himself, as nearly as a man could do who had grown three or four years older, to the old jaunty, slap-dash guise under which Tess had first known her admirer, and cousin so-called. Having decided to remain where she was Tess sat down among the bundles out of sight of the ground, and began her meal; till by and by she heard footsteps upon the ladder, and immediately after Alec appeared upon the stack—now an oblong and level platform of sheaves. He strode across them, and sat down opposite to her without a word.

Tess continued to eat her modest dinner, a slice of thick pancake which she had brought with her: the other workfolk were by this time all gathered under the rick, where the loose straw formed a comfortable retreat.

"I am here again, as you see," said d'Urberville.

"Why do you trouble me so!" she cried, reproach flashing from her very finger-ends.

"*I* trouble *you*? I think I may ask, why do you trouble me?"

"Sure, I don't trouble you any-when!"

"You say you don't? But you do! You haunt me. Those very eyes that you turned upon me with such a bitter flash a moment ago, they come to me, just as you showed them then, in the night and in the day. Tess, ever since you told me of that child of ours, it is just as if my feelings, which have been flowing in a strong puritanical stream, had suddenly found a way open in the direction of you and had all at once gushed through. The religious channel is left dry forthwith; and it is you who have done it!"

She gazed in silence. "What—you have given up your preaching entirely?" she asked. She had gathered from Angel sufficient of the incredulity of modern thought to despise flash enthusiasms; but as a woman she was somewhat appalled.

In affected severity d'Urberville continued: "Entirely. I have broken every engagement since that afternoon I was to address the drunkards at Casterbridge Fair. The deuce only knows what I am thought of by the brethren. Ah-ha! The brethren! No doubt they pray for me, weep for me; for they are kind people in their way. But what do I care? How could I go on with the thing when I had lost my faith in it?—it would have been hypocrisy of the basest kind! Among them I should have stood like Hymenæus and Alexander, who were delivered over to Satan that they might learn not to blaspheme.* What a grand revenge you have taken! I saw you innocent, and I deceived you. Four years after, you find me a Christian enthusiast; you then work upon me, perhaps to my complete perdition. . . . But Tess, my coz, as I used to call you, this is only my way of talking, and you must not look so horribly concerned. Of course you have done nothing except retain your pretty face and shapely figure. I saw it on the rick before you saw me—that tight pinafore-thing sets it off, and that wing-bonnet—you field-girls should never wear those bonnets if you wish to keep out of danger." He regarded her silently for a few moments, and with a short cynical laugh resumed: "I believe that if the bachelor apostle, whose deputy I thought I was, had been tempted by such a pretty face, he would have let go the plough for her sake as I do."*

Tess attempted to expostulate, but at this juncture all her fluency failed her, and without heeding he added: "Well, this paradise that you supply is perhaps as good as any other, after all. But to speak seriously, Tess." D'Urberville rose and came nearer, reclining sideways amid the sheaves and resting upon his elbow. "Since I last saw you I have been thinking of what you said that *he* said. I have come to the conclusion that there does seem rather a want of common-sense in these threadbare old propositions: how I could have been so fired by poor Parson Clare's enthusiasm, and have gone so madly to work, transcending even him, I cannot make out. As for what you said last time, on the strength of your wonderful husband's intelligence— whose name you have never told me—about having what they call an ethical system without any dogma; I don't see my way to that at all."

"Why, you can have the religion of loving-kindness and purity at least, if you can't have—what do you call it—dogma."

"O no. I'm a different sort of fellow from that! If there's nobody to say, 'Do this, and it will be a good thing for you after you are dead: do that, and it will be a bad thing for you', I can't warm up. Hang it, I am not going to feel responsible for my deeds and passions if there's nobody to be responsible to; and if I were you, my dear, I wouldn't either."

She tried to argue, and tell him that he had mixed in his dull brain two matters, theology and morals, which in the primitive days of mankind had been quite distinct. But owing to Angel Clare's reticence, to her absolute want of training, and to her being a vessel of emotions rather than reasons, she could not get on.

"Well—never mind"—he resumed, "here I am, my love, as in the old times!"

"Not as then—never as then—'tis different!" she entreated. "And there was never warmth with me. O why didn't you keep your faith, if the loss of it has brought you to speak to me like this!"

"Because you've knocked it out of me; so the evil be upon your sweet head. Your husband little thought how his teaching would recoil upon him. Ha-ha—I'm awfully glad you have made an apostate of me, all the same. . . . Tess I am more taken with you than ever. And I pity you, too. For all your closeness I see you are in a bad way—neglected by one who ought to cherish you."

She could not get her morsels of food down her throat; her lips were dry, and she was ready to choke. The voices and laughs of the workfolk eating and drinking under the rick came to her as if they were a quarter of a mile off.

"It is cruelty to me!" she said. "How—how can you treat me to this talk, if you care ever so little for me?"

"True, true," he said, wincing a little. "I did not come to reproach you for my deeds. I came, Tess, to say that I don't like you to be working like this, and I have come on purpose for you. You say you have a husband who is not I. Well, perhaps you have; but I've never seen him, and you've not told me his name; and altogether he seems rather a mythological personage. However, even if you have one, I think I am nearer to you than he is. I, at any rate, try to help you out of trouble, but he does not, bless his invisible face! The words of the stern prophet Hosea* that I used to read come back to me. Don't you know them, Tess?—'And she shall follow after her lover, but she shall not overtake him; and she shall seek him, but shall not find him: then shall she say, I will go and return to my first husband; for then was it better with me than now.' . . . Tess, my trap is waiting just under the hill, and—darling mine, not his!—you know the rest."

Her face had been rising to a dull crimson fire while he spoke; but she did not answer.

"You have been the cause of my backsliding," he continued, stretching his arm towards her waist; "you should be willing to share it, and leave that mule you call husband for ever."

One of her leather gloves, which she had taken off to eat her skimmer-cake, lay in her lap, and without the slightest warning she passionately swung the glove by the gauntlet directly in his face. It was heavy and thick as a warrior's, and it struck him flat on the mouth. Fancy might have regarded the act as the recrudescence of a trick in which her armed progenitors were not unpractised. Alec fiercely started up from his reclining position. A scarlet oozing appeared where her blow had alighted, and in a moment the blood began dropping from his mouth upon the straw. But he soon controlled himself, calmly drew his handkerchief from his pocket, and mopped his bleeding lips.

She too had sprung up; but she sank down again. "Now punish me!" she said, turning up her eyes to him with the hopeless defiance of the sparrow's gaze before its captor twists its neck. "Whip me, crush me; you need not mind those people under the rick. I shall not cry out. Once victim, always victim: that's the law."

"O no, no, Tess," he said blandly. "I can make full allowance for this. Yet you most unjustly forget one thing, that I would have married you if you had not put it out of my power to do so. Did I not ask you flatly to be my wife—hey?—answer me."

"You did."

"And you cannot be. But remember one thing:" his voice hardened as his temper got the better of him with the recollection of his sincerity in asking her, and her present ingratitude; and he stepped across to her side and held her by the shoulders, so that she shook under his grasp: "Remember, my lady, I was your master once; I will be your master again. If you are any man's wife you are mine!"

The threshers now began to stir below. "So much for our quarrel," he said, letting her go. "Now I shall leave you; and shall come again for your answer during the afternoon. You don't know me yet. But I know you."

She had not spoken again, remaining as if stunned. D'Urberville retreated over the sheaves and descended the ladder, while the workers below rose and stretched their arms, and shook down the beer they had drunk. Then the threshing-machine started afresh; and amid the renewed rustle of the straw Tess resumed her position by the buzzing drum as one in a dream, untying sheaf after sheaf in endless succession.

XLVIII

IN the afternoon the farmer made it known that the rick was to be finished that night, since there was a moon by which they could see to work, and the man with the engine was engaged for another farm on the morrow. Hence the twanging and humming and rustling proceeded with even less intermission than usual.

It was not till "nammet"-time, about three o'clock, that Tess raised her eyes and gave a momentary glance round. She felt but little surprise at seeing that Alec d'Urberville had come back, and was standing under the hedge by the gate. He had seen her lift her eyes, and waved his hand urbanely to her, while he blew her a kiss. It meant that their quarrel was over. Tess looked down again, and carefully abstained from gazing in that direction.

Thus the afternoon dragged on. The wheat-rick shrank lower, and the straw-rick grew higher, and the corn-sacks were carted away. At six o'clock the wheat-rick was about shoulder-high from the ground. But the unthreshed sheaves remaining untouched seemed countless still, notwithstanding the enormous numbers that had been gulped down by the insatiable swallower, fed by the man and Tess, through whose two young hands the greater part of them had passed; and the immense stack of straw where in the morning there had been nothing appeared as the *fæces* of the same buzzing red glutton. From the west sky a wrathful shine—all that wild March could afford in the way of sunset—had burst forth after the cloudy day flooding the tired and sticky faces of the threshers, and dyeing them with a coppery light, as also the flapping garments of the women, which clung to them like dull flames.

A panting ache ran through the rick. The man who fed was weary, and Tess could see that the red nape of his neck was encrusted with dirt and husks. She still stood at her post, her flushed and perspiring face coated with the corn-dust, and her white bonnet embrowned by it. She was the only woman whose place was upon the machine, so as to be shaken bodily by its spinning, and the decrease of the stack now separated her from Marian and Izz, and prevented their changing duties with her as they had done. The incessant quivering in which every fibre of her frame participated had thrown her into a stupefied reverie, in which her arms worked on independently of her consciousness. She hardly knew where she was, and did not hear Izz Huett tell her from below that her hair was tumbling down.

By degrees the freshest among them began to grow cadaverous and saucer-eyed. Whenever Tess lifted her head she beheld always the great upgrown straw-stack, with the men in shirt-sleeves upon it against the grey north sky: in front of it the long red elevator like a Jacob's ladder,* on which a perpetual stream of threshed straw ascended; a yellow river running up-hill, and spouting out on the top of the rick.

She knew that Alec d'Urberville was still on the scene, observing her from some point or other, though she could not say where. There was an excuse for his remaining, for when the threshed rick drew near its final sheaves a little ratting was always done, and men unconnected with the threshing sometimes dropped in for that performance—sporting characters of all descriptions, gents with terriers and facetious pipes, roughs with sticks and stones.

But there was another hour's work before the layer of live rats at the base of the stack would be reached; and as the evening light in the direction of the Giant's Hill by Abbot's-Cernel dissolved away, the white-faced moon of the season arose from the horizon that lay towards Middleton Abbey and Shottsford on the other side. For the last hour or two Marian had felt uneasy about Tess, whom she could not get near enough to speak to; the other women having kept up their strength by drinking ale, and Tess having done without it through traditionary dread, owing to its results at her home in childhood. But Tess still kept going: if she could not fill her part she would have to leave, and this contingency, which she would have regarded with equanimity, and even with relief, a month or two earlier, had become a terror since d'Urberville had begun to hover round her.

The sheaf-pitchers and feeders had now worked the rick so low that people on the ground could talk to them. To Tess's surprise Farmer Groby came up on the machine to her, and said that if she desired to join her friend he did not wish her to keep on any longer, and would send somebody else to take her place. The "friend" was d'Urberville, she knew, and also that this concession had been granted in obedience to the request of that friend, or enemy. She shook her head, and toiled on.

The time for the rat-catching arrived at last, and the hunt began. The creatures had crept downwards with the subsidence of the rick till they were all together at the bottom, and being now uncovered from their last refuge they ran across the open ground in all directions, a loud shriek from the by-this-time half-tipsy Marian informing her companions that one of the rats had invaded her person—a terror which the rest of the women had guarded against by various schemes of skirt-tucking and self-elevation. The rat was at last dislodged, and amid the barking of dogs, masculine shouts, feminine screams, oaths, stampings, and confusion as of pandæmonium* Tess untied her last sheaf; the drum slowed, the whizzing ceased, and she stepped from the machine to the ground.

Her lover—who had only looked on at the rat-catching—was promptly at her side.

"What—after all?—my insulting slap too?" said she in an underbreath. She was so utterly exhausted that she had not strength to speak louder.

"I should indeed be foolish to feel offended at anything you say or do," he answered in the seductive voice of the Trantridge time. "How the little limbs tremble! You are as weak as a bled calf, you know you are; and yet you need have done nothing since I arrived. How could you be so obstinate! However, I have told the farmer that he has no right to employ women at steam-threshing. It is not proper work for them, and on all the better class of farms it has been given up, as he knows very well. I will walk with you as far as your house."

"O yes," she answered with a jaded gait. "Walk wi' me if you will! I do bear in mind that you came to marry me, before you knew o' my state. Perhaps—perhaps you are a little better and kinder than I have been thinking you were. Whatever is meant as kindness I am grateful for; whatever is meant in any other way I am angered at. . . . I cannot sense your meaning sometimes."

"If I cannot legitimize our former relations at least I can assist you. And I will do it with much more regard for your feelings than I formerly showed. My religious mania, or whatever it was, is over. But I retain a little good-nature; I hope I do. Now, Tess; by all that's tender and strong between man and woman, trust me. I have enough and more than enough to put you out of anxiety, both for yourself and your brothers and sisters. I can make them all comfortable, if you will only show confidence in me."

"Have you seen 'em lately?" she quickly inquired.

"Yes. They didn't know where you were. It was only by chance that I found you here."

The cold moon looked aslant upon Tess's fagged face between the twigs of the garden-hedge, as she paused outside the cottage which was her temporary home, d'Urberville pausing beside her. "Don't mention my little brothers and sisters—don't make me break down quite!" she said. "If you want to help them—God knows they need it—do it without telling me. But no, no!" she cried. "I will take nothing from you, either for them or for me."

He did not accompany her further, since as she lived with the household all was public indoors. No sooner had she herself entered, laved herself in a washing-tub, and shared supper with the family, than she fell into thought, and, withdrawing to the table under the wall, by the light of her own little lamp wrote in a passionate mood:—

My own husband! Let me call you so—I must—even if it makes you angry to think of such an unworthy wife as I. I must cry to you in my trouble—I have no one else. I am so exposed to temptation, Angel! I fear to say who it is, and I do not like to write about it all. But I cling to you in a way you cannot think. Can you not come to me now, at once, before anything terrible happens? O I know you cannot, because you are so far away. I think I must die if you do not come soon, or tell me to come to you. The punishment you have measured out to me is deserved—I do know that—well deserved, and you are right and just to be angry with me. But Angel, please, please, not to be just—only a little kind to me, even if I do not deserve it, and come to me. If you would come I could die in your arms. I would be well content to do that if so be you had forgiven me.

Angel, I live entirely for you. I love you too much to blame you for going away, and I know it was necessary you should find a farm. Do not think I shall say a word of sting or bitterness. Only come back to me. I am desolate without you, my darling, O so desolate! I do not mind having to work; but if you will send me one little line and say, *I am coming soon*, I will bide on, Angel: O so cheerfully!

It has been so much my religion ever since we were married, to be faithful to you in every thought and look that even when a man speaks a compliment to me before I am aware, it seems wronging you. Have you never felt one little bit of what you used to feel when we were at the dairy? If you have, how can you keep away from me? I am the same woman, Angel, as you fell in love with; yes, the very same! not the one you disliked, but never saw. What was the past to me as soon as I met you? It was a dead thing altogether. I became another woman, filled full of new life from you. How could I be the early one? Why do you not see this? Dear, if you would only be a little more conceited, and believe in yourself so far as to see that you were strong enough to work this change in me, you would perhaps be in a mind to come to me, your poor wife.

How silly I was in my happiness when I thought I could trust you always to love me! I ought to have known that such as that was not for poor me. But I am sick at heart, not only for old times, but for the present. Think, think how it do hurt my heart not to see you ever, ever! Ah, if I could only make your dear heart ache one little minute of each day as mine does every day and all day long, it might lead you to show pity to your poor lonely one.

People still say that I am rather pretty, Angel (handsome is the word they use, since I wish to be truthful). Perhaps I am what they say. But I do not value my good looks: I only like to have them because they belong to you, my dear, and that there may be at least one thing about me worth your having. So much have I felt this that when I met with annoyance on account of the same I tied up my face in a bandage as long as people would believe in it. O Angel, I tell you all this not from vanity—you will certainly know I do not—but only that you may come to me.

If you really cannot come to me will you let me come to you? I am, as I say, worried, pressed to do what I will not. It cannot be that I shall yield one inch, yet I am in terror as to what an accident might lead to, and I so defenceless on account of my first error. I cannot say more about this—it makes me too miserable. But if I break down by falling into some fearful snare my last state will be worse than my first.* O God—I cannot think of it! Let me come at once, or at once come to me!

I would be content, ay glad, to live with you as your servant, if I may not as your wife; so that I could only be near you, and get glimpses of you, and think of you as mine.

The daylight has nothing to show me, since you are not here, and I don't like to see the rooks and starlings in the fields, because I grieve and grieve to miss you who used to see them with me. I long for only one thing in heaven or earth or under the earth, to meet you, my own dear. Come to me, come to me, and save me from what threatens me!

Your faithful heartbroken TESS.

XLIX

THE appeal duly found its way to the breakfast-table of the quiet vicarage to the westward, in that valley where the air is so soft and the soil so rich that the effort of growth requires but superficial aid by comparison with the tillage at Flintcomb-Ash, and where to Tess the human world seemed so different (though it was much the same). It was purely for security that she had been requested by Angel to send her communications through his father, whom he kept pretty well informed of his changing addresses in the country he had gone to exploit for himself with a heavy heart.

"Now," said old Mr Clare to his wife, when he had read the envelope, "if Angel proposes leaving Rio for a visit home at the end of next month, as he told us that he hoped to do, I think this may hasten his plans; for I believe it to be from his wife." He breathed deeply at the thought of her; and the letter was redirected to be promptly sent on to Angel.

"Dear fellow—I hope he will get home safely," murmured Mrs Clare. "To my dying day I shall feel that he has been ill-used. You should have sent him to Cambridge in spite of his want of faith, and given him the same chance as the other boys had. He would have grown out of it under proper influence, and perhaps would have taken orders after all. Church or no Church, it would have been fairer to him."

This was the only wail with which Mrs Clare ever disturbed her husband's peace in respect of their sons. And she did not vent this often; for she was as considerate as she was devout, and knew that his mind, too, was troubled by doubts as to his justice in this matter. Only too often had she heard him lying awake at night, stifling sighs for Angel with prayers. But the uncompromising Evangelical did not even now hold that he would have been justified in giving his son, an unbeliever, the same academic advantages that he had given to the two others, when it was possible, if not probable, that those very advantages might have been used to decry the doctrines which he had made it his life's mission and desire to propagate, and the mission of his ordained sons likewise. To put with one hand a pedestal under the feet of the two faithful ones, and with the other to exalt the

unfaithful by the same artificial means, he deemed to be alike incon-
sistent with his convictions, his position, and his hopes. Nevertheless
he loved his misnamed Angel, and in secret mourned over this
treatment of him as Abraham might have mourned over the doomed
Isaac while they went up the hill together.* His silent self-generated
regrets were far bitterer than the reproaches which his wife rendered
audible.

They blamed themselves for this unlucky marriage. If Angel
had never been destined for a farmer he would never have been
thrown with agricultural girls. They did not distinctly know what
had separated him and his wife, nor the date on which the separation had taken place. At first they had supposed it must be something of the nature of a serious aversion. But in his later letters he
occasionally alluded to his intention of coming home to fetch her;
from which expressions they hoped the division might not owe its
origin to anything so hopelessly permanent as that. He had told
them that she was with her relatives, and in their doubts they had
decided not to intrude into a situation which they knew no way of
bettering.

The eyes for which Tess's letter was intended were gazing at this
time on a limitless expanse of country from the back of a mule which
was bearing him from the interior of the South-American Continent
towards the coast. His experiences of this strange land had been sad.
The severe illness from which he had suffered shortly after his
arrival, had never wholly left him, and he had by degrees almost
decided to relinquish his hope of farming here, though, as long as
the bare possibility existed of his remaining, he kept this change of
view a secret from his parents.

The crowds of agricultural labourers who had come out to the
country in his wake, dazzled by representations of easy independence, had suffered, died, and wasted away. He would see mothers
from English farms, trudging along with their infants in their arms;
when the child would be stricken with fever and would die: the
mother would pause to dig a hole in the loose earth with her
bare hands, would bury the babe therein with the same natural
grave-tools, shed one tear, and again trudge on.

Angel's original intention had not been emigration to Brazil, but a
northern or eastern farm in his own country. He had come to this
place in a fit of desperation, the Brazil movement among the English

agriculturists having by chance coincided with his desire to escape from his past existence.

During this time of absence he had mentally aged a dozen years. What arrested him now as of value in life was less its beauty than its pathos. Having long discredited the old systems of mysticism he now began to discredit the old appraisements of morality. He thought they wanted readjusting. Who was the moral man? Still more pertinently, who was the moral woman? The beauty or ugliness of a character lay not only in its achievements, but in its aims and impulses; its true history lay not among things done, but among things willed.

How, then, about Tess?

Viewing her in these lights a regret for his hasty judgment began to oppress him. Did he reject her eternally, or did he not? He could no longer say that he would always reject her, and not to say that was in spirit to accept her now.

This growing fondness for her memory coincided in point of time with her residence at Flintcomb-Ash, but it was before she had felt herself at liberty to trouble him with a word about her circumstances or her feelings. He was greatly perplexed; and in his perplexity as to her motives in withholding intelligence he did not inquire. Thus her silence of docility was misinterpreted. How much it really said, if he had understood! That she adhered with literal exactness to orders which he had given and forgotten; that despite her natural fearlessness she asserted no rights, admitted his judgment to be in every respect the true one, and bent her head dumbly thereto.

In the before-mentioned journey by mules through the interior of the country another man rode beside him. Angel's companion was also an Englishman, bent on the same errand, though he came from another part of the island. They were both in a state of mental depression, and they spoke of home affairs. Confidence begat confidence. With that curious tendency evinced by men, more especially when in distant lands, to entrust to strangers details of their lives which they would on no account mention to friends, Angel admitted to this man as they rode along the sorrowful facts of his marriage.

The stranger had sojourned in many more lands and among many more peoples than Angel; to his cosmopolitan mind such deviations from the social norm, so immense to domesticity, were no more than are the irregularities of vale and mountain-chain to the whole terrestrial curve. He viewed the matter in quite a different light from

Angel; thought that what Tess had been was of no importance beside what she would be, and plainly told Clare that he was wrong in coming away from her.

The next day they were drenched in a thunderstorm: Angel's companion was struck down with fever, and died by the week's end. Clare waited a few hours to bury him, and then went on his way.

The cursory remarks of the large-minded stranger, of whom he knew absolutely nothing beyond a commonplace name, were sublimed by his death, and influenced Clare more than all the reasoned ethics of the philosophers. His own parochialism made him ashamed by its contrast. His inconsistencies rushed upon him in a flood. He had persistently elevated Hellenic Paganism at the expense of Christianity; yet in that civilization an illegal surrender was not certain disesteem. Surely then he might have regarded that abhorrence of the un-intact state, which he had inherited with the creed of mysticism, as at least open to correction when the result was due to treachery. A remorse struck into him. The words of Izz Huett, never quite stilled in his memory, came back to him. He had asked Izz if she loved him, and she had replied in the affirmative. Did she love him more than Tess did? No, she had replied; Tess would lay down her life for him; and she herself could do no more.

He thought of Tess as she had appeared on the day of the wedding. How her eyes had lingered upon him; how she had hung upon his words as if they were a god's. And during the terrible evening over the hearth, when her simple soul uncovered itself to his, how pitiful her face had looked by the rays of the fire, in her inability to realize that his love and protection could possibly be withdrawn.

Thus from being her critic he grew to be her advocate. Cynical things he had uttered to himself about her; but no man can be always a cynic and live; and he withdrew them. The mistake of expressing them had arisen from his allowing himself to be influenced by general principles, to the disregard of the particular instance.

But the reasoning is somewhat musty; lovers and husbands have gone over the ground before today. Clare had been harsh towards her; there is no doubt of it. Men are too often harsh with women they love or have loved; women with men. And yet these harshnesses are tenderness itself when compared with the universal harshness out of which they grow; the harshness of the position towards the temperament, of the means towards the aims, of to-day towards yesterday, of hereafter towards to-day.

The historic interest of her family—that masterful line of d'Urbervilles—whom he had despised as a spent force, touched his sentiments now. Why had he not known the difference between the political value and the imaginative value of these things? In the latter aspect her d'Urberville descent was a fact of great dimensions: worthless to economics it was a most useful ingredient to the dreamer, to the moralizer on declines and falls. It was a fact that would soon be forgotten—that bit of distinction in poor Tess's blood and name—and oblivion would fall upon her hereditary link with the marble monuments and leaded skeletons at Kingsbere. So does Time ruthlessly destroy his own romances. In recalling her face again and again, he thought now that he could see therein a flash of the dignity which must have graced her grand-dames; and the vision sent that *aura* through his veins which he had formerly felt, and which left behind it a sense of sickness.

Despite her not inviolate past, what still abode in such a woman as Tess outvalued the freshness of her fellows. Was not the gleaning of the grapes of Ephraim better than the vintage of Abi-ezer?*

So spoke love renascent, preparing the way for Tess's devoted outpouring, which was then just being forwarded to him by his father; though owing to his distance inland it was to be a long time in reaching him.

Meanwhile the writer's expectation that Angel would come in response to the entreaty was alternately great and small. What lessened it was that the facts of her life which had led to the parting had not changed—could never change; and that, if her presence had not attenuated them, her absence could not. Nevertheless she addressed her mind to the tender question of what she could do to please him best if he should arrive.

Sighs were expended on the wish that she had taken more notice of the tunes he played on his harp; that she had inquired more curiously of him which were his favourite ballads among those the country girls sang. She indirectly inquired of Amby Seedling, who had followed Izz from Talbothays, and by chance Amby remembered that amongst the snatches of melody in which they had indulged at the dairyman's, to induce the cows to let down their milk, Clare had seemed to like "Cupid's Gardens", "I have parks I have hounds", and "The break o' the day"; and had seemed not to care for "The Tailor's Breeches", and "Such a beauty I did grow",* excellent ditties as they were.

To perfect the ballads was now her whimsical desire. She practised them privately at odd moments, especially "The break o' the day":

> Arise, arise, arise,
> And pick your love a posy
> All o' the sweetest flowers
> That in the garden grow.
> The turtle doves and sma' birds
> In every bough a building
> So early in the May-time
> At the break o' the day.

It would have melted the heart of a stone to hear her singing these ditties, whenever she worked apart from the rest of the girls; in this cold dry time; the tears running down her cheeks all the while at the thought that perhaps he would not after all come to hear her, and the simple silly words of the songs resounding in painful mockery of the aching heart of the singer.

Tess was so wrapt up in this fanciful dream that she seemed not to know how the season was advancing; that the days had lengthened, that Lady-Day was at hand, and would soon be followed by Old Lady-Day,* the end of her term here.

But before the quarter-day had quite come something happened which made Tess think of far different matters. She was at her lodging as usual one evening, sitting in the downstairs room with the rest of the family, when somebody knocked at the door, and inquired for Tess. Through the doorway she saw against the declining light a figure with the height of a woman and the breadth of a child; a tall, thin, girlish creature whom she did not recognize in the twilight till the girl said "Tess!"

"What—is it Liza-Lu?" asked Tess, in startled accents. Her sister whom, a little over a year ago, she had left at home as a child, had sprung up by a sudden shoot to a form of this presentation, of which as yet Lu seemed herself scarce able to understand the meaning. Her thin legs, visible below her once long frock now short by her growing, and her uncomfortable hands and arms, revealed her youth and inexperience.

"Yes. I have been traipsing about all day, Tess," said Lu, with unemotional gravity, "a trying to find 'ee; and I'm very tired."

"What is the matter at home?"

"Mother is took very bad, and the doctor says she's dying, and as father is not very well neither and says 'tis wrong for a man of such a high family as his to slave and drave at common labouring work, we don't know what to do."

Tess stood in reverie a long time before she thought of asking Liza-Lu to come in and sit down. When she had done so, and Liza-Lu was having some tea, she came to a decision. It was imperative that she should go home. Her agreement did not end till Old Lady-Day, the sixth of April, but as the interval thereto was not a long one, she resolved to run the risk of starting at once.

To go that night would be a gain of twelve hours; but her sister was too tired to undertake such a distance till the morrow. Tess ran down to where Marian and Izz lived, informed them of what had happened, and begged them to make the best of her case to the farmer. Returning she got Lu a supper, and after that, having tucked the younger into her own bed, packed up as many of her belongings as would go into a withy basket, and started, directing Lu to follow her next morning.

L

SHE plunged into the chilly equinoctial darkness as the clock struck ten, for her fifteen miles' walk under the steely stars. In lonely districts night is a protection rather than a danger to the noiseless pedestrian, and knowing this Tess pursued the nearest course along by-lanes that she would almost have feared in the day-time; but marauders were wanting now, and spectral fears were driven out of her mind by thoughts of her mother. Thus she proceeded mile after mile, ascending and descending till she came to Bulbarrow, and, about midnight, looked from that height into the abyss of chaotic shade which was all that revealed itself of the vale on whose further side she was born. Having already traversed about five miles on the upland she had now some ten or eleven in the lowland before her journey would be finished. The winding road downwards became just visible to her under the wan starlight as she followed it; and soon she paced a soil so contrasting with that above it that the difference was perceptible to the tread and to the smell. It was the heavy clay land of Blackmoor Vale, and a part of the Vale to which turnpike-roads had never penetrated. Superstitions linger longest on these heavy soils. Having once been forest, at this shadowy time it seemed to assert something of its old character, the far and the near being blended, and every tree and tall hedge making the most of its presence. The harts that had been hunted here; the witches that had been pricked and ducked, the green-spangled fairies that "whickered" at you as you passed;* the place teemed with beliefs in them still, and they formed an impish multitude now.

At Nuttlebury she passed the village inn, whose sign creaked in response to the greeting of her footsteps, which not a human soul heard but herself. Under the thatched roofs her mind's-eye beheld relaxed tendons and flaccid muscles spread out in the darkness beneath coverlets made of little purple patchwork squares, and undergoing a bracing process at the hands of sleep for renewed labour on the morrow, as soon as a hint of pink nebulosity appeared on Hambledon Hill.

At three she turned the last corner of the maze of lanes she had threaded, and entered Marlott, passing the field in which, as a club-girl, she had first seen Angel Clare, when he had not danced with her: the sense of disappointment remained with her yet. In the direction of her mother's house she saw a light. It came from the bedroom window, and a branch waved in front of it and made it wink at her. As soon as she could discern the outline of the house—newly thatched with her money—it had all its old effect upon Tess's imagination. Part of her body and life it ever seemed to be: the slope of its dormers, the finish of its gables, the broken courses of brick which topped the chimney, all had something in common with her personal character. A stupefaction had come into these features, to her regard; it meant the illness of her mother.

She opened the door so softly as to disturb nobody: the lower room was vacant, but the neighbour who was sitting up with her mother came to the top of the stairs, and whispered that Mrs Durbeyfield was no better, though she was sleeping just then. Tess prepared herself a breakfast, and then took her place as nurse in her mother's chamber.

In the morning when she contemplated the children they had all a curiously elongated look: although she had been away little more than a year their growth was astounding; and the necessity of applying herself heart and soul to their needs took her out of her own cares.

Her father's ill-health was of the same indefinite kind, and he sat in his chair as usual. But the day after her arrival he was unusually bright; he had a rational scheme for living, and Tess asked him what it was.

"I'm thinking of sending round to all the old antiqueerians in this part of England," he said; "asking them to subscribe to a fund to maintain me. I'm sure they'd see it as a romantical, artistical, and proper thing to do. They spend lots o' money in keeping up old ruins, and finding the bones o' things, and such like; and living remains must be more interesting to 'em still, if they only knowed of me. Would that somebody would go round and tell 'em what there is living among 'em, and they thinking nothing of him! If Pa'son Tringham, who discovered me, had lived, he'd ha' done it, I'm sure."

Tess postponed her arguments on this high project till she had grappled with pressing matters in hand, which seemed little improved by her remittances. When indoor necessities had been eased, she turned her attention to external things. It was now the season for planting and sowing; many gardens and allotments of the villagers had already received their spring tillage; but the garden and the allotment of the Durbeyfields were behindhand. She found, to her dismay, that this was owing to their having eaten all the seed potatoes,—that last lapse of the improvident. At the earliest moment she obtained what others she could procure, and in a few days her father was well enough to see to the garden, under Tess's persuasive efforts: while she herself undertook the allotment-plot which they rented in a field a couple of hundred yards out of the village.

She liked doing it, after the confinement of the sick chamber, where she was not now required by reason of her mother's improvement. Violent motion relieved thought. The plot of ground was in a high, dry, open enclosure, where there were forty or fifty such pieces, and where labour was at its briskest when the hired labour of the day had ended. Digging began usually at six o' clock, and extended indefinitely into the dusk or moonlight. Just now heaps of dead weeds and refuse were burning on many of the plots, the dry weather favouring their combustion.

One fine day Tess and Liza-Lu worked on here with their neighbours till the last rays of the sun smote flat upon the white pegs that divided the plots. As soon as twilight succeeded to sunset the flare of the couch-grass and cabbage-stalk fires began to light up the allotments fitfully, their outlines appearing and disappearing under the dense smoke as wafted by the wind. When a fire glowed, banks of smoke blown level along the ground would themselves become illuminated to an opaque lustre, screening the workpeople from one another; and the meaning of the "pillar of a cloud", which was a wall by day and a light by night,* could be understood.

As evening thickened some of the gardening men and women gave over for the night, but the greater number remained to get their planting done, Tess being among them, though she sent her sister home. It was on one of the couch-burning plots that she laboured with her fork, its four shining prongs resounding against the stones and dry clods in little clicks. Sometimes she was completely involved in the smoke of her fire; then it would leave her figure free, irradiated by the brassy glare from the heap. She was oddly dressed to-night, and presented a somewhat staring aspect, her attire being a gown bleached by many washings, with a short black jacket over it, the effect of the whole being that of a wedding and funeral guest in one.

The women further back wore white aprons which, with their pale faces, were all that could be seen of them in the gloom, except when, at moments they caught a flash from the flames.

Westward, the wiry boughs of the bare thorn hedge, which formed the boundary of the field, rose against the pale opalescence of the lower sky. Above, Jupiter hung like a full-blown jonquil, so bright as almost to throw a shade. A few small nondescript stars were appearing elsewhere. In the distance a dog barked, and wheels occasionally rattled along the dry road.

Still the prongs continued to click assiduously, for it was not late, and though the air was fresh and keen there was a whisper of spring in it that cheered the workers on. Something in the place, the hour, the crackling fires, the fantastic mysteries of light and shade, made others as well as Tess enjoy being there. Nightfall, which in the frost of winter comes as a fiend, and in the warmth of summer as a lover, came as a tranquilizer on this March day.

Nobody looked at his or her companions. The eyes of all were on the soil as its turned surface was revealed by the fires. Hence, as Tess stirred the clods, and sang her foolish little songs with scarce now a hope that Clare would ever hear them, she did not for a long time notice the person who worked nearest to her—a man in a long smockfrock who, she found, was forking the same plot as herself, and whom she supposed her father had sent there to advance the work. She became more conscious of him when the direction of his digging brought him closer. Sometimes the smoke divided them; then it swerved, and the two were visible to each other but divided from all the rest.

Tess did not speak to her fellow-worker, nor did he speak to her. Nor did she think of him further than to recollect that he had not been there when it was broad daylight, and that she did not know him as any one of the Marlott labourers, which was no wonder, her absences having been so long and frequent of late years. By-and-by he dug so close to her that the fire-beams were reflected as distinctly from the steel prongs of his fork as from her own. On going up to the fire to throw a pitch of dead weeds upon it she found that he did the same on the other side. The fire flared up, and she beheld the face of d'Urberville.

The unexpectedness of his presence, the grotesqueness of his appearance in a gathered smockfrock, such as was now worn only by the most old-fashioned of the labourers, had a ghastly comicality that chilled her as to its bearing. D'Urberville emitted a low long laugh.

"If I were inclined to joke I should say, How much this seems like Paradise!" he remarked, whimsically looking at her with an inclined head.

"What do you say?" she weakly asked.

"A jester might say this is just like Paradise. You are Eve, and I am the old other one, come to tempt you in the disguise of an inferior animal. I used to be quite up in that scene of Milton's when I was theological. Some of it goes,

> "Empress, the way is ready, and not long;
> Beyond a row of myrtles . . .
> . . . If thou accept
> My conduct I can bring thee thither soon."
> "Lead then", said Eve.*

And so on. My dear dear Tess, I am only putting this to you as a thing that you might have supposed or said quite untruly, because you think so badly of me."

"I never said you were Satan or thought it. I don't think of you in that way at all. My thoughts of you are quite cold, except when you affront me. . . . What, did you come digging here entirely because of me?"

"Entirely. To see you: nothing more. The smockfrock, which I saw hanging for sale as I came along, was an after-thought, that I mightn't be noticed. I come to protest against your working like this."

"But I like doing it—it is for my father."

"Your engagement at the other place is ended?"

"Yes."

"Where are you going to next? To join your dear husband?"

She could not bear the humiliating reminder. "O—I don't know!" she said bitterly. "I have no husband!"

"It is quite true—in the sense you mean. But you have a friend; and I have determined that you shall be comfortable in spite of yourself. When you get down to your house you will see what I have sent there for you."

"O Alec—I wish you wouldn't give me anything at all! I cannot take it from you! I don't like—it is not right!"

"It *is* right!" he cried lightly. "I am not going to see a woman, whom I feel so tenderly for as I do for you, in trouble without trying to help her."

"But I am very well off! I am only in trouble about—about—not about living at all!" She turned and desperately resumed her digging, tears dripping upon the fork-handle and upon the clods.

"About the children—your brothers and sisters," he resumed. "I've been thinking of them."

Tess's heart quivered: he was touching her in a weak place. He had divined her chief anxiety. Since returning home her soul had gone out to those children with an affection that was passionate.

"If your mother does not recover, somebody ought to do something for them; since your father will not be able to do much I suppose."

"He can with my assistance. He must!"

"And with mine."

"No sir!"

"How damned foolish this is!" burst out d'Urberville. "Why, he thinks we are the same family; and will be quite satisfied."

"He don't. I've undeceived him."

"The more fool you!" D'Urberville, in anger, retreated from her to the hedge, where he pulled off the long smockfrock which had disguised him; and rolling it up and pushing it into the couch-fire, went away.

Tess could not get on with her digging after this; she felt restless: she wondered if he had gone back to her father's house; and taking the fork in her hand proceeded homewards.

Some twenty yards from the house she was met by one of her sisters. "O Tessy—what do you think! Liza-Lu is a crying, and there's a lot of folk in the house, and mother is a good deal better, but they think father is dead!"

The child realized the grandeur of the news, but not as yet its sadness; and stood looking at Tess with round-eyed importance, till, beholding the effect produced upon her she said "What—Tess—shan't we talk to father never no more?"

"But father was only a little bit ill!" exclaimed Tess distractedly.

Liza-Lu came up. "He dropped down just now: and the doctor who was there for mother said there was no chance for him, because his heart was growed in."

Yes: the Durbeyfield couple had changed places: the dying one was out of danger, and the indisposed one was dead. The news meant even more than it sounded. Her father's life had a value apart from his personal achievements, or perhaps it would not have had much. It was the last of the three lives for whose duration the house and premises were held under a lease; and it had long been coveted by the tenant-farmer for his regular labourers, who were stinted in cottage-accommodation. Moreover "liviers" were disapproved of in villages almost as much as little freeholders, because of their independence of manner, and when a lease determined it was never renewed.

Thus the Durbeyfields, once d'Urbervilles, saw descending upon them the destiny which, no doubt, when they were among the Olympians of the county, they had caused to descend many a time, and severely enough, upon the heads of such landless ones as they themselves were now. So do flux and reflux—the rhythm of change—alternate and persist in everything under the sky.*

LI

A T length it was the eve of Old Lady-Day, and the agricultural world was in a fever of mobility such as only occurs at that particular date of the year. It is a day of fulfilment; agreements for outdoor service during the ensuing year, entered into at Candlemas, are to be now carried out. The labourers—or "workfolk", as they used to call themselves immemorially, till the other word was introduced from without—who wish to remain no longer in old places, are removing to the new farms.

These annual migrations from farm to farm were on the increase here. When Tess's mother was a child the majority of the field-folk about Marlott had remained all their lives on one farm, which had been the home also of their fathers and grandfathers; but latterly the desire for yearly removal had risen to a high pitch. With the younger families it was a pleasant excitement which might possibly be an advantage. The Egypt of one family was the land of promise to the family who saw it from a distance; till by residence there it became in turn their Egypt also; and so they changed and changed.*

However, all the mutations so increasingly discernible in village life did not originate entirely in the agricultural unrest. A depopulation was also going on. The village had formerly contained, side by side with the agricultural labourers, an interesting and better-informed class, ranking distinctly above the former—the class to which Tess's father and mother had belonged—and including the carpenter, the smith, the shoemaker, the huckster,* together with nondescript workers other than farm-labourers; a set of people who owed a certain stability of aim and conduct to the fact of their being life-holders like Tess's father, or copyholders, or, occasionally, small freeholders. But as the long holdings fell in they were seldom again let to similar tenants, and were mostly pulled down, if not absolutely required by the farmer for his hands. Cottagers who were not directly employed on the land were looked upon with disfavour, and the banishment of some starved the trade of the others, who were thus obliged to follow. These families, who had formed the backbone of the village life in the past, who were the depositaries of the village traditions, had to seek refuge in the large centres; the process, humorously designated by statisticians as "the tendency of the rural population towards the large towns", being really the tendency of water to flow uphill when forced by machinery.

The cottage accommodation at Marlott, having been in this manner considerably curtailed by demolitions, every house which remained standing was required by the agriculturist for his work-people. Ever since the occurrence of the event which had cast such a shadow over Tess's life, the Durbeyfield family (whose descent was not credited) had been tacitly looked on as one which would have to go, when their lease ended, if only in the interests of morality. It was, indeed, quite true that the household had not been shining examples either of temperance, soberness, or chastity. The father, and even the mother, had got drunk at times, the younger children seldom had gone to church, and the eldest daughter had made queer unions. By some means the village had to be kept pure. So on this the first Lady-Day on which the Durbeyfields were expellable, the house, being roomy, was required for a carter with a large family; and widow Joan, her daughters Tess and Liza-Lu, the boy Abraham and the younger children, had to go elsewhere.

On the evening preceeding their removal it was getting dark betimes, by reason of a drizzling rain which blurred the sky. As it was the last night they would spend in the village which had been their home and birthplace Mrs Durbeyfield, Liza-Lu, and Abraham had gone out to bid some friends good-bye, and Tess was keeping house till they should return.

She was kneeling in the window-bench, her face close to the casement, where an outer pane of rainwater was sliding down the inner pane of glass. Her eyes rested on the web of a spider, probably starved long ago, which had been mistakenly placed in a corner where no flies ever came, and shivered in the slight draught through the casement. Tess was reflecting on the position of the household, in which she perceived her own evil influence. Had she not come home her mother and the children might probably have been allowed to stay on as weekly tenants. But she had been observed almost immediately on her return by some people of scrupulous character and great influence; they had seen her in the churchyard, restoring as well as she could, with a little trowel, a baby's obliterated grave. By this means they had found that she was living here again; her mother was scolded for "harbouring" her; sharp retorts had ensued from

Joan, who had independently offered to leave at once; she had been taken at her word; and here was the result.

"I ought never to have come home!" said Tess to herself bitterly.

She was so intent upon these thoughts that she hardly at first took note of a man in a white mackintosh whom she saw riding down the street. Possibly it was owing to her face being near to the pane that he saw her so quickly, and directed his horse so close to the cottage-front that his hoofs were almost upon the narrow border for plants growing under the wall. It was not till he touched the window with his riding-crop that she observed him. The rain had nearly ceased, and she opened the casement in obedience to his gesture.

"Didn't you see me?" asked d'Urberville.

"I was not attending," she said. "I heard you, I believe, though I fancied it was a carriage and horses. I was in a sort of dream."

"Ah—you heard the d'Urberville Coach, perhaps. You know the legend, I suppose?"

"No. My—somebody was going to tell it me once; but didn't."

"If you are a genuine d'Urberville I ought not to tell you either, I suppose. As for me, I'm a sham one, so it doesn't matter. It is rather dismal. It is that this sound of a non-existent coach can only be heard by one of d'Urberville blood, and it is held to be of ill-omen to the one who hears it. It has to do with a murder, committed by one of the family, centuries ago."

"Now you have begun it, finish it."

"Very well. One of the family is said to have abducted some beautiful woman, who tried to escape from the coach in which he was carrying her off, and in the struggle he killed her—or she killed him—I forget which. Such is one version of the tale. . . . I see that your tubs and buckets are packed. Going away, aren't you?"

"Yes. To-morrow—Old Lady-Day."

"I heard you were, but could hardly believe it; it seems so sudden. Why is it?"

"Father's was the last life on the property, and when that dropped we had no further right to stay. Though we might perhaps have stayed as weekly tenants—if it had not been for me."

"What about you?"

"I am not a—proper woman."

D'Urberville's face flushed. "What a blasted shame! Miserable snobs! May their dirty souls be burnt to cinders!" he exclaimed in tones of ironical resentment. "That's why you are going, is it! Turned out!"

"We are not turned out, exactly; but as they said we should have to go soon it was best to go now everybody is moving, because there are better chances."

"Where are you going to?"

"Kingsbere. We have taken rooms there. Mother is so foolish about father's people that she will go there."

"But your mother's family are not fit for lodgings, and in a little hole of a town like that? Now why not come to my garden-house at Trantridge? There are hardly any poultry now, since my mother's death; but there's the house, as you know it, and the garden. It can be whitewashed in a day, and your mother can live there quite comfortably; and I will put the children to a good school. Really I ought to do something for you!"

"But we have already taken the rooms at Kingsbere!" she declared. "And we can wait there—"

"Wait—what for? For that nice husband, no doubt. Now look here, Tess, I know what men are, and, bearing in mind the *grounds* of your separation, I am quite positive he will never make it up with you. Now; though I have been your enemy, I am your friend, even if you won't believe it. Come to this cottage of mine. We'll get up a regular colony of fowls, and your mother can attend to them excellently; and the children can go to school."

Tess breathed more and more quickly, and at length she said "How do I know that you would do all this? Your views may change—and then—we should be—my mother would be—homeless again."

"O no, no. I would guarantee you against such as that in writing, if necessary. Think it over."

Tess shook her head. But d'Urberville persisted; she had seldom seen him so determined; he would not take a negative. "Please just tell your mother," he said, in emphatic tones. "It is her business to judge—not yours. I shall get the house swept out and whitened to-morrow morning, and fires lit; and it will be dry by the evening, so that you can come straight there. Now mind, I shall expect you."

Tess again shook her head, her throat swelling with complicated emotion. She could not look up at d'Urberville.

"I owe you something for the past, you know," he resumed. "And you cured me, too, of that craze; so I am glad—"

"I would rather you had kept the craze, so that you had kept the practice which went with it!"

"I am glad of this opportunity of repaying you a little. To-morrow I shall expect to hear your mother's goods unloading. . . . Give me your hand on it now—dear, beautiful Tess!"

With the last sentence he had dropped his voice to a murmur, and put his hand in at the half-open casement. With stormy eyes she pulled the stay-bar quickly, and in doing so caught his arm between the casement and the stone mullion.*

"Damnation—you are very cruel!" he said snatching out his arm. "No, no!—I know you didn't do it on purpose. Well, I shall expect you, or your mother and the children at least."

"I shall not come—I have plenty of money!" she cried.

"Where?"

"At my father-in-law's, if I ask for it."

"*If* you ask for it. But you won't, Tess; I know you; you'll never ask for it: you'll starve first!"

With these words he rode off. Just at the corner of the street he met the man with the paint-pot, who asked him if he had deserted the brethren.

"You go to the devil!" said d'Urberville.

Tess remained where she was a long while, till a sudden rebellious sense of injustice caused the region of her eyes to swell with the rush of hot tears thither. Her husband, Angel Clare himself, had, like others, dealt out hard measure to her—surely he had! She had never before admitted such a thought; but he had, surely! Never in her life—she could swear it from the bottom of her soul—had she ever intended to do wrong; yet these hard judgments had come. Whatever her sins, they were not sins of intention, but of inadvertence, and why should she have been punished so persistently?

She passionately seized the first piece of paper that came to hand, and scribbled the following lines:

O why have you treated me so monstrously, Angel! I do not deserve it. I have thought it all over carefully, and I can never, never forgive you! You know that I did not intend to wrong you—why have you so wronged me? You are cruel, cruel indeed! I will try to forget you. It is all injustice I have received at your hands!   T.

She watched till the postman passed by, ran out to him with her epistle, and then again took her listless place inside the window-panes.

It was just as well to write like that as to write tenderly. How could he give way to entreaty? The facts had not changed: there was no new event to alter his opinion.

It grew darker, the firelight shining over the room. The two biggest of the younger children had gone out with their mother; the four smallest, their ages ranging from three-and-a-half years to eleven, all in black frocks, were gathered round the hearth, babbling their own little subjects. Tess at length joined them, without lighting a candle.

"This is the last night that we shall sleep here, dears, in the house where we were born," she said. "We ought to think of it, oughtn't we?"

They all became silent; with the impressibility of their age, they were ready to burst into tears at the picture of finality she had conjured up, though all the day hitherto they had been rejoicing in the idea of a new place. Tess changed the subject. "Sing to me, dears," she said.

"What shall we sing?"

"Anything you know; I don't mind."

There was a momentary pause; it was broken first, by one little tentative note; then a second voice strengthened it, and a third and a fourth chimed in in unison, with words they had learnt at the Sunday-school:

> Here we suffer grief and pain,
> Here we meet to part again:
> In Heaven we part no more.*

The four sang on with the phlegmatic passivity of persons who had long ago settled the question, and, there being no mistake about it, felt that further thought was not required. With features strained hard to enunciate the syllables they continued to regard the centre of the flickering fire, the notes of the youngest straying over into the pauses of the rest.

Tess turned from them and went to the window again. Darkness had now fallen without, but she put her face to the pane as though to peer into the gloom. It was really to hide her tears. If she could only believe what the children were singing; if she were only sure, how different all would now be; how confidently she would leave them to Providence and their future kingdom! But in default of that it behoved her to do something; to be their Providence; for to Tess, as to not a few millions of others, there was ghastly satire in the poet's lines:

> Not in utter nakedness
> But trailing clouds of glory do we come.*

To her, and to her like, birth itself was an ordeal of degrading personal compulsion whose gratuitousness nothing in the result seemed to justify, and at best could only palliate.

In the shades of the wet road she soon discerned her mother with tall Liza-Lu and Abraham. Mrs Durbeyfield's pattens clicked up to the door, and Tess opened it.

"I see the tracks of a horse outside the window," said Joan. "Hev somebody called?"

"No," said Tess.

The children by the fire looked gravely at her, and one murmured, "Why, Tess—the gentleman a-horseback!"

"He didn't call," said Tess. "He spoke to me in passing."

"Who was the gentleman?" asked her mother. "Your husband?"

"No. He'll never, never come," answered Tess in stony hopelessness.

"Then who was it?"

"O—you needn't ask. You've seen him before—and so have I."

"Ah—what did he say?" said Joan curiously.

"I will tell you when we are settled in our lodgings at Kingsbere to-morrow—every word."

It was not her husband, she had said. Yet a consciousness that in a physical sense this man alone was her husband seemed to weigh on her more and more.

LII

DURING the small hours of the next morning, while it was still dark, dwellers near the highways were conscious of a disturbance of their night's rest by rumbling noises, intermittently continuing till daylight; noises as certain to recur in this particular first week of the month as the voice of the cuckoo in the third week of the same. They were the preliminaries of the general removal, the passing of the empty waggons and teams to fetch the goods of the migrating families, for it was always by the vehicle of the farmer who required his services that the hired man was conveyed to his destination. That this might be accomplished within the day was the explanation of the reverberation occurring so soon after midnight, the aim of the carters being to reach the door of the outgoing households by six o'clock, when the loading of their movables at once began.

But to Tess and her mother's household no such anxious farmer sent his team. They were only women; they were not regular labourers; they were not particularly required anywhere; hence they had to hire a waggon at their own expense, and got nothing sent gratuitously.

It was a relief to Tess, when she looked out of the window that morning, to find that though the weather was windy and louring it did not rain, and that the waggon had come. A wet Lady-Day was a spectre which removing families never forgot: damp furniture, damp bedding, damp clothing, accompanied it, and left a long train of ills.

Her mother, Liza-Lu, and Abraham were also awake, but the younger children were let sleep on. The four breakfasted by the thin light, and the "house-ridding" was taken in hand.

It proceeded with some cheerfulness, a friendly neighbour or two assisting. When the large articles of furniture had been packed in position a circular nest was made of the beds and bedding, in which Joan Durbeyfield and the young children were to sit through the journey. After loading there was a long delay before the horses were brought, these having been unharnessed during the ridding, but at length, about two o'clock, the whole was under way, the cooking-pot swinging from the axle of the waggon, Mrs Durbeyfield and family at the top, the matron having in her lap, to prevent injury to its works, the head of the clock which, at any exceptional lurch of the waggon, struck one, or one-and-a-half, in hurt tones. Tess and the next eldest girl walked alongside till they were out of the village.

They had called on a few neighbours that morning and the previous evening, and some came to see them off; all wishing them well, though, in their secret hearts, hardly expecting welfare possible to such a family, harmless as the Durbeyfields were to all except themselves. Soon the equipage began to ascend to higher ground, and the wind grew keener with the change of level and soil.

The day being the sixth of April the Durbeyfield waggon met many other waggons with families on the summit of the load, which was built on a well-nigh unvarying principle, as peculiar, probably, to the rural labourer as the hexagon to the bee.* The groundwork of the arrangement was the family dresser which, with its shining handles, and finger-marks, and domestic evidences thick upon it, stood importantly in front, over the tails of the shaft horses, in its erect and natural position, like some Ark of the Covenant* that they were bound to carry reverently.

Some of the households were lively, some mournful; some were stopping at the doors of wayside inns; where, in due time, the Durbeyfield menagerie also drew up, to bait horses, and refresh the travellers.

During the halt Tess's eyes fell upon a three-pint blue mug, which was ascending and descending through the air to and from the feminine section of a household, sitting on the summit of a load that had also drawn up at a little distance from the same inn. She followed one of the mug's journeys upward, and perceived it to be clasped by hands whose owner she well knew. Tess went towards the waggon.

"Marian, and Izz!" she cried to the girls, for it was they, sitting with the moving family at whose house they had lodged. "Are you house-ridding to-day like everybody else?"

They were, they said. It had been too rough a life for them at Flintcomb-Ash, and they had come away, almost without notice, leaving Groby to prosecute them if he chose. They told Tess their destination, and Tess told them hers.

Marian leant over the load and lowered her voice. "Do you know that the gentleman who follows 'ee—you'll guess who I mean— came to ask for 'ee at Flintcomb after you had gone? We didn't tell 'n where you was, knowing you wouldn't wish to see him."

"Ah—but I did see him," Tess murmured. "He found me."

"And do he know—where you be going?"

"I think so."

"Husband come back?"

"No."

She bade her acquaintance good-bye—for the respective carters had now come out from the inn—and the two waggons resumed their journey in opposite directions; the vehicle whereon sat Marian, Izz, and the ploughman's family with whom they had thrown in their lot, being brightly painted, and drawn by three powerful horses with shining brass ornaments on their harness; while the waggon on which Mrs Durbeyfield and her family rode was a creaking erection that would scarcely bear the weight of the superincumbent load; one which had known no paint since it was made, and drawn by two horses only. The contrast well marked the difference between being fetched by a thriving farmer, and conveying one's self whither no hirer waited one's coming.

The distance was great—too great for a day's journey—and it was with the utmost difficulty that the horses performed it. Though they had started so early it was quite late in the afternoon when they turned the flank of an eminence which formed part of the upland called Greenhill. While the horses stood to stale* and breathe themselves Tess looked around. Under the hill, and just ahead of them, was the half-dead townlet of their pilgrimage, Kingsbere, where lay those ancestors of whom her father had spoken and sung to painfulness: Kingsbere, the spot of all spots in the world which could be considered the d'Urbervilles' home, since they had resided there for full five hundred years.

A man could be seen advancing from the outskirts towards them, and when he beheld the nature of their waggon-load he quickened his steps.

"You be the woman they call Mrs Durbeyfield, I reckon?" he said to Tess's mother, who had descended to walk the remainder of the way.

She nodded. "Though widow of the late Sir John d'Urberville, poor nobleman, if I cared for my rights; and returning to the domain of his forefathers."

"Oh? Well, I know nothing about that; but if you be Mrs Durbeyfield, I am sent to tell 'ee that the rooms you wanted be let. We didn't know you was coming till we got your letter this morning—when 'twas too late. But no doubt you can get other lodgings somewhere."

The man had noticed the face of Tess, which had become ash-pale at his intelligence. Her mother looked hopelessly at fault. "What shall we do now, Tess?" she said bitterly. "Here's a welcome to your ancestors' lands! However, let's try further."

They moved on into the town, and tried with all their might, Tess remaining with the waggon to take care of the children whilst her mother and Liza-Lu made inquiries. At the last return of Joan to the vehicle, an hour later, when her search for accommodation had still been fruitless, the driver of the waggon said the goods must be unloaded, as the horses were half-dead, and he was bound to return part of the way at least that night.

"Very well, unload it here," said Joan recklessly. "I'll get shelter somewhere."

The waggon had drawn up under the churchyard wall, in a spot screened from view, and the driver, nothing loth, soon hauled down the poor heap of household goods. This done she paid him, reducing herself to almost her last shilling thereby, and he moved off and left them, only too glad to get out of further dealings with such a family. It was a dry night, and he guessed that they would come to no harm.

Tess gazed desperately at the pile of furniture. The cold sunlight of this spring evening peered invidiously upon the crocks and kettles, upon the bunches of dried herbs shivering in the breeze, upon the brass handles of the dresser, upon the wicker-cradle they had all been rocked in, and upon the well-rubbed clock-case, all of which gave out the reproachful gleam of indoor articles abandoned to the vicissitudes of a roofless exposure for which they were never made. Round about were deparked hills and slopes*—now cut up into little paddocks—and the green foundations that showed where the d'Urberville mansion once had stood; also an outlying stretch of Egdon Heath that had always belonged to the estate. Hard by, the aisle of the church called the d'Urberville Aisle looked on imperturbably.

"Isn't your family vault your own freehold?" said Tess's mother, as she returned from a reconnoitre of the church and graveyard. "Why of course 'tis. And that's where we will camp, girls, till the place of your ancestors finds us a roof. Now, Tess and Liza and

Abraham, you help me. We'll make a nest for these children, and then we'll have another look round."

Tess listlessly lent a hand, and in a quarter of an hour the old four-post bedstead was dissociated from the heap of goods and erected under the south wall of the church, the part of the building known as the d'Urberville Aisle, beneath which the huge vaults lay. Over the tester of the bedstead was a beautifully traceried window of many lights, its date being the fifteenth century. It was called the d'Urberville Window, and in the upper part could be discerned heraldic emblems like those on Durbeyfield's old seal and spoon.

Joan drew the curtains round the bed so as to make an excellent tent of it, and put the smaller children inside. "If it comes to the worst we can sleep there too, for one night," she said. "But let us try further on, and get something for the dears to eat. O, Tess, what's the use of your playing at marrying gentlemen, if it leaves us like this?"

Accompanied by Liza-Lu and the boy she again ascended the little lane which secluded the church from the townlet. As soon as they got into the street they beheld a man on horseback gazing up and down. "Ah, I'm looking for you," he said, riding up to them. "This is indeed a family gathering on the historic spot!" It was Alec d'Urberville. "Where is Tess?" he asked.

Personally Joan had no liking for Alec. She cursorily signified the direction of the church, and went on, d'Urberville saying that he would see them again in case they should be still unsuccessful in their search for shelter, of which he had just heard. When they had gone d'Urberville rode on to the inn, and shortly after came out on foot.

In the interim Tess, left with the children inside the bedstead, remained talking with them awhile, till, seeing that no more could be done to make them comfortable just then, she walked about the churchyard, now beginning to be embrowned by the shades of night-fall. The door of the church was unfastened, and she entered it for the first time in her life.

Within the window under which the bedstead stood were the tombs of the family, covering in their dates several centuries. They were canopied, altar-shaped, and plain; their carvings being defaced and broken; their brasses torn from the matrices, the rivet-holes remaining like martin-holes in a sand-cliff. Of all the reminders that she had ever received that her people were socially extinct there was none so forcible as this spoliation.

She drew near to a dark stone on which was inscribed:

Ostium sepulchri antiquæ familiæ D'Urberville.

Tess did not read Church Latin like a Cardinal, but she knew that this was the door of her ancestral sepulchre, and that the tall knights of whom her father had chanted in his cups lay inside.

She musingly turned to withdraw, passing near an altar-tomb, the oldest of them all, on which was a recumbent figure. In the dusk she had not noticed it before, and would hardly have noticed it now but for an odd fancy that the effigy moved. As soon as she drew close to it she discovered all in a moment that the figure was a living person; and the shock to her sense of not having been alone was so violent that she was quite overcome, and sank down nigh to fainting, not however till she had recognized Alec d'Urberville in the form.

He leapt off the slab and supported her. "I saw you come in," he said smiling, "and got up there not to interrupt your meditations. A family gathering, is it not, with these old fellows under us here? Listen." He stamped with his heel heavily on the floor; whereupon there arose a hollow echo from below.

"That shook them a bit, I'll warrant," he continued. "And you thought I was the mere stone reproduction of one of them. But no. The old order changeth. The little finger of the sham d'Urberville can do more for you than the whole dynasty of the real underneath. . . . Now command me. What shall I do?"

"Go away," she murmured.

"I will—I'll look for your mother," said he blandly. But in passing her he whispered, "Mind this; you'll be civil yet!"

When he was gone she bent down upon the entrance to the vaults, and said, "Why am I on the wrong side of this door!"

In the meantime Marian and Izz Huett had journeyed onward with the chattels of the ploughman in the direction of their land of Canaan—the Egypt* of some other family who had left it only that morning. But the girls did not for a long time think of where they were going. Their talk was of Angel Clare, and Tess, and Tess's persistent lover, whose connection with her previous history they had partly heard and partly guessed ere this.

" 'Tisn't as though she had never known him afore," said Marian. "His having won her once makes all the difference in the world. 'Twould be a thousand pities if he were to tole her away again. Mr Clare can never be anything to us, Izz; and why should we grudge him to her, and not try to mend this quarrel? If he could on'y know what straits she's put to, and what's hovering round, he might come to take care of his own."

"Could we let him know?"

They thought of this all the way to their destination; but the bustle of re-establishment in their new place took up all their attention then. But when they were settled, a month later, they heard of Clare's approaching return, though they had learnt nothing more of Tess. Upon that, agitated anew by their attachment to him, yet honourably disposed to her, Marian uncorked the penny ink-bottle they shared, and a few lines were concocted between the two girls.

Honour'd Sir,

Look to your Wife if you do love her as much as she do love you. For she is sore put to by an Enemy in the shape of a Friend. Sir, there is one near her who ought to be Away. A woman should not be try'd beyond her Strength, and continual dropping will wear away a Stone—ay, more, a Diamond.

From Two Well-wishers.

This they addressed to Angel Clare at the only place they had ever heard him to be connected with, Emminster Vicarage; after which they continued in a mood of emotional exaltation at their own generosity, which made them sing in hysterical snatches and weep at the same time.

END OF PHASE THE SIXTH

PHASE THE SEVENTH

FULFILMENT

PHASE THE SEVENTH

FULFILMENT

LIII

It was evening at Emminster Vicarage. The two customary candles were burning under their green shades in the Vicar's study, but he had not been sitting there. Occasionally he came in, stirred the small fire which sufficed for the increasing mildness of the spring, and went out again; sometimes pausing at the front door, going on to the drawing-room, then returning again to the front door.

It faced westward, and though gloom prevailed inside, there was still light enough without to see with distinctness. Mrs Clare, who had been sitting in the drawing-room, followed him hither.

"Plenty of time yet," said the Vicar. "He doesn't reach Chalk-Newton till six, even if the train should be punctual, and ten miles of country-road, five of them in Crimmercrock Lane, are not jogged over in a hurry by our old horse."

"But he has done it in an hour with us, my dear?"

"Years ago."

Thus they passed the minutes, each well knowing that this was only waste of breath, the one essential being simply to wait.

At length there was a slight noise in the lane, and the old pony-chaise appeared indeed outside the railings. They saw alight therefrom a form which they affected to recognize, but would actually have passed by in the street without identifying had he not got out of their carriage at the particular moment when a particular person was due.

Mrs Clare rushed through the dark passage to the door, and her husband came more slowly after her. The new arrival, who was just about to enter, saw their anxious faces in the doorway, and the gleam of the west in their spectacles, because they confronted the last rays of day; but they could only see his shape against the light.

"O my boy, my boy—home again at last!" cried Mrs Clare, who cared no more at that moment for the stains of heterodoxy which had caused all this separation than for the dust upon his clothes. What woman, indeed, among the most faithful adherents of the truth, believes the promises and threats of the Word in the sense in which she believes in her own children, or would not throw her theology to the wind if weighed against their happiness? As soon as they reached the room where the candles were lighted she looked at his face.

"O it is not Angel—not my son—the Angel who went away!" she cried in all the irony of sorrow as she turned herself aside.

His father, too, was shocked to see him, so reduced was that figure from its former contours by worry and the bad season that Clare had experienced in the climate to which he had so rashly hurried in his first aversion to the mockery of events at home. You could see the skeleton behind the man, and almost the ghost behind the skeleton. He matched Crivelli's dead *Christus*.* His sunken eye-pits were of morbid hue, and the light in his eyes had waned. The angular hollows and lines of his aged ancestors had succeeded to their reign in his face twenty years before their time.

"I was ill over there, you know," he said. "I am all right now."

As if, however, to falsify this assertion, his legs seemed to give way, and he suddenly sat down to save himself from falling. It was only a slight attack of faintness, resulting from the tedious day's journey, and the excitement of arrival.

"Has any letter come for me lately?" he asked. "I received the last you sent on by the merest chance, and after considerable delay through being inland; or I might have come sooner."

"It was from your wife, we supposed?"

"It was."

Only one other had recently come. They had not sent it on to him, knowing he would start for home so soon.

He hastily opened the letter produced, and was much disturbed to read in Tess's handwriting the sentiments expressed in her last hurried scrawl to him.

O why have you treated me so monstrously, Angel! I do not deserve it. I have thought it all over carefully, and I can never, never forgive you! You know that I did not intend to wrong you—why have you so wronged me? You are cruel, cruel indeed! I will try to forget you. It is all injustice I have received at your hands!   T.

"It is quite true!" said Angel, throwing down the letter. "Perhaps she will never be reconciled to me!"

"Don't, Angel, be so anxious about a mere child of the soil!" said his mother.

"Child of the soil! Well, we all are children of the soil. I wish she were so in the sense you mean; but let me now explain to you what I have never explained before, that her father is a descendant in the male line of one of the oldest Norman houses, like a good many others who lead obscure agricultural lives in our villages and are dubbed 'sons of the soil'."

He soon retired to bed; and the next morning feeling exceedingly unwell he remained in his room pondering. The circumstances amid which he had left Tess were such that though, while on the south of the Equator and just in receipt of her loving epistle, it had seemed the easiest thing in the world to rush back into her arms the moment he chose to forgive her, now that he had arrived it was not so easy as it had seemed. She was passionate, and her present letter, showing that her estimate of him had changed under his delay—too justly changed, he sadly owned,—made him ask himself if it would be wise to confront her unannounced in the presence of her parents. Supposing that her love had indeed turned to dislike during the last weeks of separation, a sudden meeting might lead to bitter words.

Clare therefore thought it would be best to prepare Tess and her family by sending a line to Marlott announcing his return, and his hope that she was still living with them there, as he had arranged for her to do when he left England. He dispatched the inquiry that very day, and before the week was out there came a short reply from Mrs Durbeyfield which did not remove his embarrassment, for it bore no address, though to his surprise it was not written from Marlott.

Sir: J write these few lines to say that my Daughter is away from me at present, and J am not sure when she will return, but J will let you know as Soon as she do. J do not feel at liberty to tell you Where she is temperly biding. J should say that me and my Family have left Marlott for some Time.

Yours

J. Durbeyfield.

It was such a relief to Clare to learn that Tess was at least apparently well that her mother's stiff reticence as to her whereabouts did not long distress him. They were all angry with him, evidently. He would wait till Mrs Durbeyfield could inform him of Tess's return, which her letter implied to be soon. He deserved no more. His had been a love "which alters when it alteration finds".* He had undergone some strange experiences in his absence; he had seen the virtual Faustina in the literal Cornelia, a spiritual Lucretia in a corporeal Phryne; he had thought of the woman taken and set in the midst as one deserving to be stoned, and of the wife of Uriah being made a queen;* and he had asked himself why he had not judged Tess constructively rather than biographically, by the will rather than by the deed?

A day or two passed while he waited at his father's house for the promised second note from Joan Durbeyfield, and indirectly to recover a little more strength. The strength showed signs of coming back, but there was no sign of Joan's letter. Then he hunted up the old letter sent on to him in Brazil, which Tess had written from Flintcomb-Ash, and re-read it. The sentences touched him now as much as when he had first perused them.

I must cry to you in my trouble—I have no one else. . . . I think I must die if you do not come soon, or tell me to come to you. . . . please, please, not to be just—only a little kind to me. . . . If you would come I could die in your arms. I would be well content to do that if so be you had forgiven me. . . . if you will send me one little line and say, *I am coming soon*, I will bide on, Angel: O so cheerfully! . . . think how it do hurt my heart not to see you ever, ever! Ah, if I could only make your dear heart ache one little minute of each day as mine does every day and all day long, it might lead you to show pity to your poor lonely one. . . . I would be content, ay glad, to live with you as your servant, if I may not as your wife; so that I could only be near you, and get glimpses of you, and think of you as mine. . . . I long for only one thing in heaven or earth or under the earth, to meet you, my own dear. Come to me, come to me, and save me from what threatens me!

Clare determined that he would no longer believe in her more recent and severer regard of him; but would go and find her immediately. He asked his father if she had applied for any money during his absence. His father returned a negative, and then for the first time it occurred to Angel that her pride had stood in her way, and that she had suffered privation. From his remarks his parents now gathered the real reason of the separation; and their Christianity was such that, reprobates being their especial care, the tenderness towards Tess which her blood, her simplicity, even her poverty, had not engendered, was instantly excited by her sin.

Whilst he was hastily packing together a few articles for his journey, he glanced over a poor plain missive also lately come to hand—the one from Marian and Izz Huett, beginning

"Honour'd Sir,

Look to your Wife if you do love her as much as she do love you", and signed, "From Two Well-wishers".

LIV

IN a quarter of an hour Clare was leaving the house, whence his mother watched his thin figure as it disappeared into the street. He had declined to borrow his father's old mare, well knowing of its necessity to the household. He went to the inn, where he hired a trap, and could hardly wait during the harnessing. In a very few minutes after he was driving up the hill out of the town, which three or four months earlier in the year Tess had descended with such hopes and ascended with such shattered purposes.

Benvill Lane soon stretched before him, its hedges and trees purple with buds; but he was looking at other things, and only recalled himself to the scene sufficiently to enable him to keep the way. In something less than an hour-and-a-half he had skirted the south of the King's Hintock estates and ascended to the untoward solitude of Cross-in-Hand, the unholy stone whereon Tess had been compelled by Alec d'Urberville, in his whim of reform, to swear the strange oath that she would never wilfully tempt him again. The pale and blasted nettle-stems of the preceding year even now lingered nakedly in the banks, young green nettles of the present spring growing from their roots.

Thence he went along the verge of the upland over-hanging the other Hintocks, and turning to the right plunged into the bracing calcareous region of Flintcomb-Ash, the address from which she had written to him in one of the letters, and which he supposed to be the place of sojourn referred to by her mother. Here, of course, he did not find her; and what added to his depression was the discovery that no "Mrs Clare" had ever been heard of by the cottagers, or by the farmer himself, though Tess was remembered well enough by her Christian name. His name she had obviously never used during their separation, and her dignified sense of their total severance was shown not much less by this abstention than by the hardships she had chosen to undergo (of which he now learnt for the first time) rather than apply to his father for more funds.

From this place, they told him, Tess Durbeyfield had gone, without due notice, to the home of her parents on the other side of Blackmoor, and it therefore became necessary to find Mrs Durbeyfield. She had told him she was not now at Marlott, but had been curiously reticent as to her actual address, and the only course was to go to Marlott and inquire for it. The farmer who had been so churlish with Tess, was quite smooth-tongued to Clare, and lent him a horse and man to drive him towards Marlott, the gig he had arrived in being sent back to Emminster; for the limit of a day's journey with that horse was reached.

Clare would not accept the loan of the farmer's vehicle for a further distance than to the outskirts of the Vale, and sending it back with the man who had driven him he put up at an inn, and next day entered on foot the region wherein was the spot of his dear Tess's birth. It was as yet too early in the year for much colour to appear in the gardens and foliage; the so-called spring was but winter overlaid with a thin coat of greenness; and it was of a parcel with his expectations.

The house in which Tess had passed the years of her childhood was now inhabited by another family who had never known her. The new residents were in the garden, taking as much interest in their own doings as if the homestead had never passed its primal time in conjunction with the histories of others, beside which (to him) the histories of these were but as a tale told by an idiot.* They walked about the garden paths with thoughts of their own concerns entirely uppermost, bringing their actions at every moment into jarring collision with the dim ghosts behind them, talking as though the time when Tess lived there were not one whit intenser in story than now. Even the spring birds sang over their heads as if they thought there was nobody missing in particular.

On inquiry of these precious innocents, to whom even the name of their predecessors was a fading memory, Clare learned that John Durbeyfield was dead; that his widow and children had left Marlott, declaring that they were going to live at Kingsbere, but instead of doing so had gone on to another place they mentioned. By this time Clare abhorred the house for ceasing to contain Tess, and hastened away from its hated presence without once looking back.

His way was by the field in which he had first beheld her at the dance. It was as bad as the house; even worse. He passed on through the churchyard, where, amongst the new headstones, he saw one of a somewhat superior design to the rest. The inscription ran thus:

In Memory of John Durbeyfield, rightly d'Urberville, of the once Powerful Family of that Name; and direct Descendant through an illustrious Line from Sir Pagan d'Urberville, one of the Knights of the Conqueror. Died March 10, 18—

How are the Mighty fallen.

Some man, apparently the sexton, had observed Clare standing there, and drew nigh. "Ah, sir, now that's a man who didn't want to lie here, but wished to be carried to Kingsbere where his ancestors be."

"And why didn't they respect his wish?"

"Oh—no money. Bless your soul, sir, why—even this headstone, for all the flourish wrote upon en, is not paid for."

"Ah—who put it up?"

The man told the name of a mason in the village, and on leaving the churchyard Clare called at the mason's house. He found that the statement was true, and paid the bill. This done he turned in the direction of the migrants.

The distance was too long for a walk, but Clare felt such a strong desire for isolation that at first he would neither hire a conveyance, nor go to a circuitous line of railway by which he might eventually reach the place. At Shaston, however, he found he must hire; but the way was such that he did not enter Joan's place till about seven o'clock in the evening, having traversed a distance of over twenty miles since leaving Marlott.

The village being small he had little difficulty in finding Mrs Durbeyfield's tenement, which was a house in a walled garden, remote from the main road, where she had stowed away her clumsy old furniture as best she could. It was plain that for some reason or other she had not wished him to visit her, and he felt his call to be somewhat of an intrusion. She came to the door herself, and the light from the evening sky fell upon her face.

This was the first time that Clare had ever met her, but he was too preoccupied to observe more than that she was still a handsome woman, in the garb of a respectable widow. He was obliged to explain that he was Tess's husband, and his object in coming there, and he did it awkwardly enough. "I want to see her at once," he added. "You said you would write to me again, but you have not done so."

"Because she've not come home," said Joan.

"Do you know if she is well?"

"I don't. But you ought to, sir," said she.

"I admit it. Where is she staying?"

From the beginning of the interview Joan had disclosed her embarrassment by keeping her hand to the side of her cheek. "I—don't know exactly where she is staying," she answered. "She was—. But—"

"Where was she?"

"Well, she is not there now." In her evasiveness she paused again, and the younger children had by this time crept to the door, where, pulling at his mother's skirts, the youngest murmured "Is this the gentleman who is going to marry Tess?"

"He has married her," Joan whispered. "Go inside."

Clare saw her efforts for reticence, and asked "Do you think Tess would wish me to try to find her? If not, of course—"

"I don't think she would."

"Are you sure?"

"I am sure she wouldn't."

He was turning away; and then he thought of Tess's tender letter. "I am sure she would!" he retorted passionately. "I know her better than you do."

"That's very likely, sir; for I have never really known her."

"Please tell me her address, Mrs Durbeyfield, in kindness to a lonely wretched man."

Tess's mother again restlessly swept her cheek with her vertical hand, and seeing that he suffered she at last said in a low voice, "She is at Sandbourne."

"Ah—where there? Sandbourne has become a large place, they say."

"I don't know more particularly than I have said—Sandbourne. For myself, I was never there."

It was apparent that Joan spoke the truth in this, and he pressed her no further.

"Are you in want of anything?" he said gently.

"No sir," she replied. "We are fairly well provided for."

Without entering the house Clare turned away. There was a station three miles ahead, and paying off his coachman he walked thither. The last train to Sandbourne left shortly after, and it bore Clare on its wheels.

LV

At eleven o'clock that night, having secured a bed at one of the hotels and telegraphed his address to his father immediately on his arrival, he walked out into the streets of Sandbourne. It was too late to call on or inquire for anyone, and he reluctantly postponed his purpose till the morning. But he could not retire to rest just yet.

This fashionable watering-place, with its eastern and its western stations, its piers, its groves of pines, its promenades, and its covered gardens, was to Angel Clare like a fairy place suddenly created by the stroke of a wand, and allowed to get a little dusty. An outlying, eastern tract of the enormous Egdon Waste was close at hand, yet on the very verge of that tawny piece of antiquity such a glittering novelty as this pleasure-city had chosen to spring up. Within the space of a mile from its outskirts every irregularity of the soil was prehistoric, every channel an undisturbed British trackway; not a sod having been turned there since the days of the Cæsars. Yet the exotic had grown here, suddenly as the prophet's gourd;* and had drawn hither Tess.

By the midnight lamps he went up and down the winding ways of this new world in an old one, and could discern between the trees and against the stars the lofty roofs, chimneys, gazebos, and towers, of the numerous fanciful residences of which the place was composed. It was a city of detached mansions; a Mediterranean lounging-place on the English Channel; and as seen now by night it seemed even more imposing than it was.

The sea was near at hand, but not intrusive: it murmured, and he thought it was the pines; the pines murmured in precisely the same tones, and he thought they were the sea.

Where could Tess possibly be, a cottage girl, his young wife, amidst all this wealth and fashion? The more he pondered the more was he puzzled. Were there any cows to milk here? There certainly were no fields to till. She was most probably engaged to do something in one of these large houses; and he sauntered along, looking at the chamber-windows, and their lights going out one by one, and wondered which of them might be hers.

Conjecture was useless, and just after twelve o'clock he entered and went to bed. Before putting out his light he re-read Tess's impassioned letter. Sleep however he could not—so near her yet so far from her—and he continually lifted the window-blind and regarded the backs of the opposite houses, and wondered behind which of the sashes she reposed at that moment.

He might almost as well have sat up all night. In the morning he arose at seven, and shortly after went out, taking the direction of the chief post-office. At the door he met an intelligent postman coming out with letters for the morning delivery.

"Do you know the address of a Mrs Clare?" asked Angel.

The postman shook his head. Then, remembering that she would have been likely to continue the use of her maiden name Clare said: "Or of Miss Durbeyfield?"

"Durbeyfield." This also was strange to the postman addressed. "There's visitors coming and going every day, as you know, sir," he said; "and without the name of the house 'tis impossible to find 'em."

One of his comrades hastening out at that moment the name was repeated to him.

"I know no name of Durbeyfield; but there is the name of d'Urberville at The Herons," said the second.

"That's it," cried Clare, pleased to think that she had reverted to the real pronunciation. "What place is The Herons?"

"A stylish lodging-house. 'Tis all lodging-houses here, bless 'ee."

Clare received directions how to find the house, and hastened thither, arriving with the milkman. The Herons, though an ordinary villa, stood in its own grounds, and was certainly the last place in which one would have expected to find lodgings, so private was its appearance. If poor Tess was a servant here, as he feared, she would go to the back door to that milkman, and he was inclined to go thither also. However, in his doubts he turned to the front, and rang.

The hour being early the landlady herself opened the door. Clare inquired for Teresa d'Urberville or Durbeyfield.

"Mrs d'Urberville?"

"Yes."

Tess then passed as a married woman, and he felt glad, even though she had not adopted his name. "Will you kindly tell her, that a relative is anxious to see her."

"It is rather early. What name shall I give, sir?"

"Angel."

"Mr Angel?"

"No, Angel. It is my Christian name. She'll understand."

"I'll see if she is awake."

He was shown into the front room, the dining-room, and looked out through the spring curtains at the little lawn, and the rhododendrons and other shrubs upon it. Obviously her position was by no means so bad as he had feared, and it crossed his mind that she must somehow have claimed and sold the jewels to attain it. He did not blame her for one moment. Soon his sharpened ear detected footsteps upon the stairs, at which his heart thumped so painfully that he could hardly stand firm. "Dear me—what will she think of me—so altered as I am!" he said to himself; and the door opened.

Tess appeared on the threshold—not at all as he had expected to see her—bewilderingly otherwise, indeed. Her great natural beauty was, if not heightened, rendered more obvious by her attire. She was loosely wrapped in a cashmere dressing-gown of grey-white, embroidered in half-mourning tints, and she wore slippers of the same hue. Her neck rose out of a frill of down, and her well-remembered cable of dark-brown hair was partially coiled up in a mass at the back of her head, and partly hanging on her shoulder, the evident result of haste.

He had held out his arms, but they had fallen again to his side; for she had not come forward, remaining still in the opening of the doorway. Mere yellow skeleton that he was now, he felt the contrast between them, and thought his appearance distasteful to her.

"Tess!" he said huskily. "Can you forgive me for going away? Can't you—come to me? How do you get to be—like this?"

"It is too late!" said she, her voice sounding hard through the room, her eyes shining unnaturally.

"I did not think rightly of you—I did not see you as you were," he continued to plead. "I have learnt to since, dearest Tessy mine!"

"Too late, too late!" she said, waving her hand in the impatience of a person whose tortures cause every instant to seem an hour. "Don't come close to me, Angel! No—you must not. Keep away!"

"But don't you love me, my dear wife, because I have been so pulled down by illness? You are not so fickle—I am come on purpose for you—my mother and father will welcome you now."

"Yes—O yes, yes! But I say, I say, it is too late." She seemed to feel like a fugitive in a dream, who tries to move away, but cannot. "Don't you know all—don't you know it? Yet how do you come here if you do not know?"

"I inquired here and there—and I found the way."

"I waited and waited for you," she went on, her tones suddenly resuming their old fluty pathos. "But you did not come. And I wrote to you; and you did not come. He kept on saying you would never come any more, and that I was a foolish woman. He was very kind to me, and to mother, and to all of us after father's death. He—"

"I don't understand?"

"He has won me back—to him."

Clare looked at her keenly, then gathering her meaning flagged like one plague-stricken, and his glance sank: it fell on her hands, which, once rosy, were now white and more delicate.

She continued: "He is upstairs. I hate him now, because he told me a lie—that you would not come again; and you *have* come! These clothes are what he's put upon me: I didn't care what he did wi' me! The step back to him was not so great as it seems. He had been as husband to me: you never had! But—will you go away, Angel, please, and never come any more?"

They stood, fixed, their baffled hearts looking out of their eyes with a joylessness pitiful to see. Both seemed to implore something to shelter them from reality.

"Ah—it is my fault!" said Clare.

But he could not get on. Speech was as inexpressive as silence. But he had a vague consciousness of one thing, though it was not clear to him till later; that his original Tess had spiritually ceased to recognize the body before him as hers—allowing it to drift, like a corpse upon the current, in a direction dissociated from its living will.

A few instants passed, and he found that Tess was gone. His face grew colder and more shrunken as he stood, concentrated on the moment; and a minute or two after he found himself in the street, walking along, he did not know whither.

LVI

MRS BROOKS, the lady who was the householder at The Herons, and owner of all the handsome furniture, was not a person of an unusually curious turn of mind. She was too deeply materialized, poor woman, by her long and enforced bondage to that arithmetical demon, profit-and-loss, to retain much curiosity for its own sake, and apart from possible lodgers' pockets. Nevertheless, the visit of Angel Clare to her well-paying tenants Mr and Mrs d'Urberville (as she deemed them) was sufficiently exceptional in point of time and manner, to reinvigorate the feminine proclivity which had been stifled down as useless, save in its bearings on the letting trade.

Tess had spoken to her husband from the doorway, without entering the dining-room, and Mrs Brooks, who stood within the partly closed door of her own sitting-room at the back of the passage, could hear fragments of the conversation—if conversation it could be called—between those two wretched souls. She heard Tess reascend the stairs to the first floor, and the departure of Clare, and the closing of the front door behind him. Then the door of the room above was shut, and Mrs Brooks knew that Tess had re-entered her apartment. As the young lady was not fully dressed Mrs Brooks knew that she would not emerge again for some time.

She accordingly ascended the staircase softly, and stood at the door of the front room, a drawing-room, connected with the room immediately behind it, which was a bedroom, by folding-doors in the common manner. This first floor, containing Mrs Brooks's best apartments, had been taken by the week by the d'Urbervilles. The back room was now in silence, but from the drawing-room there came sounds.

All that she could at first distinguish of them was one syllable, continually repeated, in a low note of moaning, as if it came from a soul bound to some Ixionian wheel:*

"Oh—oh—oh!"

Then a silence, then a heavy sigh; and again,

"Oh—oh—oh!"

The landlady looked through the keyhole. Only a small space of the room inside was visible, but within that space came a corner of the breakfast-table, which was already spread for the meal; and also a chair beside it. Over the seat of the chair Tess's face was bowed, her posture being a kneeling one in front of it: her hands were clasped over her head, the skirts of her dressing-gown and the embroidery of her night-gown flowed upon the floor behind her, and her stocking-less feet, from which the slippers had fallen, protruded upon the carpet. It was from her lips that came the murmur of unspeakable despair.

Then a man's voice from the adjoining bedroom: "What's the matter?"

She did not answer, but went on in a tone which was a soliloquy rather than an exclamation, and a dirge rather than a soliloquy. Mrs Brooks could only catch a portion:

". . . . . And then my dear dear husband came home to me . . . . and I did not know it . . . . and you had used your cruel persuasion upon me . . . . you did not stop using it—no—you did not stop! My little sisters and brother, and my mother's needs . . . . they were the things you moved me by . . . . and you said my husband would never come back—never; and you taunted me, and said what a simpleton I was to expect him . . . . . And at last I believed you and gave way! . . . . . And then he came back! Now he is gone, gone! A second time, and I have lost him now for ever . . . . and he will not love me the littlest bit ever any more—only hate me . . . O yes, I have lost him now—again because of—you!" In writhing, with her head on the chair, she turned her face towards the door, and Mrs Brooks could see the pain upon it; and that her lips were bleeding from the clench of her teeth upon them, and that the long lashes of her closed eyes stuck in wet tags to her cheeks. She continued: "And he is dying—he looks as if he is dying . . . . . and my sin will kill him and not kill me! . . . O you have torn my life all in pieces . . . . made me be what I prayed you in pity not to make me be again! . . . My own true husband will never never—O God—I can't bear this! I cannot!"

There were more and sharper words from the man; then a sudden rustle; she had sprung to her feet. Mrs Brooks, thinking that the speaker was coming to rush out of the door, hastily retreated down the stairs.

She need not have done so, however, for the door of the sitting-room was not opened. But Mrs Brooks felt it unsafe to watch on the landing again, and entered her own parlour below. She could hear nothing through the floor, although she listened intently, and thereupon went to the kitchen, to finish her interrupted breakfast. Coming up presently to the front room on the ground floor she took up some sewing, waiting for her lodgers to ring that she might take away the breakfast, which she meant to do herself to discover what was the matter if possible. Overhead as she sat she could now hear the floor-boards slightly creak, as if some one were walking about, and presently the movement was explained by the rustle of garments against the bannisters, the opening and closing of the front door, and the form of Tess passing to the gate on her way into the street. She was fully dressed now, in the walking-costume of a well-to-do young lady in which she had arrived, with the sole addition that over her hat and black feathers a veil was drawn. Mrs Brooks had not been able to catch any word of farewell, temporary or otherwise, between her tenants at the door above. They might have quarrelled, or Mr d'Urberville might still be asleep, for he was not an early riser.

She went into the back room, which was more especially her own apartment, and continued her sewing there. The lady-lodger did not return, nor did the gentleman ring his bell. Mrs Brooks pondered on the delay, and on what probable relation the visitor who had called so early bore to the couple upstairs. In reflecting she leant back in her chair.

As she did so her eyes glanced casually over the ceiling, till they were arrested by a spot in the middle of its white surface which she had never noticed there before. It was about the size of a wafer when she first observed it, but it speedily grew as large as the palm of her hand, and then she could perceive that it was red. The oblong white ceiling, with this scarlet blot in the midst, had the appearance of a gigantic ace of hearts.

Mrs Brooks had strange qualms of misgiving. She got upon the table, and touched the spot in the ceiling with her fingers. It was damp, and she fancied that it was a blood-stain.

Descending from the table she left the parlour and went upstairs, intending to enter the room overhead, which was the bedchamber at the back of the drawing-room. But nerveless woman as she had now become, she could not bring herself to attempt the handle. She listened. The dead silence within was broken only by a regular beat.

Drip, drip, drip.

Mrs Brooks hastened downstairs, opened the front door and ran into the street. A man she knew, one of the workmen employed at an adjoining villa, was passing by, and she begged him to come in and go upstairs with her; she feared something had happened to one of her lodgers. The workman assented, and followed her to the landing.

She opened the door of the drawing-room, and stood back for him to pass in, entering herself behind him. The room was empty; the breakfast—a substantial repast of coffee, eggs, and a cold ham—lay spread upon the table untouched, as when she had taken it up, excepting that the carving knife was missing. She asked the man to go through the folding-doors into the adjoining bedchamber.

He opened the doors, entered a step or two, and came back almost instantly, with a rigid face. "My good God, the gentleman in bed is dead! I think he has been hurt with a knife—a lot of blood has run down upon the floor!"

The alarm was soon given, and the house which had lately been so quiet resounded with the tramp of many footsteps, a surgeon among the rest. The wound was small, but the point of the blade had touched the heart of the victim, who lay on his back, pale, fixed, dead, as if he had scarcely moved after the infliction of the blow. In a quarter of an hour the news that a gentleman who was a temporary visitor to the town had been stabbed in his bed, spread through every street and villa of the popular watering-place.

LVII

MEANWHILE Angel Clare had walked automatically along the way by which he had come, and entering his hotel sat down over the breakfast, staring at nothingness. He went on eating and drinking unconsciously till on a sudden he demanded his bill; having paid which he took his dressing-bag in his hand—the only luggage he had brought with him—and went out. At the moment of his departure a telegram was handed to him; a few words from his mother, stating that they were glad to know his address, and informing him that his brother Cuthbert had proposed to and been accepted by Mercy Chant.

Clare crumpled up the paper and followed the route to the station; reaching it, he found that there would be no train leaving for an hour and more. He sat down to wait, and having waited a quarter of an hour felt that he could wait there no longer. Broken in heart and numbed, he had nothing to hurry for, but he wished to get out of a town which had been the scene of such an experience, and turned to walk to the first station onward, and let the train pick him up there.

The highway that he followed was open, and at a little distance dipped into a valley, across which it could be seen running from edge to edge. He had traversed the greater part of this depression, and was climbing the western acclivity when, pausing for breath, he unconsciously looked back. Why he did so he could not say, but something seemed to impel him to the act. The tape-like surface of the road diminished in his rear as far as he could see, and as he gazed a moving spot intruded on the white vacuity of its perspective.

It was a human figure, running. Clare waited, with a dim sense that somebody was trying to overtake him.

The form descending the incline was a woman's, yet so entirely was his mind blinded to the idea of his wife's following him that even when she came nearer he did not recognize her under the totally changed attire in which he now beheld her. It was not till she was quite close that he could believe her to be Tess.

"I saw you—turn away from the station—just before I got there—and I have been following you all this way!"

She was so pale, so breathless, so quivering in every muscle, that he did not ask her a single question, but seizing her hand and pulling it within his arm he led her along. To avoid meeting any possible wayfarers he left the high-road, and took a footpath under some fir-trees. When they were deep among the moaning boughs he stopped, and looked at her inquiringly.

"Angel," she said, as if waiting for this; "do you know what I have been running after you for? To tell you that I have killed him!" A pitiful white smile lit her face as she spoke.

"What!" said he, thinking from the strangeness of her manner that she was in some delirium.

"I have done it—I don't know how," she continued. "Still, I owed it to you, and to myself, Angel. I feared long ago, when I struck him on the mouth with my glove, that I might do it some day for the trap he set for me in my simple youth, and his wrong to you through me. He has come between us and ruined us, and now he can never do it any more. I never loved him at all, Angel, as I loved you. You know it, don't you? You believe it? You didn't come back to me, and I was obliged to go back to him. Why did you go away—*why* did you— when I loved you so? I can't think why you did it. But I don't blame you; only, Angel, will you forgive me my sin against you, now I have killed him? I thought as I ran along that you would be sure to forgive me now I have done that. It came to me as a shining light that I should get you back that way. I could not bear the loss of you any longer—you don't know how entirely I was unable to bear your not loving me. Say you do now, dear dear husband: say you do, now I have killed him!"

"I do love you Tess—O I do—it is all come back!" he said tighten- ing his arms round her with fervid pressure. "But how do you mean—you have killed him?"

"I mean that I have," she murmured in a reverie.

"What—bodily? Is he dead?"

"Yes. He heard me crying about you, and he bitterly taunted me; and called you by a foul name; and then I did it: my heart could not bear it: he had nagged me about you before—and then I dressed myself, and came away to find you."

By degrees he was inclined to believe that she had faintly attempted, at least, what she said she had done, and his horror at her impulse was mixed with amazement at the strength of her affection for himself; and at the strangeness of its quality, which had apparently extinguished her moral sense altogether. Unable to realize the gravity of her conduct she seemed at last content; and he looked at her as she lay upon his shoulder, weeping with happiness; and wondered what obscure strain in the d'Urberville blood had led to this aberration, if it were an aberration. There momentarily flashed through his mind that the family tradition of the coach and murder might have arisen because the d'Urbervilles had been known to do these things. As well as his confused and excited ideas could reason, he supposed that in the moment of mad grief of which she spoke her mind had lost its balance, and plunged her into this abyss.

It was very terrible, if true: if a temporary hallucination, sad. But anyhow here was this deserted wife of his, this passionately fond woman, clinging to him without a suspicion that he would be anything to her but a protector. He saw that for him to be otherwise was not, in her mind, within the region of the possible. Tenderness was absolutely dominant in Clare at last. He kissed her endlessly with his white lips, and held her hand, and said, "I will not desert you; I will protect you by every means in my power, dearest love, whatever you may have done or not have done!"

They then walked on under the trees, Tess turning her head every now and then to look at him. Worn and unhandsome as he had become it was plain that she did not discern the least fault in his appearance. To her he was, as of old, all that was perfection, personally and mentally. He was still her Antinous, her Apollo even;* his sickly face was beautiful as the morning to her affectionate regard on this day no less than when she first beheld him; for was it not the face of the one man on earth who had loved her purely, and who had believed in her as pure?

With an instinct as to possibilities he did not now, as he had intended, make for the first station beyond the town, but plunged still further under the firs, which here abounded for miles. Each clasping the other round the waist they promenaded over the dry bed of fir-needles, thrown into a vague intoxicating atmosphere at the consciousness of being together at last, with no living soul between them; ignoring that there was a corpse. Thus they proceeded for several miles till Tess, arousing herself, looked about her and said timidly: "Are we going anywhere in particular?"

"I don't know, dearest. Why?"

"I don't know."

"Well—we might walk a few miles further, and when it is evening find lodgings somewhere or other—in a lonely cottage perhaps. Can you walk well, Tessy?"

"O yes! I could walk for ever and ever with your arm round me."

Upon the whole it seemed a good thing to do. Thereupon they quickened their pace, avoiding high-roads, and following obscure paths tending more or less northward. But there was an unpractical vagueness in their movements throughout the day: neither one of them seemed to consider any question of effectual escape, disguise, or long concealment. Their every idea was temporary and unforefending, like the plans of two children.

At mid-day they drew near to a roadside inn, and Tess would have entered it with him to get something to eat; but he persuaded her to remain among the trees and bushes of this half woodland, half moorland part of the country, till he should come back. Her clothes were of recent fashion; even the ivory-handled parasol that she carried was of a shape unknown in the retired spot to which they had now wandered; and the cut of such articles would have attracted attention in the settle of a tavern. He soon returned, with food enough for half-a-dozen people and two bottles of wine— enough to last them for a day or more, should any emergency arise.

They sat down upon some dead boughs and shared their meal. Between one and two o'clock they packed up the remainder and went on again.

"I feel strong enough to walk any distance," said she.

"I think we may as well steer in a general way towards the interior of the country, where we can hide for a time, and are less likely to be looked for than anywhere near the coast," Clare remarked. "Later on, when they have forgotten us, we can make for some port."

She made no reply to this, beyond that of grasping him more tightly, and straight inland they went. Though the season was an English May, the weather was serenely bright, and during the afternoon it was quite warm. Through the latter miles of their walk their footpath had taken them into the depths of the New Forest, and, towards evening, turning the corner of a lane, they perceived behind a brook and bridge a large board on which was painted in white letters, "This desirable Mansion to be Let Furnished"; particulars following, with directions to apply to some London agents. Passing through the gate they could see the house—an old brick building, of regular design, and large accommodation.

"I know it," said Clare. "It is Bramshurst Court. You can see that it is shut up: and grass is growing on the drive."

"Some of the windows are open," said Tess.

"Just to air the rooms I suppose."

"All those rooms empty, and we without a roof to our heads!"

"You are getting tired, my Tess!" he said. "We'll stop soon." And kissing her sad mouth he again led her onwards.

He was growing weary likewise, for they had wandered a dozen or fifteen miles, and it became necessary to consider what they should do for rest. They looked from afar at isolated cottages, and little inns, and were inclined to approach one of the latter, when their hearts failed them, and they sheered off. At length their gait dragged, and they stood still.

"Could we sleep under the trees?" she asked.

He thought the season insufficiently advanced. "I have been thinking of that empty mansion we passed," he said. "Let us go back towards it again."

They retraced their steps, but it was half-an-hour before they stood without the entrance-gate as earlier. He then requested her to stay where she was whilst he went to see who was within.

She sat down among the bushes within the gate, and Clare crept towards the house. His absence lasted some considerable time, and when he returned Tess was wildly anxious, not for herself, but for him. He had found out from a boy that there was only an old woman in charge as caretaker, and she only came there on fine days from the hamlet near to open and shut the windows. She would come to shut them at sunset. "Now, we can get in through one of the lower windows, and rest there," said he.

Under his escort she went hardily forward to the main front, whose shuttered windows, like sightless eyeballs, excluded the possibility of watchers. The door was reached a few steps further, and one of the windows beside it was open. Clare clambered in, and pulled Tess in after him.

Except the hall the rooms were all in darkness, and they ascended the staircase. Up here also the shutters were tightly closed, the ventilation being perfunctorily done, for this day, at least, by opening the hall window in front, and an upper window behind. Clare unlatched the door of a large chamber, felt his way across it, and parted the shutters to the width of two or three inches. A shaft of dazzling sunlight glanced into the room, revealing heavy, old-fashioned furniture, crimson damask hangings, and an enormous four-post bedstead, along the head of which were carved running figures, apparently Atalanta's race.*

"Rest at last!" said he, setting down his bag and the parcel of viands.

They remained in great quietness till the caretaker should have come to shut the windows, as a precaution putting themselves in total darkness by barring the shutters as before, lest the woman should open the door of their chamber for any casual reason. Between six and seven o'clock she came, but did not approach the wing they were in. They heard her close the windows, fasten them, lock the door, and go away. Then Clare again stole a chink of light from the window: and they shared another meal, till by and by they were enveloped in the shades of night, which they had no candle to disperse.

LVIII

THE night was strangely solemn and still. In the small hours she whispered to him the whole story of how he had walked in his sleep with her in his arms across the Froom stream, at the imminent risk of both their lives, and laid her down in the stone coffin at the ruined abbey. He had never known of that till now.

"Why didn't you tell me next day!" he said. "It might have prevented much misunderstanding and woe."

"Don't think of what's past!" said she. "I am not going to think outside of now. Why should we? Who knows what to-morrow has in store?"

But it apparently had no sorrow. The morning was wet and foggy, and Clare, rightly informed that the caretaker only opened the windows on fine days, ventured to creep out of their chamber and explore the house, leaving Tess asleep. There was no food on the premises, but there was water; and he took advantage of the fog to emerge from the mansion and fetch tea, bread, and butter, from a shop in a little place two miles beyond, as also a small tin kettle and spirit-lamp, that they might get fire without smoke. His re-entry awoke her; and they breakfasted on what he had brought.

They were indisposed to stir abroad, and the day passed; and the night following; and the next, and the next; till, almost without their being aware, five days had slipped by; in absolute seclusion, not a sight or sound of a human being disturbing their peacefulness—such as it was. The changes of the weather were their only events, the birds of the New Forest their only company. By tacit consent they hardly once spoke of any incident of the past subsequent to their wedding-day. The gloomy intervening time seemed to sink into chaos, over which the present and prior times closed as if it never had been. Whenever he suggested that they should leave their shelter and go forwards towards Southampton or London she showed a strange unwillingness to move. "Why should we put an end to all that's sweet and lovely!" she deprecated. "What must come will come." And, looking through the shutter-chink: "All is trouble outside there: inside here content."

He peeped out also. It was quite true: within was affection, union, error forgiven: outside was the inexorable.

"And—and," she said, pressing her cheek against his; "I fear that what you think of me now may not last—I do not wish to outlive your present feeling for me. I would rather not. I would rather be dead and buried when the time comes for you to despise me, so that it may never be known to me that you despised me."

"I cannot ever despise you!"

"I also hope that. But considering what my life has been I cannot see why any man should, sooner or later, be able to help despising me. . . . How wickedly mad I was! Yet formerly I never could bear to hurt a fly or worm, and the sight of a bird in a cage used often to make me cry."

They remained yet another day. In the night the dull sky cleared; and the result was that the old caretaker at the cottage awoke early. The brilliant sunrise made her unusually brisk; she decided to open the contiguous mansion immediately, and to air it thoroughly on such a day. Thus it occurred that having arrived and opened the lower rooms before six o'clock, she ascended to the bedchambers, and was about to turn the handle of the one wherein they lay.

At that moment she fancied she could hear the breathing of persons within. Her slippers and her antiquity had rendered her progress a noiseless one so far, and she made for instant retreat: then, deeming that her hearing might have deceived her she turned anew to the door and softly tried the handle. The lock was out of order, but a piece of furniture had been moved forward on the inside, which prevented her opening the door more than an inch or two. A stream of morning light through the shutter-chink fell upon the faces of the pair wrapped in profound slumber, Tess's lips being parted like a half-opened flower near his cheek.

The caretaker was so struck with their innocent appearance and with the elegance of Tess's gown hanging across a chair, her silk stockings beside it, the pretty parasol, and the other habits in which she had arrived because she had none else, that her first indignation at the effrontery of tramps and vagabonds gave way to momentary sentimentality over this genteel elopement, as it seemed. She closed the door and withdrew as softly as she had come, to go and consult with her neighbours on the odd discovery.

Not more than a minute had elapsed after her withdrawal when

Tess woke, and then Clare. Both had a sense that something had disturbed them, though they could not say what: and the uneasy feeling which it engendered grew stronger. As soon as he was dressed he narrowly scanned the lawn through the two or three inches of shutter-chink.

"I think we will leave at once," said he. "It is a fine day. And I cannot help fancying somebody is about the house. At any rate the woman will be sure to come to-day."

She passively assented, arose, clothed herself, and putting the room in order they took up the few articles that belonged to them and departed noiselessly. When they had got into the forest she turned to take a last look at the house. "Ah, happy house—good-bye!" she said. "My life can only be a question of a few weeks; why should we not have stayed there?"

"Don't say it Tess! We shall soon get out of this district altogether. We'll continue our course as we've begun it, and keep straight north. Nobody will think of looking for us there. We shall be looked for at the Wessex ports if we are sought at all. When we are in the north we will get to a port and away."

Having thus persuaded her the plan was pursued, and they kept a bee line northward. Their long repose at the manor-house lent them walking power now; and towards mid-day they found that they were approaching the steepled city of Melchester, which lay directly in their way. He decided to rest her in a clump of trees during the afternoon, and push onward under cover of darkness. At dusk Clare purchased food as usual, and their night march began, the boundary between Upper and Mid-Wessex being crossed about eight o'clock.

To walk across country without much regard to roads was not new to Tess, and she showed her old agility in the performance. The intercepting city, ancient Melchester, they were obliged to pass through in order to take advantage of the town bridge for crossing a large river that obstructed them. It was about midnight when they went along the deserted streets, lighted fitfully by the few lamps, keeping off the pavement that it might not echo their footsteps. The graceful pile of cathedral architecture rose dimly on their left hand, but it was lost upon them now. Once out of the town they followed the turnpike-road which after a few miles plunged across an open plain.

Though the sky was dense with cloud a diffused light from some fragment of a moon had hitherto helped them a little. But the moon had now sunk, the clouds seemed to settle almost on their heads, and the night grew as dark as a cave. However, they found their way along, keeping as much on the turf as possible that their tread might not resound, which it was easy to do, there being no hedge or fence of any kind. All around was open loneliness and black solitude, over which a stiff breeze blew.

They had proceeded thus gropingly two or three miles further when on a sudden, Clare became conscious of some vast erection close in his front, rising sheer from the grass. They had almost struck themselves against it.

"What monstrous place is this?" said Angel.

"It hums," said she. "Hearken!"

He listened. The wind, playing upon the edifice, produced a booming tune, like the note of some gigantic one-stringed harp. No other sound came from it, and lifting his hand and advancing a step or two Clare felt the vertical surface of the structure. It seemed to be of solid stone, without joint or moulding. Carrying his fingers onward he found that what he had come in contact with was a colossal rectangular pillar; by stretching out his left hand he could feel a similar one adjoining. At an indefinite height overhead something made the black sky blacker, which had the semblance of a vast architrave uniting the pillars horizontally. They carefully entered beneath and between; the surfaces echoed their soft rustle; but they seemed to be still out-of-doors. The place was roofless. Tess drew her breath fearfully, and Angel, perplexed, said "What can it be?"

Feeling sideways they encountered another tower-like pillar, square and uncompromising as the first; beyond it another, and another. The place was all doors and pillars, some connected above by continuous architraves.

"A very Temple of the Winds,"* he said.

The next pillar was isolated, others composed a trilithon; others were prostrate, their flanks forming a causeway wide enough for a carriage; and it was soon obvious that they made up a forest of monoliths, grouped upon the grassy expanse of the plain. The couple advanced further into this pavilion of the night, till they stood in its midst.

"It is Stonehenge!" said Clare.

"The heathen temple, you mean?"

"Yes. Older than the centuries; older than the d'Urbervilles! . . . Well, what shall we do, darling? We may find shelter further on."

But Tess, really tired by this time, flung herself upon an oblong slab that lay close at hand, and was sheltered from the wind by a pillar. Owing to the action of the sun during the preceding day, the stone was warm and dry, in comforting contrast to the rough and chill grass around, which had damped her skirts and shoes. "I don't want to go any further, Angel," she said stretching out her hand for his. "Can't we bide here?"

"I fear not. This spot is visible for miles by day, although it does not seem so now."

"One of my mother's people was a shepherd hereabout, now I think of it. And you used to say at Talbothays that I was a heathen. So now I am at home."

He knelt down beside her outstretched form, and put his lips upon hers. "Sleepy, are you dear? I think you are lying on an altar."

"I like very much to be here," she murmured. "It is so solemn and lonely—after my great happiness—with nothing but the sky above my face. It seems as if there were no folk in the world but we two. And I wish there were not—except Liza-Lu."

Clare thought she might as well rest here till it should get a little lighter, and he flung his overcoat upon her, and sat down by her side.

"Angel, if anything happens to me, will you watch over Liza-Lu for my sake?" she asked, when they had listened a long time to the wind among the pillars.

"I will."

"She is so good, and simple, and pure. . . . O Angel—I wish you would marry her, if you lose me, as you will do shortly. O if you would!"

"If I lose you I lose all. . . . And she is my sister-in-law."*

"That's nothing, dearest. People marry sister-laws continually about Marlott. And Liza-Lu is so gentle and sweet, and she is growing so beautiful. O I could share you with her willingly when we are spirits! If you would train her and teach her, Angel, and bring her up for your own self! . . . She has all the best of me without the bad of me; and if she were to become yours it would almost seem as if death had not divided us. . . . Well—I have said it. I won't mention it again."

She ceased, and he fell into thought. In the far north-east sky, he could see between the pillars a level streak of light. The uniform concavity of black cloud was lifting bodily like the lid of a pot, letting in at the earth's edge the coming day, against which the towering monoliths and trilithons began to be blackly defined.

"Did they sacrifice to God here?" asked she.

"No," said he.

"Who to?"

"I believe to the sun. That lofty stone set away by itself is in the direction of the sun, which will presently rise behind it."

"This reminds me, dear," she said. "You remember you never would interfere with any belief of mine before we were married? But I knew your mind all the same, and I thought as you thought—not from any reasons of my own, but because you thought so. Tell me now, Angel; do you think we shall meet again after we are dead? I want to know."

He kissed her, to avoid a reply at such a time.

"O Angel—I fear that means no!" said she with a suppressed sob. "And I wanted so to see you again—so much, so much! What—not even you and I Angel, who love each other so well?"

Like a greater than himself, to the critical question at the critical time he did not answer;* and they were again silent. In a minute or two her breathing became more regular, her clasp of his hand relaxed, and she fell asleep. The band of silver paleness along the east horizon made even the distant parts of the Great Plain appear dark and near; and the whole enormous landscape bore that impress of reserve, taciturnity, and hesitation which is usual just before day. The eastward pillars and their architraves stood up blackly against the light, and the great flame-shaped Sun-stone beyond them, and the stone of sacrifice midway. Presently the night wind died out, and the quivering little pools in the cup-like hollows of the stones lay still. At the same time something seemed to move on the verge of the dip eastward—a mere dot. It was the head of a man, approaching them from the hollow beyond the Sun-stone. Clare wished they had gone onward, but in the circumstances decided to remain quiet. The figure came straight towards the circle of pillars in which they were.

He heard something behind him, the brush of feet. Turning, he saw over the prostrate columns another figure; then, before he was aware, another was at hand on the right, under a trilithon, and another on the left. The dawn shone full on the front of the man westward, and Clare could discern from this that he was tall, and walked as if trained. They all closed in, with evident purpose. Her story, then, was true! Springing to his feet he looked around for a weapon, loose stone, means of escape, anything. By this time the nearest man was upon him.

"It is no use, sir," he said. "There are sixteen of us on the Plain; and the whole country is reared."

"Let her finish her sleep!" he implored in a whisper of the men, as they gathered round.

When they saw where she lay, which they had not done till then, they showed no objection; and stood watching her, as still as the pillars around. He went to the stone, and bent over her, holding one poor little hand; her breathing now was quick and small, like that of a lesser creature than a woman. All waited in the growing light, their faces and hands as if they were silvered, the remainder of their figures dark, the stones glistening green-grey, the Plain still a mass of shade. Soon the light was strong, and a ray shone upon her unconscious form, peering under her eyelids and waking her.

"What is it, Angel?" she said starting up. "Have they come for me?"

"Yes, dearest," he said. "They have come."

"It is as it should be!" she murmured. "Angel—I am almost glad—yes, glad! This happiness could not have lasted—it was too much—I have had enough; and now I shall not live for you to despise me."

She stood up, shook herself, and went forward, neither of the men having moved. "I am ready," she said quietly.

LIX

THE city of Wintoncester—that fine old city, aforetime capital of Wessex—lay amidst its convex and concave downlands in all the brightness and warmth of a July morning. The gabled brick, tile, and freestone houses had almost dried off for the season their integument of lichen, the streams in the meadows were low, and in the sloping High-street, from the West Gateway to the mediæval cross, and from the mediæval cross to the bridge, that leisurely dusting and sweeping was in progress which usually ushers in an old-fashioned market-day.

From the western gate aforesaid the highway, as every Wintoncestrian knows, ascends a long and regular incline of the exact length of a measured mile, leaving the houses gradually behind. Up this road from the precincts of the city two persons were walking rapidly, as if unconscious of the trying ascent—unconscious through preoccupation, and not through buoyancy. They had emerged upon this road through a narrow barred wicket in a high wall a little lower down. They seemed anxious to get out of the sight of the houses and of their kind, and this road appeared to offer the quickest means of doing so. Though they were young they walked with bowed heads, which gait of grief the sun's rays smiled on pitilessly.

One of the pair was Angel Clare, the other a tall budding creature, half girl, half woman—a spiritualized image of Tess, slighter than she, but with the same beautiful eyes—Clare's sister-in-law Liza-Lu. Their pale faces seemed to have shrunk to half their natural size; they moved on hand in hand, and never spoke a word, the drooping of their heads being that of Giotto's Two Apostles.*

When they had nearly reached the top of the great West Hill the clocks in the town struck eight. Each gave a start at the notes, and walking onward yet a few steps they reached the first milestone, standing whitely on the green margin of the grass, and backed by the down which here was open to the road. They entered upon the turf, and impelled by a force that seemed to overrule their will suddenly stood still, turned, and waited in paralyzed suspense beside the stone.

The prospect from this summit was almost unlimited. In the

valley beneath lay the city they had just left, its more prominent buildings showing as in an isometric drawing—among them the broad Cathedral tower, with its Norman windows, and immense length of aisle and nave, the spire of St Thomas's, the pinnacled tower of the College, and, more to the right, the tower and gables of the ancient hospice where to this day the pilgrim may receive his dole of bread and ale. Behind the city swept the rotund upland of St Catherine's Hill, further off, landscape beyond landscape, till the horizon was lost in the radiance of the sun hanging above it.

Against these far stretches of country rose, in front of the other city edifices, a large red-brick building, with level grey roofs, and rows of short barred windows bespeaking captivity—the whole contrasting greatly by its formalism with the quaint irregularities of the Gothic erections. It was somewhat disguised from the road in passing it by yews and evergreen oaks, but it was visible enough up here. The wicket from which the pair had lately emerged was in the wall of this structure. From the middle of the building an ugly flat-topped octagonal tower ascended against the east horizon, and viewed from this spot, on its shady side and against the light, it seemed the one blot on the city's beauty. Yet it was with this blot, and not with the beauty, that the two gazers were concerned.

Upon the cornice of the tower a tall staff was fixed. Their eyes were rivetted on it. A few minutes after the hour had struck something moved slowly up the staff, and extended itself upon the breeze. It was a black flag.

"Justice" was done, and the President of the Immortals (in Æschylean phrase) had ended his sport with Tess.* And the d'Urberville knights and dames slept on in their tombs unknowing. The two speechless gazers bent themselves down to the earth, as if in prayer, and remained thus a long time, absolutely motionless: the flag continued to wave silently. As soon as they had strength they arose, joined hands again, and went on.

THE END

EXPLANATORY NOTES

by Nancy Barrineau

These notes do not, unlike those in other volumes of the Oxford World's Classics Hardy series, include any of Hardy's revisions; if all those changes that are of interest were annotated here the list would become too bulky to be conveniently usable. This decision was made easier in that the interested reader can for summaries of the main patterns of revision consult J. T. Laird's *The Shaping of 'Tess of the d'Urbervilles'* (Oxford: Clarendon Press, 1975), or the introduction to the Clarendon edition of the novel edited by Juliet Grindle and Simon Gatrell. The Clarendon edition lists in its apparatus all the changes that Hardy made to the novel from the manuscript to his last alterations to his study copy of the second collected edition.

Abbreviations

Björk	*The Literary Notebooks of Thomas Hardy*, ed. Lennart Björk, 2 vols. (London and Basingstoke: Macmillan, 1995)
Bullen	J. B. Bullen, *The Expressive Eye: Fiction and Perception in the Work of Thomas Hardy* (Oxford: Clarendon Press, 1986)
'The Dorset-shire Labourer'	Thomas Hardy, 'The Dorsetshire Labourer', *Longman's Magazine*, 2 (July 1883), 252–69
Early Life	Florence Dugdale Hardy, *The Early Life of Thomas Hardy, 1840–1891* (1928; repr. with *The Later Years of Thomas Hardy* as *The Life of Thomas Hardy* (London: Macmillan, 1964)
Firor	Ruth Firor, *Folkways in Thomas Hardy* (New York: Russell & Russell, 1931)
Furbank	*Tess of the d'Urbervilles*, New Wessex Edition, ed. P. N. Furbank (London: Macmillan, 1974)
Millgate, *Life*	Michael Millgate, *The Life and Work of Thomas Hardy* (London: Macmillan, 1984)
Millgate, *TH*	Michael Millgate, *Thomas Hardy: A Biography* (London: Oxford University Press, 1982)
OED	*Oxford English Dictionary*
Springer	Marlene Springer, *Hardy's Use of Allusion* (London: Macmillan, 1983)
Weber	*Tess of the d'Urbervilles*, ed. Carl J. Weber (New York and London: Harper & Brothers Publishers, 1935)

1 *W. SHAKESPEARE*: from *Two Gentlemen of Verona*, I. ii. 115–16.

5 *Heptarchy*: the Heptarchy was the division of England by the Angles and

Saxons into seven kingdoms: Kent, Essex, Sussex, Wessex, East Anglia, Mercia, and Northumbria.

5 *As flies to wanton boys . . . kill us for their sport*: Gloucester says these lines in *King Lear*, IV. i. 36–7. Hardy here suggests a continuous thread of kinship between Shakespeare's view of the relationship between man and deity and his own.

6 *"Hammers of Heretics"*: according to Furbank (note to 29), 'This sobriquet was applied to, among others, Torquemada'. Tomás de Torquemada (1420–98), the first grand inquisitor of Spain, tortured and finally expelled from Spain all Jews who refused to be baptized. His name became synonymous with the Spanish Inquisition. Hardy refers to him in 'Science versus Man', a review of Ernst Haeckel's *The Riddle of the Universe at the Close of the Nineteenth Century*, published in *Dorset Chronicle*, 1 October 1900 (Björk, ii. 2069).

galls somebody's kibe: Hamlet says to Horatio: 'the age is grown so pick'd that the toe of the peasant comes so near the heel of the courtier, he galls his kibe' (V. i. 139–41). That is, the peasant forms a blister on the courtier's heel. The implication is that Hardy is the peasant galling the kibe of the reviewer or courtier.

8 *Melius fuerat non scribere*: (Latin) 'It would have been better not to write it.'

13 *haggler*: an itinerant dealer of goods.

14 *the Pipe Rolls in the time of King Stephen*: the Pipe Roll was the Great Roll of the Exchequer, the written accounts of the department charged with the receipt of government revenues.

King Stephen . . . Charles the Second's reign: Stephen ruled England from 1135–54; John 1199–1216; Edward II 1307–27; and Charles II 1660–85. Oliver Cromwell was Lord Protector during the Puritan Commonwealth, 1653–8. The Knights Hospitallers, founded in the twelfth century, were an order of religious knights of royal birth, also called the Knights of St John of Jerusalem, sworn to protect pilgrims and Crusaders in Jerusalem.

15 *'how are the mighty fallen'*: this line appears twice in David's lament over Saul and Jonathan after their deaths, which in essence ended the ascendency of Saul's line and began David's rule over Israel (2 Sam. 1: 19, 27). Parson Tringham applies the same sentiment to the d'Urberville family.

17 *women's club-walking*: a parish club was a society formed to raise money for the benefit of its members in case of sickness or death. During Whitsun week (see note to p. 22), club members dressed up and had processions in which they carried banners and went from house to house soliciting refreshments and contributions.

19 *Forest of White Hart . . . a heavy fine*: according to the legend, Henry III, while hunting in the Vale of Blackmore, spared a beautiful white hart

only for it to be killed by some neighbourhood gentlemen. The king not only imprisoned and fined the offenders but also established a tax on the land, thereafter known as White Hart Silver (John Symonds Udal, *Dorsetshire Folk-Lore* (St Peter Port: Toucan Press, 1970), 152–4).

Cerealia: a festival of worship to Ceres, the Roman goddess of the growth of food plants.

Old-Style days: Pope Gregory XIII replaced Old Style dating (the Julian Calendar) with New Style (Gregorian) dating in 1582. This new system was adopted in Great Britain and the colonies in 1752, so 'Old-Style days' were prior to the mid-eighteenth century.

21 *market-nitch*: market-nitch is the quantity of alcohol one can drink after market. A nitch is the amount of something one can carry.

22 *uncribbed, uncabined*: after Banquo's murder, Macbeth says, 'now I am cabined, cribbed, confined, bound in | To saucy doubts and fears' (III. iv. 24–5). *Cribbed* means confined. Hardy changes the quotation to suggest Angel's intellectual freedom.

Whitsun: Whit Sunday, or Pentecost, is the seventh Sunday after Easter in the Christian calendar. Parish festivals were traditionally held during this holiday.

A Counterblast to Agnosticism: the manuscript reads 'Answers to *Essays and Reviews*', which, as Furbank points out, is 'a title close to that of the actual *Replies to "Essays and Reviews"* (1862), a counterblast to the controversial manifesto of liberal theology *Essays and Reviews* published in 1860' (Furbank, note to 41).

25 *"the soft torments . . . the agreeable distresses"*: not identified.

"The Spotted Cow": in this English folk song, a man meets a maid who has lost her spotted cow. Mrs Durbeyfield is singing the stanza in which the teller of the story claims that he has seen the cow:

> No more complain, no longer mourn,
> Your cow's not lost, my dear!
> For I saw her down in yonder lane,
> Come, love, and I'll show you where!

He has not, in fact, found the cow, but the two become lovers in the grove; and the maid continues on other occasions to summon her 'gentle swain' with the words ' "I've lost my spotted cow." ' Hardy also alludes to the song in *The Woodlanders*, chap. XLVIII.

diment: (dialect) diamond.

Cubit's: (dialect) Cupid's.

27 *National school*: the National Society for Promoting the Education of the Poor in the Principles of the Established Church in England and Wales first founded schools in 1811. The first National school in Dorset followed in 1812.

28 *Compleat Fortune-Teller*: Firor relates this book to *Universal Fortune-*

Teller, a witchcraft book 'still very popular in England within the past century' (Firor, 99).

31 *off-licence*: a licence allowed an establishment to sell and serve alcohol on the premises. Rolliver's has an inferior kind of licence, an off-licence, so drinking there is illegal.

pattern of Polynesia: a pattern resembling a cluster of islands. (A line in *Cornhill Magazine* in July 1889, for example, reads, 'On the floor a polynesia of spittoons in a sea of sawdust' (*OED*).)

it was better . . . in a wide house: see Proverbs 21: 9 (and 25: 24): 'It is better to dwell in a corner of the housetop, than with a brawling woman in a wide house.'

the magnificent pillars of Solomon's temple: a feature of King Solomon's temple was four rows of pillars made of cedar from the forest of Lebanon (1 Kgs. 7: 2).

33 *But Joan Durbeyfield . . . floor*: 'To have "green malt in floor" means to have a daughter in childbed before she is married—green malt meaning immature malt, and a floor of malt meaning the outspread malt for steeping . . . there is hardly anyone in Dorset who would know the meaning of the saying, it having quite passed out of use' (letter of 24 Feb. 1926 from Hardy to Macmillans, in response to a reader's query; Macmillan Archive, British Library). See note in Clarendon edition.

37 *apples on our stubbard-tree*: a stubbard is 'an early codling apple', which is 'a variety of apple, in shape elongated and rather tapering towards the eye' (*OED*).

39 *cob*: 'a short-legged, stout variety of horse, usually ridden by heavy persons' (*OED*).

43 *Malthusian*: Thomas Robert Malthus (1766–1834) theorized in *An Essay on the Principle of Population* (1798) that population always increases faster than the food supply and that naturally occurring disasters like famine, disease, and war will eventually control this imbalance when it becomes great enough.

44 *chapels-of-ease*: these were built in the outlying districts of large parishes for the 'ease' of the inhabitants, and were supplied by the rector of the nearest large town.

61 *holmberry lips*: a holm tree is a holly tree; hence, her lips are red like holly berries.

64 *copyholders*: a copyholder is one who holds the land at the will of the lord of the manor, who gives him a 'copy of the manorial court-roll' (*OED*).

65 *Hamburghs . . . Dorkings*: Hamburghs and Cochins, the largest of these chickens, are both breeds belonging to the Asian group (the oldest in existence). They have thick feathers and coarse meat and are poor egg producers, but they are hardy breeds suited to cold climates. Dorkings, the next smaller breed, are English, developed in Dorking, Surrey.

Brahmas are an even smaller Mediterranean breed weighing only around five pounds. Bantams are a miniature of any breed.

67 *sitting like Im-patience on a monument*: in *Twelfth Night* (II. iv. 110–15), Viola (disguised as Cesario) describes her own love for the duke:

> She never told her love,
> But let concealment, like a worm i' the bud,
> Feed on her damask cheek. She pined in thought,
> And with a green and yellow melancholy
> She sat like Patience on a monument,
> Smiling at grief.

"Like Patience on a monument" means like a statue of Patience.

"Take O take those lips away": in *Measure for Measure* (IV. i. 1–6), Mariana and the Boy sing:

> Take, O, take those lips away
> That so sweetly were forsworn;
> And those eyes, the break of day,
> Lights that do mislead the morn.
> But my kisses bring again, bring again,
> Seals of love, but seal'd in vain, seal'd in vain

Since Tess does not recognize the tune, she does not know that Alec is flirting with her.

72 *satyrs . . . Sileni*: in Greek mythology, satyrs, lecherous human-like creatures with the legs and tails of goats, pursue nymphs, female fertility divinities usually associated with water and vegetation. Pan is the lustful Greek fertility god, a bestial creature with the horns, legs, and ears of a goat. He pursued Syrinx, but she escaped by turning into a reed out of which Pan made his famous pipe. Lotis similarly turned into a lotus flower to escape from Priapus, the lecherous god of animal and vegetable fertility who is often associated with an ass. Sileni is the plural form of Silenus, another name for a satyr.

76 *some Praxitelean creation*: Praxiteles was a fourth-century BC Greek sculptor whose work was characterized by sensuality and passion. One of his innovations was to sculpt naked gods.

82 *Perhaps, like that other god . . . not to be awaked*: Elijah, 'the ironical Tishbite', mocks the priests of Baal with these words during a contest to see whose gods can spontaneously ignite a sacrifice (1 Kgs. 18: 27). Hardy suggests that 'perhaps' the conventional Providence in which Tess believes is equal in power to these pagan gods.

sins of the fathers: see Exodus 20: 5: 'I the Lord thy God am a jealous God, visiting the iniquity of the fathers upon the children unto the third and fourth generation of them that hate me.' The narrator insists that even 'average' humans would not stoop to applying this kind of logic to Tess's case.

90 *term*: an archaic word for 'a statue or bust like those of the god Terminus,

representing the upper part of the body, sometimes without the arms, and terminating below in a pillar or pedestal out of which it appears to spring' (*OED*; cites *Tess* as an example).

93 *dripping pan*: used to catch the drippings, or melted fat, from a piece of roasting meat. Drippings are left in the pan to harden into lard and thus clog the pan.

96 *Robert South*: an English divine (1634–1716). The quotation has not been located.

   the old double chant "Langdon": Richard Langdon (1730–1803) was an English organist known for the collection *Divine Harmony* (1774). The hymn tune 'Langdon' is a setting of Psalm 102. A double chant is twice the length of an ordinary one.

99 *heliolatries*: religions that worshipped the sun.

   Maltese cross: a cross with eight points, the ends of which are indented. Furbank notes that the reaping-machine described is 'of the self-raking type, as manufactured by Woods, Hornsby or Samuelson, which replaced a more primitive type in 1862 or thereabouts, and was itself replaced by the reaper-binder after 1890' (Furbank, note to 115).

102 *quadrille*: a French square dance in which four couples perform five complete figures, or a set.

104 *gold-leaf halo of some worm-eaten Tuscan saint*: Tuscany, especially the city of Florence, was pre-eminent in the arts from the fourteenth to the sixteenth century in Italy. Gold-leaf is a very thin sheet of gold.

105 *Aholah and Aholibah*: Ezekiel 23 relates a parable about two sisters condemned as whores. Aholah represents Samaria, Aholibah Jerusalem. The story ends with the prophet's prediction of their deaths by stoning, the slaying of their children, and the burning of their homes. Tess questions the justice of punishing a child for its mother's actions.

107 *a name . . . in the book of Genesis*: Tess is remembering the passage in which God tells Adam and Eve what the results of their sin will be: 'Unto the woman he said, I will greatly multiply thy sorrow and thy conception; in sorrow thou shalt bring forth children' (Gen. 3: 16).

   stopt-diapason note: an organ note which sounds airy, like a flute.

   which will never . . . who knew her: the novel's narrative voice lapses here, and it seems as though Hardy has forgotten that Tess is his own fictional creation, not a real person.

108 *sin, the world, and the devil*: in the Litany in the Book of Common Prayer, one of the lines which alternate with 'Good Lord deliver us' is: 'From fornication and all other deadly sin, and from all the deceits of the world, the flesh, and the devil.' The allusion is ironic since Sorrow is literally delivered from all of these.

111 *"By experience . . . a long wandering"*: Roger Ascham, English scholar,

author, and tutor and adviser to Elizabeth I, writes in *The Schoolmaster* (1570): 'We know by experience itself, that it is a marvellous pain to find out but a short way by long wandering.' He is arguing that education is a more efficient teacher than experience.

gnomic texts: a gnome is a moral aphorism or proverb; collections of them are sometimes called 'gnomologia'.

Jeremy Taylor's thought: Jeremy Taylor (1613–67), an Anglican clergyman, wrote *The Rule and Exercises of Holy Living* (1650) and *The Rule and Exercises of Holy Dying* (1651) to help those deprived of regular ministry during the Commonwealth. Weber quotes this passage from *Holy Dying* as Hardy's source: 'Let our life be never so long . . . yet still the period shall be that all this shall end in death, and the people shall talk of us awhile, . . . and once it shall come to pass that concerning every one of us it shall be told in the neighborhood, that we are dead' (Weber, note to p. 125.10).

113 *d'Urberville, like Babylon, had fallen*: see Isaiah 21:9: 'Babylon is fallen, is fallen; and all the graven images of her gods he hath broken unto the ground.'

118 *Van Alsloot or Sallaert*: Denis Van Alsloot (1570?–1626) and Antoon Sallaert (1590–1657) were Flemish painters known for their treatments of gatherings of people at feasts, pageants, and processions. In *The Return of the Native* Hardy writes of 'the throngs which cover the canvases of Sallaert, Van Alsloot, and others of that school—vast masses of beings, jostling, zigzagging, and processioning in definite directions, but whose features are indistinguishable by the very comprehensiveness of the view' (III. iii).

119 *the pure River of Life shown to the Evangelist*: John the Evangelist is shown a vision of 'a new heaven and a new earth', including 'a pure river of water of life, clear as crystal, proceeding out of the throne of God and of the Lamb' (Rev. 22: 1).

crowfoot: a flower with divided leaves of the buttercup family.

"O ye Sun and Moon . . . for ever": Tess is quoting very accurately from memory some of the key parts of the Benedicite from the Order for Morning Prayer found in the Book of Common Prayer, not the Psalter as the text says.

120 *Benedicite*: see note above. Tess is referring back to what she has just recited.

129 *whey*: the watery part of milk which is left when the curd has been taken out, usually to make cheese.

131 *untenable redemptive theolatry*: theolatry is the worship of a god or gods. Angel is attacking the Church's doctrine of redemption (the doctrine that Christ died on the cross to redeem mankind).

thimble-riggers: in the game of thimblerig, a swindler takes bets on which of three thimbles a pea has supposedly been placed under. A thimblerigger can also be 'one who cheats by means of tricks, or juggles with phrases' (*OED*; cites *Tess* as an example).

132 *Article Four*: the Thirty-Nine Articles govern the Church of England. Article Four, "Of the Resurrection of Christ", states that Christ was physically raised from the dead.

'*the removing . . . may remain*': Angel is quoting Hebrews 12: 27 to argue that the Thirty-Nine Articles, especially Article Four, which he cannot literally believe, should be removed so that what is essential to the faith may remain.

134 "*A mesure . . . les hommes*": from the 'Préface Général' to Pascal's *Pensées*. They could be translated 'the more intelligence one has, the more one notices how many original men there are; common people do not notice the difference between men'.

Hodge: 'a familiar by-form and abbreviation of the name *Roger*; used as a typical name for the English agricultural labourer or rustic' (*OED*). Hardy begins 'The Dorsetshire Labourer' with a lengthy description of Hodge, but concludes that, contrary to contemporary opinion, 'the typical Hodge . . . was somehow not typical of anyone but himself' (253).

some mutely Miltonic . . . Cromwellian: Hardy is paraphrasing Thomas Gray's 'Elegy in a Country Churchyard': 'Some mute inglorious *Milton* here may rest, | Some *Cromwell* guiltless of his Country's Blood' (ll. 59–60).

140 *like Peter the Great . . . he wanted to know*: despite his royal birth, Peter the Great spent six months as a carpenter in the shipyards of Amsterdam, learning naval architecture so that later, as tsar (1682–1725), he could command the Russian navy (after he had worked his way up the ranks to Rear-Admiral). Angel is serving a similar apprenticeship in the dairy.

141 *lords and ladies*: this flower, the counterpart of the jack-in-the-pulpit in America, is also called the wake-robin in England. Firor writes that one pulls off its petals to answer the question "Am I to marry?" but that Tess (unlike Angel) is too unsophisticated to know the full import of her actions (Firor, 42).

the poor Queen of Sheba . . . in me: after the Queen of Sheba went to Jerusalem expressly to see the wealth of King Solomon, which was even greater than her own, 'there was no more spirit in her' (1 Kgs. 10: 5).

142 *why the sun do shine . . . alike*: in the Sermon on the Mount, Jesus says that God 'maketh his sun to rise on the evil and on the good, and sendeth rain on the just and on the unjust" (Matt. 5: 45). Tess wants to know why the evil are not punished on earth for their wicked deeds.

146 *Artemis, Demeter*: Artemis, the cold, chaste goddess of the hunt, slew with her arrows any men who tried to rape her. Demeter is also a goddess of chastity in some versions of the myth, but because of her close link with the arts of agriculture as the goddess of ripe grain, she is also a fertility goddess.

149 *Holy Thursday*: or Maundy Thursday, in Easter week, the most solemn time in the Christian year.

158 *That it may please Thees*: in the middle of the Litany for use on Sunday, Wednesday, and Friday in the Book of Common Prayer, lines beginning 'That it may please thee' (to do such things as bless the queen, illuminate the bishop, and defend the poor) alternate with the line 'We beseech thee to hear us good Lord'. Marian is afraid she will be hot well into the service.

thistle-spud: another name for a thistle-digger, a tool used to root up thistles.

159 *a time to embrace . . . embracing*: see Ecclesiastes 3: 5.

160 *Three Leahs to get one Rachel*: Jacob laboured seven years to marry Rachel, but her father Laban tricked him into marrying Leah, Rachel's ugly older sister, instead. After labouring seven more years, Jacob was allowed to marry Rachel also (Gen. 29). Angel has to carry the other dairy maids first in order to carry Tess, the one he really wants.

164 *Thermidorean weather*: Thermidor, which means 'month of heat', was 19 July to 17 August on the French Revolutionary Calendar, instituted in 1793 and abolished by Napoleon in 1805.

165 *Elizabethan simile . . . snow*: Angel is thinking of the second stanza of 'There is a Garden in Her Face' (sometimes entitled 'Cherry Ripe') by the English poet Thomas Campion (1567–1620), found in *Fourth Book of Airs* (1617):

> Those cherries fairly do enclose
> Of orient pearl a double row,
> Which when her lovely laughter shows,
> They look like rosebuds filled with snow.

171 *Walt Whitman*: in 'Crossing Brooklyn Ferry' (l. 3).

173 *"pleasure girdled about with pain"*: from a chorus section in *Atalanta in Calydon* by Algernon Swinburne:

> Put moans into the bridal measure
> And on the bridal wools a stain;
> And circled pain about with pleasure,
> And girdled pleasure about with pain . . .

174 *Antinomianism*: based on Paul's teachings, this doctrine holds that works are unnecessary since salvation comes by grace alone. In its extreme form, embraced in England by Anabaptists and some Nonconformists, Antinomianism defended the saved individual's right to do whatever he pleased. Mercy Chant is 'great at Antinomianism' in that she knows about it, not that she embraces it.

175 *Evangelical . . . conversionist*: Mr Clare is a Church Evangelical, a member of a conservative, moralistic, and usually anti-intellectual faction within the Church of England. Evangelicals believe that, despite baptism

and confirmation, members of the Church, like anyone else, must be converted—saved by a personal act of faith in Christ's atonement—in order to go to heaven.

175 *He loved Paul of Tarsus . . . the Articles*: apparently Mr Clare loves best those parts of the Bible which expound, as the apostle Paul often did, the doctrine of salvation by grace. He hates the book of James 'as much as he dared', for it teaches that faith alone cannot save but must be expressed in good works. He 'regarded with mixed feelings' Paul's letters to Timothy, Titus, and Philemon because they represent a fusion of the two positions. To him the New Testament is not an 'argument' but an 'intoxication'; that is, individuals believe or disbelieve because of its power to sway the emotions, not the intellect. He is also a determinist like Arthur Schopenhauer, a nineteenth-century German pessimistic philosopher who held that the universal will urges individuals to satisfy goals which can never be satisfied, resulting in an endless cycle of birth, suffering, death, and rebirth, escapable only by resignation. He also shares something philosophically with Giacomo Leopardi, a great nineteenth-century Italian lyric poet who was intensely pessimistic. Hardy's admiration for both of these writers is obvious from the many references to them in his journals. Mr Clare also dislikes the Canons and Rubrics, the laws and directions for conducting worship services in the Church of England, but is loyal to the Thirty-Nine Articles, the Church's doctrinal basis.

176 *the geocentric view . . . nadiral hell*: the traditional Christian view that the earth is the centre of the universe; thus, heaven is literally up and hell down.

177 *Diocesan Synods and Visitations*: a diocese is the area under the jurisdiction of a bishop. A synod is an assembly of all the clergy in a diocese to discuss church affairs and set policy, and visitations are the visits of a bishop to the diocese to examine it or the meetings connected with his visit.

178 *dapes inemptæ*: (Latin) 'unbought meal'; from Horace, *Epodes*, ii. 48. In other words, the food on the table all comes from what the dairyman himself can raise or grow. The passage as a whole, which extols the virtues of a home-maker, sounds much like Proverbs 31 (see note to p. 282).

184 *Some of the wise . . . as Hamlet puts it*: Angel is alluding to a passage in which Hamlet and Rosencrantz discuss the War of the Theatres (1599–1602), the rivalry between troupes of child and adult actors. The children declaim on stage against the adults, so Hamlet asks whether, when they are adult actors themselves, they will not say that 'their writers do them wrong, to exclaim against their own succession' (II. ii. 351). According to Angel, wise members of old families like the d'Urbervilles are sceptical of the value of their own lineage.

185 *'Being reviled we bless . . . unto this day'*: Mr Clare is quoting a passage in

which Paul, by listing the ways he has been persecuted, hopes to establish his authority over the Church and his right to chastise it (1 Cor. 4: 12–13). Clare compares Paul's treatment with his own at the hands of Alec d'Urberville.

189 *high*: see following note.

High, Low, or Broad: High Church and Low Church are philosophically opposing factions within the Church of England. The former advocates the use of ritualism and art (icons, candles, vestments, and genuflection) in worship while the latter, mostly Evangelicals, view these as vestiges of the Roman Catholic Church. Broad Church, also known as Latitudinarianism, is the liberal, ecumenical branch of the Church, which advocates open-minded free enquiry rather than blind faith.

190 *Tractarian as to phraseology*: Tess has inherited the phraseology of the Tractarian or Oxford Movement, that part of the Church of England most closely allied with the Roman Catholic Church. Although Hardy did not agree with the theology of John Henry Newman, a primary force in the movement, he expressed in several places his admiration for Newman's writing style. Hardy read Newman's *Apologia* and noted 'Style charming, and his logic really human' (*Early Life*, 64). Elsewhere he notes 'Newman's mind—a miracle of intellectual delicacy, wh. produces urbanity of style' (Björk, i. 1166).

Leave thou thy sister . . . melodious days: Angel is vowing to himself to take the advice of Tennyson's *In Memoriam* (xxxiii. 5–8) regarding his treatment of Tess.

drew the plugs . . . the milk: the milk was put into large pans or leads, and after the cream was skimmed off, the skim-milk was let out by pulling the plugs in the bottom of the leads.

192 *in fields and pastures . . . deemed waste*: speaking of the players who have come to perform at the court, Hamlet says 'the lover shall not sigh gratis'—that is, the actors shall be paid (II. ii. 316). The narrator's point (which Angel doesn't understand) is that love-making is of value quite apart from the reward of marriage.

195 *pollard willows*: a pollard is any tree whose foliage is cut back to the trunk so that it will grow back more thickly.

199 *broody poultry*: chickens sitting on eggs to hatch them.

204 *Caroline date*: 'Caroline' refers to the reigns of either Charles I (1625–49) or Charles II (1660–85), so the house dates, broadly speaking, from the seventeenth century.

206 *sixth standard*: the Revised Code of 1862 divided primary education into six standards. Tess would have been 11 or 12 when she left school, eligible to go on to a secondary school since she showed promise.

210 *Hogshead of Cyder*: a hogshead is a liquid measure of beer or, more commonly, cider. It equals 52.5 imperial gallons (or 63 US gallons).

211 *Though not cold-natured . . . Shelleyan*: in physical terms Alec, the dark, passionate lover, is Byronic while Angel, with his slight build and light hair, looks more like Shelley. More important are the personality traits Angel shares with Shelley. Both are dreamers with an ethereal quality about them, Platonic Idealists looking for the ideal spiritual, not merely physical relation with women, and both are sleepwalkers.

212 *champaigns*: flat open lands without hills or woods.

214 *true . . . of good report*: St Paul admonishes the brethren to 'think on these things' which Angel lists (Phil. 4: 8).

215 *on my own hook*: colloquial expression meaning to do something independently, by one's own efforts, or at one's own risk. The first citation in *OED* is from the *New York Herald*, 1845: 'The time is fast approaching when we shall have our American Pope . . . and American Catholic every thing, on our own hook.'

218 *him for whom she lived and breathed*: an echo of St Paul's words: 'in him [God] we live, and move, and have our being' (Acts 17: 28). Tess has obviously made Angel her god (see notes to pp. 233 and 293).

220 *going dry*: stop giving milk, generally because the cows have not been milked regularly or completely enough.

223 *bolting*: the process of sifting flour through a sieve or cloth, often called a bolting-cloth.

224 *banns . . . licence*: banns are the proclamations of an impending wedding issued in church on three Sundays in a row so that anyone having objections to the marriage may voice them. In *The Return of the Native*, Mrs Yeobright forbids the banns of her niece Thomasin and Wildeve. In lieu of banns, one might receive a licence, or written permission from the bishop.

225 *That never would become . . . done amiss*: from 'The Boy and the Mantle', a ballad in which a boy brings to King Arthur's court a magic mantle with the results which the narrator explains.

231 *felloes*: the curved pieces of wood used to make the rim of a wheel.

partie carrée: (French) a party of four.

233 *She tried to pray to God . . . ill-omened*: this passage is another example of Tess's deifying Angel, an act which she here recognizes as dangerous (see notes to pp. 218 and 293).

"these violent delights have violent ends": Friar Laurence speaks these words directly before he marries Romeo and Juliet (II. vi. 9). He is, of course, right, and the words point out the ill-fated nature of Tess and Angel's love.

234 *That's bad*: Firor writes that since the crowing of the cock was one of the first ways to keep time, he is always expected to be regular. Therefore, 'cockcrow at an unusual time is almost universally held ominous' (Firor, 12). Furbank writes: 'J. S. Udal, a friend of Hardy's, read a paper to the

Dorset Natural History and Antiquarian Field Club on 13 November 1889 in which he mentioned the Dorset superstition that an afternoon cockcrow portended sickness or death' (Furbank, note to 243).

235 *their own exclusive roof-tree*: literally, a roof's main beam. Often it is used more metaphorically to refer to a home.

239 *wing bonnet*: any bonnet having side appendages, or wings.

240 *folks mops and brooms from what's inside 'em*: to be mops and brooms is to be half-drunk. According to *OED*, the expression may be 'an allusion to the drinking that took place at the hiring fairs . . . at which the maids carried mops or brooms in token of the capacity in which they wished to be hired' (see note to p. 339).

withy-bed: a bed of willows.

241 *trencher-woman*: woman with a good appetite.

242 *an Aldebaran or a Sirius*: Aldebaran, which has a diameter fifty times larger than the sun's, is one of the fifteen brightest stars in the sky. Sirius, the Dog Star, associated with 'dog days', or the hottest part of the summer, is the brightest star in the sky.

243 *'Be thou an example . . . in purity'*: 1 Tim. 4: 12. Here, as elsewhere, Angel demonstrates his accurate memory of Bible passages, though he does not believe in "plenary inspiration", the doctrine that the Bible is literally accurate in all matters.

'Integer vitæ,' says a Roman poet . . . how: the first two words of Horace, *Odes*, I. xxii. 1–2, translated below. According to Springer, the ode is Horace's ironic commentary on cloistered virtue, which he rejects in favour of love of a woman (Springer, 137). Björk writes. 'Of Hardy's later uses of Horace in his fiction, the most significant may be Angel's unintentionally ironic quotation of the "integer vitae" passage' (Björk, i. annotation to 175).

249 *good-hussif*: a small sewing bag.

250 *Agape*: the Greek word for the most spiritual kind of love; it can also mean a love-feast taken part in by those who share this love.

251 *Behold . . . shall be pain*: the final lines of 'Not as with sundering of the earth', a chorus about fate from Swinburne's *Atalanta in Calydon*.

253 *Cistercian abbey*: an abbey belonging to the monastic order which Robert, abbot of Molesme, founded at Cistercium (or Cîteaux) in 1098 as an offshoot of the Benedictines.

tester of white dimity: the tester is the bed canopy; dimity is an undyed cotton fabric with raised stripes or figures woven into it.

254 *The little less, and what worlds away!*: in the first version of the manuscript Hardy quoted all of verse 39 of Robert Browning's 'By the Fire-Side' except the first word:

> [Oh] The little more, and how much it is!
> And the little less, and what worlds away!

> How a sound shall quicken content to bliss,
> Or a breath suspend the blood's best play
> And life be a proof of this!

In revision he left out the first line as quite inappropriate. In the American serialization in *Harper's Bazaar* the whole quotation was omitted. The present single line appeared in the first edition. This verse and those following, which embody the moment of crisis in a relationship when friends may become lovers, emphasize the moment's precariousness. The poem continues 'Had she willed it, still had stood the screen | So slight, so sure, 'twixt my love and her.' But the screen is smashed in a moment and the pair in the poem find love, while for Angel and Tess the moment of her confession has raised a screen. It is characteristic of Hardy to invert Browning's optimism.

261 *Apostolic Charity*: the words directly before this sentence paraphrase St Paul's description of charity in 1 Corinthians 13.

263 *in the words of M. Sully-Prudhomme . . . "you shall be born"*: reference to the poem 'Le vœu' by Sully-Prudhomme (René François Armand Prudhomme), a nineteenth-century French poet. The poem argues that the most enviable state is never to have been born. Björk shows that Hardy noted the title of the poem and a phrase from it (*Les Condamnés à naître*, or those condemned to be born) in his journal (i. 1629). Hardy's source for the poem, as Björk also shows, was Frederick W. H. Myers's 'The Disenchantment of France' (*Nineteenth Century*, 23 (May 1888), 673), where two stanzas of the poem are quoted.

272 *fly*: first introduced in 1816 at Brighton, this is any one-horse covered carriage which is hired from a livery stable.

273 *God's not . . . the world!*: Angel is emending an optimistic song of Pippa in Robert Browning's *Pippa Passes* (I, "Morning", 221–8):

> The year's at the spring
> And day's at the morn;
> Morning's at seven;
> The hill-side's dew-pearled;
> The lark's on the wing;
> The snail's on the thorn:
> God's in his heaven—
> All's right with the world!

279 *a Wiertz Museum . . . Van Beers*: Antoine Wiertz (1806–65) was a romantic Flemish painter of the bizarre and macabre. In 1850 the Belgian government built him a studio in Brussels which became after his death a museum of his works. Jan Van Beers (1852–1927) was a minor Flemish painter whose paintings were often compared to Wiertz's. Bullen shows that Hardy almost certainly visited the Wiertz Museum in 1876 and probably saw an exhibition of Beers's paintings in London in the spring of 1887 (Bullen, 24).

the Pagan moralist: Marcus Aurelius. From 1865 until his death, Hardy kept at his bedside a copy of *The Thoughts of the Emperor M. Aurelius Antoninus*, presented to him by Horace Moule with a quotation from the book inscribed: 'This is the chief thing: Be not perturbed: for all things are according to the nature of the universal' (Millgate, *TH*, 87). The quotation, which seems to have been one of Hardy's favourites, also appears in his notes and *Early Life* (p. 231).

"Let not your heart . . . afraid", said the Nazarene: these words appear in John 14: 27, part of the charge of Jesus, 'the Nazarene', to his disciples at the Last Supper, which immediately preceded his arrest and crucifixion.

281 *a good thing could come out of Nazareth*: after Jesus had chosen Philip as a disciple, Philip went in turn to Nathanael, whose first response was, 'Can there any good thing come out of Nazareth?' (John 1: 46). Angel's mother is trying not to apply the same sentiment to Tess.

282 *the words of King Lemuel . . . virtuous wife*: Proverbs 31 includes 'the words of king Lemuel, the prophecy that his mother taught him'. Starting with verse 10, the chapter, from which Mr Clare reads excerpts, describes the ideal wife whose own work complements her husband's.

283 *who knew neither . . . hearts*: see note to p. 108.

286 *what he had to complete . . . quickly*: Hardy is echoing Jesus' words to Judas immediately before Judas betrays him: "That thou doest, do quickly" (John 13: 27). The allusion underscores the fact that Angel is about to betray Tess.

288 *' 'Twas down in Cupid's Gardens', and 'The Tailor's Breeches'*: 'Cupid's Gardens' is a popular song about Cuper's Gardens, a pleasure garden forced to close in 1753 by the popularity of Vauxhall. The speaker is a sailor who goes to the gardens to look at the flowers and find a lover. 'The Tailor's Breeches' is a bawdy ballad about a tailor who loves wine and women 'exceedingly well'. He gets drunk, and in order to win a woman, trades his breeches for her petticoat. His reward is that she steals his breeches, watch, and money.

289 *the prophet on the top of Peor*: Balak, king of Moab, offers Balaam the prophet great reward if he will curse the Israelites, who are about to invade his country. Instead, God makes Balaam bless the Israelites on the top of Mount Peor (Num. 22–3). Similarly, Izz, if she speaks badly of Tess, may receive a reward, but she too is unable to do so.

293 *consecrated them to souvenirs . . . relics*: souvenirs are any tokens of remembrance. But since Angel's touch has 'consecrated' them, that is, made them holy, and since Tess thinks of them as 'relics', which are souvenirs associated with a saint or martyr, Tess is obviously canonizing Angel (see notes to pp. 218 and 233).

294 *éclat*: (French) glitter.

Curitiba . . . on Brazilian plains: Weber shows that Hardy's geography and description are in error here: ' "Curitiba" is the capital of the Brazilian state of Parana. It is situated almost 2000 miles south of the Amazon, on a plateau 3125 feet high. It enjoys a very healthy climate: temperature averages 65 degrees F., and the average rainfall is 58 inches annually' (Weber, note to 350–1).

296 *fancy-man*: a fancy-man can simply mean a man who is fancied or loved, but in slang terms it can also mean 'a man who lives upon the earnings of a prostitute' (*OED*). In Hardy's poem 'A Trampwoman's Tragedy', a trampwoman's husband-to-be is murdered by her fancy-man, the father of her unborn child.

thinking of her wasted life said "All is vanity": the first words of 'the Preacher' in Ecclesiastes are 'Vanity of Vanities . . . all is vanity'; the rest of the book illustrates this single idea. Tess reflects below on the inadequacy of this philosophy.

298 *they run amuck*: running amuck is 'engaging furiously in battle, attacking with desperate resolution, rushing into a state of frenzy to the commission of indiscriminate murder'. Originally, amuck was an adjective which was specifically 'a name for a frenzied Malay'. Sometimes such activity is associated with opium use, and Southey, in *Naval History of England* (1833), claimed that such drug use caused the Malays to run amuck (*OED*).

300 *The maiden's mouth is cold . . . her head*: stanza nine of Swinburne's 'Fragoletta' (from *Poems and Ballads*) reads:

> Ah sweet, the maiden's mouth is cold,
> Her breast-blossoms are simply red,
> Her hair mere brown or gold,
> Fold over simple fold
> Binding her head.

The speaker's purpose is to compare the maiden unfavourably to the male lover. Hardy's point is that Tess now seems passionless, like the maiden in the poem.

Cybele the Many-breasted: this passage compares the appearance of the landscape to that of the Phrygian goddess Cybele, the Great Mother of the gods, appropriately, since she is the embodiment of the earth itself. She symbolizes fertility; therefore, her worship was often characterized by orgiastic dances.

303 *plashed*: bent and interwoven to form a hedge; pleached.

305 *some early Italian conception of the two Marys*: they look like an early Italian painter's rendition of Mary the mother of Jesus and Mary Magdalen, probably, since they are hooded and pensive, going to visit Jesus' tomb.

306 *bill-hook*: a tool with a wooden handle and a long blade ending in a sharp hook for pruning and cutting.

308 *reed-drawing*: preparing wheat-straw for thatching by finely combing it and binding it into sheaves.

310 *like a bird caught in a clap-net*: a fowler caught birds in a clap-net by pulling a string to shut the trap suddenly.

314 *cretaceous tableland*: a plateau formed from chalk.

315 *crape quilling*: quilling is ribbon gathered into small folds which look like a row of quills (like those on a ruff). Tess's is made of crape, an embossed fine worsted fabric.

hogs'-backs: hills shaped with a ridge in the middle, like the back of a hog.

318 *guindée*: (French) stiff, strained, or unnatural.

321 *"O foolish Galatians . . . crucified among you?"*: Gal. 3: 1, part of a passage in which Paul is chastising the Church for returning to a doctrine of law and works rather than grace. The sermon, as the narrator notes, is 'of the extremest antinomian type; on justification by faith, as expounded in the theology of Paul'. It is 'a vehement form of the views of Angel's father' (see notes to pp. 174 and 175).

326 *as in the legend . . . well-nigh extinguished*: Weber's note reads: ' "Cyprian": referring to the worship of Venus at Paphos on the island of Cyprus' (Weber, note to 391.13). Furbank writes: 'F. B. Pinion comments in his Scholar's Library edition: "Hardy's analogy seems to be based on the intervention of Artemis (Diana) when Iphigenia was about to be sacrificed by the priest Calchas in order to propitiate the gods before the Greek fleet sailed for Troy" ' (Furbank, note to 331).

328 *'Come out from among them . . . saith the Lord'*: 2 Cor. 6: 17; Paul's quotation of Isaiah 52: 11, the prophet's command to the Israelites, to advise the Corinthians not to be "unequally yoked together with unbelievers" in marriage.

those who came to scoff . . . to pray: in *The Deserted Village* (1770), Oliver Goldsmith wrote of the pious village preacher: 'Truth from his lips prevailed with double sway, | And fools, who came to scoff, remained to pray' (ll. 179–80).

329 *fleshly tabernacle*: after advising the Corinthians to flee fornication, Paul writes, 'Know ye not that ye are the temple of God, and that the Spirit of God dwelleth in you?' (1 Cor. 3: 16).

332 *petite mort*: (French) a sudden chill, a shudder, or a shiver. Firor notes that a shiver is an omen, the common belief being that 'if you shiver, someone is walking over your future grave' (Firor, 23).

335 *in such dangerous ignorance . . . for them*: there are a number of Old Testament references about the nets of the wicked, for instance, Psalm 9: 15 ('The heathen are sunk down in the pit that they made: in the net which they hid is their own foot taken') and Psalm 31: 4 ('Pull me out of the net that they have laid privily for me').

337 *'The unbelieving husband . . . the husband'*: Alec is referring to Paul's advice to the Corinthians not to leave a spouse simply because he or she is an unbeliever (1 Cor. 7: 14).

339 *Candlemas Fair*: Candlemas is a festival of the Christian Church which commemorates Mary's trip to Jerusalem to purify herself and present her son Jesus forty days after his birth. In England, Candlemas Fair, which also figures in *The Woodlanders* and *Far from the Madding Crowd*, was one of the two annual hiring-fairs at which people offered their services by carrying symbols of their trades.

341 *Sermon on the Mount*: Jesus' Sermon on the Mount to the multitude, the most famous part of which is the Beatitudes, is considered by many to contain the essence of Christianity (Matt. 5–7). Angel has taught Tess to believe in the 'spirit' of this passage, though not its historicity. At the end of *The Return of the Native*, Clym Yeobright becomes an itinerant preacher and gives 'the first of a series of moral lectures or Sermons on the Mount'.

Dictionnaire Philosophique: a collection of essays published in 1764 by the French writer Voltaire (1694–1778), a famous sceptic and debunker of Christianity.

Huxley's Essays: Thomas Henry Huxley (1825–95), an eminent scientist, humanist, and defender of Darwinism, published *Essays on Some Controverted Questions* in 1892.

342 *like the devils I believe and tremble*: James 2: 19 reads: 'Thou believest that there is one God; thou doest well: the devils also believe, and tremble.' This allusion underscores the inadequacy of Alec's 'conversion'.

I thought I worshipped . . . in the groves: in the Old Testament, the worship of Jehovah is associated with the mountaintops and the worship of Baal with the groves (see 2 Kgs. 17).

343 *am I indeed one . . . beginning?*: Alec is quoting a description of those who have returned to the world after becoming believers (2 Pet. 2: 20). The next verse reads: 'it had been better for them not to have known the way of righteousness, than, after they have known it, to turn from the holy commandment delivered unto them.'

never was such a maddening mouth since Eve's: Alec's comparison of Tess to Eve, an archetypically beautiful woman, is appropriate since he is taking on the role of the serpent.

dear damned witch of Babylon: Alec is referring to the Whore of Babylon, the allegorical mother of harlots described in Revelation 17. With this allusion Alec shifts the blame onto Tess for his fall from grace.

345 *primum mobile*: (Latin) prime mover; the phrase originates with Aristotle. In Ptolemaic astronomy, it is the outermost sphere which surrounds the fixed stars and causes all movement in the heavens.

346 *Plutonic*: Pluto (or Hades) is the god of the underworld who could consign others to hell. The allusion emphasizes the sinister nature of the machine.

348 *hag-rode*: (dialect) to be ridden by hags (female evil spirits or witches) or afflicted by nightmares.

349 *like Hymenæus and Alexander . . . blaspheme*: Paul writes to Timothy to 'war a good warfare; Holding faith, and a good conscience; which some having put away concerning faith have made shipwreck; Of whom is Hymenæus and Alexander; whom I have delivered unto Satan, that they might learn not to blaspheme' (1 Tim. 1: 18–20). Alec fears that he, too, has been 'delivered unto Satan'.

350 *if the bachelor apostle . . . as I do*: when a man asked to go home and say farewell to his family before returning to become a disciple, Jesus replied, 'No man, having put his hand to the plough, and looking back, is fit for the kingdom of God' (Luke 9: 62). Alec justifies himself by claiming that even the apostle Paul, who is traditionally supposed to have been single, would have left the faith for Tess.

351 *The words of the stern prophet Hosea*: God tells Hosea to marry a harlot in order to allegorize the whoring of Israel after other gods. This verse (Hos. 2: 7) is Hosea's prophecy concerning both his wife and Israel. Alec applies the verse to Tess—in essence accusing her of whoring after Angel—but changes it: in the original, the wife follows many lovers, not just one.

354 *Jacob's ladder*: Jacob has a dream that angels descend and ascend on a ladder which stretches from heaven to earth (Gen. 28: 12).

355 *pandæmonium*: a wild uproar or tumult. Literally, it means the place of all demons, so Milton makes it the capital of Hell in *Paradise Lost* (see note to p. 415).

357 *my last state will be worse than my first*: Jesus tells a story about a man possessed by a demon which, after being cast out, returned with seven more demons to the same man. He concludes that 'the last state of that man is worse than the first' (Matt. 12: 45). Peter uses the same words when he claims that for those who follow Christ but then return to the world 'the latter end is worse . . . than the beginning' (2 Pet. 2: 20). Tess is echoing the words of Alec, who quotes this last verse when he accuses her of tempting him to leave the faith (see note to p. 343).

359 *as Abraham . . . the hill together*: God tells Abraham to offer his son Isaac as a sacrifice. Abraham does as he is told, but at the last minute an angel stops him and supplies a ram to be used in place of Isaac (Gen. 22).

362 *Was not the gleaning . . . of Abi-ezer?*: this is Gideon's answer to the Ephraimites' complaint that they were not called in sooner to help destroy the Midianites (Judg. 8: 2). They have joined his forces and succeeded where he, the best of the family of Abiezer, has failed. Hence, the question is whether it is not better to have Tess, who has been 'harvested' by someone else, than a woman Angel would once have considered more pure.

363 *"Cupid's Gardens" . . . "Such a beauty did grow"*: Furbank writes that ' "I have parks" is a version of "The Farmer's Toast" ' (Furbank, note to 365). It is a rollicking drinking song sung by a farmer who feels wealthy as long as his friends are around him drinking. In the last stanza he calls

for a toast to himself. Tess sings 'The Break of Day' below. See note to p. 288 for 'The Tailor's Breeches' and 'Cupid's Gardens'. 'Such a beauty I did grow' has not been located.

363 *Lady-Day . . . Old Lady-Day*: Lady Day is the Feast of the Annunciation, on 25 March. It commemorates Gabriel's announcement to Mary ('Our Lady') that she will become the mother of Jesus. It is traditionally the day when those hired at the Candlemas Fair move to their new situations (see note to p. 339). Hardy describes these movings in detail in 'The Dorsetshire Labourer'. Old Lady Day, the same holiday in the days of Old Style dating (see note to p. 19), fell on 6 April.

365 *the witches . . . as you passed*: Firor writes that 'pricking the witch' is a counter-charm against witches dating from the sixteenth-century witch trials and common in much of rural England up until the beginning of the twentieth century. Witches reputedly revealed themselves by not bleeding much. Furbank adds that any excrescence on a witch's body was pricked 'in the belief that, if it proved insensitive, it was likely to be an extra pap for the suckling of imps' (Furbank, note to 368). (In *The Return of the Native*, Eustacia Vye is pricked in church by Susan Nunsuch, who believes she is a witch.) Another test of accused witches was ducking. Women who drowned were innocent; those who survived were witches (according to Furbank because 'a witch, having rejected baptism, would in turn be rejected by water—i.e. would float'). 'Whicker' is a dialect word meaning snicker.

367 *the "pillar of a cloud" . . . by night*: to help Moses guide the Israelites through the wilderness after their flight from Egypt, God sent a pillar of cloud by day and a pillar of fire by night. When it moved, they followed it; when it did not, they stayed encamped (Exod. 13; Num. 9).

369 *Empress . . . Eve*: these are the words of Satan, disguised as a serpent, to Eve in *Paradise Lost*, ix. 626–31. Alec is trying to quote the passage ironically, but the words should show Tess that her situation and Eve's are parallel. Alec is indeed the tempting serpent.

371 *So do flux . . . the sky*: these words echo Ecclesiastes 1, especially verse 9: 'there is no new thing under the sun'.

372 *Egypt of one family . . . changed*: Exodus is the account of the escape of the Israelites from Egypt to the Promised Land, which they were not allowed to enter for forty years because of their sinfulness and disobedience to God. The point of the allusion is that families keep moving, trying in vain to find the promised land.

huckster: a pedlar or retailer of goods.

376 *mullion*: the bar which divides a window, especially in Gothic architecture.

377 *Here we suffer . . . part no more*: this hymn (sometimes entitled 'Heaven Anticipated' or 'Joyful') was Thomas Bilby's most popular hymn, first

published in *The Infant School Teachers' Assistant*, edited by Bilby and R. B. Ridgway (1831).

378 *not in utter nakedness . . . do we come*: from William Wordsworth's 'Ode: Intimations of Immortality' (ll. 63–4). The surrounding passage reads:

> Our birth is but a sleep and a forgetting:
> The Soul that rises with us, our life's Star,
>   Hath had elsewhere its setting,
>   And cometh from afar:
>   Not in entire forgetfulness,
>   And not in utter nakedness,
> But trailing clouds of glory do we come
>   From God, who is our home . . .

380 *hexagon to the bee*: bees always build their honeycombs from a mass of hexagonal cells.

Ark of the Covenant: while the Israelites were in the wilderness they carried with them a portable tabernacle containing the Ten Commandments, God's covenant with them. Hardy had made precisely this same comparison in 'The Dorsetshire Labourer' (260).

381 *stale*: (archaic dialect) urinate.

382 *deparked hills and slopes*: parks were enclosed tracts of land where, by royal decree, animals of the hunt were kept. It is a sign of the d'Urbervilles' decline that their once impressive ancestral park has been deparked—cut up into small paddocks.

384 *land of Canaan . . . the Egypt*: the land of Canaan is the Promised Land (see note to p. 372).

390 *Crivelli's dead Christus*: Hardy is apparently referring to Carlo Crivelli's fifteenth-century Pietà in the National Gallery. On 3 January 1886 Hardy wrote: 'My art is to intensify the expression of things, as is done by Crivelli, Bellini, etc., so that the heart and inner meaning is made vividly visible' (*Early Life*, 231–2).

392 *"which alters . . . finds"*: in Sonnet 116, Shakespeare writes: 'Love is not love | Which alters when it alteration finds' (ll. 2–3). Angel realizes that he did not truly love Tess in the past.

he had seen . . . made a queen: Faustina was the cousin and wife of the second-century Roman emperor Marcus Aurelius whom ancient writers made infamous, probably unfairly, for her unfaithfulness to her husband. Cornelia, the wife of Tiberius Sempronius Gracchus, a second-century BC Roman, devoted herself after her husband's death to educating her three children (the Gracci brothers were the two most famous) and refused to remarry. Lucretia was the legendary virtuous wife of the Roman Lucius Tarquinius Collatinus, who stabbed herself to death after she was raped. Phryne, Greek for toad, is the nickname of the fourth-century BC Athenian courtesan Musarete who was the lover of the sculptor Praxiteles. The woman taken in adultery is about to be stoned according to Jewish law by the scribes and Pharisees until Jesus says, 'He that is without sin among you, let him first cast a stone at her' (John 8: 1– 11). King David commits adultery with Bathsheba, the wife of Uriah the Hittite, and then arranges to have Uriah killed in battle so that he can marry her (2 Sam. 11). All the allusions serve to show that Angel now knows that he has been wrong about both Tess's character, which is really pure, and his own, which, despite his attempts to be a free-thinker, is pharisaical.

395 *a tale told by an idiot*: after the death of his wife, Macbeth says (V. v. 24–8):

> Life's but a walking shadow, a poor player
> That struts and frets his hour upon the stage
> And then is heard no more. It is a tale
> Told by an idiot, full of sound and fury,
> Signifying nothing

398 *the prophet's gourd*: God sends Jonah to the city of Nineveh to prophesy its destruction but then decides to spare it. As Jonah sits bemoaning his ill-treatment, God causes a gourd to grow up to give him shade. The next day the gourd dies as suddenly as it has appeared (Jonah 4: 6–7).

402 *a soul bound to some Ixionian wheel*: Ixion was bound to a fiery wheel as a punishment for disguising himself as a cloud and seducing Hera while he was a guest of her husband Zeus at Olympus.

408 *her Antinous, her Apollo even*: Antinous was a beautiful youth, the favourite and companion of the Roman emperor Hadrian, who drowned in the Nile. In one version of the story Antinous killed himself to outwit a prophecy that death would soon affect the emperor closely. Apollo, the offspring of Leto and Zeus and the twin brother of Artemis, is the Greek archer god and a model of male beauty. Bullen writes that Angel's 'harp-playing, his role as herdsman, his power to bring both light and destruction, are all reminiscent' of Apollo (Bullen, 212).

411 *Atalanta's race*: Atalanta is the virgin huntress who agrees to marry only the man who can beat her in a footrace. Milanion (or Hippomenes) wins by dropping a golden apple, given to him by Aphrodite, in order to delay Atalanta. They marry but commit sacrilege by lying together in a sacred place, so they are turned into a lion and lioness. Angel has overtaken Tess and won her again, but their happiness is likewise shortlived.

415 *Temple of the Winds*: the manuscript reads 'hall of Pandemonium' (see note to p. 355). Springer notes that ' "Temple of the Winds" is a reference to a building of the fourth century BC in Athens (also called "Tower of the Winds")' (Springer, 127). The Tower of the Winds, built in the first century BC, is an octagonal tower of the Waterclock of Andronikos of Kyrrhos with a sundial on each side and an elaborate twenty-four-hour clock on the inside. Perhaps the point of the comparison is that both

Stonehenge and the Tower of the Winds were ancient devices for keeping time.

416 *she is my sister-in-law*: Judith Weissman argues that Angel does not reply because he knows they cannot marry. The long-debated Deceased Wife's Sister Marriage Act was not passed until 1907; however, Weissman contends that only 'people of Tess's class' were untouched 'by the 1835 law which made marriages between certain relations automatically void' and that the novel's final irony is that 'Liza-Lu and Angel cannot be legally married in England' ('The Deceased Wife's Sister Marriage Act and the Ending of *Tess*', *American Notes and Queries*, 14 (May 1976), 133).

417 *Like a greater ... not answer*: when Jesus was called before the chief priests and elders to tell whether he claimed to be Christ, the son of God, he repeatedly refused to answer (Matt. 26, 27).

419 *Giotto's Two Apostles*: most commentators agree that Hardy is alluding to *Two Haloed Mourners*, a fresco now attributed to Spinello Aretino, not Giotto. It is housed in the National Gallery, a place which Hardy visited often beginning in the 1860s.

420 *the President of the Immortals ... Tess*: 'President of the Immortals' is a translation of Aeschylus' *Prometheus*, 169. Hardy's use of the phrase raised a critical furore, and thirty years later, in response, Hardy wrote a letter (which he apparently never mailed) to a disgruntled critic in which he explained, 'I do not hold ... the ludicrous opinions here assumed to be mine—which are really, or approximately, those of the primitive believer in his man-shaped tribal god ... I find that the writer of the estimate has harked back to a passage in a novel of mine [*Tess*] printed many years ago, in which the forces opposed to the heroine were allegorized as a personality, (a method not unusual in imaginative prose or poetry) by the use of a well-known trope, explained in that venerable work Campbell's *Philosophy of Rhetoric* as "one in which life, perception, activity, design, passion, or any property of sentient beings, is attributed to things inanimate" ' (Millgate, *Life*, 256). Hardy's response is somewhat inadequate, since he does not explain what he did mean by the phrase, which he changed from the 1891 first edition version less likely to offend: 'Time, the Arch-Satirist, had had his joke out with Tess.' The sense of the final version is consistent with the reference to *King Lear* in the Preface to the fifth and later editions (see note to p. 5).

*The
Oxford
World's
Classics
Website*

www.worldsclassics.co.uk

- Information about new titles
- Explore the full range of Oxford World's Classics
- Links to other literary sites and the main OUP webpage
- Imaginative competitions, with bookish prizes
- Peruse the Oxford World's Classics Magazine
- Articles by editors
- Extracts from Introductions
- A forum for discussion and feedback on the series
- Special information for teachers and lecturers

www.worldsclassics.co.uk

American Literature

British and Irish Literature

Children's Literature

Classics and Ancient Literature

Colonial Literature

Eastern Literature

European Literature

History

Medieval Literature

Oxford English Drama

Poetry

Philosophy

Politics

Religion

The Oxford Shakespeare

A complete list of Oxford Paperbacks, including Oxford World's Classics, Oxford Shakespeare, Oxford Drama, and Oxford Paperback Reference, is available in the UK from the Academic Division Publicity Department, Oxford University Press, Great Clarendon Street, Oxford OX2 6DP.

In the USA, complete lists are available from the Paperbacks Marketing Manager, Oxford University Press, 198 Madison Avenue, New York, NY 10016.

Oxford Paperbacks are available from all good bookshops. In case of difficulty, customers in the UK can order direct from Oxford University Press Bookshop, Freepost, 116 High Street, Oxford OX1 4BR, enclosing full payment. Please add 10 per cent of published price for postage and packing.